A MELODIC ENCHANTMENT

ISBN 979-8-9919165-0-9 (Paperback)
ISBN 979-8-9919165-1-6 (Hardcover)
ISBN 979-8-9919165-2-3 (EPUB)

Book Cover and Typography by Žana Arnautović

Editing by Kyra Rogers

Ornamental Breakers by Tabitha Marsh

Authenticity Consulting by Savannah Tenderfoot with Salt and Sage Books, Daniel Delgado, and Lyndsey Croal

First Edition 2025

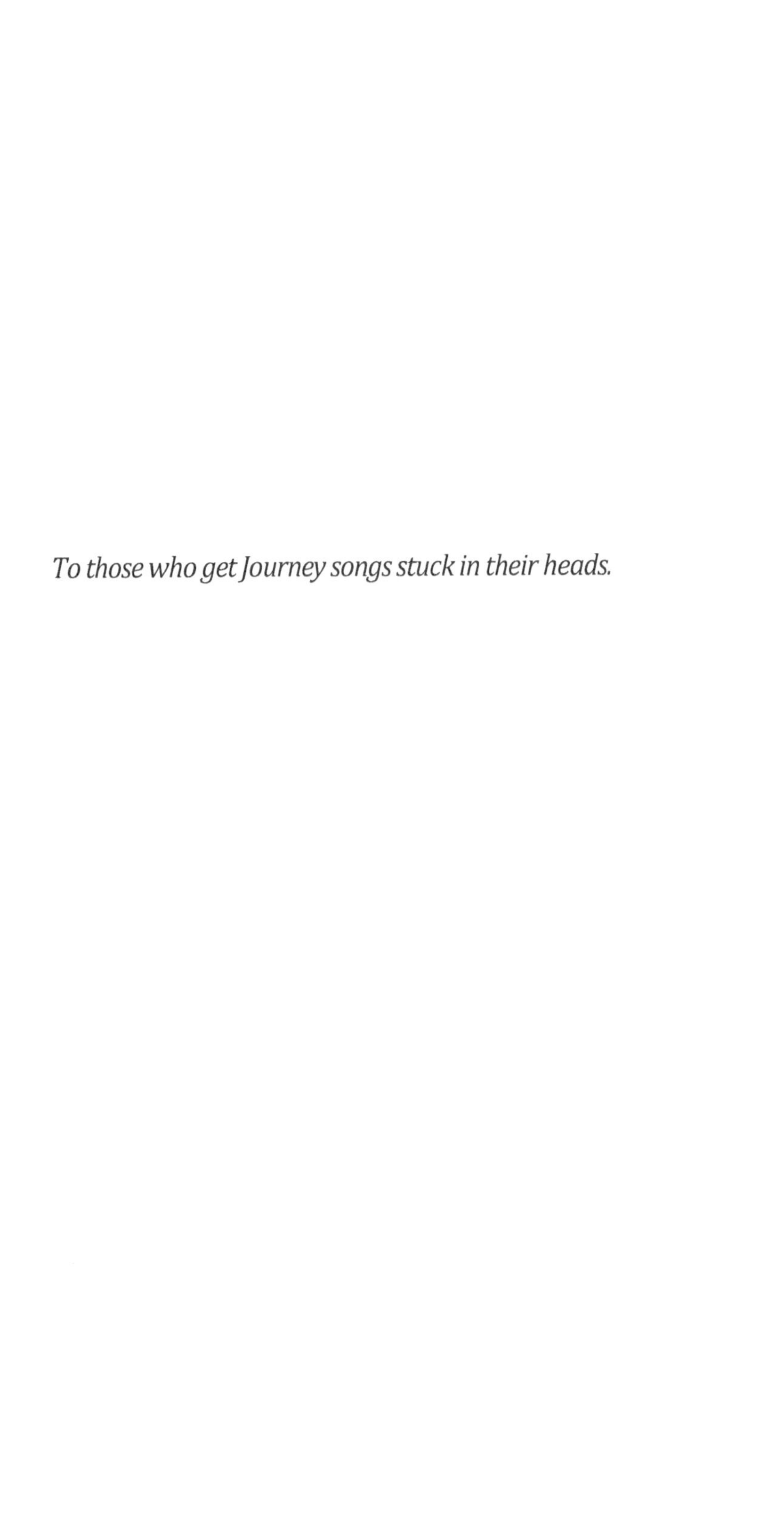

To those who get Journey songs stuck in their heads.

Author's Note

Thank you, reader, for picking up this book. Before we begin this tale, allow me to suggest for those that need it to visit my website for content warning. Please decide if and when you should proceed to read.

And while this is a fantasy world where elves and dwarves are commonplace, and fun adventures or cozy life intermingles with some "monkey fun," please do not let this be an invitation to engage with animals not from your own environment. They may look "friend-shaped", but the parasites on their coats and bacteria in their bite are certainly not.

Finally, for your convenience there is a glossary in the back of the book referencing real-world vernacular and fantasy terms.

Thank you once again, and let us begin.

Chapter One

*I*t *is a truth universally acknowledged that where festivities dwell, a bard is close at hand.*

  Soon to host such an occasion was the developing town of Goldencrest. It'd welcomed its guests with the open arms of the encompassing woods and rolling hills. Though two months stood between the festival date and the present morning, word had gone round of their first and well-renowned entertainer and mutated into a chant of his name from the wee hours of morning till dusk. Even in a week's passing, as the sun extended over a colossal tree line and its shadowed footpath could an emerging, cloaked figure hear the din. A nettled sigh left her as she lowered her hood.

  The air bore the early signs of a brisk autumn, the crispness and sweet, earthy musk of damp leaves providing a moment's reprieve. From the path carried the faint note of petrichor and wild berries, mingling with pine needles and musty straw from the farms below. Beyond the edge of the path and the forest's shroud lay the sun's domain. Pale green and golden acreage undulated over the Beinn, the name given to their mountainous hillside by Elders past. Wild heather and gorse stretched up from their sparse flower beds to greet the sky. A choir of crested tits tootled and chirped at the visitor's departure, the clucking of red squirrels not far behind.

Disappointment crumpled the expression of the lone figure, Evelot.

She ventured forth on the descending path. It opened to a wider, accessible road for wagons and their load bearers. The wind tossed at her ginger hair and tartan skirts as she peeked at the farmers' thatched-roof homes. On either side of her, their fences penned in all manner of sweet-smelling orchards, colorful crops, and noisy barns where shepherd dogs barked their commands. Granaries popped up from the sea of tilled soil and long grass like peeping gophers, watching her pass.

A ways down appeared an elongated brick building. The muddied browns and oranges of its foundations accentuated the red-and-gold doors at its sides. Atop the third story, a placard of wheat wrapped in a golden wreath sat proudly mounted, a testament to the church's deity. From its yawning glass windows, not a sign of the priestesses or monks was visible. But they'd soon throw open the doors in anticipation of donations to the Grand Granary and the bountiful year-end's harvest. Such as it was for the Harvest Maiden and her devout followers.

Evelot tugged her hood over her head as she climbed down the last incline. There, where the path dissolved, was the heart of Goldencrest's burgeon. It started at River's End, so eponymously named, the village of sturdier, mortar properties that the fishers called home. The port gave way to tall structures and shops set up by duchy officials and traders from the adjoining loch's floating city. On the hillside's left, polished stone mansions lorded over the homes of those who didn't admire the Esmoran king's coin. The farmlands may have felt the nobles' flaming ire, but Evelot knew it was the Choille, the woodlands, scalded by the erection of new homes.

With careful steps, Evelot entered the foot traffic headed toward the main square. The clack of shoes and hooves on cobblestone mixed with the surrounding chatter. Wooden business signs squealed on their hinges above log-cabin doors, deterring rather than enticing the crowd. The smell of packed bodies and oily meat pies made her nose scrunch. Evelot tugged her cloak closer, hoping to conceal her already thin form.

In the crowd there rose a sharp gasp. It muted the blether around Evelot before the others peeled back from her. Countless widened eyes fell on her with abhorrence. She lowered her head and paved her way out of the gawks and glances, leaving whispers and the tugging of arms in her wake.

Her destination couldn't come fast enough. Evelot finally stopped before the doors of a cabin storefront, where boxes of thistles and daisy wreaths decorated the windows. Their color dwindled in the cool autumnal wind that filled Evelot's ears. When the breeze faded, she heard the breathy, child-like whispers of the flowers complaining of the chill, their pleas for help. They called for her as she entered the shop, and again as she came out with one less bag of enchanted seeds. A hum in her blood wanted to answer the flowers, but eyes were on her, and nature was fickle. Evelot turned her head, and let it take its course.

Throngs of people shuffled past the small store as Evelot wove into the fray. She let them lead her into the main square where the congestion conspired. It wasn't a far-fetched notion to see it like an atrium, the center of town. The side Evelot entered was one opposing artery filled with villagers and native residents, their district lively with the smell of livestock and labor. On the other end, newcomers and vacationing duchy nobles boasted their private abodes, clean exteriors, and comely shops supplied by their outside connections. Together, they thrummed with arterial foot traffic that intersected the two boundaries.

Evelot threaded through a gaggle of children giving chase to one another as she studied the town's atmosphere. Traveling wagons and festival stages were to spring up on the same grounds where her community broke bread in religious ceremony. Of course there was a tense air between them. She glanced at the posted advertisements promising a joyous night—the ambivalent demeanors of those more fortunate were a constant reminder to Evelot and those of the Harvest Maiden of their place. Their traditions, their ways of life, weren't safe from the duchy's attempts to gentrify their home. Her expression didn't waver from one of complacency.

The smell of baker's bread and confections caught her attention. Farther into the square, the breadmaker's stall opened to the crowd gathered outside it. Her stomach growled too loudly for comfort. She sighed. It'd be a while before her next meal, but a stolen glance would stave off her hunger.

Instead, she spied a stalwart face. As the young man approached, her hunger dissipated and her skin flushed with goose pimples. His eyes, bright with a perturbed glimmer, always found her in the crowd. The boar had fooled others into thinking him knightly, but Evelot saw through the ruse. With a complexion acquainted with the shade and a gait of entitlement, he was a special kind of arse.

He gestured to Evelot with a curl of his adorned finger. "You. Come."

The familiar wash of fear doused her veins. Whatever headache he thought to start, Evelot would not take part in it. While his open summons garnered attention, she started for the flow of the crowd.

"I said—"

Evelot stifled a gasp; his chilly hand had caught her wrist. She whirled on him, careful not to drop the items she'd traded for.

He whipped his dark locks back before scowling at her.

"Don't think you can easily walk away from me, devil's harlot," he said.

Evelot yanked at her arm but his iron-like grip kept hold.

"Had we not discussed your unwelcome presence here in town? Or would you like another reminder?"

"Don't mistake dictation as conversation, Piers," Evelot replied with a coolness she did not feel. "Or would you *like* to showcase your strengths to the crowd?"

Piers regarded the people nearby. All around they whispered, an audience waiting for the spectacle to peak.

He scoffed. "Good. Let them see the next mayor take care of the problems plaguing the town. Starting with you. Go on. Show them how horrid you truly are."

Her jaw tightened; he had her cornered. Any way she moved, he'd twist the narrative. Claim the victim and bolster his reputation as the "duchy's prodigy." But his cold, putrid hands were on her.

A shiver rolled up her arm and prickled at her neck. From her nape, to her ears, to her forehead, icy pins prodded up her skin. Behind Evelot's eyes pressure built, and she squeezed them shut. The act was a mistake.

The chill pulsed downward again, and from her hands came a glass-like crack. Piers screamed in alarm and released her. She looked up to see him trying to squeeze his hand shut, encapsulated by ice. Passersby skittered back in a flurry of shocked gasps and yelps.

With her hood drawn, Evelot took her chance and fled.

Through the square and its alleys was a path connecting back to the farmer's trail. Evelot retraced her steps, and several minutes later, came across the sea of faded bronze and wildflowers dissected into gated crops. Two thinner, muddier paths led to either side of the farmers' lands. Evelot rounded to the right where the lowing of long-haired cows welcomed her. The dairy farmers there had yet to emerge from their large barn, or the leftward neighbors from their orchard.

It was mutedly tranquil, traversing past familiar homesteads. Piers's screams had faded from Evelot's thoughts, though her energy waned at the sudden expense and her wrist still burned, fiery and glacial all at once. She'd have been better off if he'd torn free the whole arm. It felt too much like how he'd once gripped her. How he sneered vile words into her ear while—

Ice stung her fingertips. It wouldn't help to lose control of her powers twice in a day. She wasn't eager to see the first incident bite her in the arse later.

Reaching the end of the lane, Evelot approached two buildings. The closest was a meager stone hut, with a thatched roof and squinting windows to match. She imagined her sister inside, doing chores as best she could with a swollen, pregnant stomach. Evelot stepped up to the other's porch, her childhood home. Standing taller than the rest, the cruck-framed establishment boasted two bay attachments to the main room. Its straw roof nearly blended into the foundation, and when winter came, the thatch would buckle under the weight of gathered snow. Through both rough and ease, Evelot had never known another home.

Upon opening the door, the smell of sliced oranges and cider greeted Evelot. She looked in the shadowed main room, stepping into the constricted quarters to find a bundled, willowy figure attending a small stove. All was quiet, with no sound from the farm life outside, or from the curtained-off second level, hardly larger than a theater box. Evelot timidly stepped up to the woman's side, holding the herbs out to her.

"Mornin', Ma," Evelot said.

Her ma's feeble smile lit up like the morning sun as she looked over her shoulder. "Mornin', my darlin'. Glad to see you've returned."

"I've brought herbs for you."

"Have you now? How wonderful."

Evelot handed them off. But not without noticing the pale color and bony outline of her ma's hands. A new symptom Evelot assumed was related to her fatigue.

"Do you need help with lunch or dinner?" Evelot asked.

"I'll be fine. Hungry? There're still some—"

"Where's that scallywag?" came a thundering voice.

The door to the back entrance blew open. Tarod Wheaton stormed into the house in a frustrated huff. His wispy, balding cap of blond hair sat in a way that reminded one of an unsettled mallard, if his disheveled cotton shirt and kilt didn't. As the patient partner, Helga Wheaton smiled at her husband from her stove.

"Has he disappeared again, lovey?"

"Aye. And that'll be the last time he does. By the Harvest Maiden's Hearth, I'll—"

"'Strap him to the mill,' 'make his bed among the pigs,' 'reforge his collection'?" Ma said.

"Ach!"

Evelot's da approached his wife. With a large sniff, he inhaled the fragrant vapors of homemade cider. His limbs loosened, and a calm washed over him.

"Why's it that when I'm ready to punish him, there's always a pot of cider waiting to stop me?" Da asked.

"Are you sure? I dinnae ken."

Ma nestled her head over his shoulder. Da's arm came up to stroke his wife's back. They exhaled in unison, and their gazes both fixed on the window looking out into the fields. Evelot remained silent as she stood back. This routine of theirs was more than commonplace. It was a gesture replacing a lengthy conversation between the heads of the household, a moment to balance their thoughts. To Evelot, it was strange, seeing Da's budding smile.

As Ma stirred the pot, he shifted. His pale eyes found Evelot to the side. She was quiet when he jolted.

"By the Maiden! You could've spoken!" Da exclaimed.

"Excuse me, Da," Evelot mumbled.

Collecting himself, he said, "Well, you're back, then. At least one of my children thinks to come home at a decent hour."

"And she's brought me herbs. Wasn't that thoughtful?" her ma asked.

To that, Da dismissively grunted. Evelot straightened her posture as he glanced back at her. A thought made his brows draw closer together. "If you aren't doing anything, then come along. There's work to do," he said.

"Oh, but Evelot only just returned. She needs to eat."

Evelot fiddled with the hood of her cloak. Her stomach rumbled in protest as she shook her head. "I can do it, Ma. Da doesn't have long before the festival."

"See?" said Da. "She'll be fine. Off we go."

Evelot felt her ma's concerned gaze as she followed Da out the back door. The fatigue in her bones was there, but she put it aside a while longer.

Tarod Wheaton's pride lay in his decades-long craft: his outdoor domain. The shed helmed all the irrigation channels with its silent watermill, and a small grain silo kept stocked for emergencies stood behind it. Twin coops of clucking chooks and their cocky protectors hadn't a single board out of place; the mud in the pigpen gleamed in the afternoon sun. Never had her da let his profession suffer from a day of rest. Evelot lost count of the times he had repainted each wee hut, of the times he had given meticulous measurements to the wood artisan for repairs. On the few occasions he had returned from the Grand Granary with a set of replacement livestock, there was a look about him. As if he'd taken a small oath to make sure that trip was his last.

Da led the way to the tiny shed before the gates to the field. All dozen of the scythes and other crop tools leaned against the wall.

"Here—" Da handed her the smallest of the scythes. Apparently, he'd yet to donate it from the years serving her and Ulleh during their youth. As Evelot accepted the tool, she took up another in the other hand.

"You'll chop off a limb, girl," warned Da.

"No, Da, I'm not wielding both."

Holding both tools out, Evelot measured their weight. Her da watched incredulously until she rotated the smaller scythe. Before her fist there mirrored the outline of a hollow hand, summoned by a muttered cantation. Its fingers closed around the tool's handle and hovered beside her, awaiting her command.

Da clucked his tongue. He turned his back to her and gave quick orders while he set off to the next lot. She should've known better than to cast magic in front of her da.

Evelot followed closely as he cut through the lineup of unharvested wheat stalks. The harvest had begun a month ago, yet half the field remained unculled, stretching back to the gate's entrance. As the two of them set to work, the autumnal chill helped cool them faster in their laborious efforts. Evelot took comfort in the humdrum rhythm of swinging scythes, the airy clunk as blade met stalk, and the swish of the wheat's fall to the earth. Like a pendulum, her arms motioned back and forth, the summoned help echoing her movements close by.

Into the early afternoon, Da called to her, letting her know he would take a break. Evelot joined him under the large apple tree, listening to his silent pants for breath as she wiped the sweat from her brow.

"Da?"

"Aye?"

"Where've all the farmhands gone?"

He grunted. "They're all setting up the festival for the next few days."

"Including Erich? Or Uto from the Granary?"

"They're helping sort the other fields before the winter."

"But you have more to harvest than—"

"We'll be fine on our own," he said adamantly, then sat up with a wince. "The work will be done on time."

Evelot solemnly nodded. She was ready to leave it at that, but Da's guard crumbled as he watched her.

"Yeh," he started. "Your. . ." He motioned with his hand toward her and the spell-summoned hand, but the gesture only confused her. "That—It appeared and—"

Evelot blinked.

"Ach, never you mind."

With a heavy frown, Da scuttled to his feet. Evelot moved to help him only for his scolding finger to dissuade her.

He returned to his work as Evelot stayed behind, lost in thought. The bite of the tree bark against her back all but distracted her from the disappointment in her heart. It was a challenge, trying to win back his favor. When the voices of nature had called to her, when they answered her wishes to bloom or wither, it'd all changed. Her da once tried to seek the clergy for help, but the High Priestess thought her alien to the church. After nothing else worked, her parents shifted their focus to Ulleh starting her own family. The chance for Evelot to put a genuine smile on her da's face scattered like dust in the wind.

She drew in a long breath. With closed eyes, Evelot bit back a swelling of emotion. A silent scream at her circumstances. A wish to change it all.

After a calming pause, Evelot shifted her focus. She'd need to replenish her supplies near the Choille's tree line. She was keen on creating a salve for strained muscles; that had to be what Da suffered from. For her ma, there were still leftover ingredients to make a tea for waning energy. Maybe a pinch of sugar or honey to dilute the bitterness.

Evelot returned to the field, where she willed her extra hand to swing faster. Her grumbling stomach quieted soon after rejoining the fray. Lightheadedness threatened to warp her vision, but Evelot took a swig from her water pouch and pushed through. The work would get done on time.

Once the spell faded, the extra scythe dropped in the middle of the culled wheat. Evelot stopped to collect what was there. She bundled the harvest into her arms and carted it back to the pile that awaited sorting by their silo. As she loaded another armful, spitting at the tufts in her mouth and swatting at bugs, a heavy swish of the wheat caught her ear. Evelot looked over, yet nothing emerged. The sound carried away into the field until it disappeared over the edge of the fence. She reasoned the wind must've been the cause, but she remembered the pig farmer across the main road had a Collie with a tendency to wander.

She rose to her feet and stalked closer to the sound. Over the dancing wheat in the breeze, there was an outline of. . . something. Something dark and shaggy, galloping on all fours like the dog in question.

Evelot sighed at the crumpled wheat stalks left

behind. Her father would pop a blood vessel to see them go to waste. The Grand Granary expected a hearty donation, too. Perfect timing.

She shook her head and opened her mouth to call for her da. But her brows drew together in confusion. Evelot crouched down. In the dirt lay not a paw, but a single footprint. It fanned out as though the person had turned too quickly. If not for its partner lying inches away, Evelot wouldn't have discerned the thick markings that pierced the ground above the toes. Thick, like claws.

The nape of her neck prickled in alarm.

As she moved to inspect it further, Da's voice echoed across the way. She jumped up to see him beckoning her. Without a second thought, Evelot scurried off and away from the field.

After depositing the last load by the silo in the dulling sunlight, both father and daughter shuffled inside. Evelot's empty stomach caught up to her, awakening at the smell of a plump roast bathing in a salted stew. From the front door came the sound of Evelot's sister, Ulleh, and her boisterous family. While setting the plates, Ma looked up with a smile, waving all of them over.

A head of brown hair on a thick little body whizzed between Ulleh's and Yahir's legs. Zachery, Evelot's nephew, rose onto the dining benches. He was a curious thing with a bottomless well of energy to tap from, insistent that his grandparents watch him do jigs and dances atop the seats. His thick-armed father, Yahir, hollered after him with a stern, low voice, too busy walking Ulleh to her seat to grab the bairn himself.

"Long day of work, Da?" Ulleh asked.

"Hmm," he grumbled.

Da took his seat at the head of the table, his fist wrapping around his knife and fork. It wasn't until Evelot eyed the open stairway in the corner that she realized what soured her da's mood. A sprightly version of him, complete with his fair hair and worn attire, froze on the staircase under his da's glare.

"Tonlin," their da said in warning.

The youngest of the siblings looked to Ma, then Ulleh. Neither of them reciprocated.

"Sit," ordered Da.

Sighing, Tonlin obeyed. He sank into the bench as Evelot seated herself, scooting away when he eyed her.

"Good evening, Father!" said Yahir.

The hardy fellow patted his father-in-law's shoulder in greeting, his jolly smile lighting up the room. Surprisingly, for a dark-haired Esmoran hailing from duchy wealth, he'd adapted well to farm life. He'd taken the Wheaton name, though soon after his surname had become nothing to those that mattered. Without his earlier privilege, he had only Evelot's sister, his son, and another bairn soon to come by the next season.

Cackling and whooping, Zachery zoomed around the table. He leaned over into Evelot's peripheral, and by his sudden silence, she knew he'd spotted her.

"Zachery."

The boy snapped his head in his father's direction.

"Come sit by me tonight, boy."

The boy snuck a peek back at her before returning to his father's side. With Ulleh's family seated opposite Evelot, Da led the table in a prayer to the Harvest Maiden. They passed the utensils after, followed by dishes of stew and roast.

Evelot kept her head lowered, listening to their blether with disinterest. There wasn't much to add to the usual talk about the weather while she'd been past the threshold of trees over several days. Her bowl of seasoned soup and sparse vegetables captured her attention more than anything else at that table.

A swollen hand waved at her in her peripheral vision. Evelot looked up to see Ulleh's smile digging into her reddened cheeks, highlighting her splotches of melasma.

"Ev," she said, low enough not to interrupt the men's chatter, "when'd you get back?"

"Just this morning," Evelot said, still spooning her soup.

"You go deeper into the woods this time?" Ulleh asked.

"No. Just went to collect herbs."

"C'mon, now. You have to tell me more. You're no' getting into trouble, are you?"

Evelot didn't need to peek at the table to know she wouldn't be able to answer that question. At Ulleh's side, Yahir turned his head and said, "Oh, no. Not in the woods. But that does not stop certain people from causing trouble in the square."

Biting into her cheek, Evelot lowered her head.

"What's this?" asked Da.

"Word has it that a crowd witnessed an attack on the mayor's son by the 'witchling,'" Yahir explained. "Graciously, the young man saw reason, and told his duchy guards to stand down. He won't be pressing the matter further."

"Aye, very gracious," Ma said.

"As much as the wee eejit can muster," Ulleh said to herself.

Evelot glimpsed her da in the corner of her eye. His knife and fork worked ever so slowly at his roast; a sign he was lost in thought over the news. She didn't dare look up any further. His disapproval was fierce like the summer sun in the fields.

"Speaking of trouble," Yahir said. "Where've you been away to, Tonlin?"

Tonlin made a noise of dismissal as he chewed his roast. "Nowhere" he finally said.

Da grumbled to himself as if to disagree. Tonlin merely glanced back down at the table.

Yahir laughed aloud. "At least you spend that energy. It's good for the spirit of a boy coming into his manhood. Perhaps it'll prepare you to best your current idol. . . That, er, 'warrior.'"

"You mean Prilthadollak? Why would I want to best the legend hersel'?"

"Because you are an underdog in the making. A human man from humble beginnings that'll show them who is more determined. No amount of Jinryuu or what have you, can overcome that."

"We'll see," muttered Da.

"Have they said anything of the visitors in town?" Ulleh asked her husband.

"What hasn't the town been talking about? As we speak, the bard and that warrior occupy the tavern with song and story."

Tonlin perked up beside Evelot.

"Of course, that won't last long. Leslie isn't pleased his tavern is filled with many a woman thirsting for song over mead."

Da scoffed. "A braw-looking bard is about as useful as a colorful strutting co—"

"Tarod." Ma tapped his arm in warning. "It's a phase, a thrill for them. Bards are known for their passion, which is a contagious emotion, aye?"

"Aye. Life is more than passion, dear. And a good day's work produces a harvest befitting the goddess."

Evelot assumed Ma smiled in agreement.

"Exactly that," said Yahir. "It's better for the youth to learn from their labor than to seek passion and pleasure, or spirits in the woods that tell them to attack others."

Evelot's fist tightened around her fork as she kept her eyes on her bowl. But without the comfort of her hood, which her ma had banned from the table, she felt stifled under Yahir's regard.

She looked up in time to see Ulleh wince, grabbing at her stomach. Yahir jumped to action, his hand at his wife's shoulder.

"What is it, love?" Yahir asked.

Ulleh squeezed his other hand, and with a puckered expression, she said, "No—" She skelped his arm with a loud smack. "Just want you to shut it," she added, sitting up.

Amid the couple's hushed argument, and Zachery's giggling and smacking at his da, Ulleh glimpsed back at Evelot. She was always the eldest sister who tended to the younger siblings. Evelot never begrudged Ulleh for it in the past, but now that she'd reached her twenty-first year, it was pathetic to let Ulleh keep championing her.

If only Evelot had her sister's strength.

Swallowing the last of her broth, she put down her spoon.

"May I be excused, Da?" Evelot murmured.

"Er, aye."

She mumbled her thanks as she rose from her seat. Like the nights previous, Evelot stole away to the washbasin, and then up the stairs, allowing her family solitude in their meal.

Chapter Two

Behind an old, dusty curtain on the top floor was Evelot's childhood bedroom. In each corner of the rickety, wooden floor sat a straw mattress draped in burlap and handmade quilts. Scant furnishings decorated the compact quarters, aside from her trunk of clothes and ingredients and a brass gas lamp dividing their floor space. Evelot stepped inside, taking a deep, quiet breath as the sound of conversation continued below. She slipped off her cloak and sat at the edge of her bed. Though the burlap was thick, bits of straw still stuck her through her skirts. After years of living as such, the pain hardly registered.

To her relief, the herbs she kept stored were still intact, if a bit stale or on the verge of molding. Evelot unwound her nerves, soothing herself with tedious organization.

Before she knew it, her family had cleared the tables below, and the curtain to the second floor whipped back.

"Hells," groaned Tonlin. "They never stop blethering."

He met Evelot's eye warily before huffing and flopping onto his bed. The wooden floorboards groaned in response.

"Da still doesn't approve?" Evelot asked.

Grumbling, Tonlin turned on his side.

Around thirteen, Tonlin was yet to be an adult that led a life of adventure and heroic battles with his mighty weapon. Their da described him as "the lad with aspirations as wild as a bairn's fancies." At least, that was one of the tamer comments Evelot heard before attending to the woods.

As she snuck a glance back at him, empathy flashed through Evelot. The memory of his first encounter with a traveling adventurer's group years ago surfaced. How his eyes lit gleefully, his wondrous smile widening at the stories regaled by a boastful bard. To the day he still collected adverts of adventuring parties and boats set on far horizons to display on his wall. It was only in the past year that his growth spurt and determination allowed him to wield an axe properly, supervised by the farmhands. The muscle for it had yet to show, all the more reason their da disapproved. But Evelot had seen the calluses forming, the various cuts and colorful bruises on his arms and legs that Tonlin tried to hide.

"Is it true?" Evelot asked. "That the bard and warrior are still in the tavern?"

"Why wouldn't it be true?" said Tonlin. "That pompous singer might be thriving off adoration alone, but. . ."

Tonlin rolled back over, a boyish grin teasing his lips. "Of all the warriors to be here in town, it's none other than Prilthadollak of Staeq Crana. The upcoming Claw of the Jinryuu, they say—a title worthy of those with the strength of a hundred men. Someone like that knows how to fight properly."

Evelot faced Tonlin, curious about his sudden silence. "What is it?"

"Da forbade me from town till the festival. Said I haven't finished my chores in the field."

"Hmmm."

Their ma may have persuaded their da against seeing through the extreme threat, but Tonlin had no chance of avoiding his field work for so long. Evelot suspected their da would make his bed on the front porch rocking chair to prevent her brother from running off. What seemed to be impossible to fix, however, wasn't as written in stone as Tonlin might think.

"If I can convince Da to let you off, will you do something for me?" Evelot asked.

Tonlin looked at her with a baffled face. "How do you convince a cow to speak the Shared Language? You don't."

"I have my ways."

"What? You'll poison your own da with something magicked?"

Her brows pinched together. "No. Nothing like that."

"Then how do I ken you're not lying?"

"Do you want to see Prilthondolla or not?"

"Prilthadollak."

She frowned back at him.

"What do you want?" Tonlin snapped. "It's not some kind of curse or hex—?"

"Forget it."

Evelot lay down on her straw bed and turned on her side. She wouldn't try to argue in her defense. It wouldn't be skin off her back to wait until morning for the harvesting she planned to do, only that the night promised better results. Tonlin could wait to meet the visitor in town for another day.

"No—wait—"

She heard him crawl out of bed, then felt his palm on her shoulder. Nudging her, Tonlin said, "Don't sleep just yet!"

"I've worked long into the day," Evelot groaned.

"Stay awake longer, then! Evelot!"

Evelot rolled over.

"What do you want in return?" Tonlin said.

Smugness curled at her lips.

"**P**uddocks?" complained Tonlin. "All you wanted were wee frogs?"

The two siblings walked the trail toward town. As promised, Evelot need only mention "herb collecting" to their da and his demeanor curdled into detachment. Tonlin tagged along to the outer rim of the wheat field where a small pond lay. There they collected samples for her craft and snuck off into the shadows of the Gloaming.

"Not just frogs. Their secretions," Evelot corrected.

"Don't call it that!" Tonlin groaned. Swiping his sticky hands on his shirt, he shuddered. "I can't believe you collect that filth!"

"You'd be surprised by their medicinal properties," Evelot said. "But. . . why do frogs unnerve you? You're a boy."

"I'm a man. And why wouldn't they? They're slimy. Those dark eyes stare into your soul, and they sound about as awful as crickets."

"And bugs?"

"Wha—? I'm not as bad as Ulleh is. Acts like the Harvest Maiden's scythe's coming to reap her every time one dives at her heid."

Evelot tried not to laugh, but Tonlin's cackle was contagious. The thought of her sister ducking and screaming from a beetle was too much.

"You're horrible," Evelot replied.

"Not as horrible as her avoiding the Blairs and their apiary."

"Maybe so, but she's still your sister."

"Oh? And what does that say about you?"

He playfully nudged her arm. Evelot chuckled. She met his gaze, stopping before the town entrance. His expression fell, and the moment dwindled. A sister, indeed. But to the public eye, she was a shadow, and he had no claim to her without the cost of his own esteem.

Raising her hood, Evelot said, "Let's see you to the tavern."

"I. . ."

Evelot started ahead only to stumble to a stop. A low, piercing howl echoed from the woods.

"Evelot?"

She turned to her brother.

"I. . ." His lips pursed before a sigh left him. "Can you. . . can you come in with me?"

"You mean it?"

"Just in case I might lose my nerve. It's. . ."

Evelot smiled. "I'll be right behind you."

He looked up at her with a small smile. "Let's go, then."

As if to answer, another ominous howl erupted into the night.

The Glistening Seed was a staple in Goldencrest in the middle of the King's Quarter. Standing at five levels, the inn boasted the tallest of the Naspington duchy's southern region. With thick stone walls and recently installed "plumbing" in each room, there was much to patronize them for besides the bevvies. Inside, Evelot and Tonlin watched the crowd shuffle and sway, astonished by the plethora of people. Beneath legs and feet wooden floorboards lined one end of the room to the other, their scuffs marking where patrons stomped to merry tunes. How they had yet to cave in to the weight, Evelot didn't know. The smell of hot, cured meats and pungent liquors carried on the warm air, and on the breath of passersby. A nervous sweat trickled down her back as she thought about wading from the comfort of the doorway into the packed room.

She turned to ask Tonlin about his mystery idol. But he wasn't at her side. Evelot peered through the crowd, rising on the tips of her toes. What looked to be visiting travelers sat at the tables, and older, regular patrons by the bar. Many were in the throes of banter and laughter, others griping about their arduous day of work. Yet no sign of Tonlin.

Evelot shifted on her feet. After another body moved, the bar became visible. At one end was a line of tankards stacked haphazardly around one individual. What looked like long dreadlocks of dark brown hung from a flat head. But then, the firelight gleamed off of their skin differently from the pale flesh that populated Goldencrest. No, not flesh. Scales.

Within her isolated human town, Evelot was one of the few to remember learning about the different species of Runlaris. In all the realm, the peoples closest to Evelot and the Duchy States of Cuthosia were the elves of Vestryae, the

Beaghans of Oglen, and farther west the Ninanuna of Acluetho. But the Jinryuu, in the country of Staeq Crana, beyond the gnome lands and dwarven mountains to the southeast, were a rare and peculiar crowd to appear in western Runlaris. Unfortunately, all Evelot could attest to was that they had appeared in the Beginning. A species of life so like the ancient dragons with tails and snouts yet as capable and similar to a humanoid.

The Jinryuu sitting at the bar drew Evelot's attention. Their demeanor appeared as serious and pensive as a wary owl with a slight hint of indifference. Taking another tankard in hand, they tipped it back and downed what might have been whiskey. Their sapphire exterior merged into smaller gray-white scales that started below their chin. When their head lowered and their cup added to the tally on the countertop, there was a glint to their eyes, golden and piercing like a flame. The warrior almost found Evelot in the distance. But they turned their gaze to the empty stage, crossing their arms sullenly. Leather armor stretched over sinew, and to Evelot's surprise, silver breastplate covered their chest.

Tonlin didn't warn her that the skilled warrior Prilthadollak was, in fact, not a man.

In the same moment, Tonlin trudged closer to his idol. He hovered behind Prilthadollak briefly with pursed lips. His hands flexed by his sides. Though his voice was muted from afar, Evelot could discern the stumble of his words as he called to the warrior. Prilthadollak craned her head toward him, and he gaped like a terrified bairn. Evelot tried to wave her hand at him, pushing deeper into the crowd. The bodies instead pushed back. She nearly dared to raise her voice, but Evelot couldn't find the courage. It was only a matter of time before anyone recognized the Witchling of the Choille.

Her brother's name slipped past her lips, drowned out by the crowd.

Heads blocked her view, and her brother and the warrior disappeared. In a dizzying blur, she stumbled into the foot traffic directed toward the stage.

Evelot finally found purchase squished between a gaggle of women near the front. They hushed one another as the curtain above fluttered. Half the room stilled as someone sauntered out into the stage lights. An elven bard.

"A fairest even, my lovely doves," said the entertainer. "Have you been waiting long for me?"

Many of the lasses blushed and squealed. Evelot heard a faint affirmation from one of them, followed by a sarcastic retort from one of the older locals. The bard's only response was an austere grin. Enclosed by squeals and delight, Evelot stood gazing at him in utter confusion.

"How humbling a sight of both familiar and new faces. Pray allow me, Zenris Aspenheart, to guide you on a journey of timelessness and nostalgia with *The Winds of Rosewick.*"

Everything around Evelot fell to a dead quiet. The bard began with a strum over his lute, falling into a slow melody. His bejeweled fingers plucked over the chords. Inclining his head with the rhythm, he sang with a lustrous timbre. It held on the notes of bittersweet memories, and grew bolder, louder with the lyrics of carrying on after love had been long lost. Fans sniffled beside Evelot; every newcomer like her numbly watched, entranced by his performance.

That is, every newcomer but Evelot.

She scrutinized the musician onstage with a curious brow. If clothing could speak, his would be as loud as an operatic bellow. Judging by the stacked heel in his boots, he couldn't have been taller than her height. Tucked into them were tight leather braies she didn't think could let his "parts" breathe, and a loose pale cotton shirt half buttoned to display a spectacle of lean dark muscle. While he plucked the strings, there sparkled small rings, blinking like the golden loop on one of his pointed ears. All of it was obviously a purposeful display to Evelot. But it amazed her that over his paughty bravado, he could still squeeze his brown hair into a tie without cutting off blood flow to his thick head.

Evelot didn't know if elves were privy to charms or ancient magical trinkets. Without the ability of the right detection spell, she assumed his musical skill was genuine. If so, Evelot might have thought his voice was exceptional. Then again, she wasn't there to listen to music and openly weep among other lasses.

With backward steps, Evelot moved away from the fans at the front. She slipped through the crowd as the bard kept their attention, the slight brush of an arm sending her hand to adjust her hood. The crowd thinned the farther she got. With the lights trained on the stage, it was difficult to see the bar toward the other wall. Evelot peeked over tall shoulders to find the silhouette of Prilthadollak in her seat. For a moment she believed Tonlin was still there with the warrior. As she reached the bar, a flash of movement closed in on her. She spotted a woman bustling with a trayful of tankards a second late.

Evelot shifted, but a solid body behind her sent her careening forward. Something thin and metal charged into her sternum before pale yellow and brown liquids sloshed into her face. Her boots slipped out from under her, and both the tray and Evelot went crashing to the floor.

She tried to look up, but the sting of alcohol in her eyes made her cry out. A hush flooded the crowd as the lights filled the tavern room. What looked like skirts swaying back and boots stomping away whirred past her. Evelot tugged her cloak around herself and attempted to stand.

But then a figure stepped up to her. Past the clearing fog, a tan hand extended downward. When she squinted up, the face of the smiling bard came into focus.

"Are you injured, little dove?" he said. "Mayhap the music was too poignant for your delicate heart?"

A sour tang on the tongue wouldn't have gagged her as much as that moment. Either because of her stalling or his inflated ego, his smile softened. Zenris Aspenheart crouched down to her level, stretching his arm toward her, too far for her liking. When she reached for her hood, she caught nothing but air; it'd fallen to her neck. She shoved it back over her head.

The surrounding crowd reared back.

"Ewgh, it's the devil's harlot," Evelot heard someone say.

"What's that thing doing here?"

"The barkeep would've stopped her at the door."

"Don't let her touch Zenris!"

A clamoring pulse thundered in her ears. Zenris turned to the crowd with a raised brow, her chance to move. Evelot stumbled to her feet in the puddle of ale and mead. She tried to correct herself as the bard glanced back at her. His hands appeared as if ready to catch her.

Sickly green energy lanced across her palms. With a sneer, she hissed, "Don't touch me!"

Only a hint of fear passed over his face. It would've launched his cavalry at her, but his fans didn't dare charge forward. Everyone in the room waited as though she'd announce a grand threat, hurl small bolts of lightning, and cackle aloud like a villainous stooge.

Instead, she whirled back and dashed for the exit, ignoring any cries or jeers that followed her out the door.

Chapter Three

Contrary to the innkeeper's sweeping declarations of attentive maintenance, the window remained glued shut. Zenris would have to have a word with her, charming as she was, if he survived the next minute.

He pulled himself up onto the window box facing the back alley. His breath hitched as he balanced on the small platform. 'Twas an anomaly, seeing his skilled hand fail to raise the blasted thing, one he was not keen to have happen again. His determination only doubled as the box creaked beneath him. He peeked up at the windows overhead. Surely there was someone in their room who would take pity on his plight and allow a bard entrance?

Zenris slowly rose on his feet, his hands outstretched for the box frame above. Another protest groaned under his boots. With little shuffles, he adjusted his footing.

His heart leapt at a splintered crack. Miraculously, 'twas only the window opening below him. From it a pair of taloned hands clenched around his ankles.

"N-no, wai—!"

The world blurred as he screamed. Wind whistled in his pointed ears, and then he was flopping onto an old, downy mattress. Zenris spat out a mouthful of yellow-stained pillow.

The list of complaints thrived as the day wore on.

"Heart of Aspen."

Zenris rolled over, folding his hands behind his head as he lay facing his Jinryuu companion. Prilthadollak glowered down at him, scaly hackles raised and posture stiff from contained rage.

"I demand answers," she said, voice husky with frustration.

"And your questions?"

"Why is it we remain here while the festivities promised have yet to be arranged? And why do you still refuse to use the entrance to your own quarters?"

"Ah, yes. How to answer such loaded questions," he said bashfully.

"What have I loaded them with if not words?" she hissed.

"Easy, friend. 'Tis a simple expression—"

"Then cease your confusing customs and answer plainly!"

He tried to hold back a laugh at the tongue that peeked out betwixt her razor-sharp bared teeth.

"Pril," Zenris said, "Admittedly, I have overestimated the days in which to travel, and the necessary coin to stay at the inn—"

"Correct. We will not last a fortnight with what is left in our coin purse."

"—but where is your sense of adventure? Do you not recall the days we had nothing but cloth and leaves for shelter alongside our other companions?"

"Yes." Pril sighed, her body relaxing. "You were surprisingly adept with the environment, for one who insists on bathing regularly in hot waters.

"But—"

Her eyes flashed contemptuously at him once more. "This conversation is not a debate of whether we can sleep outside. It is to clarify that I swore to safeguard you while our party takes a 'hiatus.' You understand that I travel by your side in order to learn your flesh-kin ways. I believed your promise of opportunity to do so. Yet you have not delivered on it, and you have not performed for the festival you claimed is 'worth the trouble.'"

"I will acknowledge my mistakes." Zenris rose to his knees, his hands up as a signal of surrender. "While I am most appreciative of your accompaniment, friend, I do have your wishes in mind. 'Twould be reasonable to acquire the coin needed for our departure. . . Without forgoing certain pleasures?"

"Very well." Pril crossed her sinewy arms. "And what do you propose?"

Zenris froze, then sheepishly grinned. "I can perform twice as often in the tavern."

"And?"

"'And'?"

"Given the outcome of your performances so far, I see no benefit to staying within one line of work."

Zenris withheld a grumble. 'Twas true; it had been nearly a week since he had taken the stage. The repetitive cycle may slightly disgruntle the barkeeper after so long, and his fans may crowd the tavern tables more than the actual patrons, but the coin was good. It should be, at least. What more was there to worry over when he was earning his keep and enrapturing listeners with his enchanting melodies? Save for one.

"As long as you bring back your earnings at the end of each night, I will accept your terms," Pril said.

"Of course."

Pril cut him off with a look. "However. Should you fall short, I will drag you back to our party who generously overlooked your departure. And we will take the long way back, mucking through muddy terrain and the filth of Esmoran waste dumps."

"Ma'am, yes, ma'am." Zenris gave an Esmoran army salute, all the while hiding the quake in his boots.

"Good. Now that one topic has been settled, you will explain why you are climbing the exterior walls."

"Ah. . . that. . ."

On cue, hushed giggles bounced across the hallway outside.

"I may not have kept quiet about my room number."

Pril cursed in her native tongue. "Have you only a brain in your nether regions?"

"I resent that remark, Pril. I would never entangle myself in a fan's sheets, according to the rulebook of professional bards. That I do not intend to break. . .again."

"Trust that you don't. But that will not stop an army of raving fanatics from hunting you like a Graulian lion would a hare."

"Ah, yes. Please do remind me of their ravenous appetite for me."

"Do you not recall the time a man snuck into camp and made off with a pair of your pantaloons?"

"The statement was rhetorical, but yes. Your concern warms my heart."

Pril mumbled her god's title, shaking her head. With ease, she threw open her door. Zenris heard the gasps of his fans crowded outside his neighboring room, others yelping.

With a beastly growl, Pril yelled, "Away with you sniveling, carnivorous pests! Before you anger me further!"

The fans screamed, and a stampede of pounding feet and bustling skirts disappeared down the staircase.

At her side, Zenris said, "You could be more delicate. They are *my* fans, after all."

"That is why you are not fit to be a true warrior. You lack the proper necessities to assert your dominance. They confuse their position thusly."

"And there is supposed to be honor and glory in dictating how they should praise me?"

"There is honor in training one's pet to be obedient."

"I. . . There is too much to unravel from that."

With a plain nod, Pril dismissed Zenris from her room. He entered the hallway, patting around for his room key. To his credit, he had remembered to lock the door behind him last.

When he stepped inside, the bitter smell of ink and dusty linens greeted him. Zenris closed the door behind himself, taking in the sight of his unkempt bed and cluttered writing desk with an aloof smile. The room, filled with his minimal possessions and bare necessities provided by the inn, was plenty cozy for relaxation. Prilthadollak was still a newcomer to humanoid-sized foundations. There are times that call for stepping around one's bags and bedposts to immerse oneself in the creature comforts of life. Not to mention, the downy mattress absorbed its sleeper in a warm embrace, more so than a pile of leaves ever could. What more could one ask for?

Pril became more irritable the longer their stay, though Zenris had not expected her ill mood to develop so soon. There were only so many embellishments and half-truths he could offer before she caught on to his true intentions, to why they were awaiting a festival in a small town like Goldencrest. Zenris was determined to maintain the ruse as long as possible.

He rounded the bed and sat at his desk. Zenris let the feel of parchment beneath his fingertips and the light from the window consume his thoughts. With a quill in hand, he stared down at his latest composition. A small collection of loose lyrics lined the upper half of the page, the bottom dotted with musical notes uncaged from the usual bracket. Despite all the slashes he had cut through them, both sheets had yet to cry out.

Zenris's sigh whistled through his nostrils.

'Twas only a few years prior that Zenris had been far from cluelessly staring at an ink-stained parchment. All he had needed was to think of a passing view, a tantalizing smell, or the melody of a chirping bird and he could compose music worthy of a ballroom audience. There was always something melodic to capture in the smallest of things. Yet the days of ease with his vernacular had passed. None of those perfect words returned, and it remained a struggle to encapsulate what he wished to share in song. This issue, insignificant in its current form, hardly troubled him. 'Twas only a matter of time before it resolved.

. . . If at all.

Zenris flipped through the other sheets, older pieces worn from age and use. A small smile crept over his lips as he reminisced on other melodies. He remembered how he stood on the Grand Stage of the Silver Strings Festival and performed them, the pieces he had toiled over for hours. The crowds had applauded him, the sound crashing through the theater as fiercely as waves over cliffsides. Their tears had shone like spotlights, and cries echoed within his mind throughout that night. They felt the same as he did; he immersed them in the beautiful complexity of his songs dedicated to journeys, hardship, and lovers. He captured their hearts, their attention.

Yet, when Zenris flipped to the last page on his desk, his earlier triumph proved inconsequential. Frail, fraying pulp brushed his fingertips. The ink was still legible, still holding the notes and lyrics he had studied religiously. Within the writer's transcription was a message to all of those amongst the city streets and dreamers riding caravans to great distances beyond their abundant or meager lives. To address the common folk of all standings with such tenderness, a song of encouragement. . .

Zenris's fingers lovingly traced over the drawn brackets. 'Twas not his penmanship. It did not seem possible for him to achieve such greatness.

As he hummed the tune aloud, something slipped past Zenris's head. It dropped onto the desk, nearly blending into the rich brown of the wood. A twig. Zenris ran his fingers through his hair. Thankfully, the stick had not given him away during Pril's earlier tongue-lashing. When he picked it up, studying it, it reminded him of his mission.

Another fruitless endeavor the night was, and those previous. Endeavors that he was not keen to perpetuate. The season's end was at hand, and time was of the essence before any evidence of his mission scattered to the winds. Until then, Zenris would bide the daylight with efforts such as his music. Yet. . .

An impatient whimper escaped Zenris. He flattened over his desk, arms folded over his head. He needed a muse. Something remarkable to reach the heights his favorite song had. Something. . . different.

His mind lingered on the thought. Zenris could pay homage to the quaint little town. Surprisingly, for a human-based civilization, they had an accent alike to the Beaghans. If a Beaghan's cadence fluttered like a butterfly's wings, then a native of Goldencrest's carried on as a bird's. The lands surrounding the town were teeming, and their abundant choice of imbibement had no competition. Yet, he did not seek "something" to write of. Rather, a "someone".

"The Witchling of the Choille" they called her out of the titles not worth repeating. None of them did justice to those few moments with her. The one who gazed upon him with those rich, verdant eyes like Oglen hills, and long hair spun of sunset colors. Her pale skin only complemented those full rose-tinted lips, so keen to loose a curse at him. Her tapered nose as poised as the ancient fae queens' and their sculptures rendered from Esmoran artisans.

Yes, that was someone worthy of song. That mystery maiden and her severe frown. However, tucked deeply away, Zenris sensed the right occasion had yet to come for her reverent smile to bloom. Unfortunately, she was an elusive creature. No amount of begging to the gods for another glimpse of her would do him well as a repeat sinner.

Sighing, Zenris took up his quill and sat up. The clouds overhead shifted, and the sun spilled into his room again. His hand rose to block the blinding light before cover finally arrived. Yet when next he opened his eyes, his mouth puckered into an astonished O.

In the alleyway behind the inn, the familiar blur of a dull brown cloak slunk past. Her pale hands secured her hood while strands of her sunray hair tumbled out.

"My. . . gods. . ."

Zenris slowly rose to his feet. The witchling looked over her shoulder. Within the depth of her hood there peeked the outline of her pointed chin, the curve of her pinkened nose. Yet the moment quickly receded as she turned and disappeared into the alley.

Zenris threw on his cloak. Climbing out the window, he said aloud, "O Forest Matron or Father Nature or whoever still watches over me, you are most gracious and kind. Pray you excuse me from paying back this favor until I clear my debt to the Esmoran magistrate, and that band of orcs. . . and that store I set aflame twice."

After a rushed climb down and a soft thud, Zenris landed in the alleyway. He spun around in her direction, checking either corner leading out of the King's Quarter. Yet his mystery witch was gone. Quickly, he jogged toward the square.

Similar to the capital city of Esmora, people were in no short supply. Farmers led their oxen-driven carts around Zenris toward River's End. The storefronts sat open, peddling their wares over the boisterous square. He laughed as children darted betwixt strangers' legs in a game of tag, before a throng of townsfolk distracted him amidst the search for the familiar cloak. Only when he trained his focus past lumbering shoulders did a sliver of the witchling catch his eye.

Zenris grinned. He started after her as she silently slipped past others. Surely their second encounter—

A gasp halted him.

"Good morning, Zenris!"

Encircling him were the familiar faces of his fans. Zenris tried to meet their eager smiles with one of his own. Many were duchy nobles with vibrant skirts and dazzling jewelry. Surprisingly they showed no qualms in uniting with the soil-dusted maidens from the farming community. If only solidarity had not taken place at that moment.

"A most glorious morn to you all, my lovely doves," Zenris greeted, trying to spy the witch ahead. Her figure receded into the crowd, and panic struck his heart.

"You must be so bored here in this small town," said a noblewoman with coiffed hair. "Why don't we show you the scenery?"

"How are you faring at the inn?"

"Is your latest song finished yet?"

Zenris puffed up proudly hearing their genuine interest, yet deflated at the last question. He felt a slight flare of annoyance warm his chest at the stifling confinement and the reminder of his poor concentration.

"Ladies, rest assured—"

"Oh, please say yes. We promise it'll be fun!"

The others chimed in just as desperately. He should have remembered his disguise spells instead of charms. With the crowd gathering, people leering, and the witch disappearing, Zenris had to act. He looked back at the inn hoping Pril would come to his rescue.

Then the idea struck him.

"Oh, no," he said.

"What is it?"

"My mannerless companion!"

Motioning for them to move, he replied, "Let us make haste before she catches us!"

They gasped and bustled away. Zenris followed behind them, pleased with himself as he ducked around a moving cart.

His quick maneuver led him opposite their direction, exactly where he last saw the witchling. Weaving under carried crates and past others, he slipped into an alley betwixt the stone-carved duchy quarters and a log-built business. To Zenris's dismay, there was nothing but discarded barrels and shadows. He was sure 'twas not a mistake. Zenris examined the alley once more, ears strained for any noise.

Faint shuffles of feet echoed nearby. He crept around the bend and stopped. In the adjoining alley was the witchling, stumbling in his direction. She must not have seen him in the flurry as she spun back around, panting.

"As if you can outrun me," said a voice from deeper within.

A ruggedly handsome youth approached, dark brown hair tied in a bun. Somehow familiar to Zenris. . .

"Your devil craft and curses will end soon enough. So hide in your pathetic woodland, if you think that'll comfort you, harlot!" the youth said.

Her shock betrayed her harsh response. "D-don't you dare blame the Choille for this!"

"'Ha! As if it matters about your precious squirrels and fawns. It'll all come down, and your plot will be exposed before long!"

Two other men waited behind the youth, cornering her in the dead end. From beyond Zenris's crate, the tension rose. The only escape was the way he had entered, but they would easily snatch her if she dared run for it. The witchling shifted, glancing at her surroundings, a sudden air teasing at the edge of her hood. A spark of light dazzled her palm, there and gone. It moved as if in tandem with a frenetic pulse, the same mana she had conjured when last facing Zenris.

"As if you have the strength of an actual hunter," she said, standing as firm as a frightened child.

"Oh, I know how to carve an animal, no less a witch and her summoned demonic horde." The youth gestured to a knife at his belt.

Without a thought, Zenris dove out of the shadows. He jumped in front of the witchling, his arms splayed.

"Stop right there!" Zenris cried.

"Who in the hells?" The reprobate's scowl disappeared as he considered Zenris. "Ah," said he. "My father's guest. How *fitting* a time to see you."

Zenris frowned. "Have we met before?"

"Once. Hardly a moment, if anything."

The way he held himself spoke of entitlement, similar to the Esmoran nobles from the capital city. Zenris fleetingly recalled someone alike to the youthful man from his arrival in Goldencrest. Whether an important figurehead or not, his behavior would have Zenris argue otherwise.

"This is the sort of customary treatment you show women?" Zenris replied. "I cannot imagine your prospects of love are exemplary."

"*That* is no ordinary woman. Take my word for it: It is wise to avoid that snake at all costs."

"A mundane magic user? Beg pardon, but there are many more in Runlaris than in this town alone."

"Perhaps they are more respectable than some. However, witches have a tendency to cause more harm than good, no?"

"What exactly would warrant a witch's punishment for a simple stroll through town?"

The young man pointed a finger, and Zenris glanced back over his own shoulder. He turned, finding that the witchling had not only made off but that the town square preserved itself in an unnerving silence. Zenris crept closer to the scene.

At the end of the alley, several men parted the crowd lumbering in from the farmer's path. They held a stretcher betwixt them, and a large burlap sack sat atop it.

No, not a sack.

A middle-aged woman cried aloud, shoving her way through the onlookers. She grasped at the pallbearers with a quivering chin, causing their load to sway. A limp hand fell out from under the cover.

As the woman wept in the arms of her neighbors, Zenris looked on at the melancholy scene. 'Twas not until the snide man had reached his side that he realized the other was speaking.

"As I said, chivalry is wasted on the witch. She'll summon whatever creature came last night and let it devour you just like that poor sap."

The youthful man and his wordless lackeys exited the alley, leaving Zenris to a gut-wrenching reality. Not after the crowd had dispersed was Zenris any clearer on the man's implications. A soul lost to a fiend loose in the wild. One would imagine it to be a bear or a lone wolf, as tragically natural as could be. The whispers in the crowd assumed as much. Yet there were plenty that glanced about, afraid to find a certain someone long vanished from the square. Accusations rose, and more derogatory names were invoked in the same breath. The air turned stale with the disturbing revelation.

In all his travel, Zenris rarely heard the term "witch" as much as the interchangeable label of "hag." The former often described a woman denied a magical college education, a woman who had gone off on her own, yet hags… Well, they were a trickier sort. Beside his party he had fought many of these residents of dank swamps and thick forests. The Witchling of the Choille lacked every characteristic of the cackling, child-eating creature. Dare he say she was unskilled, from her lack of intent to harm the other night. No, she could not have summoned something so horrid.

Weaving through the crowd of gossipmongers, Zenris returned to the tavern for respite. To his misfortune, instead of a nice goblet of wine, he found Pril seated at one of the tavern tables. More shockingly, she was with an older human gentleman.

"Ah, young man!" the stranger called.

Zenris eased toward them with a look to Pril. His companion gave nothing away with her perpetually keen eyes. He leaned against the back of Pril's seat, greeting the stranger with a practiced smile.

"Good day, sir. As well as can be," Zenris said.

"Yes, just as well. I hope your stay has been as much thus far. Given the. . . er, current events," said the stranger.

"We cannot all be fortunate, can we?" teased Zenris.

The man tried for a chuckle, yet cast his eyes to his folded hands on the table.

"Zenris," said Pril. "The mayor of Goldencrest has a request for us, being experienced adventurers."

"Indeed," he said.

Zenris studied the man closer. Ah, how rude of him. The distraction of his fans' screams had dulled his memory of the mayor. Without his previously amicable smile, the man sitting across from them looked doubly aged than he ought to be. His dark hair was grayed at the temples, and he wore a thinning beard of the same shade. Laugh lines had developed into the telltale signs of wrinkles. Yet there was an incredible resemblance in his jawline and brow to the youthful man from the alley. Sweat trickled down Zenris's back. Hopefully, 'twould not return to shame him later.

"Well, if I were seated, I would be on the edge. This sounds like a daring, heroic quest, my good sir."

"I highly doubt this will do justice to the heroics of your past triumphs, fighting wayward orc hordes or criminal syndicates. But, the heavenly Dawn King willing, this will be a swift mission for persons of your caliber," said the mayor.

Zenris nodded with a hum, taking a seat beside Pril.

The mayor loosed a heavy sigh. "I have asked your colleague here if you would take part in a hunt. We have the added strength of the duke's appointed guard, but seeing as how things have escalated, it'd be better to take the next step with more numbers to our cause."

"A hunt, you say?" asked Zenris. "Pray tell our target."

"You'll have to forgive me for being frank, but what does that matter?"

"'Twould lessen the burden of our efforts to capture the beast, of course."

"Then you'll have to ask the grieving widow who heard her husband being attacked on his own property. Whatever it is has gone too far. First the chickens and the cattle, and now we have to stitch together a devoured human corpse for a funeral—"

The mayor stopped, his fists curled as if he were tempted to slam them to the table in frustration. Zenris would have been more concerned about the mayor's fraying nerves had it not been for two looming figures by the bar. Guards, he figured, by the common attire on their large physiques.

When next he found his words, the mayor said, "If we have to empty the entire woods for the damn wolf or bear or what have you, it will be done. This cannot continue while more and more visitors come to see the festival. You cannot imagine what it would seem to outsiders, seeing the locals cower in their homes and cancel a widely advertised festival at the last minute. There is too much at stake. So, will you help us be rid of this beast?"

Zenris peeked over at Pril, his arms crossed like hers.

"We are not clerics of the Dawn King performing charity. We ask for a fair exchange: our weapons for your coin," said Pril.

"Of course. Whatever it takes."

Zenris smiled. He inched forward in his chair and offered his hand. "Beyond awaiting the written contract, 'tis settled."

The mayor nodded, shaking his hand. Zenris kept composure while bidding the mayor and his guards leave, a storm of thoughts swirling in his head. Whether exaggeration or fact, one wolf alone could not eviscerate a human so viciously, not unless threatened. Mayhap a bear, but they would hardly dare approach human territory unless absolutely starved. There had to be more at play than that.

Thus, Zenris had his excuse to avoid the writing desk further.

Chapter Four

Evelot's scowl only worsened the longer she watched the declining hillside.

Marching up the path toward the farmer's village, the able-bodied townsfolk led by the blue-scaled warrior set their dismal sights on the Choille. Few traded words with one another; their minds were full of paranoia, and they held pitchforks and rusted swords in hand. It was a sorry sight to see the inexperienced go trouncing into the woods, knowing that they wouldn't care what they'd kill in there. With Piers among them, they were all one fleeing deer away from pillaging the Choille in a panic.

It'd been a shock when the news had traveled round about the sudden and horrific massacre. She'd heard the screams that night and the widow's heartache ever since. No one had seen it come or go, whatever sort of beast was still at large. Not even a sound left in its wake. It confounded Evelot. She had to assume, given what knowledge she had, that it had been a starving, unassuming wolf strayed from the pack. One that had her taking extra care in sneaking into town, that was.

Before they could spot her, Evelot withdrew from the hills and crossed the short distance back home. However meager, her spellbook would have to help her make sense of it all.

She'd made it to the lawn when a clatter arose from the house. The door swung open and out stepped her da, with Ma tugging at his arm.

"Lovey," Ma pleaded, "let the hot-blooded youth go out there. There's no need for busy farmers to be involved."

"Theirs isn't the only blood that runs hot," Da said. "I'll go, and I won't be its dinner."

"Oh, but—"

"Da?" Evelot cautiously approached. "You're going to join the hunting party?"

His jaw visibly tightened, and his brow furrowed into a heavy line. Taking his axe, he strode past her.

"Aye," he answered. "And that's final."

She turned and stared at him as though struck. It shouldn't have been for someone like him, behind on his work and burdened by bad joints, to hunt a shifty beast. But when Tarod Wheaton made up his mind, there was no reasoning with him. Far from her to have tried to speak her piece, either way. Yet it hurt all the same.

"Evelot?"

Her ma held onto the doorframe, looking pale and wan. Whatever frustration had built inside Evelot vanished as she rushed to Ma's side.

"Ma, are you ill?"

"I'll be fine," Ma answered breathlessly.

She took Ma's arm and coaxed her inside onto the dining bench. From the garden well, Evelot fetched a cup of water and encouraged her to take a sip.

Her waning energy wasn't cured, but she appeared

better while sitting. Evelot expected the week to be as taxing on them as it was before her da's departure. Too much food had to be cured, pickled, stored, and donated—and pens always needed mucking. The fields would nearly be complete if they'd the right amount of people, but at that point it was too much to ask. It'd be another fortnight of work if the Granary wouldn't respond, and the cold would ruin their chance at threshing the grains.

"Won't you rest some more?" Evelot asked. "You've done plenty for the week as it is."

Ma slowly shook her head then took another sip. "Your da needs all the help he can get before the festival. There's much still to be done."

"Everyone else can do the heavy work. Don't fuss yersel.'"

"I may not have been born with the Wheaton strength you all have, but I can persevere. It'll be fine, bairn." Ma patted her arm with a chill-soaked hand. There was warmth and confidence in her eyes.

Evelot's lips pursed in determination; she grasped at her ma's hand. "Ma, tell me the truth. Why've you been frail these past few months? Whatever it is, I'm sure there's a way to cure it."

"Oh, darlin.'" Ma smiled.

Evelot shifted in her seat. She'd spent so long blindly brewing potions and churning thick tinctures, anything to lessen her odd fatigue. But if her ma explained herself, Evelot wouldn't waste a second in making the correct curative.

"Nothing but the weather. Once the nippy season passes, I'll be all right." Her mother's thumb drew slow circles over Evelot's hand as she continued smiling.

Evelot bit the inside of her cheek. The moment was over, brief in its time, when the front door opened and a familiar voice called out to them.

"Are you in here, Ma?" Ulleh asked.

The air shifted beside Evelot. Her sister stopped, fists to her hips as their mother smiled up at her.

"How is my eldest?" Ma said.

"Good. Now that I've come to take over for you."

"What's that?"

"Today, you're getting the day off. Now away to bed with you and let me handle it all."

"Oh, but you've your husband and wee one to look after."

"That numpty? Said he'll work today in Da's stead and go on the hunt tomorrow. He's fetching those from the Granary so we can finish the work on time."

"Is that so?"

Their ma took another sip of water, contemplating. Ulleh went to brush aside the stray hair in her face. The look she gave Evelot confirmed what she already suspected: It was all a lie.

"Of course, I could put you on bairn duty if you feel up to chasing the wee devil 'round the garden," Ulleh offered.

"I. . . I suppose I'm due for a kip." Ma rose to stand, and patted Ulleh's cheek. "Thank you, dear."

"You're welcome. Now, shoo!"

Ma shook her head, bemused. Once she'd disappeared behind the curtain over the main bedroom, Ulleh motioned for Evelot to follow.

It wasn't until the garden door shut behind them that Ulleh let out a strained sigh.

"I swear, this season has produced nothing but headless chooks and fairytale nonsense. Makes my skin itch," Ulleh said. When Evelot didn't respond, she added, "Have you seen Tonlin at all today?"

"No," Evelot said.

"Brilliant."

Ulleh marched over to the shed a yard off. Evelot followed her, watching as she opened the front entrance. All the while the back door creaked open. Grumbling, Ulleh stopped and reached down for her shoe. She hurled it, nailing Tonlin directly in the back of his head.

"Who—? Ulleh?!" said Tonlin.

"Take one more step and I'll send the other off with you to the Harvest Maiden's Fields!" Ulleh said, marching after him.

Tonlin whirled back around. "Don't stop me! This is my chance to prove mysel'. I'll be the one to kill the beast!"

"Of course. And I can knit a shirt worthy of our 'Grand' Duke of Naspington to flaunt in front of the other nobles."

"But I can! All of you doubt me and put me down, but I won't hear it!"

Tonlin moved as if to run off. But he froze in defeat at Ulleh's warning finger. Evelot silently stood by as her older sister stomped up to Tonlin.

Stopping in her tracks, Ulleh sighed. "Da has been cross with you more than not, hasn't he?"

"What's that got to—?"

"I'm sure things didn't go your way the other night when you snuck out to see that warrior. Am I right?"

Tonlin peeked over at Evelot as though betrayed.

"You can't hide a thing from me, brother. It's plain as

day on your face," Ulleh said. She opened her hand, gesturing to the axe in Tonlin's own.

With a reluctant look, Tonlin gave it up.

"Oh, Tonlin." Ulleh set it off to the side and rubbed at his arm. "You're just like Da, and it shows. But the time will come soon enough. Until then, you're the son of a farmer who needs to reap the crops before the frost settles in."

Tonlin dejectedly kicked at the hay.

"Och, don't be so put off. With Da and Yahir away, you get to be heid of the house for the day. So, what say you practice your swings on the stalks for the time being?"

Tonlin sighed. "Fine."

His noise of complaint did nothing to deter Ulleh from kissing his cheek. She handed him a nearby scythe and pointed to where he should start. Before he trotted off, he met Evelot's stare. From her quick glimpse, she noticed a pinched look about him, something scunnered in his brow but depressed in his sulking face. She was guilty for the other night, making a spectacle when it should have been his moment. She'd fled instead of being there for him. Whatever had been said, Evelot would never know as he coldly brushed past her.

"Now," Ulleh said, facing her sister, "what sort a task are you wanting to do?"

Outside, a handful of Granary representatives met Tonlin in the field. None of them would want to work beside her, the silent Witchling of the Choille.

"I'll be in the barn," Evelot said.

"Och, don't be so gloomy. Let the horses keep to their dismal stables."

"As if that matters."

She turned away from her sister, throwing over her hood and making for the opposite exit. Whatever Ulleh called after her fell on deaf ears.

Only when the natural light dimmed low did Evelot finish threshing the wheat. All of her frustration left with the wheat berries sorted and set aside for milling. Her arms shook while putting away the flail, and a sense of emptiness dulled her focus. Evelot felt herself leave the barn, heading back to the house. Neither from the windows nor the main room was there a sign of anyone. Evelot assumed dinner had already been served. With a sigh, she mentally prepared herself for another pitiful meal of granola.

Evelot perused the cabinets and wicker baskets sitting by the cooking pot, squinting into their dark crevasses and feeling for the block of honeyed oats. She slowed to a stop, hearing voices from the main entrance.

"No sign from Graham's home to the woods," said Da. "We'll be meeting again tomorrow to search further in."

"Da, let Yahir handle it this time. Take turns, even," Ulleh replied.

"We have it situated, lamb," Yahir said. "All you have to do is keep at home and look out for our little ones."

Evelot would've groaned if she dared. No sign of the beast meant no rest for the hunters; no peace for the woods, either.

The room fell silent, and Evelot wasted no time

slinking away into the shadows. She climbed up the staircase as her father entered the main bedroom below it.

Within the confines of her room, Evelot knelt before her locked chest. She shuffled through her supplies, then sat back on her bed with her findings. Biting into the stiff granola, Evelot flipped open a large leather-bound tome. A coat of dust sprung out at her. It took great effort not to sneeze while her brother lay snoring in his bed. But once she found the index page, all sensation fell to the wayside. Evelot skimmed over jaunty, slanted writing that listed all the local wildlife and their magical properties. There were many a note on the common creatures that lurked throughout western Runlaris, the majority being non-magical. Bears, foxes, wolves—the typical predatory animals. Of course, Evelot didn't stop there. She checked over the list naming various undead, blob beasts, and wandering Seelies. Either could be culprits if in a fit of bloodlust.

Yet none of them stood out to Evelot. The autumn season was encroaching, which left out the blobs that would freeze to death in the wilderness. The priestesses regularly blessed the fields, ruling out unholy beasts that roamed the night in search of flesh. With the watchful eye in the Choille, there was no chance the third could have made it into the Mortal Realm from the Fae's.

Evelot sighed. It was a night prowler that didn't care about religious boundaries or fear of human interference, but wasn't a common predator. It left few traces behind, unlike what any other creature managed—and could escalate its hunt to humans.

Nothing native to the lands fit the criteria. So the mystery beast had to be something from outside. But how did it find its way to town?

A tap on her window made her jolt.

Evelot squinted. A streak of ebony flashed past the window, and then another tap. She smiled as she got to her feet and climbed over Tonlin to open it.

"No, it lobbed a jobby at me last time," he groaned sleepily. "Keep it outside."

The dark shadow zipped under the opening and circled the ceiling. Evelot shushed and waved at the flying mass with a gesture for it to land. Chirping giddily, it obeyed. Its taloned feet caught her pointer finger and its hooked thumbs found purchase on hers.

"Aren't you a sight, my wee beauty. What sort of prey brings you out here tonight?" Evelot cooed.

Her finger stroked the underside of the little brown bat's chin as it chittered and trilled like a cicada. Beady eyes slowly blinked up at her. Its body vibrated, a sign of comfort.

"I missed you too, Jammer," she whispered, smiling.

Jammer didn't budge as Evelot spread her wings and cast a light spell to check the bones and membranous folds. For a pup left behind in the woods, Jammer acclimated well to Goldencrest's environment. Her belly was full and her teeth had come in; much bigger and healthier than two years ago.

"Is it gone yet?" Tonlin murmured.

Evelot only rolled her eyes. Jammer stayed put in her owner's palm with little trills and nuzzles. While she rubbed against Evelot's thumb, the wee beastie's fangs and teeth opened into a smile. Seeing that was always a treat for Evelot.

As Jammer carried on, a tendril of beige peeked out from her leg. Evelot unraveled the curious thing, finding it to be parchment. She unfolded it and read:

Come back on the morrow. Something is wrong.

Evelot blinked and read the parchment again. Then the shock set in.

If her mentor knew about the issue, then it was more than—

Through the silence pierced an ungodly scream. Tonlin surged upright. Jammer screeched and yanked herself up into the air. Evelot's heart thumped in her ear as she froze, waiting.

Then came a yelp, followed by her da hollering from the main room.

The siblings bolted down the stairs. There, Evelot found Ma clinging to Da. Her face was pale and desperate as she quaked, weeping.

"What happened?" Evelot asked.

"Don't let the children outside, Tarod! They can't—"

"Tend to your ma, Evelot," Da ordered. "Tonlin, c—"

Her ma shrieked again. Evelot followed her line of sight out the window.

Looking back in were a pair of feral crimson eyes.

"Demon!"

Da flew to the garden entrance. Tonlin raced past Evelot for the same door. She scrambled behind them as Ma cried out to her.

There was hardly any light in the pitch darkness. Evelot stumbled, watching as her da and brother raced into the fields with a pitchfork and axe. She hushedly commanded orbs of light to appear. They scattered into the air yet were too slow to catch them. All she could do was listen. To the fading footsteps. Da's curses and threats. Tonlin's battle cry. The swishing of wheat stalks.

The silence of the woods enveloped their farm. The absence of its voice, the lack of crickets chirping. It rang louder in her ears than her raucous heart.

"Da?" she called. "Tonlin?"

She took a few steps forward. She squinted into the darkness. The outlines of the shed and granary were only vaguely darker than the night. If her lights would only stretch farther, Evelot might see into the fields.

A swish in the wheat crawled closer.

"Da?" she yelled.

Something spun her around. Evelot screamed and batted at the frigid grip on her shoulder. A face leaned in, scowling down at her under a candlelight.

"Where is it?" Yahir said.

Ulleh flocked to his side and skelped him before tugging Evelot back to the house. Evelot pointed at the fields, and Yahir took off. With a candle in one hand, and Evelot's palm in the other, Ulleh led them to their weeping ma. But before the door opened, Evelot's magical lights returned. They illuminated the windows and ground, casting a dark shadow over the window frame. The acrid smell of iron wafted toward her. A thick shine of liquid coated the aged flowers in their bed, beneath where those haunting eyes had hovered; the tracks led from their chillingly silent pigpen.

S ilence had proved to be a repeat guest to the Wheaton farm. Upon a fitful sleep and the rise of daylight, Evelot had carefully followed her family outside. The scene was as horrific as they dared imagine. She'd stood outside the barn as her ma sobbed in Ulleh's arms, and the men came back out with the stink of blood wrinkling their noses. The faint clucking of chooks was their dismal hope for the winter. Anything else had been claimed by the beast.

As Evelot helped Tonlin heave the last of the near–skeletal pig remains into a burial ground, an idea encouraged by their sentimental sister, she glanced over at the hunting party. After an hour, the swarm of people still moved through the fields like ants cascading from a wilted apple. They poked and prodded through their barn, and followed the trodden path of wheat stalks to the woods. All while stealing glances when they thought she wasn't looking. The fabric of her cloak may have shielded her periphery from them but hardly muddled the sound of their voices. Among their mutterings, the word "wolf" echoed about. But they were wrong. Evelot had seen remnants of wolves in the woods, seen their kills and how they traveled. Whatever had spied on her family through the window left paw prints the size of a human head.

It was no ordinary wolf.

Evelot puffed for breath as she stood back from the burial plot. Tonlin brushed his hands off before turning to the investigation. She wanted to ask what her brother would do next, but came up short. Standing a few feet away was the last face she expected to be in her sanctuary.

"Boy," Piers said. "Your father asks for you."

Tonlin grumbled as he walked past him. As soon as he was gone, Piers faced Evelot with a smug grin.

"Don't think for a moment that I can't see through

you. This is all a ruse, and soon everyone will know it was you who beckoned the creature," he said.

Her blood boiled. This was Evelot's home. As if she would ever endanger her family. They'd have to do without during the brutal season as it was. To think that a half-wit shite would dare assume otherwise was outrageous. It was insulting.

The ground shifted beneath her feet. Evelot felt her body hum with mana; she heard the hushed tones of vines and earth beg her for vengeance. But Piers smirked, unimpressed by her frozen state. He turned and skulked away, leaving Evelot to writhe in her humiliation.

Evelot inhaled, exhaled. Then moved.

Past more party members and into her home, Evelot snuck to her room. Her hands snatched up her spellbook and flitted through the pages. Finally, she found the thing she swore not to use impulsively. It was her last resort as a fledgling witch. It had to work.

The gathered hunters paid her no mind as she crossed the threshold of the farmlands to the treeline. The canopied entrance of the Choille waved to her in the breeze, beckoning her to it. A humid sheen embraced her as she breached the leafy path. The sounds of wildlife had returned, a comfort that did little to settle her nerves.

After a while, she found an old oak tree sitting within a bed of orange leaves. Evelot knelt beneath it, brushing aside the coverage in her way. She opened her tome and took up a stick. In a careful hand, she recreated the sigil from the page onto the dirt.

Then, she closed her eyes and whispered the incantation.

Light danced under her eyelids in hues of blues and purples. Her body became weightless, sound and time a blur.

She took a deep breath in, counted, and slowly released it, opening her eyes.

The Traverse spell was still new to her as a fledgling witch. It took a kind of patience that tested the body, her senses numbed yet heightened all at once. In the past, she'd traveled to the Ethereal Plane with her mentor, a place only visited by nature witches and those not meant to return to the land of the living. Like before, the nauseating mixture of wading and falling twisted her gut.

All around her was the image of the woods she'd stood in. Yet color and shape blurred as though washed from a black and white canvas, her own outline dissolving at the edges. Not a sound or smell struck Evelot as she carried on, save for a misty air that held no true water: not the crunch of leaves beneath her boots, nor the crackle of branches above, nor the stamp of hooves in the distance. It was the absolute pinnacle of seclusion.

Because the Ethereal Plane took after the material realm, she traveled to the border of the warped woods and toward the fields. The trees gave way to fencing, and from there, the wispy wheat fields exuded waves of dim particles to the nonexistent wind. From afar, she vaguely discerned a blip of color marching around the other side of the field. A sign of the other plane and its occupants. Evelot had learned that the different colors represented emotions. An imprint that took longer to fade, where color bled and scorched a hole into the Ethereal, marked a recent death.

Evelot returned to her home, finding hardly an imprint by the pigpens or the coop. She'd expected as much. Two paw prints sat at the edge of the house's window, the place where those haunting eyes had looked back at her. The colors of sickly orange and beige muddled there, a sign of immense hunger. It trailed back to the woods, then quickly faded.

A regular wolf wasn't moved by emotion or self-awareness when hunting, nor when peering into a human's home. It was suspicious, but with no other sign Evelot hastened off the property.

Down the main trail from the farmers' homes, she rounded the corner to the Graham residence. Like the rising sun over the horizon, colors of all kinds emanated from the perimeter of their thatched home. Sapphire blues of mourning, greens and emeralds of illness. Sunlit reds for fury and anger bled from the windows, and faintly Evelot heard the undulating wails of the widow.

She stumbled to a halt past the corner of their home. At the back door hovered an oval-shaped being of shifting color like a candle's flame. Mutated arms hung from its sides, an open maw letting out a weak, raspy bellow. Within its ruby red shades of terror lay an orb of pure darkness; what once was living refused its death.

The hairs on her arms rose. Evelot pawed at her belt for the dagger hanging there. The husk—a being more powerful than a ghost with the potential to transform into a wraith—was one of the few threats to witches who traveled across planes. Meeting its eye would poison her with its last emotions.

Evelot wasn't keen to become ravaged by pure terror.

She fixed her hood over her eyes, the other hand wrapped around her dagger. From the edge of her vision, the husk slowly turned to her.

Its weak, echoing bellow ebbed. "Help me!" it begged. "Save! Me!"

Evelot took a breath. No emotion, no reaction. Do not meet its eye.

"What happened here?" she asked.

"Help! Me! Help!"

"What attacked you?"

The husk sucked in a shaking breath. Like a dying cry, it exhaled, "Beast! Monster! Carnage!"

"Did you see it?"

"Teeth! Claws! Pain! My gods, the pain!" it moaned.

"What did it look like?"

It paused. Evelot heard it suck in shaking breaths. Then, the husk wailed to the monochrome sky: "Death incarnate! Large maw! Those crimson eyes! Howling laughter!"

"It—what?"

Wolves can't laugh.

"'Hunger for your flesh'! Then it! It—"

Evelot faltered in covering her ears. The husk cried, a noise more feral than a dying animal. Its silhouette drew close in her periphery. She ducked away from a clawed hand ready to snatch her. As her hood fell away and her eyes squeezed shut, the image of the husk's deadly visage flashed before her. A skeletal maw opened farther than a human's ever could. Pinpoint pupils shone from wide, terror-filled eyes that peered into hers.

"It will come! It will kill! It will consume you!" it shrieked.

Its hand reached for her again.

"Enough!"

Evelot twisted away. A surge of air and sound wrapped around her body. She jolted, gasping for air as she reappeared in the Material Plane. Her hands patted at her torso, her arms. No blood, no wounds. Miraculously, she'd escaped unscathed before it mutated into a wraith.

The realization made her curl into herself. Evelot sat against the oak tree in nervous contemplation. One of the most dangerous of magical creatures had referenced another beast that howled with laughter. The same that left large tracks and had an appetite that didn't stop at animal meat. A wolf, and not a wolf.

Through a small, fragmental part of her memory, she'd learned of a beast that fit that description. A monster bred of a curse, if she was correct. Such knowledge wasn't stored in her tome, unfortunately. But deeper into the woods, there was one: where she'd been summoned to. Her mentor's keep.

Evelot peeked at the path leading back to the wheat fields. Her body craved rest in her bed only a short distance away. Da would need another hand in the field to finish the last of the work. Ma would need help in the kitchen. Too much was to be done after the slaughter of their livestock. Whatever would happen, at least it was safer with them.

Piers's last words echoed in her mind. Evelot squeezed her eyes shut. Her mother's scream crescendoed in the recesses of her memory.

Her home wasn't safe. They weren't safe. This was a danger the townsfolk's hunt couldn't contend with; Evelot didn't have a choice.

It was time to take initiative.

Evelot returned home. After taking up her traveling satchel and stowing away a block of granola, she penned a small letter to her parents. She left it on the dining table and snuck back into the woods.

With her back to the house and an urgency in her

step, Evelot hurried down the woodland path. Her pack sank with the weight of her supplies. It was an optimistic sign that the sound of bird chirps and squirrel chitters were becoming more audible. A warm welcome from her natural domain.

To say that the wilderness was her home was an understatement. Evelot never lost her way in those woods. She'd studied the course of every burn, charted all the dens in the rocks and coniferous trees, and kept note of all the seeds that regularly grew. Every object had a place, a belonging. She felt more at ease here than with people. There was a pleasantness to the air that Goldencrest didn't have, one with aromatic notes of oak and pine, wild berry and honey. The earth was softer than the recycled soil on the farmlands, and it all thrived on a heartbeat so wild, untamed and unfettered that the witchling herself sensed it in the sway of the trees and scatter of the animals.

But something was missing. Not because of the lurking evil. Something was absent in the birds' lyrical conversations. In the way she crossed paths with bucks leading their families off. In the breath of cool mist on her cheeks. That familiarity, that element she yearned for. The Choille felt like her home, but similar to her family's farmhouse, an unspoken hindrance barred her from comfort.

Though the sky was clear, the humid veil and thick foliage clogged her path with a graying darkness. The music of the Choille dimmed around her. She couldn't fathom whether the beast itself was waiting for her somewhere farther in, and her pulse clamored with terror. But it wasn't only her family's home under threat. These creatures, these woods, would be victims if the threat struck again.

She quickened her pace.

Chapter Five

Once the Gloaming settled in, Evelot surmised she was nearly halfway to her destination. A stream burbled in the vicinity; the woodland path had long since disappeared, and her legs wobbled beneath her. It was a more than fitting time to rest for the night.

She set aside her bag and unfurled a battered bedroll beneath a low-hanging branch. It'd be enough support for her to drape her cloak and to create a makeshift canopy in case a rain cloud or curious animal passed by. On that note, Evelot opened her spellbook. Walking a perimeter she marked with a stick, she recited a protection spell, which shone in a pattern on the ground. The draining of mana wearied her bones as much as the day's trek had. But she wouldn't have to worry about being attacked, at least.

At the water's edge, Evelot found her attention waning, and her spell of floating lights flickered in the dim. The water was crisp against her fingertips as she refilled her water pouch. She supposed the bite would clear her tired mind.

Evelot stripped off her top and layers of skirts then slowly sank to her knees in the stream. Her body quaked in the three feet of water, and gooseflesh made it hard to scrub the dirt and oil off her skin, but the frigidness purged her anxious thoughts.

The hunting party couldn't reach her there. They'd return home on the hour. They'd probably try again the next day and dare to go farther into the woods. Evelot couldn't imagine what sort of unassuming beast's carcass they'd bring to the square, if they hadn't done so already. Her suspicion dusted off an old memory nearly faded to time. The town had been in an uproar once before. Back when she was but a child, when Ulleh and her current husband were two teenagers skirting around their affections. Word of a strange owl, nearly tall as a man, had haunted the edges of town. The creature never breached the treeline, but it waited at the precipice, watching the farmers as they worked. Evelot used to have nightmares of its ghoulish face pressed against her bedroom window.

Like a harbinger of fate, the owl had slowly eased its way closer. It took flight over the town, and with its arrival, so too had a new face emerged. The first day Evelot's mentor had appeared was one of the few holidays they celebrated as both duchy wealth and native Harvesters. She couldn't recall which of the two had started it, only that the insults hurled at the elder witch weren't far off from what Evelot was currently accustomed to. Not even the priestesses found it in their hearts to be merciful.

But her mentor wasn't dissuaded from returning. Not while her owl familiar flew above, gazing at all the townsfolk with those dark, empty eyes.

Until one day the owl didn't return home. Not intact.

Evelot stirred from her thoughts. Splashing water resounded downstream. What sounded like a fallen branch led to ripples, then more splashes. The stream curled around foliage and large, wild shrubs that hindered her lights. She didn't think the disturbance was an animal, unless it was crossing over the stream. Perhaps puddocks were finding shelter nearby. Whatever it was waded through the water as loudly as a bloodhound. Then there was. . . humming?

No one should've been so deep into the woods, especially at night.

Evelot quickly wrung out the ends of her hair, then recounted her elemental cantations as she crawled around the bend.

The sounds came to a stop. Even with the aid of her lights, she saw nothing in the shadows of the woods, or at the shorelines. Her brows furrowed. Besides the ripples she created by her movement, Evelot was. . . alone.

"Kiss me under the lig—"

Evelot looked down to a blurred face and the shadow of a body floating closer to her chest. She screamed, fumbling back on the slick rocks beneath her feet. With the crash of water and the stranger's high-pitched scream echoing hers, all manner of wildlife escaped for cover.

Evelot struggled to the surface. When she did, she found that not only had her lights disappeared, but the shadow had, too. She summoned her lights again. They sparked to life over a man's dark skin and hair and a shining piercing on one of his pointed ears. As one light drifted lower to the water, Evelot also spotted a visible shrunken tadger.

She gasped, wrapping her arms around herself and spinning around. "Get back!" she snapped.

"W-wait!" the other said. "Fear not—I mean you no harm!"

"Oh, and I suppose you're about the woods on a daunder?" Evelot retorted.

"One could argue so." The man chuckled, soft yet confident. "And what a gift it bestowed me. For I am in the presence of a breathtaking water nymph."

"I'm no water nymph as you're no townsfolk. Who're you and why're you here?" she barked.

"Alas, how the frigid night warps the lady's tone. Mayhap my melody shall break its curse."

With that, he broke out into a short song.

"You're—" She snuck a peek back at him. "Ugh. You're the traveling bard," she said to herself.

"Zenris Aspenheart, at your service, my fair lady."

She heard the water waver as though he were taking a bow. "You are familiar with my performances in Goldencrest?"

"Not really. Now, would you turn the other way?"

"Ah, 'tis a game I am familiar with, ending with a gift from an adoring fan. Thus, I humbly oblige the lady."

With his back to her, Evelot started downstream.

"Methinks the gift is farther away than what was anticipated," Zenris said.

"There's no gift. I'm simply avoiding you."

Zenris laughed aloud, a bit theatrical for Evelot's taste. "If you wish to play indifferent, then I will say no more."

"Good. I'd rather the silence."

Evelot could have gasped in relief to find her clothing still by the shore. As she hurriedly threw the garments over her body, a trill of alarm stopped her. A hovering light revealed Jammer had snuck into her hood for warmth. Evelot hushedly cooed at her, careful to hold the wee bat while she clothed herself.

Then the water rippled behind her.

"Oh, but my lady, silence is too bleak for a night like

this," Zenris called from the bend. "Let us make merry with tunes and good company."

"If company's what was staring up at me, I'll take my chances with the bears," Evelot muttered.

"Do mine elven ears hear slander?"

Securing her cloak, she said, "If you're looking for merriment, then you're out of luck."

"Oh, you see it that way, yet the Fortune Giver cherishes me now."

"My, my, how humbly you put it," retorted Evelot.

"Where an explanation is due, I must first ask the lady's permission to approach. If I may?"

"If you don't mind," Evelot said, walking the shore to where he was, "I'd rather make my bed for the evening."

"In that case, I have a number of lullabies—"

"What the hells are you doing out here?" she snapped.

"As previously stated, my lady," the bard said. "Unless you are the mysterious beast that terrifies Goldencrest, I come in peace."

Evelot froze. "You're with the hunting party? They've come all the way out here? This far?"

"Fret not. For 'tis only us tonight," he said with a wink over his shoulder.

Evelot stormed back to her camp in a huff, her thoughts swirling in her head and Jammer crawling behind her hair. If the hunting party were to find her—if her father were to find her—what would they say? How would they react to the "witchling" creeping about the woods while the beast remained at large?

Apparently, there wouldn't be any rest that night.

She grabbed her traveling pack and tossed in her

supplies before moving to her bedroll. From the corner of her vision, the bard approached, now in his full gaudy attire.

"My lady, I do not mean to alarm you—"

"Go back to the hunters, but don't dare speak a word of me," Evelot said.

"Why would I?"

She spun back to him. "You've been about town. You must know what I am?"

"Mayhap I have heard rumors," Zenris replied, molding his attitude into a form of seriousness.

"Then you best clear off before I curse you."

He balked at her. Evelot took no joy in making threats, empty or not, that only solidified the town's impression of her. But outsider or no, she wouldn't be cornered again.

Zenris threw his head back in a guffaw. "I do not believe you," he declared.

Evelot paused. "Really?"

"I do not."

"Are you mad?"

"Enthused, simply put. And certain you have not the ability to curse others."

"Of course I do!"

His brow rose in coy defiance. "I would challenge the threat, but seeing as how ungentlemanly 'twould be to do so, I will leave it at that."

Evelot gawped. His confident look and knowing eye told her there was mischief about him. However he could read her thoughts, he knew too much.

"As I have said, I mean you no harm," Zenris continued. "I have traveled too far for my group to search for me tonight. And as neither of us wish to be found, I entreat you . . . a truce, of sorts."

"And why would I agree to anything?" Evelot asked, glaring at him.

"Because we share a common goal: to stop the townspeople from mongering fear and purging the woods."

She folded her arms across her chest. "Then why hunt with them?"

"My travel companion, she insists we aid the town out of a necessity. Though we view *safeguarding* differently."

Evelot squinted at him in disbelief.

"Naturally, as a woodland elf, I wish not to see wildlife and habitats be damned. If that does not sway you, then allow me to offer my services. As a bard, I am handy with a slim blade. Best to travel in numbers when a monster lurks about in the shadows, no? Another set of weapons on the chance it corners you?"

Evelot couldn't respond to that. He looked to have more muscle on him than her. For a traveling bard, he was used to traversing harsh grounds. Not that it would get her to say yes right away.

"Regardless of your reputation, I am sure we would make for an excellent set of adventurers," Zenris added.

She frowned. "Where I go, few can follow. Someone like yersel', I can't say you'd be any different."

"But that is the beauty of being a bard. We do not fit the common standard."

Evelot sighed. She shouldn't be considering this deal. Her mentor wouldn't blink before casting her out for bringing an outsider to her home. But the bard was stubborn, and the night was growing old.

Evelot scrutinized him once more. Zenris's assuredness

didn't falter.

"All right," she sighed. "You can act as my bodyguard. But when we get there, you'll do exactly as I say. Otherwise, you'll have more to worry about than actual curses."

"As you wish, my lady." Zenris placed his hand on his heart.

Evelot nodded. With that, she went to work remaking camp, absolutely appalled by herself.

Not a minute later, the bard asked, "Now that we are traveling companions, 'twould be appropriate to address the lady with something suitable."

"Don't my names suffice? The Witchling of the Choille? Devil's harlot? Heathen?" Evelot said. "Take your pick."

"Names for outsiders of our band," Zenris said. "What say for fellow adventurers? Acquaintances? Mayhap terms such as 'blossom' or 'kitten'?"

"It's Evelot." Her lips pressed into a frustrated line before she turned back to him. "Evelot, and nothing more."

His expression softened into a smile. With a half bow, he replied, "As you wish, Evelot."

Chapter Six

Zenris rose the next morning with a skip in his heart and a beaming smile. The logs and ash had long since dispersed. Evelot sat beside the fire's remains with her pack, eating what looked to be an apple and granola while perusing a thick leather-bound book.

Evelot. So that was her name. The witchling he had heard so little and so much of had a moniker not tied to her profession. Indeed, the Fortune Giver had blessed him with meeting her face-to-face. An oddity 'twas, his sharing words with her in the woods, and stranger still to overhear mutterings in her sleep regarding "jam." To Zenris's hope, her snark and oddities had dulled with a good night's rest.

He raised his arms in a dramatic stretch. "For one acquainted with bubbling cauldrons, how shocking a sight to find a lack of a hot breakfast," Zenris said.

"Is that your way of asking for food?" she replied from the depths of her tome.

"'Tis a simple observation."

"Whatever happened to keeping watch for the beast and having each other's backs? I don't see you doing so much of that at the moment."

"Have a heart, my lady," Zenris said. "A moment prior 'twas that your humble bard stirred awake."

"I thought elves hardly slept?" she asked.

"Of course."

"Then you were able to keep watch over night."

His cocky smile waned. Her coldness was peculiar, and rather infuriating. The possibility of her having any correlation with his dalliances or the orc clans he had fled was nonexistent. Mayhap she had seen more than her fair share of a stranger. No, Zenris was certain that was not the case. Many had taken to his stunning physique and golden personality, after all. Yet the bite of her words, and her confrontation with the townsfolk days prior, spoke of a bashfulness barbed by cynicism.

Well, that would not do for his morning.

"Tell me, Lady Evelot—"

"I'm not a lady," she insisted.

"My fair maiden Evelot?"

She raised a brow in challenge.

"Where does the lady travel?" Zenris asked. "I cannot imagine finding anything of note this far in the woods."

"Nothing to concern yersel' over. You'll see soon enough."

"Another way of answering 'I am luring you deeper into the woods so I can stuff you into a cauldron'?" he asked, hoping she would take the bait.

Evelot scowled at him. "Oh, and I suppose you believe I fly on brooms or turn people into toads?"

"That depends. If not, what difference is there of hags and witches?"

She had not hidden it well, that pout of frustration that curled up to her nose, so tantalizing and traitorous to her cause. Zenris felt the sparks of avidity ignite into something larger.

"I see you aren't as observant as you pride yersel' to be," she muttered.

"Why do you say that?"

"Because 'hags' can't fit their cloaks anymore. And even if they did, the material's dyed like pitch."

"And yours is brown," Zenris remarked.

"Aye. The color of a nature witch. Hags that broil you and eat you alive were once of the Shadow Coven. The only ones left are those who haven't gone insane."

"Interesting. This I had not heard before."

"What do you mean?" she said over a bite of apple, putting down her tome. "You're supposed to be a traveling bard. You've seen plenty out there."

"On the contrary. Though I may have fifty years' traversing western Runlaris, witches remain the more elusive of the two."

Evelot blinked. "You're… fifty?"

Zenris smiled, brushing back his hair. "A most complimentary sight, your astonishment. Alas, I am eighty and one years. 'Tis all owed to natural elven beauty."

Evelot's expression deflated into one of disinterest. A shame 'twas that she had not the sense for light humor, nor the eye for physical refinement. Yet, knowing he could easily fluster her, Zenris found it an amusing spectacle. If only he knew what exactly set her off.

Zenris fiddled with his lute, plucking the strings to dim his airy whisper of a cantation. The hum of magic tingled in his fingers. Evelot's voice crackled to full volume in his head: *Why in the Maiden's Crops did I agree to take him with me? He's as useful as far as I can toss him. That's what I get for thinking his voice was anything pleasant,* Evelot thought.

A smile crept over Zenris's lips. So, she found his music pleasant.

Evelot swallowed her next bite with a grumble and stored her granola. Tossing her apple core into the grass, she asked, "Are you ready, bard?"

"In a moment's time, if you will."

She hummed in impatient agreement. After Zenris made himself presentable and dusted off his clothes, they began walking. He found it a shame that her scowl remained. One would think the sourness in her attitude would eventually sweeten in the company of a famous bard. Yet, that was the beauty of time. Zenris bided her air of indifference in the soothing sound of his pan flute. She would smile before long.

After a time and struggle, Zenris discovered Evelot was, in fact, not a fan of the pan flute. He stowed the instrument deep in his pockets, safe from harm, amusing himself by humming along with his lute. He stayed far back from Evelot and her wrath.

The day carried on with glances stolen through the corner of Zenris's eye. Evelot was silent, leading both of them over leaf-choked grass and a fallen tree atop a cavernous river. The milky mist had blanketed the deepest parts of the woods, the sound of wildlife but an echo there. Upon ill memories of Ceblait's haglands, Zenris's skin prickled. He felt a sensation in the thick and foreboding air, akin to a building itch without salve. Yet it hardly camouflaged the familiar call of mana singing within his fae-touched blood the longer he walked. It acted as a melody from a dream, a song that eluded him the farther he went on. The feeling meant Zenris was heading in the right direction.

The trek would have been doubly dull and uneventful had Evelot not found him. Over the defensive exterior and sharpened scrutiny, there was definitely a tenderness within her, evident by the slight turn of her head to the trees and the skitters of little creatures. Her sharp gaze softened in the presence of her surroundings. Every so often Evelot stopped to examine mushroom caps and sprigs of herbs, muttering under her breath as she collected them. He smiled when he caught a semblance of words. She was quite the studious botanist, according to the potions she referenced. Once the task was done, Evelot adjusted her hood, that damned thing. It always denied him the sight of her odd, yet captivating expressions.

It felt as though hours had passed before Evelot slowed to a shuffle. She strayed off the path toward an encirclement of magnificent oak trees. There was a methodical approach to her, a wasted endeavor on an empty plot. Upon a cursory glance, Zenris saw nothing but a small open field of browning grass from where he stood. Yet she pursued some unknown goal, brandishing a random stick over the ground as she crept in slow, crab-like fashion.

"The main square in Goldencrest is quite spacious and less dangerous for children's games," Zenris called to her from the path. "Unless you find pleasure in playing in open fields?"

Evelot appeared too deeply concentrated to respond.

Amused, Zenris approached. If the lady wished it, he saw no harm in joining her endeavor. He copied her footwork through the grass until he stood at her side.

"What are we doing, my lady?"

"Avoiding war—"

She jumped away, spooked. Then she gasped, bouncing on her heels and stumbling into his arms.

Zenris laughed, pulling her a step back. "Well, well, well, I was wrong to assume them child-friendly games."

"Don't flatter yersel', bard! And don't move!"

He frowned. "Why?"

"Warding spells, you eejit! This clearing's trapped—"

If only his foot had not cramped. Zenris's boot twitched as he tried to shake off the pain.

Under his sole, a red light flashed.

"Look out!"

Evelot tugged at his arm. They tumbled away as the shriek of flame and erupting earth broke the calm. Heat scorched behind him. Zenris shut his eyes and covered his head. Bits of earth came pelting down, little nuggets of heat, hardly comforting like the stone massages in eastern Stadahl.

After a lull, no other danger emerged. Blinking away stars, Zenris groaned, barely hearing his voice over the ringing in his ears. Past the dark fog in his vision, he found Evelot below him, twigs and dirt tangled in her hair. She shook her head and squinted up at him. At close proximity, Zenris discerned no distortions of color in her emerald eyes, and her pale skin was like the spring blooms of Vestryae.

She frowned at him, and the moment of mesmerization died.

"My apologies," Zenris said breathlessly.

Her features relaxed, making his heart skip a beat.

"What are you saying?" Evelot yelled.

Zenris cried out, his eardrums fiercely throbbing. Weakly, he tried to respond, "I simply—"

"My warding spells!"

Zenris was positive 'twas not Evelot who spoke. He looked past the holes pockmarking the ground to the trees. Replacing the glade, there stood a single hulking oak that towered over the others. With several curtained windows and a small staircase leading to a door, it appeared to be a home. A home that's occupant climbed down the steps in a great splaying march.

The setting sun blended well with their fuchsia skin. Light twinkled on a gold set of bells jangling from their crooked walking staff. Dark crimson horns curled from their graying-pink hairline to the back of the head, stopping at a tip that could pierce the fabric of the sky.

A Ninanuna, Zenris realized. The pervading gleam in her aureate eyes already spoke of her unfriendly nature, but this wizened Ninanuna with tattered attire was one to cause alarm.

"Good gods, 'tis the Hells' Bell," he breathed.

"And you are a pervert!" she snapped, pointing a taloned hand at him.

"I—what?"

With a whisk of her staff, Zenris went flying. Thick bark struck him from behind before he collapsed to the ground. Zenris struggled for air as he crawled to his feet.

When he looked up, Evelot was running toward him.

"He's just a bard," Evelot said to the Hells' Bell.

"And I am an unassuming old maid. Hah!"

The elder woman waddled over behind Evelot. Zenris reached for his companion and pulled her behind him.

"Evelot," Zenris croaked. "Run…"

He moved to unsheathe his dagger. The witch scoffed with a brisk wave of her staff. An invisible force pinned Zenris to the ground. He cried for Evelot to escape once more.

"Master, wait—" Evelot stepped in front of Zenris. "He travels with me. He's harmless."

"Master?" Zenris repeated, astounded.

The witch huffed at Evelot. "He is a bard. You said so yourself, girl. He would sell your secrets for a copper on the streets of Steinstad and watch as they string you up."

"Would not," replied Zenris.

"Would, too!"

"Master, please!" Evelot said, her arms held out wider.

Falling silent, the witch studied Zenris. For a moment, he feared another attack or hex that would slowly end his life. Yet as both women held an unspoken conversation, the curl of the Hells' Bell's back convinced Zenris otherwise. Her glower did not mask the perspiration above her lip, nor her quiet pant for breath. Granted, it had been decades since anyone last laid eyes upon her, the Beluphis Lovecraft. A Ninanuna who acted as an Acluethan spy and attempted a coup on the Esmoran king three generations ago. Afterward, she turned the tide of the Logryrian War, fending off the humans from her countrymen and earning her infamous moniker.

Someone in such controversial regard, rendered feeble by time. Zenris felt his chances of survival rise.

The witch's jingling staff cut through the air. Zenris's limbs were released from their invisible shackles, allowing him freedom to rise to his feet.

"So, you received my message," said Beluphis.

"Aye. And there's more," Evelot said.

"I assume there are hunters in the woods, then. Peh." Beluphis huffed before turning back to her home. Her pointed tail aggravatingly swung as she waddled away. "Pupil, histrionic page boy!" she called. "Both of you, come! We talk indoors."

Zenris's astonished grin felt frozen across his lips. He hurried across the grass beside Evelot toward the front door.

"My lady, do you know who this is?" he whispered.

"I told you to keep quiet, didn't I?" Evelot hissed.

"That is the Hells' Bell! How does one become a pupil to the thing of legend?"

"Just haud your wheesht—"

"Any day would be lovely!" called Beluphis.

Evelot shook her head at Zenris, her lips soured in a frown. "Don't make her angry. Got it?"

Zenris glanced back at Beluphis who tapped her foot impatiently by the doorstep. To be in her presence made for the perfect tale to sing throughout the duchies. A tale of her infamy and the current warrant for her arrest. Regardless of what power she may have left, deficient as it was, Zenris was determined to follow them.

"Oh ho, for that I cannot promise," Zenris said in tow.

Beluphis spared no glance back as she led them inside. The door slammed shut behind Zenris by invisible means, yet the noise hardly registered as he gaped at the interior. The ground floor of the home could have housed a throne room. Where armor and trophies would hang from above or a red carpet would be rolled for kingly feet, bookcases and stacks of parchment split the path betwixt an open-door kitchen and a deep decline toward the basement level. Spirals and whorls of energy drifted in the air, dancing around the rafters decorated with enormous avian fossils and spinning devices. Beneath a coat of dust miscellaneous furniture tried desperately to create a makeshift parlor by the entrance windows. A large indent in the throw cushions of a chaise exhibited a creature larger than Beluphis resided beside the elder witch. However, no other clue of its identity lingered there.

"This way," Beluphis huffed.

They followed her down the steps. In her descent, grunting then shoving at the creaking door, the witch said, "Tell me, girl. What do they suppose is attacking the chak—ay, the 'fields'?"

Evelot explained the situation. With a cluck of her tongue, Beluphis stepped into a dark, dust-ridden room. "Not a wolf. No such thing," came her croaking voice.

"Tell me, o infamous Hells' Bell: By the soft rolls of your *r*'s, do you hail from the eastern plains of Acluetho?" Zenris asked.

"They roll as much as coin out of your skinny pockets," answered the witch.

Before Zenris could respond, light burst within the room. Both Zenris and Evelot entered, watching the magicked light settle into a clear glass orb hanging from the ceiling. Beluphis sifted through unlabeled bottles and parchment on a large desk by the back wall. Similar to the decor in the room above, bookcases and tomes lined the walls, and a cauldron and a writing desk stood in the room's center. Curiously,

Zenris approached one shelf. Animal specimens were on display in categories of bones, furs, and skins. Within a large bottle, a pair of eyes stared back at him. He reared back, stifling a yelp before pivoting away.

By the Hells' Bell's desk, the two witches spoke in hushed whispers. The only thing Zenris perceived were the words "husk", "ethereal" and "crimson" before he drew closer. Beluphis gawked at what Evelot whispered. She suddenly snatched her by the chin and squinted into the witchling's eyes. Zenris was ready to defend her once more, yet there was a determination about Evelot and an admiring gleam in her mentor's eye. The perceived danger quickly resolved. However, that did not stop Beluphis in her frustration.

"Damn, damn—double-damn!"

Beluphis tossed the tome in hand to the desk with a large smack. She shuffled away and doggedly searched through her shelves of tomes.

In a flurry of flings and panting, Beluphis said, "No, child, this is assuredly much, much worse. Something the farmers and duchy cannot fix."

"I do not follow," Zenris said. "Praytell the exact matter at hand?"

"You—upallay!" Beluphis pointed her finger at him, yet what was meant to be a spell only fizzled brightly atop her nail. A defeated sigh left her.

"Creatures like you should know this," Beluphis said, jutting her chin at Zenris. "When an Opening between realms appears, there bleeds magic, and more. This time, something. . . eh—cunning, broke through my wards. Yes, something disgusting."

Though the mention of Portals—otherwise called

Openings—raised some alarm, Zenris smiled facetiously at the wizened witch. Given her current exasperated state, Zenris found not the heart to pretend to quake at her vague description of a troublesome foe.

Beluphis pushed past the two and heaved a thick tome onto the desk with a slam. Flicking her fingers through the air, she willed the pages to move. Text and parchment scrambled past his vision until the book froze on a particular page. The darkly illustrated image of a wolf bore its maw back at Zenris. Red hot bloodlust blazed in its eyes as it towered over a miniature scrawled village. In common print, 'twas labeled—

"A werewolf?" Evelot and Zenris said in unison.

Another myth Zenris had only heard in songs and plays. Though he knew little details, what other bards had portrayed was that of a metamorphosis during a full moon. A man who transforms into a beast. For what sensational embellishments were worth, he was also a voracious lover in bed that kept you warm in the winter.

"They travel in a pack, but this one seems to be. . . eh —a lone traveler," said Beluphis. "The gods should have sent a comet to smite us all, instead."

"Come now, no need for the dramatics," Zenris said.

Beluphis gaped at him. "The kettle talks to the pot! Ha!"

Evelot moved to intervene; her look to Zenris was one of frustration. Then, to Beluphis, she said, "There must be something, Master. A spell or a ward?"

The elder witch nodded in thought. "Perhaps. Yes, this will be good for you to learn."

Beluphis made for the aligned bookcases. She huffed

and griped under her breath as she read the titles, yet Zenris had not his answer. If not for the dense mana surrounding her, he would have tried for his telepathy spell. He had to gain her attention.

Zenris let out a large gasp. "A duchy guard!"

Beluphis froze. "Where?"

"Away in Goldencrest, still," Zenris said. "Now, o great witch, what risk is there of a beast that simply shifts from one form to another?"

By her tone, Zenris assumed her foreign words were mere curses. Beluphis shuffled toward him, panting and wagging her staff as she replied, "If you want to face the bloodthirsty beast, then go! But that lunar crone of a goddess created it from temple thieves. They are not like stray dogs. Every day of the lunar cycle, their bodies slowly warp and their minds darken. Then, they are rabid until the full moon completes the transformation. For two days, they hunger so great that an experienced knight would struggle to contain them. Those that survive an attack will suffer the same fate. One bite, and they are joined in the accursed pack of devils."

An unexpected shiver raced down his spine, yet Zenris grinned back at her. "Then we must simply find a cure," he said.

"Ha! Unless you know a highly trained cleric or wizard, I doubt a shave of the face will mask the symptoms!"

After another search in her shelves, Beluphis returned to the desk with a dusty book. She opened it to a page with what Zenris thought was a strange, archaic hieroglyph.

"This will do it. We will make a multi-point ward. Using certain ingredients and—" Beluphis clucked her tongue. "I knew it."

"What is it?" Evelot asked.

"This will use the last of my rosehips. I wanted to use them for a nice brew during the cold—"

"Master," Evelot sighed.

"Yes, yes, it is for the 'greater good.'" Beluphis rolled her eyes. "Where was I? Yes—ingredients. All of it should be here. Except for the sample of the beast."

Evelot frowned. "A sample? As in. . ."

"Hair? Or fur?" Zenris replied.

"Finally following along, eh?" Beluphis asked him.

"Of course. 'Twill be easy," Zenris answered proudly.

As Beluphis's mouth opened in retort, Evelot interrupted, "But you said before that a bite can transform us. How do you get its fur without being within reach?"

"How should I know? I will not be hunting it," said Beluphis.

Zenris and Evelot locked eyes with one another before looking to the elder witch.

"You mean *us*?" both said simultaneously.

Evelot frowned back at him, yet Zenris was grinning from ear to ear. Surely hunting a werewolf was worthy of great triumph—of a heroic ballad and glowing accolades. As soon as he ensnared the creature.

"But, Master, it's too dangerous for a novice alone. Wouldn't it be better to work beside you to defeat the werewolf?" asked Evelot.

Beluphis grunted, leaning against the desk for support. "Yes, a crippled old bag with her plucky pupil against a fast, rabid werewolf. We know I cannot do it, not anymore. But you, girl, you will do fine."

"For shame, my lady," Zenris whispered aloud. "We

cannot ask so much of our esteemed host."

A glare darkened through Beluphis's wrinkled face, yet she turned her attention to her pupil who stared in thought at the floor.

"Think of it as training," she told her. "Find the beast, get the fur, come back in one piece. Should be easy, if you remember to use silver weaponry. They've adapted well to the other elements. It is. . . eh—evolution."

Words too faint for Zenris's ear made Evelot give a weak nod. Satisfied, Beluphis turned back to her desk and tomes.

"While you two plan, I will make the preparations. Before you ask, pupil—yes, I have made the temporary teleportation potions. They're in the kitchen by the. . . foodstuff. Use it to get back to town on the morrow."

"Splendid," Zenris said. "Might we encroach on your generous hospitality? Mayhap a cot for the night?"

"Yes, that is too much trouble for me," grumbled the elder witch.

Evelot hissed at him to follow her, and together they stepped out. Beluphis kept to her tomes, either unaware or disinterested in their doings.

Up the stairs and into the main room, all was quiet. Evelot hurried into the kitchen as Zenris smiled to himself. A new quest to undertake, another companion, and a lead to his search in the form of stronger fae-magic. His luck was changing for the better, it felt.

Upon Evelot's return, his lips spread into a sheepish grin. "Quite the first impression with the Hells' Bell, no?"

"Thank you for 'doing as I say,'" Evelot sarcastically remarked. After a deep breath, she asked him, "Why do you want to stay? We can leave now and sleep in our own beds."

"The trek," Zenris said. "'Twas strenuous upon my travel-weary limbs. Had I not worn these ill-suited boots, I would have fared better at returning to the inn at this hour."

Evelot studied him and his high heels curiously, as if waiting for him to say something else. Alas, there was a weariness in her own countenance, a weighted exhaustion in her next sigh.

"Fine. Be ready to leave at dawn, bard," Evelot said, then moved past him toward the rising staircase.

On the second floor, Evelot silently knocked at each door. One opened for her and slammed shut in Zenris's face before he could wish her pleasant dreams. Figuring it safer not to open doors at random, he attempted the same as she had. A room opened to him, veiled in pitch black.

Yet Zenris glanced back at Evelot's door then turned to the staircase.

The night would be long if he were to find the source of that familiar fae magic. The season was fading; time was of the essence. In the dark of night the Opening would shine brightest, and hopefully light his path out of certain witches' sights.

Chapter Seven

Stepping foot back on familiar soil lit by a pale gray sky, Evelot exited the portal.

After a night in a warm bed, she had a clearer mind—but she'd only an inkling as to their next course of action. Without an experienced witch to help in the hunt, capturing a werewolf felt as impossible as a hare becoming a celibate. An actual werewolf, of all things to "practice" on, and to hunt it down with the... whimsical bard. Her mentor had alluded to using him as a scapegoat should the werewolf corner them, but Evelot wasn't willing to risk it. Not yet.

He was odd, that one. All the theatrics and "gentlemanly" code nonsense unnerved her, in a way. If his posh talk reflected anything of Vestryae, then the Esmoran nobles sounded like lads at the pub in comparison. But finding him that deep in the Choille? Suspicion pawed at her, urging her to believe it was a ruse. Then again, what else would have him out in the woods flashing coy smiles and making her look daft in front of her mentor?

Whether his pan flute skills had warped her intuition or not, it didn't matter. She had more pressing issues to address.

"A moment, my lady!"

Evelot's lips pressed into a frown. As she adjusted her hood in the morning sun, Zenris jogged toward her. Apparently, the portal had enough patience to keep open for him.

His smile widened as he said, "Now that we are official party members, mayhap a toast to celebrate?"

"Party members?"

"The future heroes of Goldencrest! Sworn to save a town of innocents from the clutches of a bloodthirsty villain!" he said with gusto. "It requires libations and cheer!"

Evelot blinked at him, her brows heavy with disinterest. "I don't think so."

"Come now, do not be so wearisome."

Zenris opened his arms. Unnerved by his nearness, Evelot stepped back. Thankfully, he wasn't trying to touch her. Instead, the bard said, "On success of surviving the night, I will pay the expense at the tavern."

"Ha, that's funny," Evelot deadpanned.

"I am honest. For shame, to doubt me."

With a frown, Evelot replied, "You may walk about freely in town, but I can't do the same in the tavern because of. . ." She remembered the night Tonlin met Prilthadollak. "Well, I just can't go."

"My lady, you need only ask for assistance. For I have my ways in persuasion and illusion."

"Ah, in that case, let me plug my ears before you sing again," Evelot muttered, starting down the path once more.

"The sharpened points of my ears are not only for show," Zenris said, keeping pace.

Arguing with him felt pointless, however long he

insisted on making his case. All Evelot wanted was to sit down and think, to consider where to look for an elusive werewolf. But his lyrical voice and those perpetually jovial eyes bore into her like sweltering sunlight in the summer.

She opened her mouth to tell him where he could stick his fancy lunch when her stomach ferociously growled. Her lips twisted into a frown. She should've eaten breakfast at her mentor's house before leaving. Looking back at that self-satisfied grin of his, Evelot knew she was all the more scunnered for her oversight.

"What say you?" he asked, victory plastered over his expression of faux sincerity.

Evelot sighed. "All right, all right. I'll go with you. But" —she fixed a sharp glare on him—"no idle talk. We're going to talk about business. Aye?"

"You have my word," he said with a bow.

She sighed again. The only thing to look forward to was the fresh, warm meal she hadn't had in days. Everyone had talked about the fluffy buttermilk biscuits and roast that fell apart in your mouth. Hopefully, it was worth swallowing her pride.

Together, they traversed the path to town. It was as if nothing had happened in Zenris's eyes; he blathered on about the weather all the while she risked her neck entering town. He didn't take issue when walking the alleys, not until they reached the square. There, Evelot observed him from the shadows. The bard talked with random passersby as though he'd lived beside them for years, so easily and lackadaisical. As was his charm as a bard, naturally. All his fanciful notions and gall attracted everyone to his shiny grin.

Evelot couldn't help the heat in her chest that

crackled like a hot coal at the sight, a strange sense of jealousy she didn't like. When she looked down at her hands and the cloak that shrouded her figure, a dose of reality snuffed out that odd feeling.

When they'd finally arrived at the tavern, Zenris held open the door for her. Evelot stepped into the cheery main room, where spirits began to pour and twice as much food was served. The barkeep laughed with his regulars seated around him.

Beside Zenris, they moved toward the tables, but an interruption stopped them in their tracks.

"Youse two!" the barkeep called.

"Leslie, my good sir! Glad to see business as usual!" said Zenris.

"Aye. But what sort of businessman would I be if I allowed troublemakers into my establishment?"

"A wise decision. Luckily, I penned 'troublemaking' into my schedule for Duodies."

"Lucky you," the barkeep grunted. Squinting at Evelot, he added, "But that one disturbed my guests the other night. I'm no' keen on serving her even a garbage scrap."

Zenris looked at Evelot, then back at Leslie. "This person beside me?"

"Of course."

Zenris raised a brow. "And you know them by their hood?"

"That there's the devil's harlot. I know it by the cloak alone. What do you take me for?"

"Sir, I only ask, for—"

Zenris leaned in. Evelot's heart raced as his hand rose

to the back of her head. She batted at it, but the bard was stubborn. With a too-practiced grin, he whispered, "Pardon me, my lady."

He lifted off her hood.

"This here is my companion, most obviously a man."

Evelot blinked, as did the barkeep. She couldn't see her reflection, but by the way his regulars and the barkeep gaped, it wasn't good. Whatever flashy appearance he'd cast on her, sitting over her skin like a wet coat of sudsy soap, must've begged for hellish humiliation.

"Who in the hells is that?" one bystander asked.

"One of my traveling companions."

"You only came with the lizard woman," said Leslie.

"Jinryuu, sir. But yes, she and I were the first to arrive. My other associate, Timothee of Curray, previously wrote us of his business elsewhere. Now we celebrate his arrival with a lovely meal here at The Glistening Seed."

The barkeep examined Evelot. Her entire body stiffened under his scrutiny. She could have gone for a soak in the river and felt the slime of fish scales over her flesh with fewer jitters. Keeping eye contact was a struggle in itself.

A hand clapped her shoulder. She jolted, frowning at Zenris.

"He may not be as social, but I can attest to his fairer countenance. It seems I have a contender," Zenris laughed.

"If I didn't know any better, I'd say the laddie's no worse than a lass's doll," said another bystander.

"Like one of those extinct Proxims. Some said they were all so pretty you couldn't tell what parts they had."

"What's that word again? Rhymes with 'agog' or other."

"Since when the hells have you opened a book, you numpty?"

At that, all three men erupted with laughter. Evelot dared to breathe with their gaze elsewhere.

With a second glance their way, the barkeeper told Zenris, "Gaun, then. I'll send a barmaid out for you shortly."

Zenris sent a wink his way and steered Evelot around to the tables.

She was too stunned to speak until Zenris offered her a seat in the shadows of the sunlit room, far from the bar. Once she flopped onto a rickety wooden chair, her thoughts came rushing back.

"What kind of magic did you use on me, bard?" she whispered.

"'Twas nothing dangerous, I assure you," Zenris said smiling, taking his seat across from her. "Though, I cannot say the same of your acting skills."

Irritation bent the corners of her lips. Of all the things to say, it had to be a quip at her expense. She questioned whether the food was worth it.

The barmaid appeared a minute later. She put in their order with a toothy smile aimed at Zenris, hardly glancing at Evelot. Not that she minded, pondering on strategy in the meantime.

But it was all for naught. Sitting in a boisterous room with cheers and clinking plates, it drew up a mental barrier. All the warm lighting and salted meats nearby distracted her and her empty stomach.

"Kingspenny for your thoughts?" Zenris said.

Evelot glanced up at him. Leaning on the table, he rested his chin over his fist, the smirk on his lips brightening his spring-green eyes. But his boyish posture garnered a few wandering eyes, and the subtle cleavage of his open, latticed top made it more difficult to take him seriously.

"Aye," Evelot said, sitting up with a sigh. "Hopefully, you've got a few ideas in mind about catching the beast?"

"Ah, for there lies the serious question," he said. Zenris sat back in his seat, preening his nails and holding them up to the light. "I have not your answer. At the least, not the one you would hope for."

"What do you mean?"

"Well, one could attempt to capture the foe with a readily made strategy, yet our target is quite clever. A plan would be as useful as predicting the rain when the clouds are at their whimsy."

"So, you think we should just... wait for it to come back?" Evelot gaped at him and his lack of response. "You know that our 'clouds' have more than rain in this analogy?"

"I do. However, the 'weather' constantly changes. Until its next strike, we know not its course."

"It'll obviously be here unless we—" Evelot stopped. Her brows knit together before her jaw fixed shut. She wasn't sure if the plan she had in mind would work on something powerful, but it was better than nothing. "It..."

"You wish to set traps," finished Zenris.

Evelot frowned back at him. She shouldn't have been that obvious in her silence, but he still guessed it. Strange...

Smiling a bit too quickly, Zenris added, "A tried-and-true method, albeit a little less novel. Yet, it should do the trick."

"A-aye."

Evelot frowned down at the table, replying, "It's not

exactly the best, or clever. But… if I can manage it, I'll be able to make something better than what those hunters are using."

"Oh? Praytell."

The way Zenris smiled didn't look sarcastic. Suddenly doubtful, Evelot paused. It was madness to think he might be genuinely interested in what she had to say. But he patiently waited for an answer.

Evelot managed a murmured reply when the barmaid returned with their drinks and plates. The awkward moment quickly faded to the roar of Evelot's stomach. Steam vapors swirled into the air from the warm ceramic, carrying with them wafts of braised ham, scrambled eggs, fluffed buttermilk biscuits, and sweet syrup. Her lips pursed to prevent her own salivation.

Zenris took his salad bowl from the barmaid with a flirtatious grin. She blushed, rushing off in time for Evelot to roll her eyes and take up her cutlery in peace. With a ravenous appetite, Evelot vigorously sliced through and shoveled large forkfuls. The salted and cured ham rinds made her mouth water, and it was a struggle to slow herself down. She had no jam over her buttered biscuits, and the tankard of milk remained undrunk. Hunger was a nasty devil that haunted her plenty.

"O how the lady's passion inspires her appetite."

Zenris chuckled as he brought a bite of fruit salad to his lips. Evelot frowned, putting her fork down. That she hadn't eaten her fill in days was already bothersome, but she refused to let him think he had it better than poor farmers and their brief periods of food scarcity.

Evelot took a swig from her tankard. Cold, creamy

milk went down her throat like a pleasant chill, bringing her a second of reprieve. When she faced the bard again, she said, "Are you really wanting to do this? Set up traps and all? It's no different from what the hunters are doing, but now that you know what we're up against, it doesn't seem smart to stick your neck out for a bunch of strangers."

"As if I could refuse to do so."

Evelot's brow rose with her curiosity.

Zenris patted his lips with his napkin, then said, "I may be an outsider, yet I have much interest in Goldencrest. You have your loved ones, and I have my adoring fans. There are those and… things that we must protect. 'Tis my duty as much as yours. And so, I fully support you, the strategist and leader of our merry band."

"Leader?" Evelot asked.

"Of course," replied Zenris, smiling. "Who else could sit at the helm? You are the one to have first suggested an idea, and a reasonable one at that. Huzzah, I say! For the lady, our esteemed leader!"

He lifted his goblet to her then tilted it to his lips. Evelot stared back at him, awkwardly doing the same with her tankard. But… *leader*.

She'd never taken charge of anything before. No one had bothered to ask for her opinion in donkey's years. If it weren't for his demeanor, she'd suspect he was having a laugh at her. Evelot wished that he was; her cheeks were an inferno on her face. His complimentary words replayed in her head. It wasn't… bad, having it come from him.

Her lips pursed tightly together. As if she wanted him to see her unravel like that.

Evelot emptied her tankard and shoveled the last of

her plate into her mouth. Before Zenris could make another comment, she forced the large gulp down and said, "All right, bard. Come along, then. We've got work to do."

Chapter Eight

She was a passionate fire blazing, and Zenris an enthralled insect, transfixed by its light.

Evelot did not stop for him at the door as her disguise dissolved betwixt entering patrons. Zenris scrambled to separate kingscoins from his deficient leather coin purse and empty them onto the table before rushing after her. Only when he had waded through the entrance of the tavern did he spy Evelot. She stomped through the congregation of townsfolk without waiting for them to leap away. They veered back as though scalded before the sizzling whispers of gossip rose in her wake.

At the end of the farmer's path he fell into step with the witchling. She was quiet, an expression of serious concentration about her. At the crossroads, she stopped, putting her fists to her hips. Her emerald gaze surveyed the thatched-roof houses ahead.

"We know it marked both Graham's home and mine." She pointed at the individual homes. "But if it craves livestock more, it'll come back the way it came. You following?"

"So, we lure the beast out with live bait?" Zenris asked.

"Aye, a farmer willing to sacrifice his food stock for the winter is in large supply here," Evelot deadpanned. "Try it if you want, but no one here's as foolish as you'd think."

"You would be surprised," Zenris replied. "I can be very persuasive."

Her only retort was a snort.

"So, my lady—"

"You still haven't given that up, have you?"

"Say we do not conspire to use live bait. What then?"

Evelot turned back to the houses. Zenris tried to follow her line of sight, but then she raised her finger and began mumbling. Zenris caught a few words—"it came through", "then it was from"—and what sounded like a curse in her native tongue.

She whirled back at him. "Follow me," said Evelot.

Zenris's eyes widened in amusement as a smirk teased his lips, and so he trailed behind Evelot around the spacious outlines of homes and their fields. Providing the right words previously in the tavern was a simple act on his part. Akin to others he had once encountered, she needed a sliver of power, a mere morsel to feed the suspected desire in her heart. All the while he did not suffer the consequences of responsibility as leader.

Over the steep inclines they travelled, crossing the threshold of private property and nature lording over its subjects of town and farmland. The midday sun teased the autumn slopes, and the air was cool with the sweet, heady scent of hay and leaves. Only by the treeline did the two halt. Evelot spun around to study the distant crops and twisted back. Hardly any muttered word of hers helped Zenris's waning patience. If he was to sneak off before the hunters gathered, especially to the depths of the woods where he sensed fae magic, he needed immediate action.

Thank the gods that she spared him from using his telepathy spells once more. Evelot spun back around and said, "All right. Keep a lookout for werewolf tracks. We're going further in."

Stifling a sigh of relief, Zenris swept his arm out in a gesture for her to lead the way.

The journey was brief, considerably, as they had found the markings of claws in the sides of trees. Following them, Zenris and Evelot came across the remains of something's previous meal. Their noses wrinkled at the stench, and the buzz of flies was as audible as a shout.

They turned away, Zenris trying for a sigh.

"Have you any funerals for cattle such as this poor victim?" Zenris said.

It took a moment for Evelot to catch her breath, the smell overpowering her. Folding her arms, she replied, "We know the general area where it comes from. There aren't any tracks left to follow deeper in, so there's no use going farther. In that case… We'll try to set up traps away from this rank."

"Ah, yes," Zenris said, stepping back from the stench with her. "Traps… I assume this is where you reveal those that you had alluded to previously?"

From her traveling sack, Evelot produced her spellbook. Quietly she muttered, flitting through the pages until an image caught Zenris's eye. He tried to spy it again over her shoulder; for a moment, he swore it wriggled and writhed as though animated.

"Right here—"

Zenris straightened back to a standing position.

Evelot looked up from her book and said, "I can use this to conjure a trap. It'll be awhile, but I can put up a few. From there we can take turns watching them between the night and early morning."

"What exactly is 'a while', by your definition, my lady?" Zenris asked.

"The amount of mana this'll spend isn't something I can easily muster. Suppose it'll take a few hours. A day if I'm covering a large area."

A day. Zenris would have to guard her during that time. Time he did not have. Ah, premeditation, what a fickle curse. Yet resolve would prove mightier.

"A splendid idea," Zenris said, smiling. "Although, I cannot help but wonder how this will affect the other hunters' territory."

Evelot frowned. "What do you mean?"

"Say that we set traps as we see fit. This would surely impede upon, if not risk setting off our own. However, should the hunters 'misplace' their traps—Well, who is to say?"

"You want to *steal* them?" Evelot said.

"Oh, no, of course not. Once we have captured the werewolf, the traps shall be returned. After all, for the hunters to use them risks any creature here becoming a victim. As for us, we know to err on the side of caution."

Evelot grumbled, unconvinced. "If you're wanting to use their traps, you go right on ahead. But I won't take part in it."

"A shame." Zenris stepped away, his arms crossed and head hung to portray the downtrodden. Then he rose to full height, mischief curling his lips.

"'Tis a challenge, then," Zenris said.

"What?"

"Yes. I challenge you in a friendly trap-setting competition. I shall obtain mine by my own means, and the lady shall do as she sees most fitting. The one to trap the werewolf first may unfurl their banner of victory. 'Twill speed along the process, and the lady would not suffer as many days of exhaustion."

Her brows may have hung low in scrutiny, yet Evelot spoke not a word in dismissal.

"Of course, for the pupil of the Hells' Bell, this should be simple. Or... mayhap there is something amiss?" Zenris said with a smirk.

Her emerald eyes bore through him, a pout in her lip in tow. An internal celebration of his victory surfaced, prodding into each cheek.

"All right, bard. I'll play along. If you catch it, I'll get the fur. And if I catch it—"

"A large assumption," Zenris teased. "But I accept."

"Aye. We've got a deal then," Evelot said. "All right, let's see you set up traps first, then. With all that big talk."

"Certainly. If the lady would allow a gathering of materials."

"After you," she replied, a flicker of competitive light in her gaze.

That defiant brow of hers stayed glued to her forehead all throughout the trek back to town. Standing erect in the heart of Goldencrest was a tall, two-story building whose sign above read in bold red letters: Newall Goods and Services. Zenris felt a lightness in his steps, a confidence raising his chin as he held the door open for his companion. Evelot gripped at the edges of her hood before silently entering, a strange expression of pinched discomfort upon her visage. Such a reaction did not inspire Zenris's immediate concern, though the brick-and-mortar foundation was more polished than any lodgings she might live in. If anything, a little touch of grandeur would surely cure her ambivalence to the comforts of life.

The interior was much like the other goods store he had patroned. Standing shelves sat perpendicular to the entrance, marking aisles along the wooden floorboards. Windows in the opposite walls let in warm light and the smell of leather and parchment wafted through the air. The chime of a register's bell sounded from the back of the first floor where a few individuals stood in line. Zenris led Evelot toward the end and waited.

His companion remained silent throughout the ordeal, leaving Zenris to his observations. He studied the customers ahead, and the clerk behind the counter: the way he flicked away his long blond hair, how his unwavering smile accentuated his youthful appearance. Eager to please, and eager to serve.

Perfect.

When his turn came, a calmness washed over Zenris, his lips shifting into a small smolder.

"How can I help you?" asked the clerk.

"My good man, I must trouble you for hunting traps," Zenris said. "The jaw-like contraptions, in particular. 'Tis of the utmost importance that I acquire them."

"Hunting something ferocious, are you?"

Zenris tittered, exaggerated by his nervous gestures. "Indeed."

"Well, I'd love to help, but unfortunately, we've been bought out of our supply till the next shipment a tenday away."

Zenris leaned away from the counter, feigning shock. "Truly?"

"'Fraid so. All that talk about beasts and the wilderness has made the locals feral—pun unintended."

Evelot's small scoff was sharp in Zenris's pointed ears.

"Wish there was something more I could do, but I've been picked clean," said the clerk.

Zenris snuck a glance over the clerk's shoulder. A small section of shelves held the weightier of items, but one section appeared devoid of anything, save for a single coil of rope. He did not need a telepathy spell to know the man spoke truth.

However, it left Zenris curious regarding another peculiarity he spied. Where the clerk flicked back his hair, beneath his collar, was a spot of darkness. There looked to be a dragonfly stuck through with a dagger. To the common eye, 'twas a simple tattoo. Yet, to the fae-related and sympathizers, it resembled an Esmoran smugglers' ring steeped in bias and old political influence. The human store clerk was less likely to have crossed into the Fae Realm to hunt for rare pelts and the like than to store his true "commodities" elsewhere for the right buyer. Luckily, Zenris was in the mood to shop, knowing what would help in baiting traps for the werewolf.

Zenris leaned against the counter. Gone was his staged anxiety, a meaningful smile there upon his lips.

"A shame 'twould be to exit empty-handed. Suppose there was something in the back room—something *unaccounted for?*"

The clerk leaned closer, a smirk teasing his lips. "Maybe there's something in the back, maybe there isn't."

"Something worth. . ." Zenris retrieved his coin purse, sliding his last two kingsquarters toward him.

The clerk silently pocketed the coins. With no one else but Evelot to witness them, he said, "Go around through the alley. Knock on the cellar door and tell them 'Ilbis' sent you."

Zenris stepped away from the counter. "'Twas a pleasure, then."

Ilbis wiggled his fingers in a wave, and the two companions took their exit.

N ever again would Zenris gamble on his chances with smugglers. Not after he had been practically robbed.

Falling into step with Evelot through the alleys, he studied the little vial in hand. The smugglers had given him what he paid for, the liquidized pheromone of the infamous Cassowary from the Fae Realm. 'Twas said to make any predator, cursed or no, ravenous. That alone could be a trap on its own. However, the amount received was what infuriated him. A mere vial. It held only three traps worth, with but one extra coating. Unless he wished to poke at the proverbial bee's nest and demand his coin back, Zenris would have to make do, to his great misfortune.

"So, Sir Flops-A-Lot, you giving up the challenge already?" Evelot asked mischievously.

"Ha! You assume 'tis my last attempt," replied Zenris.

"Ah, it is a tragedy, indeed, to have failed your first," she said.

Zenris smirked. The witchling would do well to practice her diction in such an accent, yet her feeble attempt revitalized his motivation. "The day is still young, and the hunters make their traps in many a way. Follow me, my lady!"

Outside of town and before the inclining farmer's path sat a small house. Zenris and Evelot came upon its rectangular open shed with a hefty hanging sign of an anvil mounted above. The smell of hot iron and sweat mixed with the clang of metal against metal. Neither of them dared draw closer as the blacksmith dropped his tools to address an approaching patron. With a proud stature was a willowy man of fair hair; traditional garb hung from his hips that Zenris had yet to learn the name of. Though, by the way Evelot anxiously tugged at her cloak as they listened to the others' conversation, Zenris's curiosity had the better of him.

"They say that daughter of yours is wreaking havoc in the square again, Tarod," the blacksmith said.

"I'm sure they do," Tarod answered.

"Best keep an eye on that one. Not your fault she ended up the way she is. Sometimes, they're just born that way."

"And I suppose you figure it's better than the Sawneys, eh?"

There was a shared chuckle betwixt them, but a weaker note in Tarod's tone seemed perfunctory. Stranger still, Zenris peeked back at Evelot, and in her rapt focus, she had balled her hands into her cloak. The longer she watched on, the more anxiously she nibbled at her lower lip.

After the patron had left down the path, the blacksmith continued working, unaware of the two's presence.

"Is there a problem, my lady?" Zenris finally asked.

"No. I-it's… nothing. Never you mind. Just go talk up the smithy."

"Methinks the lady has not perfected the art of lying."

"Then you try being the town pariah and I'll playact the lute strummer!" she hissed.

"Who goes there?"

Zenris turned to see the blacksmith with his tools lowered, looking in his direction. Beside the bard, there was only air.

A wide grin peeled across Zenris's lips. "Well met, fine sir!"

Summoning his swagger, Zenris approached the blacksmith. The surly man was less friendly than the clerk in both appearance and demeanor. Small dark eyes stared Zenris down, and the blacksmith's arms, sturdy as oak, bulged as he held the metal rods in hand. They were thrice Zenris's weight, he was sure. Nevertheless, he would not allow himself to be intimidated, not in front of Evelot, wherever she had spirited away to.

"What do you need?" the blacksmith said.

"A trap, sir. Of the hunting variety, if you do so have them?" Zenris said.

"What's it to you?"

"Why, for hunting, of course!"

The blacksmith frowned at him. "Aren't you that bard that sings over at the inn?"

"Zenris Aspenheart, at your service," he replied with a bow.

While Zenris hoped a smile would encourage the man to warm up to him, the blacksmith's frown only deepened.

"I've got traps, all right. But they're for the official hunting party, no' for outsiders," said the smithy.

"Well, you are in luck," Zenris said. "For I am of that very party. 'Tis on the mayor's request that I and my companion act. Mayhap you heard mention of the Jinryuu warrior from the east?"

"I have."

"Fantastic. So, regarding the traps—"

"Doesn't mean I'll give them to you."

"Why not?" Zenris snapped.

"Even if you were with the hunting party, you don't look like you could carry a one of them."

"I assure you that is no problem, sir."

The blacksmith simply grunted. Waving his rod, he told Zenris, "Fetch someone else to receive 'em."

"Now see here—"

The man stood at his full height, making Zenris retreat a step. He looked up at the smithy, like an ant before a grasshopper.

"Problem?" the blacksmith growled.

Zenris was at a loss for words. While he harbored enough spiteful energy to defend himself, the survival instinct within told him to stop. Before Zenris could step away, there passed a flash of familiar orange and brown on the other side of the shack. Evelot, cloaked and as silent as a breeze, slipped behind one of his stacks of weapons. He vaguely discerned the outline of a hunting trap next to the stack.

"There is," Zenris said.

"Really?"

"Indeed, I wou—*Dormeo!*"

The blacksmith wavered on his feet. Evelot squeaked behind the rack, jumping back. In a heap and clatter, the man collapsed to the ground.

Aghast, Evelot looked back at Zenris.

"What was that?" she hissed.

"Shh!" Zenris said. "'Tis a sleep spell, not a coma spell!"

Evelot gritted her teeth. "Come help me, then!" she whispered.

Oh, Zenris did. A shame 'twas that the smithy slumbered while Zenris lifted three traps into his arms. Alas, there was no time to gloat.

His little success rewarded him the early evening air, joyously rich on Zenris's skin. With Evelot, they stole away to their spot in the woods. The dying light cast an ember-like glow over the golden hills, creating a small illumination to brighten their way.

In the forested darkness, Zenris shook his head with mirth curling at his lips.

"I believe the lady would do well to improve her stealth," he said.

"Apparently," countered Evelot, "you also need to work on your people skills."

Zenris prepared himself to retort, yet a quick hiccup of laughter silenced him. Evelot hoisted the traps in her arms. She hastened her steps. However, Zenris swore there was an etching of amusement upon her lips.

He grinned. "My, my, what a wondrous sight I glimpsed."

"No, you didn't."

She attempted to bustle away, but Zenris gave chase.

"If innocent, then why do you flee?" he laughed breathlessly.

Though she did not answer, they scurried into the depths of the woods. Upon their spot, Zenris tossed his handful of traps to the ground. Cool air filled his lungs, relief to his aching muscles.

As Evelot summoned her magicked lights and examined his traps, a thought crossed his mind. An odd revelation 'twas: her amusement and reserved air were so similar to the patron of the blacksmith.

Before he could ask about the matter, Evelot looked up at him. "It's no time for a break."

"Apologies, my lady," Zenris replied, tucking his question away for another day.

"Or… oh. You off to the hunting party?"

Drat. He had forgotten about his plans before the meeting. The hunting party would soon gather in the main square, if not upon the same path through the farmlands.

"Too long have I been absent from both the hunters

and adoring fans. 'Tis my duty to grace them with my presence. Though truthfully, I would rather not anger a Jinryuu warrior."

"All right, then."

A minor disappointment came over him at her quick relent. He supposed she would do sufficiently in setting traps alone for the evening before retiring, being the independent woman that she appeared.

Yet Zenris made it no further than a few steps before her tired voice called to him.

"Zenris?"

"Yes?"

She looked back at him and asked, "Do me a favor?"

He smiled. "Anything for the lady."

"Make sure they don't go home with the Choille."

Zenris paused. The way she looked at him in the woods' shadows, under the light of the orbs that floated about her head, spoke of genuine fear behind a mask of collectedness.

Bowing, he replied, "You have my word."

She nodded.

With her back to him, Zenris retreated toward the woodland path. He heard her mutterings, and then another odd mention of "jam," before the choir of crickets filled his ear.

A chuckle left him. Mayhap he and his new companion should attempt to rob more storefronts if they were to truly bond as such.

By the time Zenris arrived, the hunting party had doled out their assignments. Given the grim tone of their endeavors, Zenris was in lack of a friendly face. He rounded a large group and found Pril standing with several locals, armed and ready to march toward the west side of town.

"Mind if I accompany you, friend?" he said, jogging up to her.

"You are late," she stated.

"Not too late to join, I hope?"

She grumbled low in her throat. Pril handed him a meager sword and set off with their group into the woods. "You are fortunate to have been assigned to this group. That way I can prevent you from running off as you did the last time," Pril said.

"'Lost,' 'wandered,' 'run off.' Frivolous semantics, are they not?"

"You owe me much for these years of tolerating you. So let us begin with an answer, yes?"

Zenris theatrically sighed. "You think too much on trivial things."

"You and I have differing definitions of 'trivial.'"

In the thick of the trees, nightly shadows collected, hanging in place of the fallen leaves. Zenris wrapped his cloak tighter around himself. He felt as though it were any other early evening. Without the lurking threat of the beast, the cold in the air would have no bite, nor would he hold a pregnant breath after a twig snapped under his boot. The birds might have dared to sing this late into the day. Yet the patrol dragged on without a sign of their traps laid out earlier.

Dread subsided to boredom as Zenris tried to keep pace with Pril under the looming moon. A miracle 'twas that she slowed for him; he tugged at his shirt collar to fan himself, his feet nearly barking like dogs to come out of his heeled boots.

"It is a disappointment to see that our party's progress is slacking," Pril said. "We would have been farther along had unexpected obstacles not arisen."

"Oh?"

"Yes. We were expecting traps from the blacksmith. But it seems he had 'misplaced' them after taking a sudden fall and landing on his head."

Zenris felt a nervous perspiration wet his skin. "How unusual."

"You are not causing mischief after your tavern performances, are you?"

"Perish the thought. I have been Proxim-like my entire life."

"The King's Merry," Pril deadpanned.

"That was a planned event," Zenris said, frowning indignantly.

Pril chuffed at him. "No one plans to mock a duke at his own birthday party, unless they are willing to take on his battalion."

"Your point being…?"

"I will lock you in your room if you are not behaving,"

Pril said. "As is my right as the one with the majority of the gold and the labor to earn it."

"Yes, yes, of course. As I have been earning my keep, 'tis simply Goldencrest's view that I gaze upon in my spare time."

"Very well. Then that means you have coin to store in our savings."

"Well…" Zenris recalled the enormous meal he had shared with Evelot and the lack of a jangle in his coin purse since.

"Zenris."

"Strolling taxes your energy, and the inn offers many a selection—"

Pril halted. Grabbing his shoulder, she spun him around to face her. "Is there no brain matter between your ears?" she hissed.

"You cannot expect me to forage for berries and nuts like a squirrel—"

"I expect you to think and ration when necessary."

"Preposterous. How could I—"

A scream tore through the silence. Denizens of the trees took off, making Zenris jump. He looked around; the indistinct silhouettes of the other hunters and lit torches ran left toward the sound. A cacophony of voices and thudding footfalls exploded around him. Their patrol group abandoned duty in a breath, rushing after the others. Pril charged ahead before Zenris did the same.

More shouts led them to disarray. Countless others scattered around a thick gathering of trees. Zenris heard in the chatter and confusion a name being repeated. A volunteer from the village, he assumed. People frantically searched nearby, calling for their neighbor.

Pril grumbled. She swiped a racing hunter by the collar and stood him in front of her.

"What happened?" she ordered.

"One of the others—someone said he went too far ahead—heard him shout and then he just. . .gone! Disappeared!"

Upon release, the man stumbled away. Zenris stepped closer to a large cloister of hunters. They talked amongst themselves in hushed, angered tones. Only when he had followed their line of sight did he find it on the ground. A worn tree axe meant as a weapon, decorated in crimson splatter.

He studied the distance ahead. Beyond the obvious signs of a struggle in the layer of leaves, the trail had ended there. Truly, 'twas as if the hunter had vanished into the night.

Zenris shivered. He met Pril's eye, and her stoic expression showed no concern for his whereabouts in the daylight. Both of them knew the dire nature of the matter. Whether a pauper's fate was in the cards, Zenris knew not. His, and anyone else's, chances of survival hung in the balance—until that beast was caught.

Chapter Nine

"**A**rise!" called a thunderous voice through the fog of sleep.

Zenris jerked awake. He sat back in his desk chair with a groan. Daylight stretched over the cloud cover into his room, stinging his tired eyes. Before him and his clogged mind sat a sea of inked parchment. The pages had collected in the week following the first disappearance of hunters. A week of creative blocks, of rising panic, of balancing investigations in the woods alone and with his witchling companion. If only hunting a werewolf were as simple as pilfering traps from the hunters. If only writing music were as such.

Ah, with that thought—he had to check the traps that morning.

The door shook with another bang.

"Heart of Aspen!"

"Yes, yes, I have awakened!" he called back.

"Good. The barkeeper asks for you post-haste. Your fanatics demand for you."

His heart leapt in his chest—he had overslept.

Zenris cursed aloud as he threw himself into the washroom and tore down the staircase. As Pril had claimed, the barkeeper was caught amidst Zenris's fans gathered near the stage, appeasing them with more food and drink. They chanted his name as Zenris slipped behind the stage curtains.

Before he could perform, Zenris held his lute in hand. Counting to five, his mind basked in the joy of his craft. Fans cheering, singing in tandem, the flow of songs pouring out of him. That familiar spark of energy filled his chest. Zenris took a deep breath and stepped through the curtains.

"Good day, my loveliest of doves," he greeted.

The crowd raved with applause.

"As a token of appreciation for your patience, I welcome any and all requests."

Zenris listened amiably as past titles of his echoed forth until one resounded over them all.

"*A Dreamer's Renaissance*? An excellent choice," Zenris said. "Accompany me, then, on this journey."

He started on the lute and let the notes take the lead. The crowd listened in rapt focus from their seats. The slow beat relaxed both himself and his audience, a tale of trekking through the countryside in search of glory and splendor. Yes, this song was quite popular several years back, having long lived on sheet before then. Zenris remembered writing it as he had traversed the expanse of Vestryae, his homeland, into Esmora. His spirits had been great and his determination far from receding as he sought to prove himself a worthy successor to his profession, to his mentor. Opportunity was plenty in the booming, industrious lands of Esmora where he later met his current party. He had assisted in slaying many a beast, from criminals to magical foes and wayward tribes of orcs. Yet, as was in Vestryae, he left behind something important.

Zenris took a theatrical pause on a soft note, then his eager voice broke into a sprint. As the crowd stood awed, his lips stretched into his practiced smile. After so long, 'twas easier to fall into the habit and hide his splintering determination. Day by day, he disparaged his choices. He never meant to leave his party or test their patience with lies and excuses. He never meant to force their hiatus. Yet too long had Zenris been wandering in search of places similar to Goldencrest. With every encounter ending in disappointment and late arrivals, the sacrifice proved too great.

Mayhap 'twas karma at play, being stuck with a babysitter and no clue to where his goal lay; he had a pure lack of luck to be trapped in debt in a small town plagued by a contagious curse.

A twanging chord interrupted Zenris. He peered down, realizing his hands were both placed incorrectly upon the lute. He chuckled up at the audience as he searched for the right note once more. They did not appear taken aback, only soothed by his voice returning to the soft lyrics. With that, Zenris's flash of anxiety passed.

Evidently, nature intended to prove him wrong by other accounts. The stress of finding the werewolf before it could take another life must be accosting him, as well as following the hum of fae magic in the woods. Earning coin. A horrid, taxing cycle of staying in constant motion every waking day. However, upon studying the crowd, Zenris realized that with fewer familiar faces, the same wariness was present throughout Goldencrest. In that regard, he considered himself fortunate and free of maddening boredom.

The thought also brought to mind his witchling

companion. A week prior, Zenris imagined Evelot would have detested being in his presence. Though they remained in a "friendly" competition, new grounds were created betwixt them. Those small slivers of pleasant conversation and banter were slowly bearing fruit from Zenris's determination. The witchling in question still had moments of doubt, yet Zenris felt himself changed. As if another kind of seed was planted. Her biting veracity and quips were the ichor to his rebuffs, his full attention. In pride 'twas that he verbally dueled her. In victory or defeat, an odd feeling of solace was his reward.

He hoped 'twas not a curse of madness she had enchanted him with.

After several more songs and breaks for water, Zenris took a bow. His fans called to him before the rush of regular, hungered patrons drowned them out. Feeling lightheaded, he decided 'twas the time for a decent meal and drink. However, Pril's harsh warning days ago still haunted him. They had to conserve their earnings until their contract was complete, however long that took to catch the villainous werewolf. He refused to beg a farmer for a spare apple or, gods forbid, dig through the trash for scraps, but wherever his next meal lay, he hoped 'twas somewhere clean.

The smell of hot broth and honeyed wines brought on salivation. Zenris snuck away to save his pride, yet the shame burned at his heart; 'twas beneath him as a magnificent bard to do without a good meal.

"Zenris!"

Stricken with surprise, he turned around. A cherubic fan waved at him from steps away. Several others like her beamed from their table. The maiden eagerly motioned for him to draw closer.

Approaching, Zenris said, "A fair and heavenly day to you all. How may I aid in making it more so?"

One of them hopped out of her seat. "Hello, Zenris! Would you care to join us for a spell? We'd love to host you a moment more."

"Your generosity stirs my heart. Alas, I must fulfill an obligation elsewhere."

"Are you sure? We've ordered food and drink, and it won't be for long."

She gestured to their table where, to Zenris's utter delight, a display of foodstuffs and tankards lay. Sandwiches and salads, soups with vapors drifting toward his sensitive nose. Salty broth tantalized him with cubed vegetables that looked easily mashable upon his tongue. Zenris's hand flew to cover his roaring stomach, yet the maidens' titters and giggles proved there was no use.

"My apologies," he bashfully replied. "It all looks so wonderful. 'Twould. . . be a shame to let it go to waste."

His fans giddily ushered him to the vacant seat at their table. Zenris guiltily let them as he remembered his mentor's rules. Dining with his fans teetered on breaking a cardinal rule: Never allow fans the intimacy you cannot afford to lose. Well, his youth had been spent learning from his mistakes, and his fans before him simply wished to enact a charitable gesture. Surely there was nothing ill-suited about dining with fans?

However, Zenris needed not look further than his plate. The girls moved like hawks, setting before him bowls and miniature plates and a goblet of fine wine. He thanked them with as much encouragement as they had in offering it.

As he courteously broke bread, their gazes on him sat uncomfortably long, inviting an awkward pause to their table.

"How have you been, Zenris?" one of them asked.

"Splendid, now that I am basking in your jubilant countenance," he said with a grin.

She bashfully covered her cheeks, giggling. Then, the one beside her added, "Are you getting enough rest?"

Zenris blinked. "Pardon?"

"We were worried because of what happened earlier on stage." The other girls tried to shush her, but she persisted. "And, well, we'd hate to see you struggle, since you've yet to release your newest song."

Her sentiment brought a budding smile to his lips. "I would not make a lady worry over me. All is well."

She sighed in relief. "Oh, good. Then at least the bone broth is doing some good for you."

A chill went up his spine. "Bone broth?"

The girl nodded. "The cook makes a wonderfully hearty broth with whatever livestock he can use. Always helps those that are exhausted after a long day's work."

Zenris tried to answer with as much excitement as before, but the other maidens stared back at their companion in abject horror. One politely cleared her throat, motioning for the earlier speaker to join her away from the table. They stepped to the side, yet he had no difficulty overhearing their conversation. They spoke in hushed, angered tones of him and his culture: the old tales of evil fae created from "breaking their oath of a vegetarian diet" was quite audible. Where Zenris would come to his defense, he dejectedly frowned down at his bowl. Vegetables floated in the clear brown soup, not that he would find a freshly harvested eyeball or portions of actual bone there. It could be minutes or hours before the damage settled in his digestive system. He hoped there was a privy nearby whenever all hells broke loose.

His spoon dropped too quickly into his bowl. Without missing a beat, Zenris managed a grin and raised his goblet to them.

"My dear gracious, lovely doves," he said, before they could be the wiser. "A toast. To a wonderful festival and making merry."

With everyone seated, they eagerly followed suit. Cups met and laughter rose from their table. Zenris tried to join them, though he stifled his words with a sip of wine. At least 'twas not slaughtered for his benefit—

His chair budged beneath him. Zenris glanced down at his seat, but no passerby seemed to be the cause.

Then he was sliding backward, past the bar and toward the entrance. His fans called out to him. Zenris froze as he tried to make sense of the situation. He reached for the hand dragging him back, but 'twas for naught. Nothing was there. A ghost might be the culprit, if Zenris believed in such things. To his fortune, Zenris had lowered his cup before wine could sully his nice leather braies.

Sunlight enveloped him before the chair tipped back. Zenris careened into a somersault, landing face first on the solid, cobblestone outside. The hushed voices of onlookers stayed too far back to offer help. When Zenris lifted himself off the ground, he peered into a face shrouded within a drawn hood.

"Get a move on, bard," Evelot said, and walked past

him.

Zenris sighed. Not a full minute given to him and his wine. Why were the gods so cruel to him?

In tense silence they cleared the square and neared the farming community. Zenris took his time observing her; her stance was stiff, her stride quick and purposeful. He noticed the usual markings of her temper, including her little puffs of breath that blossomed into white wisps beside her hood. He knew not the predicament he was in at that moment, but a minuscule contemptuous part of him relished in having been in league with the cause for her anger.

Thankfully, the hunters' anxiety refused them to investigate every corner of the woods, especially where the traps lay. Zenris and Evelot had dispersed both man-made and conjured traps over the possible trails the beast would use to reach the farmlands. As they approached a two-limbed tree that marked the beginning of their trapped territory, Zenris awaited his chance to speak.

Finally, he asked, "Could you not have found a more appropriate way than physically removing me?"

"If you recall, I'm not allowed to set foot in that building."

Zenris let out a half-hearted hum. "Since when has that stopped anyone, including yourself, my lady?"

Evelot opened her arms at him. "Witch."

He need not have used his telepathy spell in that moment, for she had given herself away. Unlike her earlier barbs, her current reaction was livelier than usual. He must have struck a dissonant chord… by sitting in the tavern? Or…

"Tell me: Does envy of me sway you?"

"'Envy'?" she exclaimed. Evelot let out an incredulous

huff as she shuffled past mounds of dirt, covering her traps post-haste.

"You have not discounted the possibility yet," he said, inspecting his traps from the thin veil of trees separating them.

"Oh, aye, I'm green with envy at your way of life," she sarcastically retorted.

"A reference to the infamous bard Stirhooke? Here I thought you had never indulged in fantastical plays or fictional reading."

"As you say," she said dismissively.

While her reaction was underwhelming, the frustration in her frown ensnared his attention. Zenris spared a few glances at the traps in her wake as he pondered her character. That hood of hers did no favors regarding her complexion and her ability to converse with him. For no apparent reason, she was especially determined to remain secluded in her thoughts.

Well, that was to be remedied.

"If not, then what exactly dissuades you?" he asked. "I am an open book, as scholars say. Ask and you shall receive, my lady."

Evelot rolled her neck as she came to a stop. "I'm not envious," Evelot said. "I'm… I just can't go places you can. All right?"

"Strange, indeed."

Evelot put her fists to her hips. "What is?"

"Many a temple, Harvest Maiden or other humans' gods, embrace magic users warmly. As you are a member of such power and this community, 'twould be sensible that your neighbors would also be inclined."

Evelot was silent a beat too long. Then pensively, she replied, "Someone from the village who doesn't worship the Dawn King, learning magic from the shunned Ninanuna witch in the Choille, it's a threat to the Harvest Maiden. And it's a threat to the duchy's regulations. It makes sense that they'd bond over a common enemy."

Zenris scoffed in disbelief. "Come now. Is there truly no one to vouch for you? A friend or vendor, a neighbor. . . Someone not akin to that Piers fellow?"

Evelot whipped her head back and stared at Zenris. Her eyes shone wide with fright, before she quickly glanced away.

"No," she said. "They're mostly like that bastard. No one but my family supports me. The Harvesters put up with me because I'm another set of hands that tills the soil and sows the wheat, but my family. . . they've got me."

Melancholy laced her logical answer. An emotional wound yet to be cleansed was what Zenris had stumbled upon. Having no experience in such tender ways, he assumed the matter closed. However, that did not mean he was tolerant of being in a somber maiden's presence.

"Well, I suppose a witch's life is far from glamorous," Zenris said with a teasing grin. "Do they not ride upon broomsticks and turn innocents into toads?"

"Aye, and all before being drowned in the river or crushed under a slab of rock, too."

No irritated blush reddened her cheek, nor did a stubborn pout cross her lips, as Zenris remained silent. 'Twas as if a heavy thought crossed her mind, one that stifled her amusement. She turned away and made for the other traps farther off.

"Go tend to your traps, all right?" she called over her shoulder.

Zenris obliged with a bow. While he fixed one trap, leaves scattered about and a broken twig clamped in its jaw, he considered her pause. How peculiar, her circumstances. Human politics and religion were foreign concepts to Zenris, and gossip abounded within Goldencrest's precarious state of affairs. Being an elf in a land where relations with humans were fragile, he supposed Evelot's issue to be a true mystery.

However, his curiosity remained. How could one person withstand such volatile prejudice in one meaningless town? What nonsense. Why not either discard or conceal her practices? That way she would be spared mass ridicule. Surely she did not stay solely for her family? To what degree would one do so for—

No. He could not judge her for that. Not when he, too, sacrificed much for his own family.

"Are you done over there yet?"

Zenris looked up. Evelot's arms were folded; she stood by the odd tree, somehow finished her work already. With a hurried sprinkle of the last of his pheromone vial and a shuffling of the leaves, Zenris deemed his traps suitable and returned to her side.

"I've got to set another trap, and it's my turn to keep watch. Best you get back before your raging fanatics search for you," Evelot said.

"Oh, but they are patient. I have plenty of time to return," replied Zenris.

"Not concerned about breaking their hearts, eh?"

"Well, I believe 'twould do me better to keep you company."

She turned back around in disbelief. "Haven't you heard? Witches don't make good company."

"Truly? How odd. For I have seen the way they smile and can attest 'tis worth the trouble."

Zenris realized too late that he was in trouble. The rose of her cheeks lit her green eyes staring at him. Her lips slightly parted in bewilderment. When she leaned in closer, Zenris's heart fluttered. He must have broken through her barriers. The thought of her smile begged him to receive her in his arms.

Yet her expression morphed into one of fear. Her chilly hand went to his mouth, and her eyes glanced back into the woods.

"Listen."

It amazed him how she heard it first. Moaning. Not that of exhaustion, nor anything humanoid at all. It chuffed and snorted. It sounded large.

Zenris and Evelot moved in tandem, crouching low behind the small incline of the woods' edge. The thing in question trudged closer, panting like a horse.

Then, it struck him. Zenris had not encountered as many in Vestryae or the large cities of Esmora, but he remembered those that he had met. Still as frightening as a werewolf, and more vicious.

"A bear?" Evelot breathed. "What's it doing this close to town?"

Her hand slipped from his mouth and curled in the dank leaves beneath them. Zenris shifted, watching with her.

The bear, all dark fur and a beige snout, moved as if stumbling home from the tavern. Its ragged breath tore from its throat, and the usual weight of such a creature hardly hung below its ribs. Judging by the way it scanned the trees, it searched for something.

Zenris's heart raced as the bear shuffled closer to their traps. Save for the witchling's spells and his songs, they were not armed. If it became ensnared, they would have to kill the beast. Zenris should not have left his daggers in his room. Evelot's face showed the same panic, and he was certain: Neither were prepared.

The beast came to a noisy stop in front of an obscure metal trap. Its claws slid dangerously close to tricking the jaws beneath the unnatural mound of leaves. Groaning, it turned to its side, and began scratching its back against the tree. One of its paws adjusted, another tease toward the traps. Evelot's whispered worries nearly gave them away as it scooted up and down the tree's bark.

Then, the bear stopped. It looked as though 'twould carry on back into the woods whence it came. It lowered to the ground.

Zenris grinned in relief.

A splintered crack broke the silence. The bear turned to look at the tree as it leaned. A paw sank into the trap. With a metallic thunk, it snapped shut.

The bear's roar shook the air. One tug at the loose trap post and the chain fell away. Ferociously, the animal sailed back into the tree. The previous crack morphed into a yielding of the trunk itself. The tree plummeted, landing in the direction of Zenris's own metal traps. With similar clicks and snaps, the contraptions snatched up the bark and its limbs.

In a panic, the bear fled. Its legs fumbled beside a magicked trap. Though the snares had been widely divided, the explosive effect of one set multiple in the entire line. Dirt rained down; vines grasped at air meters above. One missed the log, yet sent it leaning toward a decline. As the bear limped to the safety of the deep woods, the trap's chain links snapped, and the log tumbled into the valley.

Mouths agape, the two stared into the trees.

"Well, that went horribly wrong," Zenris said.

Evelot flew out from their cover. Though Zenris joined her, there was no need to study the damage. He stayed by the edges of the valley as Evelot raced off for signs of any surviving traps. With the bear long gone, the only thing to take in was the disturbance of leaves and the rotting stump of the tree. The valley he peered into below was not cavernous, yet the decline was too steep to climb. There was no point in trying for the traps.

Zenris looked down at his feet to see one still left in mayhem's wake.

Evelot called out as she jogged back to him. "I've only got two vine traps at the end," she said.

"And here, one of mine," Zenris replied.

In response to her pained expression, Zenris assured her lightheartedly, "I'm sure more traps have been forged by the blacksmith. Shall we overtake him once more?"

Of course, 'twas partly in jest. Zenris laughed to himself, thoroughly amused. The outcome had proved better than putting the bear out of its misery. However, Evelot was silent in those few precious seconds. Her head stayed directed to the ground where the traps had once been. As Zenris sobered, he suspected his humor was in ill taste.

"My lady?" he asked.

For a split second, green energy flickered to life over

her curled fists. Though her hood remained over her head, Zenris imagined dark lines beneath her eyes from the mana spent conjuring her own traps. Or mayhap 'twas a sign of deep concentration. She was the logical, collected leader, after all.

As he raised his hand to wave at her, Evelot looked up with a calmness too… poised. Unnervingly so.

"We'll have to start over," she said. "Stay more alert for traps to steal while I make more."

"Naturally. I assume our little 'competition' will be delayed for a 'spell'?" Zenris said, smirking at his smaller jest.

"Aye. That also means we'll need to do more. Patrolling more often, arming ourselves properly."

"As you wish, my lady."

That was, if Zenris attempted to do so with a full schedule. He smiled at her, nonetheless, before she turned to assess their remaining traps once more. Surely their werewolf would make an appearance later on. Then their undetermined window of time would be in their favor yet. Yes, they could make it work—

A sickly rumble stirred to life within Zenris. His hand flew to his stomach. By the Pantheon, why must his body turn on him now?

Yet, 'twas his time; another angry grumble traveled downward. He had to find a privy. With Evelot's back to him, Zenris stole back to the farmer's path. To whichever deity would listen, he prayed for a swift recovery of his organs and pride.

Chapter Ten

It was more than apparent that they weren't going to work well together, after all.

Evelot should've split off on her own after the incident with the traps. It'd been three days of spiraling downward since. Exhaustion clouded her mind after so long of casting more traps and trying to set a plan for when they encountered the beast. Zenris had offered wee help with such planning, including going on patrol in the woods. It infuriated her more that work wasn't any different from the hunting party yet he couldn't be bothered. He had the nerve not to show until after the midday sun was high in the sky, and he pretended to have only "lost track of time".

The knots in her temples twisted as she headed toward the square. Hours of waiting and observing, sitting by their traps did nothing to ease her. If she found him dining and *making merry* with that boyish grin, or sauntering out of the woods' depth again, she'd make mince of him more than his fancy wines could.

It'd been strange, seeing him enjoy his "fans" company the first time, and even stranger was the sort of sadness that twisted in her chest. It felt like. . . another exclusion of her. Which was outrageous. Zenris Aspenheart was an unreliable bard who, if the sneak, would be sent packing on the morrow with her boot still planted up his bahoochie.

In record time, she'd made it to The Glistening Seed, which welcomed the usual crowd. Evelot had a minute to blend into the foot traffic and look for Zenris, a minute before Leslie would likely spot her. But her chances of finding Zenris quickly vanished. Piers and two of his men from the last standoff exited the tavern. Her heart seized, breath halted, and she dove away into a nearby alley.

Behind a crate, Evelot listened for racing footsteps. Her pursuers hollered indistinguishably to one another, and after a pause, she peeked up. Only unassuming townsfolk passed by, but she wouldn't take her chances again. She'd have to sneak around the long way to get into the tavern.

Evelot crept off in the opposite direction. The advantage of learning disguise or invisibility spells became apparent, however far advanced they were for someone like her. Not that she'd give Zenris any credit. Having to merge into yet another crowd was only stalling their efforts, and who knew how long—

Commotion sounded from the main square, and Evelot moved in careful strides. At the edge of the plaza, she stopped. The square was hoaching with onlookers who applauded, cheering for what looked like the heads of a small group entering from the farmlands. When standing back from the center, Evelot struggled to see what they'd stepped aside for. She wedged herself between people and fought toward the front.

She fumbled to a stop, her mouth agape.

Evelot came face-to-face with the wide-eyed stares of several bucks stacked on top of the other. Gathered in hasty piles and divided by species were similar kills; their blood pooled into the cobblestone beneath them. Hunters and villagers from the crowd went over to collect the meats and pelts, others standing atop the miniature mountains of death. Under one drunkard's boot she spotted the woolly lumps of dog-sized bears—of cubs. Her breath was stifled; bile threatened to rise in her throat.

The group of hunters displayed their freshest kills, several wolves and a doe. As they dumped them into their proper piles, Piers reappeared from the crowd. He stood in front of the massacre and shook hands with each hunter. Her ringing ears couldn't pick up a single word, not when the crowd had yet to stop in their celebration. His head tilted, then Piers saw her in the throng.

His lips peeled back into a smirk.

It was cold—more unbearable than winter and its spiteful gusts. It was cold in her veins, her mind, her chest. She was hollow, and yet heavy like stone. None of it, their joy, their hunts, were natural. It wasn't nature's design, and Piers had the audacity to inspire madness further.

Her breaths came unevenly. Something caught her fingers. Evelot looked down. Verdant vines sprouted from between stones and earth as if tugging at her for an answer. Evelot wanted Piers's vicious, disgusting face to be a smudge on the pavement. She wished for the earth to open up under the entire town and swallow them all.

That thought snapped Evelot back into action. One foot, then the other, through the alley and out to the wilderness. Breathe in, breathe out.

It wasn't Piers she should think on, no matter how much he taunted her. The werewolf was the true menace. She needed to dispose of it.

With concentrated breaths and tearful eyes, Evelot forced herself to focus on the hills ahead.

Zenris didn't appear until the sun was a trace of ember red fading beneath a lilac sky. Evelot had summoned orbs of light, away from the woodland path, when she spotted him coming from the Choille's depths. His posh, tousled shirt hung loosely over his torso and his knee-high boots were muddied beneath his braies and a cummerbund-sized corset. He looked like the cheery, unassuming party member of their ragtag group, but Evelot knew there wasn't any mud within a mile of the path.

Strange.

"Good even, my lady," he said.

"Bard," she said.

"Shall we?" With a gracious wave of his arm, Evelot took the lead.

Like the previous days, they aimed to travel as far as possible looking for signs of the werewolf's tracks. Off the beaten path, crickets in the foliage chirped weakly, a sign of the ending season. The dense layer of decaying leaves on the ground made trekking undetected rather difficult. Of course, it wouldn't have been that way had Zenris not taken his sweet time arriving. Soon enough they'd be forced to return to town through the dark woods in the dead of night. After her separate patrol throughout the day and the making of her traps, Evelot had no more energy to spend.

As they wove around the denser leaves piled below, Zenris sauntered closer to her.

"How are you faring today, my lady?"

"Not your lady," she gritted through her teeth. It was good that she didn't have as much mana left. It would've been crackling over her hand in irritation.

"I do appreciate your patience. 'Twas almost a challenge to meet you here, yet here we are. Alone together!"

"You don't say?" she mumbled.

"I take it you have also been busy?"

Evelot groaned low in her throat.

"I imagine there were difficulties, then?" he asked.

"Nothing you mind," Evelot answered.

"Oh?"

"Aye. Unless you have the werewolf in one of your fancy pockets—"

The foliage stirred to her left. A quiet hush fell over them. Evelot held her breath as another bout of noise shook the nearest bush.

"Do you have any spells on you?" Evelot breathed.

Zenris leaned toward her ear. "Have you no mana to spare?" he whispered.

"No."

Evelot scanned the woods with Zenris as the bush jostled again. Without knowing what he was going to do, Evelot wished she knew a useful spell. A sphere of flame or even a simple bolt of lightning—anything to fight against whatever was closing in.

Footfalls charged toward them. Zenris thrust out one arm to shove her back. Evelot closed her eyes as his other hand rose. The words of his sleep spell spilled past his lips.

After a hollow thud, there was a beat of silence.

Zenris laughed.

"Poor thing," he said.

Evelot opened her eyes to see Zenris approach a small bundle. When he turned back to her, there slumped a common hare in his arms.

"'Twas more in need of a carrot than our flesh," Zenris joked.

Evelot exhaled in relief.

The cry of a buck pierced the air. Evelot leapt as violently as her hammering heart. It echoed and shifted through the woods; the creature screamed as if fighting something off. Before her, Zenris gently set down the hare on a bed of leaves.

"Could be our perpetrator. Let us make haste!"

Evelot opened her mouth to speak, but Zenris dashed into the thick of the woods, leaving her behind. When she called out to him, summoning her lights to follow him, it was all for naught. It must've been the elven blood pumping through his veins that carried him further ahead. Or the skirts that fluttered and flapped around Evelot's ankles muddling her speed. She growled in frustration as she picked up her pace.

Yards off, Zenris stood at the entrance of a den beneath a rock surface. Evelot puffed and panted, stumbling in beside him. Her lights hovered overhead, outlining a thick sticky liquid trailing into the hollow. The whiff of rank brought on the image of those crimson eyes. A shiver rocked her shoulders.

"We can lure it out," Zenris said, pulling Evelot out of her thoughts.

"While it's feasting?"

To her shock, Zenris then stepped toward the entrance.

"Stop!" Evelot harshly whispered. "You can't be serious!"

"Why not? With the beast distracted, stealth shall be on our side."

"What for? If it's the werewolf, we can trap it in there rather than feed ourselves to it."

"What if 'tis not our beast? We might trap an innocent predator inside."

"Ah, an oxymoron. Glad to see you joining us for craic!" Evelot said sarcastically.

"In that case, I shall leave the two of you to get acquainted. Excuse me."

"Are you—? Zenris!"

His figure receded into the shadows of the cave.

She felt like an eejit, shifting from foot to foot and wrapping her cloak tighter around herself. The chill wind scraped between the trees. Not a sound rang out inside the den; there was no cry for help as she waited for him in the safety of the woods.

That bard had been naïve all for a fool's dream of glory. He was nothing but a radge, running into that hellshole. Technically, he'd pronounced himself dead. Absolutely no chance he was coming out of that one. Evelot would've walked away if not for her churning thoughts. He might've been alive. . . and if so, what did that make her for abandoning him? It's not like she hated the elf. He was annoying and full of himself, but he'd been a companion who'd stuck up for her on past occasions.

Sucking in a breath, Evelot stepped into the cave. No warmth followed her in, not even a speck of moonlight. All her senses stalled; she was almost too afraid to cross the barrier until she heard a distant sound. In the pitch black, she held her arms aloft and listened, her breath bated. The even drip of water plunked down from above. Her boots stepped on something that crunched and scraped. Deeper in echoed snorts and chomps, gnashing and thunking and breaking—

A hand covered her mouth. Her shriek died in their palm as they pulled her away from the noisemaker.

Stop, said a familiar voice. *'Tis I.*

Evelot tried calling for Zenris, but his hand stayed in place.

Refrain from vocally responding. This telepathy spell allows us to communicate.

What? she wondered.

There you have it!

Evelot recognized the spell. Beluphis had used it once or twice before, but in the den it sounded more crisp, like waves crashing against cliffs. However—

You've got that sort of magic? That means you've been able to read my mind this entire time! she snapped.

'Tis no time to address such things. We need to leave.

You don't say? Suppose it's another hare—

'Tis not a hare, he answered gravely.

Evelot let him guide her by the wrist. She wasn't eager to discover the beast or its meal, not that she'd changed her mind in the past few minutes. Neither dared speak as they stepped around what Evelot surmised to be bones. She hurried to keep Zenris's pace. The faint moonlight grew closer.

Just a little ways, Zenris encouraged.

Evelot stepped forward.

The crunch of bone reverberated off the unseeable walls.

An animalistic groan rumbled in the air. It chuffed and puffed, a familiar scrape of metal accompanied a heightened growl.

"Make haste!" Zenris said.

She wasn't sure whose scream she heard as they dashed out of the den. The bear roared at their heels and charged, and with Zenris's hand still wrapped around her wrist, the two fled to the safety of the woods.

"Though I know not the lady's distress, I apologize for my action once more!"

"Then what's the point when you clearly don't mean it?" she snapped back.

Evelot stomped down the path, homebound. The dim silhouette of her house lay ahead, its fences drawing close as she trudged toward them. Peace of mind and a warm bed were near.

"To assuage you," Zenris said. "To put you at ease."

"Oh, but *sir*, you've proven yersel' lacking in that degree altogether!"

"Were it that my companion had stayed in place…"

Evelot whirled back on him. "Don't you turn this around on me. You didn't say a thing! This isn't my fault!"

"No, not the entirety of the fault. Only part of it."

Her tartan skirts caught onto the wooden fencing as she climbed over. Yanking them free, she scoffed. "I can't believe I went back to help you."

"Did you?" Zenris asked, infuriatingly easing over the fence.

"Clearly, I shouldn't have."

"Yet you did."

Having made it to the garden, Evelot refused to look back at him. There wasn't a slim hope of watching her words when her patience was long gone. They'd lost their traps because of his shite work at checking and gathering them, they'd no clue where the werewolf hid, and they'd almost been mauled by a bear—because of him. Of all the things she could do that night, having that conversation with him was long down the list. Especially when she suspected he'd spin it in his favor: He'd smile and joke, say something sugar-coated meant to make her blush, and she'd fall for it. Or she might, if she continued being around him.

"Evelot, wait!"

Bolts of magic sizzled across her white-knuckled fists. Evelot sneered at the back door.

"To know that you acted on my account is hum—"

"G'night," she muttered.

"Is it so hard to believe—?"

"I trusted you!" She spun around in a flurry of green energy. The earth rumbled beneath her boots, and vines sprouted in waves as she trembled with rage.

"You want to know what my problem is?" she

snapped. "It's working with a bard that creeps into my heid and disappears into the Choille while tossing his responsibilities to the wind. It's hoping he'd keep his word and then seeing dead cubs in the square! It's seeing Piers throw it all back in my face because—Because—"

She squeezed her eyes shut. Evelot wouldn't think about that night with Piers or what happened. She wouldn't let it come crawling back into her mind.

Sucking in a breath, she said, "Tell me: Why does a materialistic, silver-tongued bard play pretend at caring about something other than himself?"

The ground settled. For a second, Evelot thought she might collapse in front of him in a heap of quaking limbs and gasps of breath. But she was still standing, still gaping at the awestruck elf whose gaze looked more terrifying than a glower from Piers. Oh so subtly, his jaw loosened and his eyes widened. His usually carefree face showed nothing but shock.

Zenris pursed his lips, blinking back to reality. "Well, if that is your honest opinion, Evelot," he said, "then mayhap you understand me as much as Goldencrest does you."

He turned and silently walked away. His words doused her in ice; the nippy wind that blew back her hood was just as horrible. The absoluteness in his tone told her plenty. Zenris was walking away for good. She'd finally spoken her piece, and it took crossing both their boundaries to get there.

Surrounded by the chill night, and Jammer's concerned titters, Evelot felt a wrongness weigh heavily on her conscience.

Chapter Eleven

Everything hurt: from the edge of the bar counter biting into his forehead, his limbs that had long since fallen asleep, and his pride after several days of fruitless recovery. Zenris groaned. His current remedy flooded his veins, attempting to lull him into a long, blissful sleep. Shame 'twas hardly noon. His bed was a short distance up the stairs, but because of the pin-pricks numbing him, he supposed 'twould not hurt to close his eyes where he sat. If only a set of encroaching, sturdy footsteps would cease thundering in his ears.

In the corner of his vision, Pril's outline took the seat beside him. Sapphire arms leaned against the counter, fingers bridged under her elongated chin. Inebriated or no, Zenris recognized her distempered expression.

"Whatever the matter, I am innocent," Zenris said.

She raised a suspicious brow at him. "I am not here for you," grumbled Pril.

"Oh… then praytell what summons you here?"

"I wish to imbibe."

With one swipe, Pril stole the goblet in his hand and downed the rest of its contents. Her lips curled in distaste. "Your preference is displeasing to my palette," she said.

"How dare you!" Zenris slurred. "That is superb wine!"

Zenris dared to sit up only to suck in wind. For a moment, the tavern room shifted like a rocking ship. He balanced himself against the counter as Pril adjusted in her seat.

"You look horrible."

"How modest you phrase it," Zenris sarcastically replied. He squinted up at Pril and then asked, "Why did you steal the last of my Mytalin Sweet Wheat? 'Twas a good year, that one."

"You will not be needing it, unless you plan on avoiding the stage another night."

"Are you certain you are not here on my account?"

Pril grumbled, yet said nothing. Zenris wiped at his oily face. A relief 'twas that his fans were nowhere in sight to see him in such disgrace. He was no better in appearance than a haggard pauper, though he had not the smell other than the sharp sweetness of wine upon him. Fortunately, he wore "mussed and unkempt" better than any beggar.

With a huff, Pril waved to the barkeeper and gave him her order. After receiving her tankard and partaking, she became wearied.

"The hunting party is being called off," she said.

Zenris frowned to himself. "And that is disagreeable?"

"The mystery creature has been outwitting us. Sneaking past our defenses and stealing more livestock and hunters. Civilian volunteers have been dismissed, and there are talks of putting the entire town on a curfew. Because we signed a contract, we do not need to fear losing our wage. But the mayor keeps secret of our next course of action. If they do not maintain the numbers necessary to hunt the beast, we will continue to be thwarted."

Through his muddled thoughts, Zenris understood her point of view. Pril's concern over their curtailed defenses was valid. There was the chance the mayor would find other means of protection, stripping the two of potential earnings. 'Twas the consequence of signing a contract allowing them pay only per "each patrol."

Had he thought to include her on his separate hunt —rather, past hunt—would they have stood a better chance in ridding the problem altogether?

In the temporary pause of his secret mission through the woods, Zenris hoped the hunters' "other means" did not include burning down every tree in zealous mania. The fate of becoming a town fool would be more relieving than being proven right.

"And for what purpose are you drinking today?" Pril asked.

Zenris folded his arms and rested his head on them. "'Tis complicated."

"Make it not complicated."

"I would rather forget it."

"Yes, because your method so far has worked perfectly for you," Pril said.

"You... I must be well inebriated to think you could be sarcastic."

"I have been practicing."

Zenris stared at her. She was right; he needed to sober before he saw her dancing a jig.

Pril's sigh formed a slight crinkle in her brow, a rare occurrence upon her taught, scaly features. "For too many days you have been distracted from your duties. You look elsewhere, your energy is insufficient for combat, and you whittle away your time here in the tavern. You are the colorful bard of our operation. What is it that can upset you?"

"'Tis only a… personal matter concerning another."

"Ah." Pril sagely closed her eyes, a look of understanding crossing her features. Zenris had not thought her to be someone who could empathize with another, but it appeared she would have a word of advice to offer.

"I see. So, one of your dalliances finally caught up to you and demands recompense for a child you sired."

"Good gods, no!"

"A shame. I was hoping to see how feeble your offspring would be."

Zenris groaned under his breath. "Let it alone, Pril."

"Your tone is different, as well. Is this what you call 'hysterical'?"

"I am not hysterical!" he snapped, albeit a pitch too high. "I am… downcast."

"All the more reason, then, to explain yourself and this 'other' you've been associating with."

"You cannot leave things be, can you?"

"No."

Zenris sighed. He knew not if he should spare her his own matters or speak truth to his comrade. He blinked back his inebriated fog and leaned over the counter. "I had met an… interesting person. We exchanged words, and after much toil, I had for a time won their trust.

"Several nights ago, all my efforts were in vain. She— they said things, and I… said something in return. Only now do I realize that in defending myself, I spoke words unworthy of a bard." Zenris sighed. "It feels as if the chance to make amends has been lost."

"What was it she said first?" said Pril.

With a deep breath, Zenris replied, "She said that I was an arrogant, irresponsible, materialistic bard who lies all the time."

"Finally, a woman who speaks the truth," Pril said into her cup.

"Wha—? I am a gentleman!"

"Do not fool yourself. You are as at fault for selfishness as anyone else. Perhaps more so. Your fans do not know how to critique you, and their praise has spoiled you to the point of gluttony. It is a shame that More of Gray has also done so. The party bit their tongues for his sake, and now you struggle like a hatchling from their shell."

Zenris could not find the words to respond. There was a flash of betrayal within his chest, yet it faded as Pril leaned in to speak once more.

"You have flaws, and strengths," she replied, "and you have learned from your eighty plus years of life. Anyone who has fought by your side knows this, but for this 'female,' she has only a temporary impression of you."

"And you?" Zenris asked. "Why had you not spoken?"

"It was not my place until you had asked."

Pril returned to her tankard. Masked in mud and dirt, her sharp, taloned hands nearly blended into the wooden cup. 'Twas then he recalled Pril had disappeared more often after their last hunt together.

Zenris turned his head in shame. He had allowed himself to be blinded by fame. For too long his pride and reputation remained intertwined. Worse yet, his secret cause hindered his duty to capture the werewolf, his duty to his witchling companion and Pril.

What Evelot had said was truth: He was selfish.

Zenris rose from his seat and signaled the barkeeper. With a fresh goblet of water in hand, he imbibed in greedy gulps.

"Forgive me, Pril. I have been a fool. I must make amends," Zenris said. "Will you—?"

"I will arrange for your performance tonight. See that you finish your quest post-haste and report back in a timely manner."

Zenris smiled before making for the stairs. He was to be presentable, after all. Thus, he started with a fresh bath and clean clothes.

He left the tavern with a clearer mind. Zenris donned a more humble attire of starched layers under a vest and cloak, paired with a simple golden loop in his ear. A true refreshment indeed. With a click of his low heels, he sought after Evelot.

Unsure of where to find her, Zenris returned to their last meeting place. After a meager trek through the woods, he found mounds of enchanted vines set as traps. Akin to a trail of breadcrumbs, they led him to the familiar tartan-skirted figure of his companion. She silently knelt in the leaves amidst the forming mist, her hands aloft as green mana ebbed from her palms. Seeing her there, solemnly at work, Zenris paused. Evelot made no indication of hearing him approach with her back turned. While danger was afoot and a watchful eye necessary, he was grateful for the respite to collect himself.

Zenris cleared his throat. Evelot startled, and her mana faded into the evening. She turned back to him, her visage shifting from shocked to crestfallen.

"Good even," Zenris said.

"Bard," she greeted.

"May I join you?"

She furrowed her brow. "Why?"

"I come offering my assistance. . . if you would have me?"

Evelot said nothing. Zenris wondered whether she would snap at him again. He hoped 'twould not come to that, though he was prepared to hear her discrepancies if so.

Instead, she rose with a small nod. "Patrol with me?"

Astonished, Zenris joined her side. They waded through the gathering fog, the silence betwixt them stifling. The need to clear the tension with jovial words or a brief mention of the weather would have more than sufficed for Zenris. Yet Evelot did not meet his eye, her gaze too focused on the trees ahead. The moonlit night reflected in her complexion, outlining exhaustion beneath her eyes and the nervous nibble at her lips. Her hands gripped each side of her cloak, a cocoon to shield her from the chill, or likely from Zenris. Those hands that summoned a ferocious response from the earth nights prior.

At the time, Zenris considered not the cause for the rage she had displayed. Whether she had truly attempted to smite him was beyond his imagination, though Zenris did not think it possible. As she had not the strength of her mentor, neither her energy nor her mana reached him. It hovered at the edge of an invisible barrier akin to a dog leashed behind a fence; it incurred fear, not injury. To know that she had kept so much bottled in her heart, masked by logic and sarcasm, placed a mark of shame upon Zenris's name for his inconsideration. He could not bear for her to suffer any longer.

The afternoon sun was retiring and the background wildlife hurried to do the same as the two returned to the path. In a hidden glance, there remained a far-off look in her eye, her fingers forlornly curled around her hood. A sight that encouraged Zenris to speak.

"May I confess something?" Zenris said.

Her jaw tightened but her eyes stayed trained ahead. "Aye?"

"I wish to beg your forgiveness and be held accountable for my actions. To have disregarded your previous concerns, and the lack of care to my current duties. . . 'Twas horrendously inappropriate of me."

Evelot shook her head. "It's nothing."

Zenris paused. "You are. . . certain?"

"What does it matter?"

She still had yet to look at him, and her hood prevented him from sneaking another glance at her full expression.

"Well, for one, I had insulted you," Zenris alluded.

"And I'm telling you, it's fine."

"How so?"

With a scoff, Evelot stepped away. She turned back to

him only to say, "I'll keep watch a while longer. Go on back to town."

What an absurdity. Zenris gaped at her. Evelot was stubborn, yet he had not accounted for the limits of that stubbornness, or lack thereof. Trying for patience, Zenris insisted, "You can speak plainly here. I wish to hear your full thoughts."

"J-just stop."

"Why?" he asked.

In a small voice he nearly missed, Evelot said, "I can't do this."

Evelot marched deeper into the woods. Zenris called out to her, giving chase. The ground was shockingly flat in their stretch of the woods, unlike the hills and divots outside. It made for an easier setting to run, however foolish Zenris felt doing so for a simple apology. Had it not been for such an environment, Zenris would have missed the receding haze and the odd markings within the leaves: coiled squares, the telltale signs of a net masked by nature.

It stood in her path a mere meter ahead.

"Evelot, stop!"

Zenris sped toward her. Muffled sniffles resounded from under her hood hung over her lowered head.

Reaching out, his hand grazed hers—

Something snapped beneath her boot. Zenris caught her arm.

The trees whirled around him. Evelot screamed in his ear. Air whistled in their descent until a creaking, fibrous object caught his fall. When nothing else stirred, Zenris opened his eyes. He lay on his back within a large, humanoid-sized net. Atop him, Evelot sputtered for breath, their limbs tangled and protruding out of their prison.

"Wha-what's?" she panted.

"Stay calm," Zenris said. "We have been caught."

Evelot struggled onto her knees, her eyes cast down at the netting. "T-this isn't mine."

"Is this not a hunter's trap?"

"No. It can't be. N-none of them made it this far out."

"Your hesitant tone says otherwise."

"I'm sure!" she insisted.

"Very well, 'tis as you say," Zenris relented.

"If I had my knife—" Evelot groaned. "Not here with me."

"Allow me."

Zenris slid his hands down to his pocket as Evelot struggled to rise. He slowly pried his knife free. 'Twas but a moment he held it in hand. It slipped from his grasp, and their saving grace fell through the netting. A collective breath left the two as the knife hit the ground with a soft thud.

Evelot's eyes squeezed shut. Her breath escaped her in a whimper, and her body leaned away from Zenris in the tangle of netting.

"Evelot?" Zenris said.

"I'm fine. Fine. . ."

Taking a deep breath, she looked up at him. "Let me think. Just… don't touch me."

Hers was an odd reaction, but Zenris recalled learning of a condition that invoked a fear of closed spaces. Or mayhap the other "knife" in his pocket, visible through his braies, unsettled her. He was not keen to admit to its presence. Someone atop him, breathing close to his ear. . . Well. . .

With that in mind, Zenris clumsily rose to his knees and turned his back to her. He listened to Evelot's dejected sigh, the shuffle of her skirts and the jostling of the net in unison with her movements. In the distance, the sun disappeared behind the trees; its ember halo gently pierced through shadow and fog. Surely Pril would notice his absence by nightfall and sic an army of duchy soldiers after him. Preferably before Evelot crafted a plan that involved her current mutterings of "notes," "inkwell," and "jam." By the gods, she must have a ravenous craving for jam in times of stress.

"Have you an idea in mind?" Zenris asked impatiently. "If not, we can swing the net toward the tree limb?"

"Fine."

He felt her gentle tug upon his sleeve. Zenris turned around to his companion. Her gaze fell to their knees, a weary expression in place of discomfort.

Zenris internally chided himself. Of all the circumstances, 'twas being tossed into a net where a bard like him could make peace with a sharp-tongued witch. . . a maiden such as she. After seeing her distress, he decided the time for a gentlemanly conduct was at hand.

"Beg pardon, for I must be twice the fool in your eyes," he said.

"What do you have to apologize for? It was a trap, and I. . ."

She sighed once more. One would think Zenris truly was the instigator of offenses in their petty argument, though he knew not the extremity of her grievances. With no ability to erase his mistakes, he could only summon the patience to understand.

"Happens to the best of us, no?" he asked, smiling light-heartedly.

"I-it's not that." Evelot tipped her head to the sky. Her hardened expression threatened to become melancholic.

"I am all pointy ears, if you wish."

When she looked back at him, she said, "What're you being kind to me for? I've been nothing but a—well, 'witch' to you. No point in offering apologies."

"I have offended a lady. Would not that be the appropriate answer?"

"I've told you before, I'm no lady. I'm a witch."

Zenris could not help the smirk curling his lips. "Lady, witch, squirrel, amoeba, 'tis all the same, frankly."

"If that's the case, then nothing would get done. We'd have to apologize to every dust mite in the air."

There was a shine in her eyes as she smiled that spoke of more than the glimmering hope of laughter. It told of nights helplessly alone. She wore it in stride for someone society cast out of its graces. The shame lay in Goldencrest: 'Twas a most enrapturing sight they shunned, her smile victoriously rising above pain.

Her amusement hardened, crumbling into vulnerability that refused another word to leave her parted lips. All the while, Zenris awaited her next response.

"It's," she began, "so much easier to hide behind a reputation than to let others see. . . you. Isn't it?"

Like in the song from the bard band Trimming Team, it truly must have been her words that caused his old self to expire. Where a favorable or humorous response would have easily sprouted from his lips, Zenris found his jaw agape, struggling for words in the ensuing silence.

"Zenris?"

"I. . . know that feeling well," he said.

"You do?"

"Of course. There is a privilege in being a bard, and with it a duty to create music that inspires, that speaks to individuals far and wide. 'Tis truly an honor, but I endure much for that sake. My fans' expectations of me can be exaggerated. They expect me to smell of a spring meadow, day and night, and to have a smile that makes the heavenly Dawn King jealous. . . and I must watch as they order the same foods at the tavern for the sake of imagery, not of shared customs.

"To perpetuate this idolatry is. . . taxing. Yet, I do so to avoid the same fate as elder or unfavorable bards: of being forgotten. One day, 'twill be all gone. The illusion will fade, and they will forget my voice. As it petrifies me. . . I ponder the weight of either fate."

A feeling of wistfulness warped his smile as he added, "Mayhap 'tis the daily toil we face. That which we sacrifice, and what we yearn for. If the lady questions it, then I can only assume she seeks what was unfairly taken."

Her parted lips pursed as she leaned her head against her knees, staring back at Zenris. The way Evelot beheld him was as though she were stepping into his shoes and walking his path in slivers of seconds. 'Twas empathy that churned a feeling within, greater than countless stage lights or applause. As much as he could be emotionally exposed, that tenderness was warmth, breathing new life into his soul.

Her smile wavered at an interruptive thought. "Will

you forgive me for acting like an arse, Zenris?" Evelot said.

"A mutual pardon, then?"

"All right. All's forgiven," she replied, her smile glowing brighter than the setting sun.

The sight was overwhelming for Zenris. He looked away, praying for Pril's search party before he lost his composure.

"Ach! We've wasted enough time. Gotta get out of here!" Evelot said. "You were talking about swinging toward the limb earlier?"

"Yes. Oddly enough, I am adept at being caught in nets such as these. However, we have not the Jinryuu to catch our fall."

"You still survived it in one piece, though?"

"Well, I have also been told I have a skull forged of dwarven ore. 'Twould do well to absorb our fall," he teased.

Her laugh was like fireflies: effervescent lights that illuminated on their grassy stage, gone too quickly to appreciate.

"All right, bard. On the count of three, we swing together."

Zenris felt a grin widen as the two leaned back, side by side.

"One," Evelot announced. "Two. Thr—"

An abrupt lurch of the net sent them jostling into each other.

"What was—?"

Zenris heard a resounding snap below. The net gave way, and the two plunged toward the ground. He pulled Evelot into his arms. In a heap of screams and tangled limbs, they fell.

His back struck the leafy ground.

Stars flittered above as Zenris gasped for breath, opening his eyes. He felt about his spiraling surroundings. The netting scratched at his bare skin; a bed of leaves had softened their fall. Evelot sucked in a breath, rolling onto her side beside him. Zenris's every muscle protested with his attempt to face her.

"Are you injured?" he rasped.

"I'll—I'll be fine."

An unhinged cackle echoed from behind the trees.

"No running, no hiding, tasties."

Zenris's hand stiffened on her arm, his heart clenched tightly. Another hiccup of laughter resonated nearby, then another. He squinted into the darkness. From the shadows, three figures jogged closer.

Evelot looked up and screamed. A crack thudded against Zenris's head, heavy and thick. The stars returned with a vengeance, and in their dark hold Zenris collapsed.

Chapter Twelve

Her mind scrambled to come up with a solution through a throbbing headache.

The dark figures had swarmed her and Zenris like starving vultures. One second Evelot was struggling to summon a spell, the next a club beat at hers and Zenris's heads before four shadowed strangers stuffed them into a net and dragged them both off.

As they continued through the Choille, the moonlight highlighted their outlines. There was a smaller werewolf, about Beaghan-sized, and three humanoids. Cloaked or not, their hoods didn't hide dog-like snouts protruding outward. Four werewolves. . .

There was wee chance of escape. They had no weapon to cut through the net, and she had an unconscious companion she'd spent the last of her mana trying to heal with a vaguely remembered spell. There was no running, and no fighting back. If only she'd spotted Jammer to send a message to her mentor, although it'd be difficult without parchment—and she'd have eyes on her.

Evelot spared a glance at her companion. Zenris groaned, slowly waking in her arms as their sides scraped against mud and leaves in the net. After all that they'd shared earlier, his facade dropping and her hearing his story, they were going to be carted off to Goddess knows where to be eaten. She should've stopped feeling sorry for herself and listened to him. Because of her mistake, Zenris was literally and figuratively being dragged into the same fate she was.

The density of the trees cleared to a large, open field. A grass-enveloped dirt path led north toward a crumbled structure. As they approached, a church came into view. Beyond a surviving bell tower, there was no sign of which religious order it once housed; it'd been long since ransacked by time and nature. With the ancient doors looming over them, Evelot envisioned the open jaws of a beast more than a place of worship.

Zenris groaned aloud. "Evelot. . ."

"Shut it!" one werewolf snapped.

Evelot held Zenris close as the werewolves dragged them further down the path and to the church's doors.

"Are you hurt?" Zenris whispered.

"I don't have a plan," Evelot quietly answered. "Zenris, I'm so—"

The tallest, their leader, stopped them and hollered to the open ceiling of the church. Several shadowed faces appeared in the portals and smashed windows, here and gone again before Evelot could catch them.

The doors heaved open, and their group entered. Greeting them within was a scene out of her nightmares. A large nave teemed with voices, howls, and monstrous bodies. From the dimly lit corners and a hanging iron chandelier of dripping candles, the remnants of pews dined and sat similar figures.

Evelot's blood ran cold. A whole horde of the beasts that had plagued her home, gathered under one roof. She wasn't sure whether to be frightened by their appearances or the bloodied, rank corpses they feasted on. Whether it was proper to call them "werewolves" or "mutants," Evelot didn't know. Most of them were men, a few were women, but all wore tattered clothes and squinted through feral eyes. They cackled and nipped at what was close at hand; sneering and shoving, picking fights over scraps of human and livestock. Unnaturally thick fur covered their exposed limbs. Several had full snouts for mouths. It was as if the gods couldn't decide the boundary between man and beast.

Their eyes fixed on Evelot's group as they marched to the altar. On a rickety clergy chair there sat a lone figure, their Alpha. His gait and stature commanded attention, his oak-like build and thick arms proving fatal results when crossed. Salt-and-pepper hair had been combed over an oblong head, and the same smatterings covered his unkempt beard. Ravenous red eyes bore into her as the other werewolves opened the net, exposing Evelot and Zenris.

Her jaw clenched shut against her building scream.

A pleased grin split across his face. "Smells like you brought me meat," their Alpha said.

"Found the magic user you were complaining about, Boss," said the troupe leader.

With a black-tipped claw, he ordered her closer. Her captors yanked her out of the netting, away from her protesting companion and to the altar. Hands gripped at her arms. A scrape at her back made her lurch forward. It was like the pawing and jeering from years ago, disgusting touches that summoned a scream behind her bit lips.

Coming face-to-face with the Alpha, the fight drained out of her. The old stench of gore and sweat watered her eyes while he sniffed at her, scaring off her volatile recollection.

"Yes," the Alpha said, "just like the magic that tried to keep us at bay." His grin dwindled as he stared at her. His eyes were the only red ones in the room. "But this little twig can't be the only user. She is too young for such old magic. Tell me, little witch, who else is guarding the Portal?"

Evelot's jaw stayed clamped shut.

"Another in your coven. . .? A sibling? A passing wizard?" With a keen eye, he added, "A mentor, perhaps?"

She stared at the wall behind him. She'd rather die than speak.

"Answer!" growled the troupe leader, jolting her.

Evelot didn't see the Alpha's hand, but it flew out and latched onto the other's face.

"I'll be the one giving orders!" he roared.

With a thrust of his arm, the underling went sailing backward, crashing into the opposite wall. Evelot didn't hear it stir.

Louring, the Alpha composed himself into an unsettling silence. Evelot's heart was a tempest in her chest. When he turned back to her, it crashed to a halt.

"Have it your way. Let's see how silent you are while I suck the marrow from your bones.

"Put her in my chambers," he told another underling.

She spun around. The mutant lackey was already pulling her toward an open doorway behind the altar. Evelot couldn't hold back her next scream as she twisted and turned in its grasp. Another set of claws sank into her other arm, shoving her forward.

"Halt!"

Evelot peeked over her shoulder. Zenris rose to his full height, addressing the Alpha.

"Look no further," he said. "For 'twas I, the spellcaster."

"I am not a fool. You reek of bard magic, not witch," the leader deadpanned.

Zenris looked shocked, then chuckled self-deprecatingly. "True. You have a keen mind. It must come easily to such a sharp-eyed master of the woods."

"Of course."

"Amazing. Have you always been so clever, or was it an enhancement from your condition?"

The leader studied him; the room fell to a stupefied quiet. As the Alpha laughed, a sound that ominously thundered through the dilapidated rafters, no one dared budge from their perch.

Circling Zenris, the werewolf took a long whiff of his neck. Then he stopped, crossing his arms. "I care not for names, but yours piques my interest. What do they call you, 'half-elf'?"

"The magnificent, illustrious Zenris Aspenheart, o fearless Alpha of the werewolves," Zenris said with a bow.

"As if my betas are of the same ilk. Do not mistake jackal-kin for the purer form."

"My apologies, sir."

How Zenris kept composure was a mystery to Evelot. It was the same demeanor he maintained on stage that kept him alive. Unless the Alpha changed his mind, that was.

"It seems you are famous, for even I have heard that name," the Alpha said.

"How kind of you. Alas, I am but a humble traveler always with a song in my heart."

"He's that singer that women threw their underwear at!" said a voice in the crowd.

The interrupting minion raised hushes around him, but their leader looked more incredulous than enraged.

"Feral Lord's Bane—Is that true?" asked the Alpha.

Zenris's hand went to his cheek. "That story is a bit. . . complicated. The maiden responsible, name forgone for her respect, was quite swept up in the melody of a *saucy* lyric."

"You've a sizable array of songs in that heart of yours, then?"

"Absolutely," Zenris said with a smirk. "And mine ears do catch all manner of whispers about Goldencrest."

The Alpha perked up. "Anything about the mysterious magic user protecting the Portal you'd care to share?"

Evelot numbly shook her head at Zenris. He wouldn't sell her and her mentor out to the werewolf that easily. Not after everything. Would he?

"A shame! For whomsoever cast such spells has caused me agony." Zenris gestured to his head with a sigh. "The sensitivity to darker magic offends me. Dreadful business, I assure you."

The leader considered Zenris with a serious look. "Then you don't know where they are?"

"Though I had not laid eyes upon them, I can attest from my many strolls within the wilderness. I sensed them coming from"—Zenris pointed to the left wall—"that direction."

"That direction?" The Alpha pointed with him.

"Exactly."

"We checked there, Boss!" someone in the crowd said. "No way we didn't scope thoroughly!"

"Except for Dirk. They was sleepin' on the job."

"Hey!" the captor behind Zenris exclaimed.

The werewolf snarled at them in warning. After the crowd settled, he replied, "Are you sure of this, bard?"

"On my honor, sir!"

The Alpha fell back into his seat. Not a sound echoed in that large room, save for Evelot's thundering heart. It hammered at the realization that Zenris was playing the fool to help them escape. His concentration was too sharp, too different from his real demeanor.

But the werewolves wouldn't fall for Zenris's plan so easily. Was he considering the outcome?

"Very well, Aspenheart. You have my thanks."

A flash of relief filled Evelot's chest.

Then, the Alpha turned to his lackeys—

"You may eat him now."

The room erupted into a frenzied cacophony. The jackal-kin yanked Zenris into the crowd as Evelot fought against her captors shoving her the opposite way. She tried in vain to call on her powers, to nature, anything to create a distraction. It couldn't be the end.

Over the roar of voices, Zenris's rose, stopping them all.

"I beg pardon, sir," Zenris said to the leader. "But did not that information warrant us a release?"

The Alpha guffawed. "You hardly told me a thing."

Zenris hung his head in dejection.

The werewolf scoffed at him then turned to Evelot.

She reared back from the starving eyes that rolled up her body. His nails dug into her cheeks as he held her jaws, bringing her in for another long sniff over her neck. His putrid, hot breath puffed against her skin as a laugh rocked from his chest.

"I think you should scream a little longer, witchling," he said, releasing her. "Both of you." The Alpha looked back at Zenris. With a wave of his hand, he ordered the bard back onto the altar. "Yes. The bard will play until his voice is a croak, and the witchling's legs have fallen off. We like them slick with sweat, don't we?"

A celebratory cheer rose to meet his announcement. The jackal-kin put away their utensils and weapons, flitting around the chapel to set a stage. Without their attention, Evelot felt a strange sense of freedom. Freedom that spared her a few steps closer to Zenris.

Zenris gaped at her as she stumbled into his arms. He held her up by the elbows and leaned in close.

"Zenris, what did you—"

"Ah, ah, ah!"

To her surprise, Zenris pulled her into an embrace. He didn't speak, but a crackle in her head made her freeze.

Beg pardon, my lady, for this intrusion, he said within his telepathy spell. *'Tis the only way I can maintain our cover.*

What do you mean 'cover'? Zenris, it's over. We're—

Evelot.

She waited. His hand slid up her back, making her jolt.

My apologies once more. I . . . Though I have not been reliable within this fortnight, I am determined to see us survive. There is a plan in this, I promise you. You will not suffer this alone.

There was the bear's cave, Evelot reminded him.

Zenris held back a chuckle as he pulled away. His smile eased the fearful pounding of her heart.

Please trust me through this endeavor. You need only follow my lead. Will you do that for me?

Tears pricked at the corner of her eyes. Evelot nodded. *All right. Tell me what to do.*

"Bard boy!" interrupted one jackal. "We got you a lute!"

Zenris turned back to the famished crowd, putting on a terrified smile. "Splendid! Let me tune it and we can begin the festivity!" Then Zenris turned back to Evelot. "Well, my lady, I offer only one piece of advice," he said.

"What's that?"

"Dance like your life depends on it."

Before she could respond, impatient jackal-kin whisked him away to the stage atop the altar. Evelot shuffled after them in a stunned panic. The thought of dancing in front of others, in front of a starving pack of beasts, fleetingly crossed her mind. There wasn't a chance on this plane or the next for her to do what Zenris expected of her.

But, Evelot had no choice.

Soon, Zenris had his lute tuned, and a select few pack members to support him with provisional instruments. Evelot stood stiffly beside him, glancing at the audience. A horde of mutants returned the gesture, whispering to each other and awaiting their leader's command. She felt his gaze on her from his seat relocated to the chapel's crossing, a front row view so he could pluck her when he wished.

Her hands balled into her skirts.

The crowd was silenced by Zenris's raised palm.

"Thanks to your cohort, I wish to treat you to a. . . 'witchy' rendition of a song that a colleague, Sir Ricardo of Martine, graciously permitted me to sing long ago. Like my rabid fans, may you also find that same wild spark in this crazed melody of life."

Zenris smirked at the accompaniment, and the stage erupted with song. The jackal-kin performers followed suit with brass horns, tambourines, and drums to his energetic beat. In a lower range, Zenris suavely sang of black bats and spells. It enchanted the crowd into hip swivels and guffaws, but Evelot felt no comfort. Not while the Alpha focused solely on her.

With a turn of his head, Zenris slipped Evelot a wink between lyrics and signaled for her to dance. Her cheeks flared as she tried swaying stiffly. His chin jutted out, and a long moment passed before she realized he meant for her to copy him. But he only smiled.

In soft shuffles and steps, he moved. Evelot shadowed him with her rustling skirts and loosened limbs. Each step lifted a weight off her. When Zenris's smile widened, his voice a mixture of relief and encouragement, she felt herself grinning back.

His hips rocked side to side like hers.

Her heart skipped a beat in tandem to his voice.

The crowd cried out in excitement.

She twirled about Zenris, appearing over his shoulder, then the other. The fabric of her cloak slipped from her back, its clasp coming undone in a matter of shakes and circles. For once, Evelot wasn't bothered to fix it.

Zenris faced the crowd once again. Evelot glanced

out at the audience with him, content to ruffle her skirts in thought. She laughed to herself. Her fear fell away, and a new sensation of determination filled her. That nonsensical positivity of Zenris's was becoming contagious.

While he continued singing, Evelot shimmied around him. She counted eleven heads, the Alpha still in his seat, and an unguarded front door. It took two jackals to pry it open. Luckily, Evelot had a second set of hands.

As the crowd sang the chorus's lyrics, Evelot winked at Zenris. Then she leapt off the stage.

Evelot felt herself lowered to the ground before seeing mutants surrounding her. A second of morbid realization passed while she looked at all the revelers distracted by the performance. She maneuvered around them in rollicking steps. They guffawed and pawed in play; Evelot was careful not to get caught by their claws. She spun, her head tilted to the ceiling. The iron chandelier swung slowly above, its lit candles dripping wax onto the floor.

The chandelier.

Tracing its rope lead, Evelot spotted its hook sticking up from the worn cobbled floor like a hangnail. It sat a leap away. A cache of weapons was not far, either.

Evelot slunk toward the shadows. Her hands gripped at the hilt of an abandoned sword.

Zenris belted out the last of the chorus.

She raised the sword, eyes trained on the fixture's taut rope.

Jackals sung back at him.

She swung downward.

"I think not!"

A clawed hand caught her wrist. The music

screeched to a stop. Evelot whipped around to find the Alpha holding her in place, his glowering crimson eyes burning like hellish fire.

Their chance was gone. She'd failed.

"*Inicio!*"

Both the werewolf and Evelot looked at Zenris standing on stage. His hand was outstretched, and gold bardic magic receded into the tips of his fingers. He offered a sheepish grin to the crowd, but snuck a wink to Evelot.

"Nice try," the Alpha said.

No. Not "nice try." An odd courage flooded Evelot, hot like the adrenaline and magic coursing through her. With a thrust of her knee between his legs, Evelot fell out of his grasp.

She clutched her sword and swung down.

One swing was all it took for the rope to sever. The chandelier plummeted to the ground. Mutants and humanoids scattered, several of them pinned under iron rings and inferno. A nearby puddle of brandy caught flame—then a stool, and then the moldy banners.

A rapid assault of fire began swallowing the chapel whole.

With her weapon in hand, Evelot called to Zenris over the chaos. Jackal-kin scrambled all around to put out the flame or escape the onslaught. Flashes of fiery color and acrid smoke clouded her vision. She desperately listened for a response.

"Evelot!" Zenris called faintly.

"Zenris!" she yelled. "I'm over here!"

"Stay—"

She rose on her feet to glimpse him. His silhouette

shambled across the stage. The fires allowed her one shuffling step before they lunged at her in whips of smoky air.

She shouted his name—

An ear-piercing roar filled the chapel.

Evelot spun around. The Alpha fell to his knees as he tried to claw at her, trembling arms only just catching himself. His heavy grunts morphed into something feral, something inhumane. Muscle and sinew expanded. Hands stretched and curled into paws. Hair tore from his flesh, growing into thick furs. A snout surged out from his face.

On its haunches stood the thing of legend, the fearsome werewolf. The beast shuddered and grunted for breath before throwing its head back, nose nearly touching the crumbled ceiling. What escaped from its throat was beyond an anguished wail, hellishly deep and ricocheting in the ear.

The werewolf looked down at Evelot and growled.

Other mutants nearby stumbled and fell, curling into themselves. They faced the same fate of disfigurement: their bodies writhed until nothing but humanoid-sized jackals were left. They whimpered and nervously cackled as the flames continued to sprout.

Evelot's grip tightened around the sword's hilt.

The werewolf surged forth. Zenris hollered to her over the din. Evelot forced out a breath before whispering a cantation. To her relief, blue frost enveloped her before the beast's claws slashed at her. The blow struck her sword, close enough to her fist that the reverberations stung. The werewolf howled; magicked ice coated its paw in retaliation.

Seeing it shrink back, Evelot swung at the beast. Its

body shifted away. She spotted the doors being yanked open behind it.

Before the beast could chomp down, Evelot raised her sword. Its jaw snapped onto the rusted metal. They struggled for purchase. With one more tug, the sword went flying from Evelot's grasp.

The air faintly rumbled with the werewolf's growl as it stalked after each of her retreating steps.

"Evelot!"

From the smoke barreled Zenris. He skittered to a halt beside Evelot. The werewolf lunged at him as if in challenge. Energy charged into Zenris's hands. With a resounding snap of the bard's fingers, blinding electricity pulsed through the air. Howls of pain rang out as the werewolf flew back several feet.

"Zenris—"

"Go!" he exclaimed.

She grabbed his wrist, and together, they ran for the exit.

Behind them their enemy howled. Heavy pants chased after them. Orange, red and gray flashed in her periphery. With her lungs burning, Evelot felt energy thrum in her veins. Voices whispered in her ear. She blindly took aim backward and fired off a spell. Vines burst through the floors with thunderous crumbles and cracks. Stones rained down in their wake.

Evelot slipped through the gap in the doorway. With both her feet on the dirt and gravel, she turned and pulled at Zenris's arm. He scrambled to follow. But then, Evelot saw a flash of claws and teeth behind him. An agonizing scream ripped out of Zenris.

"Zenris!" she exclaimed.

She pulled him through, the werewolf clawing its way out.

Zenris turned in her arms and held up his hand. *"Caligo!"*

A splotch of bright color flooded into the beast's eyes. It yelped, stumbling back. Both Evelot and Zenris rammed into the door, shutting it in its face.

The echoes of howls and crackling wood emanated in the night as they bolted into the woods. Slivers of moonlight yielded to the foliage. Evelot couldn't see past the burn of smoke in her eyes, but she didn't care. Zenris's wrist was still in her grip, and his breath heaved as much as hers in exhaustion. They had to put the chapel far behind them.

Only when all had stilled and her lungs scalded did they crawl to a stop. Evelot leaned against a tree, gasping for fresh air. It was so cool, too cool for her at first, but it was a brilliant sign—a sign of freedom.

"We—" she panted. "We've done it! We've actually done it!" She turned around with a weak grin. "Zenris, w—"

"I feel slightly. . ."

He collapsed to his knees with wee gasps of pain. Evelot stumbled toward him and knelt by his side. She gaped. Down the length of his back were three deep claw marks staining his shirt crimson.

"Zenris, it'll be fine! It's not a bite!" she said.

"Thank the gods," he tried to say.

"Don't worry. It's just a little blood."

"Oh?"

He reached behind his back, then studied his bloodied fingers. "Ah, that is quite a sight. . ."

His eyes rolled into the back of his head, and his body slumped over.

Evelot patted his cheeks, but he refused to stir.

"Z-Zenris!" Evelot snapped. She shook his shoulders. "Zenris!"

Chapter Thirteen

Morning had risen long before Zenris when he came to. The smell of cooking meat and damp earth penetrated his foggy thoughts, a cold, humid breeze causing him to violently shiver. He wrapped his arms around himself—only to discover, in place of his blouse, the thicker textile of. . . tartan fabric? Something dried and chalky glued it to his back, and a knot secured his front. Atop 'twas his cloak, falling away as he sat up. He did not recall removing any clothing the night prior, nor had he imbibed anything odorous or distasteful. Only images of warped bodies and blurred trees came to mind.

"Zenris!"

In front of a small campfire before him knelt his magically-inclined companion. She turned to him with a sigh before her lips pressed into a line of frustration.

"You scared me," she breathed.

"Pardon?" Zenris asked, his voice hoarse from a parched throat.

She shook her head. "You're squeamish, aren't you?"

"I. . . cannot deny it."

"By Her Golden Fields! I thought you were dead!"

"As if I would leave this plane so undignified." Zenris

laughed. "But all the same, I apologize."

He shifted onto his side to face the fire. The sudden movement compelled a sudden inhale—the fiery burn of fresh wounds cascaded to his hips.

"Does it sting?" she asked. Evelot moved over to him as if to check his bandages.

Zenris attempted a smile and rolled his shoulders. "'Tis nothing I have not experienced. Although, if you wish a look underneath, you need only ask."

Where a snide remark would arise, Evelot rolled her eyes. Yet there was a hint of timidity upon her lips that she failed to suppress.

"We've survived the night, but don't get cocky over it," Evelot said. "Better hope that coat of paste will keep for the day."

Zenris's retort caught in his throat. Evelot patted her torn skirt, the scraps of sleeves and threads drifting over her bare arms. The dark bags under her eyes were more prominent on her pale skin in the early morning light. Under a chill wind from the woods' depths her body shivered. All of which was a sacrifice made for his sake.

"Thank you," Zenris said.

Evelot returned from the fire with a small lump of steaming browned meat on a spit that appeared obliquely squirrel-shaped. She sat before him with a confused brow.

"What do you mean?" she said.

"Thank you for not abandoning me to the wolves? For giving aid to my injuries?"

"Of course I wouldn't have. Abandoned you... I mean. You might be a radge at times, but we're party members and all."

Zenris chuckled. "At least my spontaneity has done us good, past experiences notwithstanding?"

Her small laugh stirred relief in his heart, and he detected a hint of amusement, as well.

"I dinnae ken. You'd been the one to save us with your *quirk*," she said.

"In that case, 'tis my 'quirk' to thank for allowing me the privilege of the lady's radiant smile."

No furious shade of pink blossomed upon her cheeks, yet her wayward glance and curled lips spoke of mild vexation. "If you have time to flirt, bard, then I assume you're ready to move on?" she said. "We're still exposed out here, remember?"

"As exposed as you have made me?" Zenris asked.

She frowned at him.

Zenris raised his hands in surrender with a laugh. "Peace, peace, I withdraw," he said in jest. "Before we depart, might I also forage for victuals?"

"You mean food? No need."

Evelot untied one of her hip pouches and handed it over to him. Zenris curiously opened it, finding inside an array of berries and nuts.

"Should be enough for both of us if we ration it properly. Assuming we can reach my master's home by nightfall."

Zenris nodded in agreement before popping a berry into his mouth. Evelot joined him, and he did not pretend to overlook her thoughtful glimpses at him.

"Yes, my lady?" he asked.

"You... um..." A frown crumpled her features as she tried for words. "It isn't true about elves turning into blights or. . . seebies if they eat meat?"

"You mean to say 'seelies'?"

"A-aye."

Zenris smiled to himself. Chewing on a bitterly earthy-tasting seed, he regarded her with grim amusement.

"No. Though 'tis not a surprise that little shreds of Esmoran propaganda have survived in the duchies longer than my years. In reality, only a kernel of it is factual. An ill elf is no better than a blight, especially when locked in a room with their chamberpot."

"You get sick that easily?" Evelot asked.

"Depending on the elf. . . or half-elf, 'tis simply harsh on digestion. Although, I doubt you would wish to test the theory on my wounded, fragile person?"

Evelot shook her head in disbelief. "As if we needed 'shite your braies' on the pile of troubles we've got."

A peal of laughter erupted from Zenris. Evelot shyly fell victim to the same mirth, and there was no helping their cover. Thankfully, there was nary a sight of stampeding jackals as they sobered.

Once they deemed it an appropriate time to move, Evelot stoked the campfire while Zenris stretched to his feet, careful to put on his blouse. Though the garments were damaged, he needed whatever layers were available. To see them go was a heavy shame he could not bear. His olive vest may have absorbed the majority of damage, yet his lilac blouse remained intact. There was still use of it in bringing out the color of his eyes.

"You ready?"

Evelot stood facing him with a fist to her hip. Her bare arms looked as pallid as the brewing fog.

"One moment."

Zenris held out his blouse to Evelot. "Here, for the cold," he said.

"I'll be fine. You just put your cloak on to cover yersel'."

"You need not worry over me, my lady. But, if to spare me the same, would you do me this favor?"

With a nasally sigh, Evelot accepted it. It slid over her seamlessly, albeit with her layers puffing like duck feathers underneath. Mayhap 'twas their similar height, or his ego having another brutal reminder of its limits, for there was a difference in seeing her wearing his decorative garb. Their realities were vastly at odds. She was from the farmlands and he from an elven citadel. Such a shirt would likely cost several months' worth of work for her, and yet... it suited her better.

"We off, then?" said Evelot.

Zenris smiled. "Homeward, we go."

The air was choked with fog during their trek over the rising and falling crests of the woods. By nightfall, they warmed their hands over a humble fire beneath a tall oak, and the mist cleared to the scent of petrichor, alluding to the impending rain. He attempted to hide his concern as Evelot insisted on checking his wounds, despite his protests. Though, 'twas hardly a difficult endeavor; a hint of tantalizing heat danced over his skin with each brush of her hand.

Betwixt her tender touches, Zenris managed to hold his end of their conversation of cultural celebrations. At his declaration of partaking in her duchy festivities, Evelot laughed, shaking her head. "Don't say you weren't warned. There's a reason no one stands downwind from a kilt."

"Ha! As if I was threatened by such merriment," Zenris replied. "If 'tis anything like elven garb during Bloomtide, I will fare well. However, this 'Last Sunset' you spoke of? 'Tis only a large banquet with a 'kay-lee' afterward?"

"To worship and give thanks to the Harvest Maiden's generous bounty with her 'faithful,' as the High Priestess would describe it," Evelot said. "If anything, the cèilidh is the main event, as is any dance."

"An exclusivity to your village, then?"

"Once upon a time, aye. But each year, the mayor kept pushing for us to open up for 'guests' more and more. With every holiday, we've obeyed. This year will be the first time our banquet table won't come out of the Granary."

Her stare carried dread, and a bare sense of longing. The idea of someone powerful dictating your customs was not one he had experienced, nor considered before. 'Twas far from a cheery reality, to put it lightly.

Zenris offered a smile. "Do the women also wear 'kilts'?"

"No, just gowns and flower crowns. To 'attract affection,' if they're not already married and all," Evelot answered.

"You speak as if you have never tried?"

"Not in years, no."

His smile soured into a frown. "Do you mean to say

they withheld you from participating in your own customs?"

"They didn't have to. After a while, I stopped trying."

Zenris turned to face the trees as she had. Though she did not face him, he saw a pained grimace upon her lips.

"There be no need for melancholy, my lady," Zenris said. "For we are their debtors, you see. I am most curious of how large a celebration they will hold in our honor. Mayhap with banners of our likeness strewn through every street?"

Evelot peeked back at him with a raised brow. "Perhaps the bard's right," she said with a thoughtful look.

Before he could ask what she meant, Evelot fished from her belt loop a cinched pouch. From it, she pulled out a corked vial containing—

"Fur?" Zenris asked. A moment passed before he beamed. "You collected the sample!"

"Aye. I have you to thank. Found it stuck to your clothing."

Zenris laughed aloud. "Huzzah! They will sing your praises most fervently. Evelot, they will cry!"

"I-it was only my duty," she said with a flustered expression. "It's not a big deal."

"My lady, do you know how few are as skilled at thwarting foes as you? This comes from a bard that thrives off praise, as you can recall!"

She scrambled to tie the vial back to her hip. Evelot looked as though she wished to speak, yet her lips would not let loose a single word. Zenris was ready to celebrate; his arms widened to catch her in an embrace, when pain lanced through his back. He bit back a grunt as he curled into his bed of leaves. Her soothing hands brushed over the salve, checking his wounds.

"We should be close to my master's home," she said beside him. "She'll have a spell or potion that'll heal you right up."

"Would Beluphis have the same gentle touch when treating wounds?" Zenris asked.

"Not exactly."

He whimpered aloud, his pride fleeing at the thought of returning to Beluphis's home.

A small sigh left Evelot. "I know she seems intimidating, but she'll warm up to you soon."

"A stray would be more likely to warm to me. The Hells' Bell herself? I think not."

"I wouldn't use that name around her, if I were you," Evelot said. "There's a reason she stays hidden in the Choille."

"I can imagine so, for one who is wanted by the monarchy."

Evelot shook her head with an exasperated look.

"Or mayhap another reason?" Zenris replied.

"My master doesn't take well to others. It was a struggle in itself when I first showed up on her doorstep."

"Well, you are living proof of an exception."

"Only because I had an affinity to magic," Evelot countered. "Before that, I was as stupid as the rest of the town. Always staring at her all the time."

"Had none bothered to approach her?"

Evelot raised a brow. "A Ninanuna witch that suddenly appears and tries to buy produce from a human town? No chance. The women could've caught a farm's worth of flies with their gaping mouths. Save for the mayor's wife who started the rampant rumor mill. She was… unique."

"I have noticed a touch of boredom amongst the

wealthy.”

“Who knows if boredom had anything to do with it. One second she was doting on her husband and openly whispering within the square, then suddenly she’d left a note at home saying how Master and her were eloping together in Acluetho. Master told me this year she didn’t know the mayor’s wife was holding the torch for her. Said she slammed the door in her face as she would ‘any other upa.’”

Zenris gaped in amazement at the imagery. “My lady, I rescind my statement. I wish to sit with your master and discuss her wonderfully exciting life.”

Evelot smirked. “Ach, try to have some dignity.”

“Do not play innocent. Surely you find Beluphis Lovecraft in some manner disagreeable?”

Her smile waned. There came a pause before she replied, “I think she’s experienced life so differently from me. She came to Goldencrest on a Pilgrimage—her calling as a nature witch. She found her purpose, and yet she’s still bitter. Whether it’s from years of an old war or prejudice from a small-minded town, something stops her. I wonder if that’ll be my fate.”

“Absolutely not.”

Evelot turned back to him, gobsmacked.

“This is your life. Believe in fate, if you must, but deny not the opportunities afforded only to you. Otherwise, you merely shake the chains of a self-fulfilled prophecy,” replied Zenris.

Her head rested on her knees, and she fell into such ruminating thoughts she appeared to look through Zenris. Always thinking, that one. If not for her words, ’twould have greatly frustrated him. Zenris knew not if his statement held any sway over her. However, he felt it right to have spoken his piece.

Evelot blinked, unpursing her lips. "Zenris, what do you travel for?"

"What do you mean?" he said.

"That. What opportunity is out there for you?"

"I. . ."

He immediately thought of his search, its limited window of time closing with each hour. Oh, it had been easy to ignore when a werewolf threatened one's life, moreso because none were the wiser to his plot. However, Evelot. . . She was not them. He had not asked for help previously on the chance she would not understand, yet he thought she might now, after all they had survived. He felt the words forming on the tip of his tongue.

"My fa—"

Evelot waited.

Zenris only smirked. "I wish for the world to see me as I am: a handsome devil that can perform at any venue."

"All right, then, Sir Handsome Devil. We'll have you back on stage soon enough. For now, try to rest before those wounds turn into scars, aye?"

"Though I may be half elf, I still take comparatively little sleep," Zenris said. "To take first watch this night would be most fitting for me."

"If you insist."

Evelot curled onto her side, her back turned to him. Eventually her shoulders rose and fell in an even tempo. Though his wounds still stung, and his stomach was far from full, he stirred the fire while seated by her side. The wind sank through his layers of clothing, nipping coldly at his flesh.

Yet his heart leapt, as panicked as a startled hare.

He had almost said it aloud. The reason he was visiting Goldencrest. He had nearly confided everything to her: his true motivations, his travels through every corner of woodland in western Runlaris. To think that he would have given it all away freely.

Zenris folded his hands and stared off into the darkness beyond their fire. If he had been blunt, Evelot may have reacted poorly. Or thought him pitiful. The woods were her territory, after all, and he was a visitor in search of the Opening the werewolf had utilized.

The image of his prized possession, that old composition, flitted to mind. It reminded Zenris he was far from a handsome devil, let alone a talented bard.

Mayhap he was more the fool for not following his own advice.

Through the shiver down his spine, Zenris felt the swell of freezing rain in the clouds. With a fresh dressing on his wounds and a good sum of berries in his stomach, he set about his path with Evelot at his side. Their pace was quick this quiet morning, though as the foreboding weather loomed over each stream and incline, their hopes dwindled. Evelot's sights scanned ahead while Zenris concerned himself with what lay on either side of them.

Carcasses and rotting remains blended in with the

colors of autumn like a macabre decoration. 'Twas a common sign of predators having feasted long ago. Yet several were fresh, and his fear of encountering survivors from that hellish chapel persisted. No amount of bravado prevented his terror of Evelot being dragged away into that back room, nor the impending doom of being ripped apart in the crossing. Evelot had called it his "quirk," as though heroics had anything to do with spontaneously rushing to her aid. Truthfully, Zenris did not thrive on danger as much as other adventurers. He simply did not wish to die, nor Evelot. He was far from brave. . . or creative for that matter. Having been reminded of his shortcomings, Zenris turned away from the bones left to the elements, and carried on with what little pride was left of his.

By late afternoon, they had circled several glades in the woods for signs of Beluphis's home in vain; no explosive wards or paths appeared to connect back to her corner of the wilderness. As they both raggedly trekked betwixt the trees, Zenris felt the toll on his body tenfold. His mind reeled at how many blackberry and raspberry bushes they had passed, the sound of a woodpecker's hammering forever grating on his nerves. Their circuit of insanity had only squandered precious daylight, and as Evelot desperately searched, it had shortened the window of time to make shelter before the oncoming storm.

"I don't understand," Evelot said. "It should be here!"

"I do not doubt you. But we must come away from the open wild," replied Zenris.

"But what if—"

Cold droplets splattered upon his head. Zenris looked up to see the gray light of storm clouds through the trees' awnings. Evelot sighed, her head downcast as steady rain began to fall. She let him lead her to the cover of a nearby tree without complaint. Feeling the cold numb him, Zenris wrapped his cloak closer around his shoulders. It did little to help as the wind rose, and Evelot had only one more layer to protect herself against the chill.

Zenris opened his cloak with an extended arm. He motioned for her to approach.

"I—erm . . . I'll be all right," Evelot said.

"You are shaking," said Zenris.

"I'm fine."

"Evelot?"

She avoided his gaze, turning her head away.

"Let me help you, please," Zenris gently said.

She peeked over her shoulder at him. With a sigh, she shuffled closer.

"I cannot reach you from there," Zenris said.

Another inch toward him.

"A little more."

She complied with a huff.

Zenris did not move so quickly to enfold her in his arms. Her shoulders were stiff, her head kept turned away from him. Previously, he had suspected she was merely self-conscious. Yet Evelot's hesitancy was. . . odd, compared to his fans. Whatever the matter, he would not give his hubris reign over his judgment.

"Do not be alarmed," Zenris said. "My arms will stay around your waist and nowhere else."

"A-all right," she said with a shiver.

He did as he had said and stood behind her, wrapping both of them in the warmth he could provide. It hardly deterred the rain-fall, rolling down the bark and through the back of his clothes. His cloak was sturdy and thick, but inadequate for another brutal season. If he collected the funds in Goldencrest, he would find more appropriate attire for autumnal weather. In the meantime, Zenris was determined to keep himself and his companion preoccupied.

"This will let up soon," Zenris offered. "Then mayhap her ward will wane in time for us to find her."

"I hope so," Evelot said.

"Of course! There will be a bubbling cauldron to sit by with food and drink. Warm, soft beds up the stairs. If she is feeling gracious, a change of clothes and a bath."

"Are you imagining her home or the inn?" Evelot said with a laugh.

"Either would sound like paradise. However, I would rather patronize the establishment that allows you entrance."

Amidst the silence surrounding them, Zenris satisfied himself with studying his cloak. It brought to mind their first encounter: how shadowed her face had been to the observer, how ghoulish her hood had made her seem in the middle of the crowd, how naked she must feel without it.

"Will Beluphis have another cloak for you?" Zenris asked.

"More than likely."

"And you would still wear the hood over your head?"

Evelot did not answer. He hoped, deep down, that she would say no. She could change her mind and try something new. As the town's champion, she could hold her head high, and go on in a new light. If they knew what she had done, there was hope that her reputation would improve.

Yet, secretly, he only hoped she would abandon the hood for selfish reasons. To see it over her was a shame, day after day, for—

"It conceals such a beautiful smile."

Evelot went rigid in his loose hold. Zenris dared to look at her. Her jaw hung open and her eyes wide in a stunned stare.

Zenris cleared his throat. His traitorous thoughts and lips were, hopefully, not a sign of fatigue.

"I apo—" A horrid crack rendered his voice useless. Try as he might to clear it, shame burned hot in his face. "I apologize," he tried again. "That was uncalled for. Not that you do not deserve to be complimented. You are truly beautiful—oh, no.

"I-I am not of sound mind tonight. Why not we—?"

His stomach dropped at a distant howl. When all fell silent, the chillingly familiar cackle of a jackal rose. One, then two, then numerous cries followed. Zenris's heart raced. Evelot's hand reached for his.

"Where else do you think her lodgings could be?" Zenris whispered in her ear.

"O-off to the right?" Evelot quietly responded.

In proximity to the howls.

Zenris lowered his arms and offered a hand to Evelot. "Will you follow me?" he asked.

"You want to go near them?" she replied incredulously.

"No. Yet, I cannot make such a promise."

Another howl, followed by a growl, echoed through the woods. A second passed too quickly for her to weigh her options before she faintly nodded.

Her palm fell into his, and he gently squeezed it back.

Zenris was careful to step around the fallen leaves and twigs. With his heightened vision, the outlines of shadowed objects in the distance were perceivable. Evelot had her human eyesight that allowed only his tracks for her to follow in the dark. She whispered directions, and the two crept away. The howling stayed in place for seconds, minutes. Being captured by the jackal-kin would only lead him back to the werewolf. He was sure that—unlike his confrontation with the orc chieftain he had royally upset years ago—no party member would save him from being boiled alive, or from being the food that beasts played with before consumption. He did not believe Evelot would enjoy such a fate, either.

The howling cut off, and a yipe pierced the air. Zenris and Evelot froze.

A human-like shout caught Zenris's ear. Then another distant howl.

Then another close by.

Zenris gave a small tug on Evelot's hand. He wove them through the dying grass and brush as the thudding of feet and howling neared. Her arm went slack, and Zenris's heart leapt. He grasped for her for a moment until she patted his arm.

"There should be a stream nearby. To the left," she whispered.

Zenris turned—

A howl from their right nearly sent him sprawling. Zenris heard the thundering charge of a jackal. He looked around. A tree stood merely a sprint away.

Adrenaline stirred him forth; Zenris pulled his companion in a deer's charge toward safety. Twigs and branches snapped beneath their feet. A grunting pant followed.

Zenris enveloped Evelot in his arms and dove into the brush. He landed on his back, withholding a pained cry at the burn and scrape of his recovering injuries. An audible sniff and a low growl resounded behind the foliage.

Zenris silently hovered over Evelot, who leaned against the tree. Elven magic hummed in his veins, coming to life. Without the daylight, he could only imagine how the camouflaging illusion painted his skin, how it blended the outline of his contorted position into the natural shape of the tree. The sound of the jackal encroaching nearly deafened to the rapid beating of his heart. Evelot stiffened beneath him as the beast grunted. Slowly, Zenris opened his mouth for a quiet breath.

The grunt soured into frustration, then leaves crunched farther off. Zenris waited.

One beat.

Two beats.

Three. . .

Silence.

Zenris looked down at Evelot, his lips stretched into a relieved grin.

"'Tis gone," he whispered, helping her up. Zenris crouched on his knees as he peeked out around the brush. He saw no sign of movement ahead. "Just a ways yet before the house. Let us—"

"Zenris!"

He froze at Evelot's shriek. Her finger pointed upward.

A jackal-kin lunged for him with its jaw hung wide.

Chapter Fourteen

Her body couldn't move. She was too paralyzed in fear, seeing Zenris meet his end in front of her. The chance to act, to shield him or shove him out of the way, was gone. Wasted on a damned scream.

Rapidly, it's jaw closed in—

With a yelp, Zenris rolled out of the way. The beast tumbled and crashed into the tree he'd leaned against.

Evelot sprung to her feet.

"Z-Zenris?" she said. "We n-need to go. Now!"

Their hunter righted itself on all fours and bared its fangs.

Evelot reached for Zenris's hand as they blindly ran through the dark. A rush of air above made her stumble. Something crashed, then a growl rumbled ahead.

Faintly, it crept closer. In her panic, magic flickered and dulled in her palms. Neither of them had weapons. Zenris was too weak to put up a fight. He'd done so much already, and there was nothing she could do. Not unless she threw herself at the beast. It'd be enough of a distraction for Zenris to get away. It couldn't be much farther until he reached her mentor's home. She had to make his efforts count, even if it were for only one of them.

"Heart of Aspen!"

Evelot glanced over her shoulder. In the darkness, the silhouette of a large figure charged through the woods in their direction. The beast stopped snarling, stupefied by the sight.

"How dare you deceive me again!" roared a low female voice.

Zenris gaped as though he'd summoned a god. But then the Jinryuu's fist clenched the hilt of a thick claymore sword, and his smile dropped to a horrified gape.

"No, no! Pril, I am not the—"

Prilthadollak plowed past him and swung her sword at the beast. It yipped, sailing back several feet.

" —enemy. Sweet, melodic Minstrel, I thought you meant to kill me!"

"Do not discount that possibility yet, fool of a bard!" the warrior snapped.

The three of them turned their heads at the sound of snarls and yips. The jackal emerged from the distance, charging straight for them. Prilthadollak blocked its lunge at the last second. Feeling courageous, Evelot sucked in a breath and concentrated on her mana. The Choille was quiet, but a heat in her chest sparked. It crackled over her arms and faintly lit her palms, but died off as soon as it'd come. Before the beast could strike, Evelot summoned the vines beneath them. A thorned edge struck the jackal-kin's head. It cried out as it cowered to the ground.

"At least this one has the sense to fight the opponent," Prilthadollak commented. "She will be more useful than you, Heart of Aspen. Stand back!"

"Wha—!"

As Evelot focused on the beast rearing back, Zenris's voice rose from the warrior's other side. His hushed cantation created sparks of gold bursting over his open palm. Like dandelion seeds, he blew them forth. The hiss of air met a disembodied scrape of metal on metal. A wooden pole appeared in front of the jackal, and large ropes lashed out at the creature. They wrapped around its limbs, pulling it in. The beast shrieked, bound to the pole, as unseen lances, cut across its body one small nick at a time.

Within seconds, the beast no longer stirred.

"Here come more!" Prilthadollak shouted.

The sound of howling clogged her ears. Evelot turned around to see three other jackal-kin close in on them. The warrior rushed forward and swung her sword to slash at the three. Two of them leapt away, but the third dodged too late; its head rolled to the side, feet from its body.

One took a chance and nipped at Prilthadollak. Its teeth sank into her leather vambraces before the beast retreated.

The second snapped at the warrior's legs. Evelot scrambled through the leaves for a stone or a surviving vine, anything to get the jackal-kin's attention. Instead, a wee titter rang down from the canopy of trees. A shadow plunged toward the beast. The jackal-kin yipped before the dark speck, her bonnie Jammer, came swinging back down into the safety of her collar.

Once the beast shook off the pain, it twisted to face Evelot. But she smiled, welcoming its charge.

When the white of its fangs flashed, she ducked down. Behind her Zenris's spell still twirled in a miniature tornado. Cries and howls met each slash of Prilthadollak's claymore until the smell of iron stung Evelot's nostrils.

The last standing opponent recoiled, hiccuping in terrified laughter.

Zenris raced past his companion. Evelot vaguely heard him say, "Need to borrow this."

Something reflective flashed in his palm. The warrior exclaimed in frustration before Zenris sliced at the beast with a dagger. It howled, then tried to nip at him. With its attention drawn away, Prilthadollak raised her sword and brought the final blow down on the jackal.

No longer in danger, the party's spells dissipated and they sheathed their weapons. Evelot sighed a long breath of relief, feeling her own body ache from the exertion. She turned to Zenris hunched over a step away. His hands went to his hips as he gasped for air. But seeing him grinning, she felt at ease.

"They were more bark than bite," he said lamely.

Prilthadollak grabbed his collar and lifted him off his feet.

"I ask little of you, and now look where we are!" she snapped. "No excuse will rectify the situation this time!"

"Ack! Pril," Zenris gasped. "My-my throat—"

"Do you not understand the term 'consequence,' bard, or are you too distracted by a skirt in the woods to put it into perspective?"

"Pril! Air—!"

Prilthadollak snarled in frustration. She furiously flicked her tail and threw Zenris over her shoulder. He gasped for breath and desperately tried to reason with the Jinryuu. Evelot clamped her jaw shut. She had to step in. She couldn't let Zenris be whisked off before getting him help.

"Stop!"

Prilthadollak whipped her head back at Evelot, halting. The Jinryuu's flaring nostrils and glowing serpentine eyes were as horrifying as telling Beluphis they'd run out of roasted pumpkin seeds.

"P-please, wait!" Evelot said. "He was aiding me on a quest from my master. We need to—"

"I care not for your master nor your cause. This bard here is to be disciplined accordingly, and that is that."

"Pril, wait," Zenris said. "There is more than meets the eye."

"Is my name Heiser More of Gray? No. Now shut your mouth."

"No!" snapped Evelot. With extended arms, she jumped in front of the warrior. "That bard is coming with me!"

"I respect your willingness to fight when cornered, but that respect ended in battle. Do not attempt to stop me further, human!"

Prilthadollak stomped off into the thick of the trees. In the crosshairs of her own thoughts and emotions, Evelot felt her mana channeled through her limbs to her hands. She slowed her breath, dismissing the voices of the woods from tempting her with magic. She would be in control—she would speak her mind.

All she needed was a rock.

After a quick search, Evelot picked one up and chucked it straight at Prilthadollak. It simply pinged off the warrior's armor, but the message was *well* received. A deep growl faded into a breath of irritation. In a blink, Evelot was staring down the face of absolute fury. But she would not cower before the warrior.

"Enough of your—"

"No! You'll listen to me!" yelled Evelot.

The warrior regarded her with a crooked frown. Her tail swished behind her slowly, like the tail of a cat waiting for the chance to snag its prey.

"Whatever you assumed, it's wrong," Evelot said. "Zenris wasn't out here for some tryst. He was here helping me find the beast that's been picking off the villagers of Goldencrest. He didn't need to volunteer, but he did. And even if we'd been butting heads like oxen, he still risked his life to save us. So, if you don't mind, I'd like to return the favor by treating his wounds at my master's home and preventing this—this *shite* from happening again!"

With an intimidatingly stoic expression, Prilthadollak asked, "I assume you are this 'interesting person' he referred to before, correct?"

"I-I'm what?" Evelot said.

"Umm," started Zenris, still on his companion's shoulder.

"And the person in question is the 'witch' everyone takes disinterest in."

"I—aye," answered Evelot.

"I see." Prilthadollak's tail swayed as her head tipped thoughtfully.

The warrior took too long for Evelot's patience. "If all the tossing he's been through has opened his wounds, I don't have much time to get him to my master. Are you letting him go or not?"

Evelot assumed Prilthadollak was in agreement by

the hard set of her brow and lack of response. Then, the warrior answered, "Because my charge is infantile when near blood, I will accompany you. If either you or your master do anything to harm him, I will not hesitate to slit your throats."

"So we're in agreement, then?" Evelot said.

Prilthadollak curtly nodded. "Lead on, witchling."

"Her name is Evelot," Zenris said from behind the Jinryuu.

"It's fine. If we aren't going by names, I'll settle for calling you 'warrior,' aye?"

"However you see fit," grumbled the warrior.

With that, Evelot turned to lead their group deeper into the woods.

It'd taken nearly an hour for Evelot to make sense of her surroundings. Without the sound of howling rattling her nerves, and summoned lights to brighten their path, she recognized more of the landscape. The trees clumped closer together the farther they pressed on. Squinting, Evelot spotted the familiar tree-trunk bridge off to the side.

Prilthadollak followed surprisingly obediently, with Zenris captive over her shoulder. Evelot suspected that was the reason for her own bewilderment. The earlier buzz of adrenaline must've numbed her judgment when she'd suddenly had free rein over her actions. It was Zenris's kind of gallus behavior, facing off the female warrior of Runlaris's legend with no hesitation. But Evelot had done it. Done something. . . unexpected. It didn't feel appropriate to feel victorious, but all the same it budded into a smile on her lips.

Evelot looked up at the canopy of leaves yards above their heads. Surprisingly beautiful, the stars blinked through the dark veil of iridescent obsidian.

A massive fog entered the clearing of her mentor's home as they approached. Evelot carefully stepped inside the thick of it. It felt. . . wrong to do so. So wrong that she should go back unless she sought death. The feeling was too foreign, as thought it were someone else's thoughts twisting around in her head urging her to leave.

There was no other place her mentor could be. No sigils were lit up under Evelot's feet, but she suspected another kind of magic at hand, protecting her mentor.

"That is your master's domain, witch?" Prilthadollak asked.

"Aye. But don't—"

She shoved an arm in front of the warrior, making Jammer squeak against the nape of her neck. Evelot waited for a sign in the fog that didn't fade.

Nothing came.

"What is the matter?" Zenris called from Prilthadollak's shoulder. "I cannot see a thing. Turn me around!"

"You will sprint off into the distance for your next charity case. I think not," said his companion.

"As if I have the energy to do so. I lost feeling in my abdomen ages ago."

Evelot shushed them. She took a deep breath, closing her eyes. Beluphis had once pushed her to memorize a cousin spell to the diagnostic magic few spellcasters used. It had been too long since her last test, but Evelot recalled the cantation enough to whisper its arcane words. Magic ran deep in the veins of the body like the roots of a tree. She extended her arms, imagining her and her mentor's roots stretching past illusion and wildlife, connecting.

Dimly, she sensed her mentor. Her magic pulsed nearby with the warmth of a candlelight. Evelot sought forward, pushing her palms toward the faint source.

The sound of Prilthadollak sharply inhaling snapped her out of her trance. The fog dissipated, and in its place, the familiar view of her mentor's home undulated into visibility.

Her front door opened, but only a long limb-like staff peeked out from the doorway.

"Get off my lawn, you filthy, mangy—eh. . . dogs!"

Prilthadollak reached for her claymore, but Evelot jumped in front of her.

"Master!" she called.

Beluphis poked her head out with wide eyes. Seeing Evelot, she slammed the tail end into the floorboards. "You nearly scared me half to death, girl!" Beluphis exclaimed. "So, you've survived the hunt, eh?"

"Aye. Master, can we come in? One of us is—"

"Ah, the fiddly bard met his maker?"

Beluphis cackled as she peered over Evelot's shoulder. "At least he spent it for some shred of honor."

"Madam, I have yet to breathe my last," Zenris said defensively, arse forward while Prilthadollak still kept hold of him.

Beluphis deflated with disappointment before cocking her head. "Well, so there is a way to 'talk out of your siki' besides the—eh. . . bilge you sing."

"Master," Evelot cut in.

"Come, come along, inside you go," Beluphis said impatiently. "Before the gods' forsaken mutts sniff us out!"

Evelot waved to Prilthadollak, and the warrior

marched up the steps. She ducked her head beneath the door frame, passing Beluphis who loudly whispered, "My gods, there are too many people."

Once Zenris settled to his feet, Beluphis slammed the door with a wave of her staff.

"Let's look at what your bard got himself into, shall we?" she asked a bit too eagerly. Beluphis waddled to him. Her spindly fingers gripped his shoulder as she inspected him with a quick glance. Upon noticing his back, she gasped.

"What is it?" Zenris asked.

"It's horrible! Infected from top to bottom. Ah, look at that! Pus oozing and skin turning green!"

Zenris gagged into his fist. "Is-is it—? Oh, gods."

Evelot sighed. "Master, that's the paste I made to cover his wounds."

"Yes, yes, I know," Beluphis said. To her pupil, she whispered, "Spoilsport."

Zenris laughed in relief. "Oh, great witch, how you blithely jest!"

"Of course, of course. We can fix you up in no time. I'll need sewing thread and—oh ho, ho, ho, what have we here? A bit of bone among all the blood."

His complexion turned ashy before he went limp. Prilthadollak caught him and set him over the chaise lounge, glaring down at Evelot's mentor.

Beluphis cackled aloud. "The bard has some use as entertainment! Ha!"

"Did you move the healing salves into the kitchen or are they still in your study, Master?" Evelot asked.

"Lower cabinet, to the right of the kitchen counter. Bring towels, too."

"A moment!" Zenris called. "Is a needle truly required?"

Without answering, Evelot moved past Beluphis and scavenged in the kitchen. Jammer fled upstairs as Evelot returned to her mentor's side, balancing the items in hand while untying the vial from her belt. It was better to turn over the sample than let the proverbial kitten play with its new ball of yarn.

As Evelot knelt beside Zenris and washed away the old salve, Beluphis studied her findings.

"Incredible. The two of you have truly done it," Beluphis said, holding the vial up to the ceiling light.

"How were you injured?" Prilthadollak asked.

"Ah, after a heroic battle involving quick wits and a random scabbard—"

Evelot gave Zenris a look that told him to shut it. While she dabbed at his wounds, the witchling recounted the details to the other women.

"Good. Now that those pests are out of the way, I can attend to my usual business," said Beluphis.

"You won't be needing the samples anymore, Master?" Evelot asked.

"You did not kill all of them, did you?" Beluphis said.

"If they hadn't, my men and I have," answered Prilthadollak.

"Oh?"

"On our search for this 'deserter,' the jackal-like creatures cornered us. There were at least four more that the twenty of us battled. In the heat of the fight, I had lost track of my men. We agreed to regroup in Goldencrest, and I am confident they marched home victoriously."

"And the werewolf?" Beluphis asked.

"There was a difference?" the warrior replied.

"One eats you, and one turns you into its pack member with a bite. How could there not be?"

"Then it was amongst the vanquished. Suppose it was the more difficult one I had taken on. It did not survive long against my blade."

"Hmm. . ."

Evelot glanced back at Prilthadollak, suspicious. It should've been impossible for that many regular hunters to take on the werewolf. But then she remembered how Zenris had blinded it and the few strikes she'd gotten in herself. Maybe they'd weakened the beast for the others to take down. Maybe not. Knowing the villagers, they'd divide its corpse in the square like any other kill. That'd be the proof to seal the deal, for Evelot to assure herself that it was over. She'd have to return to town and keep an eye out. Until then, Evelot stayed silent.

Beluphis harrumphed. "Fine. I will need this if those dogs return. So, yes, I will make the wards."

Prilthadollak nodded. To Evelot and Zenris, she asked, "You had been cornered by the werewolf's pack. How did you escape so easily?"

"Ha! Fatal injuries surely cause no issue," Zenris said sarcastically through winces.

Evelot dipped her finger in the egg-white, balmy salve. As she gently coated Zenris's wounds, a smile bloomed on her lips. "It required a bit of dancing," she said quietly.

The other two peered at her, baffled. Zenris smiled over the discomfort before meeting her eye.

"As well as singing," he added.

Beluphis and Prilthadollak may have still been confused, but between Evelot and Zenris, the joke was still amusing. When the fresh memory should've been terrifying, a part of her found it the opposite. Those rabid red eyes didn't summon a shred of fear in her anymore. It made her feel courageous, uplifted. Because of his gallus stupidity, Zenris was to thank for that.

After Evelot exchanged more words with her mentor, Beluphis retreated into her study down below. The three left in the main room had free rein, more or less. Evelot was far from put off by the lack of conversation. She couldn't help but let her suspicions about the werewolf's demise run rampant in her mind. Her mentor was getting started on the wards. In a matter of a week, there'd be no more trouble in Goldencrest. Life would return to normal if all went well.

How bizarre. After all the trouble, Evelot didn't know how to envision a normal day. The thought of donning her cloak to enact secret deals in town for her mentor, or of using what meager coin she had to buy food for her family, was surreal and comforting all at once.

Evelot peeked over at Zenris. He'd also have to return to his life. While she worked, he'd probably have all the free time in the world. Without the beast, they'd have no reason to meet by the woodland path anymore. Would he find it easy to go back to singing in the tavern or daundering by the fields until the festival? Would he want to stay behind after it was over? Or would he also forget about her town and move on to the next adventure? All before he'd finally tell her about his secret mission he'd been on during their hunt.

Her heart twisted sadly at the thought.

"Witchling."

Evelot looked up at Prilthadollak. She stood by the doorway, somehow having moved while Evelot was away in her ponderings.

"Aye?" Evelot said.

"You have my thanks for defending my companion. Will you do me this favor of watching over him another night?"

"You're leaving so soon?"

"I have my duties to report to."

"'Tis a shame," Zenris said. "There are clean beds here, and mayhap a bath. You could take advantage of this limited opportunity, Pril."

"Such luxuries are unnecessary for a traveling fighter. In the meantime, be on your best behavior here."

"You speak as if I am a dog," Zenris replied.

"See that you won't be."

Prilthadollak turned to leave. Before she could open the door, a sudden thought dawned on Evelot.

"Prilthadollak?" she said.

The warrior looked over her shoulder at Evelot. "Yes?"

"A month ago, you'd spoken with a boy with fair hair."

"Yes, the one who asked that I train him."

"What exactly did you say to him?" Evelot asked.

"The truth," Prilthadollak said. "He is not ready for battle, nor does he have the physique for the training necessary."

"But you've not watched him train?" Evelot said.

"I have not."

"Then how can you be sure? What if there's more to him than meets the eye?"

Prilthadollak glanced back at the door. For a beat, the warrior stood there as if in deep thought. Her taloned fingers fisted the doorknob before she hummed in consideration. "I will see you two in Goldencrest," was all she said, and then the door shut behind her.

Evelot leaned against the wall. That sort of reaction wasn't what she expected, but it didn't feel promising, either. With a solemn exhale, she cast her eyes to the ground.

"My lady Evelot, you are a marvel."

She looked up at Zenris, at a loss for words. The smile on his lips warmed her through her rain-soaked clothing.

"W-why do you say that?" she asked, her hands fiddling with her skirts.

"In all my years, I had seen none confound my companion to such a degree. Knowing her, she might consider training the boy."

"I . . ." His confidence in her made something stir in her chest. But she rolled her eyes, shaking her head. "How are you feeling?" she asked.

"Much better. I am in your debt, my lady."

Zenris adjusted himself. His arm cushioned his head on the chair's armrest, the rest of him spread out over the chaise lounge. Evelot suspected he was used to positioning himself in a way that would scandalize a chaste noblewoman. The way he watched her was obnoxiously purposeful: heavy-lidded eyes and lips slightly parted in a provocative smirk. He still hadn't put on his blouse. Evelot felt a sweet heat in her stomach, clouding her mind with its pluming smoke. This had been the longest she'd seen a man exposed like that, as if solely for her sake.

When next she blinked, the idea was snuffed out, and his expression became one of masked discomfort. Her whole body burned with guilt for her former presumption.

Zenris chuckled to himself. "Do I but dream," he said, "or would it that our struggle has come to an end?"

"Want to douse your heid out in the rain again for good measure?" Evelot joked.

He gave a tiny laugh. "Goodness, no. I simply find it remarkable. The town will not have to waste another moment fearing for its livelihood, and the festival will be back in production."

"I'm sure the mayor'll be pleased about that," Evelot said sardonically. That man'd most likely return to butchering the border of the Choille after saving face with his governmental superiors.

"And what of you?" Zenris asked.

"As if I'd show my face round there. Nothing but an earsplitting din to keep you up into the wee hours. Can't imagine fancying myself deaf and pished on a good day."

"Come now, it cannot be so horrid?"

"All right, bard. Since you're the expert, what would I be expecting at a festival that size?" Evelot asked, amused.

"Ah, 'tis not wise to answer. Only in person can one truly understand," he answered.

"Ach, you eejit!" Evelot laughed. "Fine, have it your way, then."

"Is that so?" Zenris rose from the lounge. With a

mischievous grin, he said, "You will accompany me there?"

"To. . . the festival?" she said.

Her cheeks flushed at the thought. Was he seriously inviting her to a party?

"Your hesitancy is understandable. As I had not specified either the Last Sunset or the Harvest Festival, allow me to correct my words: Why not we attend both together?"

"I—"

Her brows crinkled into a frown. It didn't help that she'd been drenched for the past hour when a heat crawled over her skin. It could've been an oncoming fever, but she was still unable to answer. Going with a beloved bard to a party? That'd be a sight.

She wanted to lie and say she couldn't, but the Granary had sent their people to help with the field work and whittled down the chores. Another part of her felt bashful. Zenris was inviting her and while the need to hide and draw her hood up was still there, what would happen if she went with him? What if, for once, she opened herself up to adventure? She'd done it before in hunting the werewolf. How bad could it be to do something for herself?

His smile was warm when she failed to reply. "There is no need for an answer so quickly, my lady."

"A-all right. After all, we need to see you healed up first."

"Of course. And where not a place for rest than such warm beds upstairs?"

Zenris moved toward the staircase. When Evelot didn't budge, he looked around and asked, "Will you not be joining me?"

Evelot stared at him. "I-in bed?"

"I—"

Zenris turned a shade darker. Evelot's jaw hung open.

"That was. . . no. Oh, my."

When she thought the situation couldn't be worse, Evelot heard chitters and crickets bounding down the stairs. Her wee Jammer darted through the air nervously only to zip up when Zenris's head turned. She screeched, flittering back and forth as he exclaimed, looking around. Evelot tried to calm the bard and get his attention. But then Jammer plopped onto his head and sprawled out, nestling into his fluffy hair.

"Evelot, what is on my head?" Zenris asked, stiffly frozen while Jammer rounded his scalp.

He looked up at the wee brown bat peeking down from the crown of his head. His mouth opened in a scream, but nothing came out. His body swooned toward the ground. Evelot reached out to catch him. Only Jammer made it into her hand.

She sucked in a breath at the heavy thud of Zenris's fall. Jammer licked at her palm, hardly bothered.

"Not exactly what either of us pictured for 'getting into bed,'" Evelot said to the bat, and turned to Zenris with an exhausted exhale.

Chapter Fifteen

Oh, how Zenris was an utter, tremendous, outrageous fool.

Night had crept past the curtains, morning alight on the horizon. Zenris had struggled with sleep in a blind state of shame and perturbation. Staring out through the brightening window, he questioned his ability to so much as speak. As a celebrity, he had held plenty of banter with all kinds of individuals. His own notoriety allowed him the privilege of wooing paramours with as little as a smile and a flicker of recognition on their part. He offered passion, a thrilling tale of a personal encounter with such an icon. So why was it that Evelot's very nature rendered his modus operandi moot? What power gave her the right to do so?

It frustrated him not to know. If he believed in Goldencrest's rumors about her, he would think he'd been bewitched. It felt as though there was no other explanation than that. The intoxication her smile caused still lingered in his veins; her laughter like wind chimes constantly stirring in his memory. The phantom imprints of her fingers danced along his back; the color of her lips offered a refuge for his restless sight. Yes, it had to be a strange magic. Or delusion set by an oncoming fever.

Oh, yet 'twas a magnificent delusion. He imagined Evelot entering from the doorway with salve in hand. She would offer to treat his wounds, and he would bare himself before her without question. In witnessing her blushing cheeks and feigned ignorance of it, Zenris would tease her lightly. That reticent smile would surface and allow him to revel in the way her rosy lips perfectly curved at the corners.

He could nearly feel those soft little buds under his thumbs. He wondered if her kiss would be as—

Zenris blinked, looking down. He cleared his throat and placed an extra pillow over his lap.

"I cannot rest on my back nor front," he grumbled to himself. "By His Bushy Beard, I have lost the plot."

To linger on such thoughts was unbecoming of a gentleman bard. He truly had forgotten himself. Another weakness sundered by this enchantment, he imagined. Thank the gods there was a washroom in this treehouse. Hopefully, a bath and pampering would do him good.

From what Zenris surmised, he had spent the better portion of an hour preparing himself for the day. With damp hair naturally drying and modest attire of braies and a peasant blouse, he exited his room. Not one sound disturbed the hallway outside in the early hours of the day. The home's keeper was likely downstairs or withdrawn to the basement, and Evelot in her own quarters. He hoped she had risen for the morning. Having drawn a bath, Zenris would need more of that salve Evelot had used. His wounds did not burn as they had, yet the itch spurred him to listen closely for either door to reveal the whereabouts of the witchling.

When the house remained silent, Zenris started for the door across from him. After a few knocks down the hallway doors and hushed calls, he heard Evelot answer.

"May I come in?" he asked.

"It's unlocked," he heard her say.

Zenris turned the knob and entered. Evelot looked up from the edge of a four-poster bed. The down-feather mattress consumed her slowly, and in her lap Zenris spotted her spellbook opened to yellowed pages.

"Did you sleep well?" she asked.

"Comfortably," Zenris lied. "And you?"

"As much as can be. Can't say I'll be used to this type of mattress."

"Do they not favor feather mattresses in Goldencrest?" Zenris asked.

"Besides the innkeepers and those vacationing nobles, no. Only my master's magic and imagination can afford it, for what it's worth."

"I see."

Evelot closed her book. "How're your wounds?"

"I wished for the lady's assistance as I cannot tend them."

"Good thing I thought to keep the salve on me. Come on over."

Evelot motioned for Zenris, and he obeyed. Sitting beside her, he turned his back and lowered his blouse. He heard the suction of the salve's pot lid open and Evelot's concentrated hum. Her calloused, icy fingers brushed his skin. Before any wayward thoughts distracted him, he stopped himself there.

When she finished, Zenris covered himself, smiling in relief. The itching had subsided.

"Tell me: How does the wound seem to you?" he

asked.

"It's healing fairly well," Evelot answered. "Master's salves aren't as fanciful as you'd see in cities, but it'll clear away the rest of your scarring in a day or so."

Zenris smiled. He had been curious if he would have battle scars worth making a spectacle over. They might have made for an interesting story on stage, but he preferred smooth, unblemished skin rather than a war-torn, leather-like exterior.

"You aren't going to faint on me again, are you?" Evelot teased.

"No, no . . ."

Zenris would have gladly lost himself in her smile had it not been for the smudge of black beyond her shoulder. It writhed in the ceiling's corner. He looked up, expecting it to be a mote of dust. Its outline stirred, proving him wrong.

"Zenris?" Evelot said.

"Hmm—yes?"

The speck then dropped from the ceiling. Zenris froze. The thing flapped its little wings, diving to the floor. At the last second, it swooped up and disappeared behind Evelot.

Zenris leaned over, yet found nothing by the end of the bed.

"What is it?" asked Evelot.

Zenris tried for a smile. "I do not mean to alarm you . . ."

"Aye?"

"Mayhap I am imagining it."

"Imagining what?" she insisted.

Zenris turned to her. There, on her shoulder, was the

thing he wished had stayed forgotten: a tiny devilish face with lips peeled back in a beady-eyed snarl. A high-pitched scream, Evelot's, Zenris was sure, erupted as he gallantly retreated beneath the bed. The barking of a cricket or chipmunk erupted inside the room. Little flaps of wings beating the air mixed with the sound of Evelot's voice.

"It's all right!" Evelot exclaimed.

"Take care, Evelot! It carries diseases!"

Instead, Zenris heard her coo and softly coax the little beastie into submission. Zenris peeked out from under the bed to see its infernal wings flapping about, as if to dive straight for him.

"Would you like to come out, or will you be taking up with the dust bunnies under the damned bed?" Evelot asked.

Zenris climbed to his feet. Brushing lint and dust from his shoulders, he eyed Evelot's palm cupped to her chest. A little squawk of sorts arose from there. The black speck, no bigger than an apple up close, scuttled and jerked until it saw him. Obsidian eyes glinted back at Zenris. He blinked, and inconsistently, so too did the shadow.

"You've spooked our guest, Jam-Jam. What do you have to say for yersel'?" she asked it.

The creature clung to her fingers, answering with excited chirps. Membranous wings threatened to open as it celebrated its owner's return. With ears that looked too large for its head and an upturned fuzzy snout, the little brown bat was no more feral than an attached pup. Yet there was a look of evil about it, Zenris felt. 'Twas in the way it bore its fangs in a feral-like smile, with a joy that did not meet its eyes.

"You call it 'Jam-Jam'?" he asked.

"Her name," Evelot answered. "Short for 'Jammer'."

"An. . . interesting name."

"She. . . makes jam out of the bugs I feed her," Evelot answered bashfully.

The bat and Zenris continued staring each other down.

"I was trying to socialize her, but I suppose you can keep on scaring her."

"Hmm—"

Zenris blinked. Seeing how Evelot disappointedly frowned at him, he realized the threat of disease was less dire than his current situation.

"You wound me, my lady. Are you suggesting that I, Zenris Aspenheart, could disturb not one, but two women in Goldencrest?" Zenris joked.

Evelot eyed him skeptically, albeit with a blossoming smile. "Guess we'll have to blame the bard on that one," she said. With that, Jammer added a squeal of agreement.

Zenris dared approach them. The bat, Jammer, did not appear to spring for him. Difficult 'twas, the search for anything winsome about a face wrinkled and scrunched and ears that stuck out from the sides of its squat, little head. Mayhap if he focused on the fluffy brown fur on its body, he could envision a familiarly doggish image about it.

"How may I—err. . .?" Zenris motioned to Jammer.

The little bat opened her wings and slammed them down on the air. Away she flew, circling the two with clicking noises made in assumed irritation. Zenris jolted, his hands instinctively reaching for something to hold as he forced himself to stand still. Evelot squeaked in alarm. To his credit, and fortune, 'twas her hand that he had found. Her fingers were cool on his palm, and slim in his grasp; for reasons he knew not, they fit perfectly there.

Little Jammer found a perch on the ceiling beams above, yet the way Evelot observed Zenris ceased his hesitant thoughts regarding her pet.

"You act as if you haven't lived in nature," Evelot said with an inquisitive look.

"Careful, my lady. That is quite the statement to make about elves," Zenris chuckled.

"I'll have to tell Jammer the bad news. A shame, considering how she's eager to meet new people."

Zenris smiled. "I would not relinquish the possibility yet. For 'twould be dishonorable to shatter a fair maiden's humble wish."

"How chivalrous."

Jammer dipped in the air and landed on Evelot's back. She scuttled over the stretch of Evelot's arm until she came to their hands still intertwined. Zenris felt the warmth and wetness of her little tongue seeking food or salt on their skin. She proved his assumption correct: the beast truly was like a flying pup. Then again, he was more inclined to consider how long it had been since he had taken Evelot's hand, and to wonder how long she would allow it to continue.

"Since you're staying. . ." she said.

"Yes?" said Zenris.

Her mouth opened, yet she stalled. Zenris's eyes peeked down at her lower lip pursed in thought. He assumed her words became lost to the wind. He did not mind it, either way.

"How's about some scran downstairs?"

Evelot took back her hand. Jammer cried out in

dismay before returning to her perch on the rafters. Her chirps were loud in Zenris's ear as he rubbed his thumb over his other fingers, the absence of her hand stirring a sense of mourning within him.

Another peculiarity. Where many others' hands created only warmth, Evelot's summoned a tingling energy in his wrist that flittered down to his palm. Had hers stayed, Zenris felt he would not have let go. For the sake of curiosity, he wished she would change her mind. Alas, 'twas not so.

"Very well. Lead on, my lady," replied Zenris, following in withheld dejection.

Chapter Sixteen

Downstairs, Zenris put his thoughts to other things. Important topics such as their next course of action, and what sort of foodstuff Beluphis kept in her cupboards. As if reading his thoughts, the absent witch reappeared by the top of the staircase leading to her study. She hollered at both of them as Zenris's jaw hung open for a bite of apple. Evelot answered her call, and after another clipped summons, so had a pouting, full-mouthed Zenris.

The tidiness and lack of pungent herbs and old potions in her study advised Zenris to take heed. Beluphis stood by her cauldron, empty of popping bubbles or toes, and huffed.

"Are we getting to work on the ward, Master?" Evelot asked.

Beluphis crossed her arms. "Today, you are not assisting me, girl. You will do something else."

Evelot said nothing. Zenris looked from the witchling to her mentor. "This 'something' requires me?"

"Yes, a witness," answered Beluphis.

"Beg pardon?"

Beluphis moved to one of her discarded desks off to

the side. She rummaged through the drawers for a moment, then let out a hoot when she found what she was looking for. In Evelot's hands, she placed a black-handled knife. Its hilt looked to be too wide to hold in a serious fight, but the metal engravings suggested the weapon was ceremonial.

"Hold it tight in your hands, girl," ordered Beluphis. "And repeat after me."

The words they spoke were not ones Zenris had heard before; the language seemed to be an old human dialect. When they were done, a green glow emanated betwixt Evelot's clenched hand and the blade. When it faded, a surprising smile passed over Beluphis's face.

"You are now ready to take the next steps of your witchhood. You remember what I told you about studying?" Beluphis asked.

"'The brain is the arm holding the sword. Without the proper training, your abilities are useless,'" Evelot said.

"Good. You have an athame, so you can train by performing rituals and making deals with others, humanoid or not. I had better see you copying text in this library more often, as well. Do you understand?"

"M-Master, I . . ."

Evelot gaped at her new tool. Zenris smiled at her. He could imagine her shock, for 'twas a reward to be acknowledged by one's mentor. However, the occasion called for celebration and her gratitude took too long to form upon her visage. Her lips pinched, reluctant to move. She looked up at her mentor and held the blade to her chest, the picture of appreciation suddenly come over her.

"Thank you, Master. I'm forever grateful," she said.

Zenris knew not if the tears on her lashes were

genuine, or a symptom of something left unspoken—but Beluphis was sure to notice. Before that could happen, Zenris leaned into Evelot and nudged her.

"Make haste," he said, "before she changes her mind."

"I never change my mind!" Beluphis snapped.

Evelot giggled, tying her tool to her belt. "Would you like for me to do anything today, Master?"

"Eh, if you're feeling grateful, fetch me the rest of the harvest in the garden and get started on your studies. Go, I have things to do now!" She gestured impatiently for both of them to leave as she went back to her cauldron. With nothing to add, they made their exit.

They wound their way back up the stairs and through the kitchen to a door Zenris was sure was not there before. To find a maintained garden outside it left him shocked. A log fence penned in several plots of earth, rich with the last of the harvest: swollen aubergines, pumpkins, and small bushels of berries next to rosemary and thyme. The scents surrounding him reminded Zenris of the Fae Realm and its bounty, how the endless sun and greenery nurtured immeasurable life. To his own mentor, a garden such as Beluphis's would seem as limited as a miniature terrarium.

His mentor. . .

The sound of Evelot's boots stirred him from his thoughts. She stopped before the rows of bushes, her hands clasped together behind her back. With her chin tipped to the sky, a forlorn expression swept over her countenance. A pity, the sight, for her joy should have been visible. He wished to celebrate with her, feel her giddiness like a melody on the wind. More importantly, he was curious of her complex reaction.

"Tell me," Zenris said. "How does it feel, now that you have elevated your status as a witch?"

"Suppose it'd be cause for celebration," Evelot answered.

"Suppose?"

Evelot looked back at him. Whatever form of happiness she wore in that moment, 'twas a facade.

"Given your occupation, I think I'll refrain. I don't have the coin for it, sir," she said, a humorous glint in her eyes.

"Well, for the lady, I would arrange an agreeable price."

"How's about a bushel of raspberries, then?"

"And what of the owner of the garden?" Zenris replied with a grin.

"She's nearsighted, if that eases your conscience."

Zenris dipped his head with a bow. The witchling took a nearby basket and handed him a pair of large shears.

"Care to help tend the pumpkins while I fetch your payment?" she asked.

"With pleasure."

He set to work on the closest row, well within view of her as she foraged from the bushes.

Her task was hardly difficult compared to snipping pumpkins from their vines. In the last stretch of the season, the surviving berries were flush with fervor to leave the near-hibernating bush. Zenris was glad the task was her own, as he felt salivation pooling in his mouth every time the wind carried the berries' scent to him. The elder witch would have had his head for eating her entire supply.

All the while he was patient. He knew not if Evelot

would say anything of particular interest, or so much as hint at her ruminations. The more he peeked at her, the less confident he was of her feelings. She hardly uttered a single word, only concentrating on her chore. Her brows were fixed in such a way that Zenris feared they would become stuck.

He quickened his pace, severing vines and rolling pumpkins to the side of the house. Back and forth. Snip and shuffle. A melodic tune Zenris felt was familiar. If he remembered correctly, his mentor had penned it many decades ago. Zenris closed his eyes and envisioned its creation. The two of them had sat in the shadows of a tavern, away from prying eyes, sharing ideas and a bowl of baked bread chips. His mentor's finger curled around his quill. Their laughter was muffled in their full mouths.

It should not have been performed at a grand ball where nobles shared not its sentiment. Eventually, it grew out of favor, and out of mind; a terrible fate for a lovely tune.

"That isn't your song," Evelot said.

"Pardon?"

Zenris looked up from the soil to Evelot coming out of the kitchen, her basket emptied and the bushes plucked.

"Whatever it was you were singing under your breath. It isn't yours, is it?"

"I was. . ." Zenris paused. "How is it you are certain?"

"You usually sing about beautiful things, but that was about 'lonely worlds' and 'never ceasing belief' to yersel'."

Zenris gaped at her. To hear confirmation that she had listened to his music was a happy shock upon his heart. Yet, she rendered him flabbergasted with her words.

"Surely, you jest," he said. "No one has avoided the great melodies of Ykos, the satyr bard."

"A 'satyr'? As in someone from the Fae Realm?"

"Yes. Come now. Ykos, the first bard to travel across realms? The first of adventuring heroes on the Material Plane? The Million-Hit Wonder?"

Evelot shook her head.

"He lulled a dragon to sleep, for Father Nature's sake!"

"Hardly rings a bell," she said.

"Good gods," Zenris mumbled to himself. "To have erased Ykos's legend from the duchies proves only how ill in taste the current king of Esmora has in music."

"You must admire him a great deal," Evelot observed.

"Of course! Would not anyone admire their idol? Without him, I would have no profession."

"What do you mean?"

Evelot sat on the stoop of the back door. Zenris stayed kneeling beside the rows of pumpkins as he smiled at old memories.

"'Tis not an exciting story. My mother and I lived in the Citadel of Thalthaes in Vestryae, in the pauper districts. You could hardly call it luxurious compared to the image of elven culture. Within our solitary, unfortunate life, the two of us endured. One day, Ykos arrived in Vestryae with his party. He was to perform on stage at venues so grand my young, spry self had not the dream of affording entrance. Luckily, I was quite agile in sneaking inside.

"When I heard him playing for the first time, 'twas. . . greater than any magic in this world. His songs had captured the essence of my life so clearly I thought he had somehow lived it before I had. His passion was tangible, from the way his voice cherished each lyric gifted to his listeners through the careful handwork of his notes. Until that point, I had not truly felt alive. I had not that same passion for anything.

"At that moment, my sole purpose was to study every note he played. I returned home and regaled my mother by recreating his performance as painstakingly accurate as my untried hands could. What little embers of passion stirred that day, she stoked to life. I remember when she surprised me the next year with a lute. From then on, I played nothing but his works. Retrospectively, 'twas far from my brightest idea, nearly impersonating the legend from my window and in the taverns hiring performers. There were plenty of objections from the audience. But. . . my mother believed in my dream, and so too did I."

Evelot was quiet. She watched him with a pensive face, absorbing his words. It terrified him, in a way. The first person to listen to his complete life story hung onto every word. He felt strangely self-conscious.

"Where's Ykos now?" Evelot asked. "Does he still play music?"

Zenris's spirits fell with his gaze. "No. He returned to the Fae Realm over four decades ago."

"Because he wasn't from this plane. . . He wouldn't have survived that long outside his own realm."

"Yes."

The silence hung over them like a drenched cloak. Zenris continued on with his task until all the pumpkins sat inside the kitchen. Then, he took a seat beside Evelot on the stoop and stretched out his arms.

"And your ma?" she asked.

"She rests in the Father's Endless Forest."

Evelot nodded. Once those words had spilled from

his lips, Zenris lost confidence in his secret endeavors. In traversing a great deal of woods he had learned 'twas a fruitless mission to seek the Portal during the eve of the season. The last remnants of its magic would fade to the wind, reopening upon Athbreith months later.

A wistful calm washed over him upon the reminder that he was truly alone.

Evelot rose to her feet. With a determined brow, she said, "Come with me."

Zenris did not ask their destination, nor did he think he should have. The way Evelot carried herself as she led him out the garden gate was answer enough.

They followed a footpath toward a cove of trees, past a decorated grave marker carved with the blurred image of an owl into it. Zenris did not recognize the area, nor the bay willows and their magicked floral shawls, ceasing the whispers that had clouded his mind. Delving deeper into their shade, he recognized a change in the atmosphere. A layer of humidity gave way to a luminous, spring-like environment; the crunch of twigs and leaves shifted into the swish and hiss of long grass, and the scent of sun-basked flora wafted on the air. Then, a sense of familiarity in his soul. Fae magic, coursing through the foliage answering as a thunderous, heavenly cry his body fought akin to a headache.

From within the shroud of forestry, a splendorous light blinked into existence. Zenris assumed 'twas Evelot's orbs of mana lighting their way until the glow grew in size, and the pair drew to a stop. The tree before them stood wreathed in decadent canvases of colorful flora. Around its trunk stretched foliage, perfumed berry bushes, and ponds dotting the base. With sinewy arms, it reached for the stars.

Had the canopy of greens and golds not shrouded Zenris's vision, he might have seen its true height.

Yet the light Zenris had seen was not in the air like Evelot's cantation. His eyes fell to the tree's base. There, as if a mirror erected by the gods, the oak's flesh was split atwain and repurposed as an opening spacious enough for a circus caravan to enter. A wall of infinite color flashed and twisted, swirling like the hues on pond water. Zenris peered inside, seeing not a hint of visibility; only a hollow shadow and meaningless light stared back.

Evelot exhaled. She reached for the pouch at her hip and produced a hand-sized object. Though gray and slim, it shone a similar color to the Portal within its cavities. He felt the magic connecting them; like two pipes of a pan flute, they echoed the same tune.

"What is it you have there?" he asked.

"A witch stone from my master. Supposed to protect me from the Portal's magic."

"To pluck its mana and place it in a trinket. . . 'Twould have been a tremendous effort," Zenris said.

"I don't make light of what she did. Without the Call or heritage from the Fae Wilds, I would've been entranced into an empty plane of existence. Much like any half-human or relation. Neither the Choille nor the Portal simply give. This. . ." Evelot held the witch stone up to eyeline. "This cost something. For me."

Zenris glanced at Evelot. A blank face came over her, one that teetered on the edges of thought and drifting memories. Those verdant eyes fell to the pale stone for a moment that carried on too long in silence.

She shook her head and looked back at him.

"Zenris, is this what you're really here in Goldencrest for?" she asked.

A lump in his throat proved difficult to swallow. "I suppose I cannot keep it secret any longer, then?"

She did not answer. Gone was his smile as Zenris faced the truth.

"Yes. In the few decades past, I have been searching every single Portal on this plane for him."

"Because of. . .?"

He smiled ruefully and gestured to the Portal. "My father, of course! He raised me when my mother departed. When 'twas his choice to chastise me for stealing his art, or have me locked away, he took me off the streets and taught me everything I know. The satyr bard who won the hearts of all Runlaris, that very legend, was my mentor, my idol. It has been too long since his crossing into a realm that allows no entrance for half-blooded creatures. Yet I. . . wish to speak with him again."

Evelot nodded solemnly. "The Opening's fickle when it comes to closing. It chooses when it shuts for the season. Might be days or hours. You up for waiting here a while longer?"

Zenris despondently gestured for her to move first. Evelot was quiet as they took a seat on a patch of green grass. She stared at the Portal as though it were a passing farmer's wagon, with no other regard for its existence. Through the precarious light above and the Portal's shifting colors, Evelot's eyes dulled, her lips drawing ever so slightly tighter in its presence.

"Evelot?" he said.

"Hmm?"

"What does this place mean to you?"

She did not meet his eye. "What do you mean?"

"Exactly that."

"You want to know?"

Zenris leaned over to peer closer at her. "If I may," he said.

Her brows furrowed carefully, her hands fiddling with the witch stone.

"I wanted so desperately to belong," she started quietly. "I thought my magic was meant for the Harvest Maiden. I'd stood before the High Priestess... the whole village. They were all watching me, expecting something grand. Until I killed an entire meadow. Then they... they watched me like I was going to take their lives next. It was so unbearable that I just ran.

"But then my master found me half dead. Took me under her wing. She was so confident witchcraft was my calling that she told me I had the makings of being the next Guardian of the Choille. The coven would've been summoned from all across the duchies to witness it, too. I wanted it. I was ready for the responsibility, for something to call my own.

"She told me the Portal sings more loudly than a choir of Proxims praising their Devas, like the pulse of magic in your veins.

"I've made peace with the silence now."

A hush fell softly over them.

Long after she had finished, his heart still trembled in fear. His eyes sought the Portal, though he struggled to imagine such a fate. Zenris could almost see himself standing before it like she had, waiting for its reply as his patience wore thin. He had prepared himself for so long, ready for when the Portal would sing, a glorious melody filling the woods. But it regarded him like a small pebble, a wisp in the air meant only to continue past it.

"Zenris?"

He blinked, turning back to her. "Yes?"

"Have you thought about what you'd say to him? Your da?"

"I cannot say," he answered.

"Nothing?"

Zenris studied the canopy of leaves above him. "My father and I need say very little. In my first years with him, he had a sense about him. It told him when I needed help and when to leave me to my study. Mayhap he will know what to say when he appears."

Evelot wordlessly nodded. Zenris's mind wandered on the possibility. Once, he had been confident in greeting Ykos with a smile and a jest. Yet time had passed. Zenris was decades older. He had written and performed many effortless compositions Ykos had not witnessed, had not critiqued. Many feelings had come and gone, returning and then taking flight to gods know where. All that remained were embittered memories of his failed attempts to enter a Portal. Ykos had never warned him of such struggles.

Zenris thoughtlessly asked Evelot, "Suppose if I had something in mind?"

Evelot tipped her head toward him, waiting.

"I would reprimand him, tell him what an ass he was without sending word or returning. For not explaining what makes a great bard, or putting to words if he believed I could be one of them. And for abandoning me to all these unanswered questions!"

Zenris took a breath, mulling over the words that had escaped him. Then he chuckled.

"What is it?" Evelot asked, facing him.

"'Tis. . . ridiculous."

"Do you think so?"

He gazed back up at the trees with a fading smile. "Of course."

Evelot did not push the subject any further. Neither did Zenris have the motivation to remedy the downtrodden atmosphere surrounding them. Time in the woods' heartbeat passed without sign or sound, save for the Portal that stirred in its seat. When Evelot had run out of berries from the bushes and closed her eyes, Zenris persevered in their wait.

The silence unnerved him. The hope of seeing Ykos, of speaking with him, wormed its way into his mind. 'Twas a childish thought, too unimportant to share, yet it refused to subside. It absorbed his energy, manifesting into doubt. Would this truly be it? Was this the moment where Ykos would finally emerge from the Portal with his warm smile and soothing voice?

Or was another impasse in store? Another arduous journey to another Portal in vain, repeating the taxing cycle once more?

Zenris was not confident his heart could take the disappointment.

A vibration in the earth stirred him from thought. Zenris sat up, looking to the Portal. Its evanescent doorway flickered with light, fading. Evelot stirred at the shaking of tree limbs and the faint rumble of earth to watch beside him.

Neither one said a word as the Portal closed. Its hum in Zenris's ear retreated to an echo, light giving way to the dark of the night. With its exit, a crushing, icy reality engulfed him.

No hand would outstretch from that path; no tall silhouette of a satyr would enter the Mortal Realm. The light finally died out, breathing its last, and a silence was cast over them.

Zenris gently squeezed his eyelids shut. He counted to five and then rose to his feet.

"Let us return to your master," he said.

Evelot silently cast a spell, creating dancing lights to hover around them. Zenris turned to offer his hand. In those little lights, her eyes glistened. Evelot looked at him, utter disappointment awash on her face. She was. . . upset for him.

Zenris found it in himself to smile.

"Are you ready?" he asked.

That vale of tears was gone in a blink. Evelot turned her head, yet her attempt to hide her sadness was plain by the quick swipes at her eyes. To think that she empathized with him. Well, Zenris supposed it another commonality betwixt them: having faced countless rejection.

With a faint nod, she rose to stand at his side, and the two journeyed back to Beluphis and her home.

Chapter Seventeen

Green energy flickered to life, a response to her incantation. A low hum emanated from a bulb wedged in the middle of a branch-like wooden stake. After a beat, the light dimmed, a signal of the ward taking root.

Evelot looked up and considered her surroundings. Daylight warmed the Beinn and thin treeline beside her. Several yards ahead, where a gathering of trees still crowned the hill, lay the outskirts of the festival grounds. The air was slightly warmer, the breeze gentle. A perfect time for a daunder where the workers weren't, and for working where hammering and hollering were ripe. No one within view would notice her.

Like a shadow, she fell into motion. She crept down the hill where the grass would camouflage her. By the dark canopy of trees, her worn, shaking hands held the ward's stake as she tacked it into the ground. Another uttered cantation, and it was done. The ward was in full effect.

Evelot stared down at the post.

Somehow, some way, she'd protected her home from the invading beasts. Now that she'd finished the deed, she was back to... what exactly? The monotonous routine of studying, making tinctures and potions, collecting supplies from the Choille? That was what she found comfort in for so long. But. . . the idea of returning to her everyday tasks felt like an itch, a flourish of hot, prickly panic that made her limbs seize. In a blink, she no longer saw herself kneeling in the shallow reach of the trees, but at the precipice of two planes of existence. Nature's shade, and the light of a grassy clearing. There, where the birdsong eased her, and the Choille was ripe with comforting scents. In the distance, workers erected the festival grounds in the midday's mellow sun. New perspective, more faces, more ideas.

To choose one felt treacherous. To ignore the choice was no longer an option. After facing the threat of death and lost hopes, Evelot wanted for more, even if that change was small. Anything to change her perspective for a minute or a month; maybe it wouldn't be so bad.

She trudged toward the open field. The sun was blinding, and the breeze tossed back her hood. Inching away from the shadows, Evelot couldn't find it in herself to adjust it. She let the wind tease her hair and kiss her cheeks, welcoming her into a new day.

The grass opened to a yawning space of packed earth forever marked by the soles of strangers' feet. Evelot stood at the edge of a smaller foot-path, observing the large scene in front of her. No one bothered to look at her as she crept through what looked to be the woodworking section. Oaky chimes jostled in the cool breeze as a darker-skinned human went about hanging them from his sturdy booth. Under a canvas tarp and a placard display, a half-elf woman was carving into a slab of wood. Many of their designs looked to be from other duchies of Cuthosia with their similar circular patterns, a few intricate and obvious religious symbols of the surviving "lesser" gods.

Hollering caught her ear. Farther to the right, Evelot glimpsed the makings of stages. Like ants, lumberjacks carried massive planks in single files to the section of open-air stages. Most were small, enough for a few people to play for a dozen. These modest venues encircled one massive theater, all of them with curtain rods being installed as a final measure.

She followed the path straight ahead, also empty of customers. It had to have been a special occasion for Goldencrest, inviting many nonhuman folk to come visit and sell their products. Half-humans of different forms and colors, neighboring Beaghans, and travel-weary gnomes put up their gadgetry shops and prepared foodstuffs and bevvies.

As she passed the food stalls and their mouthwatering aromas, Evelot felt a smile creep over her. She wondered if Zenris felt the same in his limbs from his travels. It was strange to see others who were different, to watch them craft and display their livelihoods. She imagined it wasn't easy to do so, and she found it more admirable. But Zenris wasn't at her side to share the same thought. He was back at the inn, taking his depressing reality as well as could be.

Someone shouted nearby. Evelot blinked, and a townsman charged toward her with a heavy plank over his shoulder. She dipped out of the way, her hip colliding with a wooden panel. Over her pained hiss, a sharp creak wailed. Rickety boards inside a traveling wagon groaned under two feet coming toward her.

From within the canopy, there stepped out a Beaghan man. His tawny skin nearly matched the shade of the wagon's exterior, and his limbs were like a knobby tree, thicker at the joints. There were similarities she saw between elves and Beaghans in him: his garb and the pointed edges of his ears. But that was where they ended. Where Zenris wore vests and cotton shirts for appearances, the other dressed for comfort with breeks and an added cloak.

When the stranger hopped down to the dirt, Evelot couldn't help but notice that not only did he rise to her ribcage but the gray of his thick head of hair didn't match the youthfulness in his round face.

"You have a tumble there, lassie?" asked the stranger, smiling in jest.

Evelot rubbed at her hip and answered, "Just passing through."

"That's a shame. Was hoping you'd come to take a gawk at the Hazel Salmon."

"The *what*?"

"My shop." He pointed up at the signboard hanging from the side of the wagon. Evelot looked up; encircling the symbol of an open book was that exact title.

"You sell books?" Evelot wondered aloud.

It was difficult to understand when the shopkeeper's lilt bounced like a hare and his *t*'s stabbed into *h*'s, but Evelot managed to interpret, "You bet your coin purse, I do! And not just any random tome—well, scratch that. Anything's a fair go when you find it in the rubbish. But! I can promise I have about every subject you can think of. Go on, give me one."

"A subject?"

"Of course!"

Amused, Evelot paused in thought. "How's about botany?"

"Several, in fact. Most being from outside the duchies."

Eagerly, the shop owner zipped into his wagon. Not a heartbeat had passed when he reappeared with an armful. Four tomes went onto the panel Evelot had crashed into, all clattering on top with a heavy thunk.

"Here we go: *The Unknown Uses of Western Herbs*, *A Complete Collection of Acluethan Flora*, *The Mysterious Greenery of Graulia*, and *How to Survive the Treacherous Landscape of the Mountainous Theydor*. You'll be sure to get your money's worth from that last one."

Evelot marveled at the simple covers. "Can I look?"

"Be my guest."

Her hands grasped at the first tome, careful to open the worn cover and flip through the beige pages. Though the text looked like chook scratches, the detailed sketches of herbs garnered a grin from her. As did the other tomes as she peeked through them.

Evelot then asked the tome-seller, "Do you have anything on beastology? Or potion-brewing?"

"Would that be mythological beasts or guides on known animals?" he said.

"Both?"

"Let me check."

When the shopkeeper returned, there were only two other tomes offered.

"Only one for the eastern coast's fauna. As for potions. . . eh."

Evelot glimpsed the title scooted her way: *Ilemerth Collegiate's Guide to Wizardry and Magicks Vol. 12*.

"Those haughty school folk in Stadahl toss out

textbooks every single year. Hear they're on volume forty-six or other. 'Outdated' or not, 'tis still worth something of learning."

Evelot took a cursory glance inside the textbook. It was a little more worn than the others, and heftier, but the print was still legible and some of the potion-brewing techniques her mentor had taught her appeared to be accurate. She didn't know what came about her as her lips stretched into a small smile, but it was an opportunity she couldn't pass up.

"A-are you selling anything before the festival?" Evelot asked.

"I'd be remiss not to," laughed the shopkeeper.

"How much would it be for the ones here?"

"Really?" he said in disbelief. "Are you sure?"

Evelot nodded.

"In that case, just two kingsnickels."

It was a relief Evelot remembered her coin purse before leaving home. She opened the little satchel and handed over the change.

"Thank you, lassie. If you ever need any more reading, be sure to find my traveling wagon, the Hazel Salmon. Just give a holler to old Clovis Brandywood!"

"Thank you. Ta!" she said.

Evelot turned away with her purchases in hand, and Clovis waved back to her cheerily before disappearing into his wagon.

She scurried onto the farmer's path toward home, past the rolling carts and wagons going the opposite way. Among the passing faces, she recognized one of her father's farmhands. Thankfully, their deliveries were going to the town and its buyers, and with that, hopefully a source of income for the farm to support the imminent winter.

A wave of excitement and doubt overtook Evelot as she traveled back up the hills. She didn't think she could feel so thrilled to read, to want to learn. It reminded her of too many years ago when she'd felt confident in controlling her magic through her mentor's tutelage. Her magic hadn't failed her until she'd faced the Portal. She'd assumed her confidence would never return. But somehow, it'd found her again. Though she meant to study in the library, like she promised her mentor, Evelot supposed she could make do at home with her new findings in hand.

A racing figure headed her way from the homestead. She jumped aside in time to see Tonlin with a budding grin, whooping joyously. Nothing stopped him; he was carrying on the wind toward town. A spark of hope filled Evelot. Whatever good news had hit him, she internally wished him luck with his new venture.

But it wasn't all sunshine for Tonlin, or her. The familiar sound of her da's booming voice made Evelot's head turn. Standing at the entrance of the family home, his face burned with rage, all a scunnered.

"I wasn't finished with you, boy!" he bellowed. "Don't think we're done here yet!"

Evelot neared the front porch. Whatever kind of happiness had visited her sped after Tonlin as Da's ire fixed on her.

"And you!"

Evelot stopped. His wagging finger hardly did justice to the scowl on his face.

"Have you lost your heid, girl, or just your voice? I

don't speak in 'scrawled notes left on the dining table,' and you certainly don't speak the native tongue! You directly disobeyed me when I told you to stay put. And now you've come crawling back as though nothing's wrong!"

He started for her. Evelot took a breath, steeling herself for the onslaught of nagging and the threats of no meals. She'd ignored his orders before setting off the last night of hers and Zenris's werewolf hunt. Inevitably, she'd have to face Da again.

What Evelot didn't expect was her ma rushing out of the doorway. Her arms opened, and the scent of cider and spices, of comfort, enveloped Evelot.

"I thought you were gone," Ma murmured.

"I'm sorry, Ma," she weakly replied, wrapping her arms around her.

The tomes tumbled to Evelot's feet. Ma rocked her gently, her hand stroking Evelot's head. They stood silently in the pathway for far too long in silence, but Evelot was far from caring about the neighbors.

Over Ma's shoulder, Da watched them from the porch. With a screwed up look on his face, he balled his fists and quietly fumed. He met Evelot's eye and then stormed inside the house.

Evelot hugged her ma tighter. At least someone was relieved to see her home.

With dinner on the table that evening, the whole family gathered together. Evelot sat in her usual seat, a tome placed precariously under the table on her lap. She picked at her plate, secretly flipping through pages as the sound of their voices droned on through one ear and out the other. The fascinating world of herbology preoccupied her mind. That was until an interesting conversation gave her pause.

"Those girls will finally unclog the streets here shortly," said her brother-in-law. "Can't wait to have peace in town."

"Many a them will prolly follow Aspenheart to his next jaunt. Where do you think he'll trot off to next?" said her sister.

Evelot peeked up from her book. "What's it about Zenris?"

"Most of the people in town were talking about when he'll leave," Ulleh said. "Hasn't said so himsel', but none seem to mind him leaving the day after the festival."

"Leaving?"

Disappointment weighed heavily in her chest. It'd been too long since anyone had spoken of his departure, and there'd always been a time limit. It was only shocking to realize how quickly it was coming up. But... No. She shouldn't be concerned. He was a traveling bard, and she a village girl. Wasn't any of her business.

"Don't tell me: You've fallen for his charm, too?" Yahir sneered.

"You asking if I hold the torch for him?" Evelot asked.

"What else would I have asked you?"

She fixed a cynical brow at him. "You've already got a wife, so why the need to ask if you've not the means to change anything?"

Ulleh covered her mouth as she sputtered a laugh around a bite of potato. Evelot blinked back at Yahir and turned her head to the rest of the table, who sat in astonished silence with raised brows. It amazed her she'd said anything back, but even more amazing was how easy it'd been.

Yahir managed a scoff, then said, "As I said, no love lost when that bard leaves."

Evelot rolled her eyes and returned to her book. She spooned at her bowl of broth, waiting for the usual chatter to start up again while she perused her tome. Instead, she felt Tonlin nudge at her side then gesture to their ma.

"Evelot," she said.

"Aye?"

"You aren't wearing your cloak today, dear?"

"Hmm?"

Evelot felt for the edges of her garment only to find her shoulders bare. That was right. She'd left it on her bed upstairs.

Ma's face showed as much surprise as Evelot felt internally. Anxiety made her want to run back up the stairs for her cloak, but she kept in her seat.

"Don't need it," Evelot answered. She smiled at Ma, and the anxious feeling was gone.

Chapter Eighteen

The air was damp and the sunlight a candle's warmth when Evelot stepped outside the next morning. It would've been nice to read outside, according to her original plan, but there were ingredients to fetch for her ma and warding posts to check before the weather turned more dreich. All was well after a visit to the apothecary and a brief check on the outskirts of the festival grounds.

But the daunder Evelot took into the square held more purpose. She lingered in the shadows of the alleys, watching the comings and goings of hunters and townsfolk. Dark stains muddled the cobblestone where the carcasses had been butchered and handed off. Tradesfolk and tanners hollered over the chatter for the last of the pelts and horns; the villagers were just as vocal in trading what they could for the meats.

With some struggle onto a haphazard stack of boxes, Evelot laid eyes on a bellowing hunter calling for passersby. He stood behind a large carcass dark as pitch and coated with thick fur. His next words were muffled, but the word "wolf" caught her ear. He raised the head toward those nearby. The maw fell open, the jagged teeth bared in an empty snarl.

The coat, the head—it had to be. The beast... was gone. A feeling of relief, of satisfaction flooded Evelot. She could move on.

Unconsciously, Evelot followed the foot traffic toward The Glistening Seed. She waded through the crowd, coming up to the inn's side and hovering close by. Chatter and laughter floated past its doors, but without the faint notes of music intertwined, Evelot couldn't help but feel dismayed. Zenris was still hidden away.

A shoulder scraped past her, sending Evelot teetering on her feet. A lass around her age made off to the other side of the entrance to mingle with others like her. They all peeked up at the top floor with taut expressions on their faces. Ah, his fans. Evelot wasn't the only one noting his absence.

Evelot stood back. She couldn't catch a word they'd said, but the way they peered around the alleys and the building had Evelot curiously sneaking toward them.

"Maybe we should call on the tavern owner to do something," Evelot heard the first say.

"And disturb his rest? That wouldn't be right," replied the second.

"She has a point. What if the hunt has finally gotten to him and he needs a doctor? What if he hasn't woken yet?" said the third.

"It's been several days. How awful a condition he must be in to be sleeping that long."

"I thought elves didn't need sleep," said the first.

"Just like you thought they ate meat. I wouldn't be surprised if he's still suffering the consequences of your ignorance," the second retorted.

Evelot looked up at the second level of the inn. Zenris had tried to hide his disappointment over the Portal closing to the Fae Realm, wearing a smile that didn't reach his eyes. After traversing Goldencrest in lonely, awkward silence for a time, she understood that he'd been wallowing about more than that. What does a bard do after searching for his da and coming across another dead end? Face enough disappointment, and hope quickly becomes a distant memory.

Evelot remembered her past struggles, all the ones she'd told him about and the ones she held onto privately. Those wounds were still fresh, no matter how much time had passed. She hadn't been blessed by the Harvest Maiden, nor bequeathed any responsibility by the Portal. She had little to go on for besides her family. Maybe Zenris felt as hopeless as she did over the future.

Wordlessly, Evelot walked around the tavern up the steps. The establishment played host to many locals of Goldencrest and tourists alike, all seated at the bar and at the tables. A cloud of conversation carried over the long room, and amid the movement of the crowd, Evelot found it effortless to sneak past the bar and toward the staircase leading to the rooms. But the inn's check-in desk wasn't as easy to keep clear of.

With a shrill whistle, the hostess beckoned Evelot nearer and put on a smile too sharp to be inviting.

"Hello, there! What can I do for you?" she asked.

"Have you seen the bard Zenris come out of his room at all?" said Evelot.

"Zenris? Maybe. I can't be sure."

"Is he expecting anyone right now? Like a doctor?"

"Now, lass, don't fuss yersel' over him. Go tell your friends that he'll be performing soon enough."

"I—No. I'm no fan."

"Sure. As neither one of you is his long-lost sister or secret wife, eh? You can't fool me."

"I—Wait—"

From behind Evelot, an enormous shadow eclipsed the desk. She turned around, seeing the barkeep's sneer before the rest of him.

"She's not one of them, all right," he said. "This one's different, hen."

"How so?" the innkeeper asked.

To Evelot, he demanded, "I thought I told you to stay out, witchling. I won't have you casting any of that shadow magic in my business again."

"Och, for goddess's sake, I'm not here to spook your patrons!" Evelot snapped.

"Do you think I care? You're lucky your Tarod's daughter, otherwise I'd a skelped your heid and tossed you out to the garbage as you deserve."

He pointed her to the doors. Evelot grumbled under her breath, marching past the patrons, scunnered.

After exiting the tavern, Evelot stormed toward the alleyways. A small part of her chided herself for not expecting the hostess, and another part cursed the barkeep for being a bastard. If she was going to check on Zenris, she'd need to take the hard way.

Evelot turned down the alley and came to a screeching halt. More whispered chatter came from the back of the building. Leaning out from the shadows, she spotted a few of the earlier lasses squinting up at the third level. They pointed to a center window, and she heard them talking about a ladder. Evelot's brow shot up. The term *fanatic* might be used loosely, but it was another thing to live up to the namesake.

Evelot suspected Zenris was too troubled to be taking on unhinged lasses from the window.

But it wasn't as if they couldn't be avoided.

With a whispered cantation, she pointed at the ground. A swarm of grasshoppers appeared from thin air. They gathered in a swath, flying and hopping in the lasses' direction. One of them gasped, and the others shrieked; they couldn't race out of the alley fast enough.

Evelot stepped out from her hiding spot and observed the back of the tavern. From where she stood, Zenris's room was high enough to make her squint against the daylight. Many of the windows above were curtained off from the inside, save for the one his fans had pointed out. Nothing stirred within, not before or after Evelot summoned her phantom hand and knocked on the glass. She sighed, dismissing the spell.

On closer inspection, the window frames were bulky enough for her to wedge her boot on top of one and climb up. But she wasn't that daft. A building wouldn't be as easy to climb as a tree. She didn't have the physical strength to scale the wall.

Luckily, Evelot had something else in mind.

She knelt to the ground and ran her fingers over the cracks and grooves of the cobblestone. With closed eyes, she concentrated, imagining what coils of vines were still stuck down there. A burst of mana pinched at her temples, and warmed her palms. Something leafy brushed her fingertips.

"Witchling."

Evelot opened her eyes, her mana creeping back into her veins. She looked over her shoulder. With a swishing tail, Prilthadollak observed her a few paces away.

"What is it you are doing?" she asked.

Evelot cocked her head. "I could ask the same of you. Aren't you supposed to be practicing your sword skills?"

"I have concluded my training for the day. All in time to watch you sneak around like his fanatics usually do."

"Good thing I'm not one of them, then."

"Then what is it you mean to do, if not something similar?"

"Well, I'm. . ."

She didn't know how to phrase her plan in a way that wouldn't sound as ridiculous as what those lasses were about to do. *I was going to climb up a magicked vine and check on Zenris?* Evelot kept quiet in fear of the warrior thinking her a radge.

Prilthadollak looked up at the building, a pensive look about her. "I assume your purpose is to reach Zenris's room, yes?" she asked.

"Erm, I suppose so."

"You do not want to watch him for hours as he works, steal locks of his hair, or make off with his undergarments?"

"No," Evelot answered, too afraid to speak further.

"I see. . ."

The warrior stepped up to her. Evelot rose to her feet, suspicious of a confrontation or sizing up similar to several nights ago.

To her amazement, Prilthadollak said, "Then I will

allow you to continue. Please tell him that if he does not perform tonight as he promised, I will have him sleep in a shared room with me for the rest of the month."

"Oh. . ."

"I have been told that it is unpleasant. Thus, a fitting punishment," Prilthadollak replied. Not a hint of emotion colored her face as she waited for Evelot's response.

"A-all right."

Prilthadollak nodded, and then curtly left Evelot standing in the alley with more questions than answers. However strange a request, it was better than being sent off by a Jinryuu warrior.

After a minute more of coaxing the greenery below through spell-casting, Evelot manifested a thick vine and stepped onto a sturdy foothold. It stretched up along the wall, stopping at the center window. Her temples pounded, and her breath was heavy, but Evelot kept hold.

She swung around and pushed off the vine, flopping onto the empty window box as a makeshift seat. Through the glass, she spotted Zenris lying over his desk. A mountain of parchment cradled his head, his body rising and falling with steady breaths. If he didn't hear her previous attempts at entry, it must've been a long night for him.

It took several tries of lifting the jammed window and rapping her knuckles on the glass, but finally, her plan worked. Zenris startled awake, and when he met her eyes, a yelp jolted through him.

"Evelot?" he exclaimed.

"Let me in, will you?" she said, yanking at the bottom of the frame.

The wood groaned under her. Evelot panicked,

feeling the weight of the window box budge.

"Zenris!"

He hoisted the window up, and she grabbed hold of his outstretched arms. The box buckled. Zenris tried tugging her inside. As the plank gave way, her body was only halfway inside, and her boot caught something slippery. Parchment scattered everywhere as she went flying into the room with him.

Evelot grunted at the force of impact, the breath in Zenris's lungs bolting past her ear. She felt his arms slip off her waist before her eyes blinked open. Beneath Evelot, Zenris hissed in pain. The curl of his lip led her gaze across the planes of his cheekbones. She'd thought his eyes had always been pure green, the kind that stained your skirts after a rollick in the spring grass, but a rim of daffodil yellow rounded his pupils. She sat mesmerized. His nose sloped like a steep hill, and below were the full lips she'd seen blush the same mauvish rose as summer blossoms.

The smell of green cypress and sweet cedar begged her to lean in further. That was, until Evelot realized he was blinking up at her, waiting.

"Evelot?" Zenris said.

She blinked and threw herself off him.

"I-I came to make sure you were still alive," Evelot said too quickly.

He chuckled as he sat up. Before Zenris could speak, the sound of shifting parchment caught their attention. A breeze flew in, tossing the stacks about the room. The pair moved to catch them.

As Zenris shut the window, Evelot gathered her stack into a pile. The scrawls on the parchment stood out among the pale-colored pulp. She hadn't learned about musical compositions before, but she recognized lyrics written beneath bars and squiggles. He'd written in the Shared Language, but she guessed the other parts of it were in Elvish.

Smiling, Evelot murmured the lyrics to herself. *"Betwixt the sheets—"*

Zenris squeaked. Quickly, he plucked the parchment from her hand and shuffled it into another pile on his desk. Evelot rose to her feet in stupefied silence.

"My apologies," he said. "'Twould be a bother to you, this unfinished—"

Evelot shook her head. "No, no, that's all right. I-I shouldn't have snooped."

"Hardly so, when it sits out in the open," Zenris said.

Her face felt warm as her hands balled into her skirts.

"What brings you here?"

"Are you all right?"

The two stared at one another, gobsmacked. But it was Zenris who burst into laughter, easing the tension with one of his enormous smiles.

"Do forgive me," Zenris said, sobering. "But may I ask: Is it every day that you climb into people's rooms?"

"Aye. It so happened to be yours today," Evelot quipped with a grin.

"Then I should pay respects to the Fortune Giver. For They have blessed me not with a storm from the clouds, but a beguiling witch from the alley."

She rolled her eyes, her cheeks near scalding with bashfulness. "I came to check on you," Evelot said.

"Oh?" Zenris perked up at that.

"Apparently, you've to keep your promise with the barkeep to provide entertainment. And something about you bunking with Prilthadollak if you don't?"

"My, my, how frightening," he said with a surprisingly uninterested tone. Tidying his desk, he added, "So, you come only on behalf of others?"

"I. . ."

She couldn't look at him. No matter how ridiculously childish it was, her nerves bundled at the thought of telling him the truth. It took a moment to remember he still had his ego, and she wasn't there to stroke it any more than necessary.

With a huff, she tried again. "Well, I came to check on you for everyone's sake, mine included. All right?"

"Really?" Zenris looked back at her. The smile he wore was appreciative, bright, and oddly more enchanting than it had been previously.

"You've been holed away in this room for days now. Of course I'd be worried. Any longer and I'd have to drag you out in a burlap sack."

"Methinks you would not hesitate to do so were I amongst the living or the dead," Zenris said with a teasing grin.

That radiance in him didn't last long. His grip on his desk chair was loose, but stayed put as if to anchor himself. In the daylight, faint tired lines stretched over the planes of his face; a shade of ash paled his complexion.

"The gesture is most appreciated, my lady," Zenris said. "Now that my warning has been issued, I will see to gracing those most distraught over my absence."

If Zenris not meeting her gaze wasn't any clue, the

state of the room spoke the truth of his emotional state. For something larger than her bedroom, he'd crammed it with discarded shite and all. Parchment teaming in the corner, bedsheets torn off the mattress left scattered to be tripped on, and clothes bleaching in the window's light. She didn't want to know if the connecting bathroom in the corner was any worse. It was a miracle that there wasn't a smell to all of it. Save for the rank of depression and melancholy coming off the bard.

As if reading her thoughts, Zenris replied, "My apologies, once more, for the state of my quarters."

A nervous quiver broke through his smile as Zenris moved to tackle the clothing on the floor. It wouldn't do him any good to be left alone in his state.

"Let me help you," Evelot said.

"What?"

"Look, I understand that you 'gentlemen' have your codes and all, but if anything, let me try to help you with the room."

His laugh trembled. "I dare not trouble a fair lady with something beneath her."

"You ken where I live? My boots are mucky every day stepping out the barn." Evelot shook her head. "And for another thing, we're a team, aye?"

He paused, wee thoughts churning under the surface of his charismatic mask. It wasn't as if she was in it for a snoop—or Goddess forbid, his trousers—but she couldn't go on only feeling sorry for the poor bastard. They'd been through hells and back, and she'd been in the same state ages ago. It was the least she could do.

After ruminating, Zenris cheerily said, "If the lady

insists."

They set to work in the cramped room, organizing piles and airing out the bedsheets. Evelot left him to the clothing, and he entrusted her with the desk. She made sure not to peruse any of the writing again as she evenly stacked loose parchment. Thankfully, there were actual paperweights to use instead of half-dried inkwells and quills. She reopened the window to a damp breeze carrying through the alley, the scent of baker's goods and spices in tow.

When all was done, Zenris's smile dazzled with approval. He observed their work and acknowledged her with a dip of his head.

"Thank you, my lady," he said. "This would have been quite the challenge without a fellow companion."

"*Companion.*" A pang of disappointment caught Evelot off guard. She was sure that was what they were, companions. But the feeling told her otherwise. If not that, what exactly had she expected him to call her?

Whatever was coming over her, she wouldn't bother him with it.

Smiling, Evelot said, "You're welcome, as long as you remember to eat, eh?"

His smile waned, and she supposed her invitation was worn. Evelot moved to leave, reaching for the window frame.

"Evelot?"

She glanced back over at Zenris.

"You are aglow with optimism. More so than the norm," he said. When Evelot furrowed her brows quizzically at him, he added, "'Tis a lovely thing on you."

She tried for a frown, but she couldn't hide the amusement on her lips. "Thought there was going to be a catch."

Zenris chuckled under his breath. "Nothing of the sort from your honest, humble bard."

"Hmm." Evelot turned back to him and leaned against the wall. Then she asked, "Is that bad? Me being different for a change?"

"On the contrary. Such optimism could inspire many a thing."

"How's about inspiring a certain someone?"

A mischievous grin teased his lips. "And who might this individual be?"

"Someone who's been feeling sorry for himsel' for the past few days," Evelot said softly. She peeked up at Zenris. "As a 'companion,' I think it's time to put the past aside and do something else now, even if it's ridiculous, aye?"

Evelot tried to think of an idea to give him. If writing on all that paper or playing instruments wasn't inspiring him, then he had to start elsewhere. So, she blurted out, "Come on a daunder with me tomorrow."

"Pardon?" Zenris said.

"What you call a 'strr-oll,'" she answered in a fake Elvish accent. "I mean it. Come find me at the outskirts of the festival grounds. I'll sit under one of the trees and wait all day if I have to. Regale me with all your stories of grandiose adventures and harrowing romances. Just get some fresh air."

It felt like the sun was directly on her when he lit up with a grin. Whatever that arse had done to make his teeth sparkle or the locks of his hair frame his half-lidded eyes, it made her heart skip a beat. Her lips pulled into a frown, and she felt flustered that he had caught her off guard then of all times.

"Very well. 'Tis a promise," Zenris replied.

Evelot awkwardly nodded as she reached behind her for the window frame. Her arm flailed in midair for a second before she latched on and summoned the vines closer. She almost forgot the window box's state. A lack of mana may have made her swoon with exhaustion after shrinking her ladder back into the ground, but journeying home, she struggled to walk at the thought of his damned smile.

True to her word, Evelot settled herself under a shaded tree the next morning, watching the view of the developing festival. Oddly enough, the hollers and sounds of construction created static noise that helped her to absorb her notes. But even while scribbling them from her collegiate textbook into her tome, there was something keeping her from full concentration.

While she tried to fall asleep the previous night, that tricky "companion" nonsense had reared its ugly head, and now it kept up into the day. Her cheeks burned and her heart skipped when his smile reappeared. Maybe it was all the songs he sang about passion and freedom that finally broke her down. She didn't want to become a bashful eejit, but it wasn't all bad. There was a calmness to being beside him that inspired her hope for change.

If only it was easy to remember that he'd be leaving

after the festival when he gave her something to smile about.

Her hand had been cramped around a quill too long, and a grumble echoed from her stomach. Evelot sat up against the tree and huffed. The only signs of life nearby were the lumberers and stall owners. Wherever Zenris skulked, it wasn't anywhere close to her. Luckily for her and her tome of trusty spells, she wouldn't have to leave her spot for food. Evelot raised her good hand to the apple tree's branch above and closed her eyes. In a blink and a whispered spell, one of its ripe fruit dangled there, ready to fall into her palm.

She reached up—

Another hand snatched it. Evelot gaped up at the tree branch where the bard triumphantly bit into her breakfast.

"A pleasant morn to you, my fair lady," he greeted after a swallow. "Or mayhap I should say 'a good midday'?"

"How long have you been sitting there?" Evelot said. "No sound or whiff of you came past me at all!"

"Not long, I assure you. There is much of Goldencrest to observe and too many faces to see. Especially the radiant one sitting below me."

Evelot hid her embarrassment with a pout. "Och, no," she grumbled. "You've managed to hide away from all your fans."

"Ah, no, no, no. Not hiding. Merely enjoying the shade from a certain, unnoticeable angle," Zenris said, peeking out at the festival grounds.

"A roundabout way of saying 'hiding.'"

Zenris harrumphed. With cat-like grace, he landed beside her and leaned in to glimpse her tome. A panic seized her, seeing him that close. But it quickly faded, leaving Evelot pondering another matter to distract from her reaction.

"How'd you do that?" she asked.

"Do what?" he said.

"Get past me. Was it some sorta bardic spell?"

"Ah, that." Zenris snuck in another bite before answering, "'Tis a wonderful thing to have elven heritage when one requires stealth in the wilderness. Unfortunately, 'tis not a magic that can be replicated."

"Suppose not. Then again, I've no reason to turn mysel' into a leaf."

Zenris laughed aloud. "I assure you 'tis more complex than that."

Before Evelot could ask, Zenris peeked down at her tome again. "Care to share any of your latest studies?"

"Wouldn't have thought you had an interest in Acluethan plants," she said.

"Indeed, I do, as a being of nature itself. Would you care to test the mettle of my mind as a demonstration?"

Evelot laughed, pulling her tome to her chest. "Maybe I will, then. Tell me, bard: What's the color of the veins of the Qaras?"

"If you mean to say the large, sentient plant-monster that prefers one's backside, I recall it having blue veins."

"You ken the tea leaves found in the northern region of Waswayu?" she asked.

"Mm, I know it well. The Uchuy Achkiy is light-bodied with a hint of spice afterward."

"You eejit!" Evelot laughed. "You've been holding out on me!"

Zenris cheekily smiled. "Ask and you shall receive, as they say. Yet I see more than one tome here."

"Aye. I was studying my spells, but had to take a

break," Evelot said.

"No athame or cauldron required for this sort of practice?"

"Not unless I'm willing to lose the pot." Evelot pointed to a wee dirt mound in the grass in front of them and explained, "Trying to sprout a new seed from the loam. Hasn't blossomed yet."

"I see. Quite the shame," Zenris said. He picked out a seed from the core of his eaten apple and held it up to the light.

"In my youth, my mother taught me of the elements and nature. Amongst the Elven Pantheon, the gods and goddesses influence all forms of life by different means. The apple tree, for example, is a symbol of the Handmaid, servant of Our Lady of the Wilds, the Forest Matron. The Handmaid tends to the Eternal Forests' orchards and worshippers bearing their own fruit, quenching all's thirst. As the sustenance of all, one must correctly. . . pray. . ."

Zenris closed his palm around the seed. Shutting his eyes, he breathed words that sounded gibberish in Evelot's ear. When he opened his hand and eyes, a small bubble of water floated up.

"Would you care to do the honors?" Zenris asked her.

"Wha—? Like, hold out my hands?" Evelot said.

Zenris nodded, and Evelot gingerly obeyed. The bubble acted like a droplet of water sliding off his hand, yet it rolled to a stop above her palm. Faintly, she heard a wee sigh come from the mana within it, different from the breathy sound her vines made. The water jostled as she moved to kneel before the planted seed in the dirt. She dipped her hand toward it, and the water slowly absorbed into the earth.

A flash of pearly-blue light sparked up from underground. A second of silence passed, and then, a little stalk of green emerged. Its point curved and swelled into a leaf.

When Evelot glanced back at Zenris over her shoulder, his boastful grin stretched ear to ear.

"All right, bard," Evelot said with a laugh. "What else you got for me?"

"Come now, the lady did all the work. I know not what you speak of," he said, though his smile was unconvincing.

"As you say."

"Of course, mayhap it the time to make good on my promise?" he asked.

"And what's that?" Evelot said.

Zenris stood on his feet and offered his hand. "Why, to 'regale you with my tales of grandiose adventures,' naturally."

Evelot chuckled. She should've expected such a quip from him, though it was nice to see he hadn't forgotten her request. But she was glad to see him smiling again.

Putting her hand in his, Evelot rose to her feet. She stumbled for a second, enough for Zenris to reach around and put his hand on her back. Evelot tried to warn him, but she felt the little lump in her hood squeak in alarm. Zenris jolted back.

"Was that—?" he said.

"Aye. It's all right."

Evelot reached over her shoulder and patted at Jammer. The wee bat chittered and scuffled about, frustrated someone had woken her. She popped her head out on Evelot's shoulder, chastising Zenris with angry clicks that pierced Evelot's ear.

Stroking her head, Evelot cooed, "He didn't mean it. You'll be fine, my wee beauty."

Zenris tried for a smile only for Jammer to turn her plump, furry buttocks at him and scuttle back into the safety of Evelot's hood.

"May she swiftly recover," Zenris said apologetically.

"Aye, she will. Just a wee bit spooked, is all. You ready for that daunder?"

Zenris nodded, offering his arm. Evelot chuckled at the gesture, but took it all the same. Together they left behind the apple tree and seedling and cut through the festival grounds to the outskirts of town. Avoiding the crowded streets, Zenris told her of orc clans swarming his camp in the dead of night and treks on the highways, stories that made her heart race excitedly.

It wasn't until Zenris stopped on the slope of a hill that she realized how far they'd gone. The land past the right of the farmer's path cascaded with strands of long golden grass and wildflowers, the nippy wind caressing them with a gentle breeze. That soft sound mingled with that of her dafty heartbeat. The view encapsulated all that Goldencrest was named for, worthy of all the praise and admiration. While it usually calmed her, Evelot couldn't stop thinking of life outside of town. Or of Zenris's smile finally meeting the light in his eyes like the sun's reflection on the Beinn. His shoulders relaxed with an awed breath, and he turned to her with a merry expression. He asked her something she didn't catch, but she nodded anyway. Her heart was singing too loudly to hear.

However erratic its beat, Evelot didn't mind at all.

Chapter Nineteen

Marvelous, the new day was. The mounted sun bade Zenris warmth amidst the chill autumnal season, and a view as spectacular as 'twas several days prior. Not only was this the perfect weather for a stroll but also a distraction from Goldencrest's populace.

He slipped through the shadows of town, his lute in hand as he trekked the well-trodden path up the hill and breached the top of the incline. Zenris peered through the wild long grass to his right, wavering in the soft wind. The reed-like stalks enveloped him into their secret world of sweet, earthy musk. Dipping his head under the surface, Zenris braced his lute and pack close to his chest.

An orangish-red flashed through the veil of pale gold and green, and a smile crept across his lips. Zenris followed the sound of a turning page until he stood a little ways behind her. She flipped through her tome, facing the receding grass and the decline into the moorlands of purple heather. The wind teased her sunlit hair, coaxing the long grass with it. Those pompous stalks flaunted how easily they raked through her tresses and dared to caress her cheek, and oh, how he wished to do the same.

Ever since the pair had discovered this hidden

basking spot, Zenris's every minute with her was a dream. She had stolen away from her duties to share in conversation and practice her spells. The traces of her smile had embedded in his memory, and her laughter was as refreshing as crisp air in his lungs. That wit of hers seized his heart in ecstasy. He was enchanted, surely, yet she had not used her witchcraft to capture him.

Carefully, he raised his lute. He then belted out, "*She'll cause thee to strip thy braies—*"

Evelot's head whipped back at him and she let out a sharp gasp. She tried to smother her laughter under her palm, yet Zenris saw plenty. He lifted his hands in surrender, chuckling as he lowered to her side.

"I apologize. Have I offended the lady?" he laughed.

"You nearly sent me off to the Maiden's Fields!" she said, sobering.

"Ah, but there lies the trick. To catch a beauty off guard is the remedy for dull work."

Evelot shook her head in bemused disbelief. Noticing his pack hanging from his side, she asked, "What's that you got there?"

Zenris grinned, seating himself on the ground. From his traveling pack, he withdrew a clean towel torn atwain. He hid the tavern's inscription on his own half and offered the plainer strip to her.

"I wish to make amends with Jammer for the previous rude awakening. Though long has it been since my last words with her kind, I am confident I have something of use for her."

"Is that right?" asked Evelot.

From her hood, a squat, furred face peeked out at

him. Jammer's eyes kept shut, save for the minute squint that deepened the perpetual frown below her thick forehead. Now that she was in plain sight, Zenris focused on her. The necessary spell ached in his eardrums and jaw, his own price to pay for neglecting to use it. He spent a fraction of his energy and mana to sift through Jammer's trills and clicks, until finally he pieced together a semblance of speech.

Warmth, complained Jammer. *Momma not give. Need warmth. Tired.*

"Would you care for an extra layer, little one?" Zenris asked.

With shut eyes, Jammer barked, *Who? Where? Where?*

He held out the cloth to Evelot's shoulder where a quivering Jammer tried to climb out into the chill. Her nose touched the fabric, and her clawed little hand squeezed at it.

New. New. Thick. Need warmth.

"Yes, your warmth is here," Zenris cooed.

Warmth.

Jammer scuttled onto the cloth over his palm, tucking her wings into her sides. Zenris gently wrapped her inside the fabric, until only her head was visible. He heard her little mutterings of *Tired. Tired. Momma.* before she fell silent, and the little bat nestled into her new bed.

Zenris smiled, handing over the small bundle to Evelot. She watched him in amazement. "What's it like, being attuned to nature as an elf?" she asked.

Zenris had to collect his thoughts before answering, "I imagine it as a second heartbeat. Its passions and thralls coalesce and divide from your own at whim. Do you know of this same connection?"

"I dinnae ken. You could say it's more like patter with your friend than anything. But with what you can do, you might have a fair chance at taking up witchcraft."

"I fear my heart could not bear the weight of another occupation," Zenris said. "My hands would ache to write lyrics. My mind would be filled only with music as I toiled at a cauldron."

"Suppose I can see that."

"And what of yourself, my lady?"

"What about me?" Evelot asked with a quizzical brow.

"How would you see yourself faring in another occupation?"

Evelot smiled bemusedly. "Like if I sang and danced with a lute or something? Created lyrics like I'm plucking them out of thin air?"

"Only in experience can you be certain," Zenris said, grinning.

"I-I don't have that kind of talent." Evelot busied herself with cradling little Jammer to her chest.

"As if the courageous Witchling of the Choille were to yield to simple practice."

"Is that a challenge, bard?" Evelot said in mock defiance.

"Not so," Zenris answered. "Here. A demonstration before the real challenge, my lady."

He took up his lute and placed his hands accordingly, moving to sit in front of her. When Zenris looked back up, he said, "Would you grant your bard a word that comes to mind?"

Flustered, Evelot looked around. She peeked up at

the sky and replied, "Ah. . . b-blue."

Zenris strummed slowly, singing, "*You grew so blue, a sad, sad hue. 'Twas true, on your cheek, that melancholy dew.*"

There was an air of humor about her when Zenris finished.

"Gold?" she asked.

"*Untold treasure was it foretold. This golden idol, one I could not hold. This tale it doth remain of old.*"

Her eyes lingered on him as his hands rested over the instrument. The smile on her lips gave way to mesmerization, bringing sunlight to that verdant stare. He wished to know if 'twas that same sensation calling him to her.

"Green," she said.

Zenris withheld a grin, already taking inspiration from the view before him. In careful measure, he sang, "*Her eyes, evergreen, oh that serene gleam. 'Twould forever linger in my heart so keen. O'er mountains and oceans between, ne'er would there be a color as pristine.*"

"All right, bard," Evelot said with a laugh. "Maybe I'll start with the lute, if you teach me?"

Were it his soul or his lute she asked for, he happily began by offering his lady the latter.

Once she tucked little Jammer into her hood, Evelot delicately held the lute and watched him mimic the chords. Her enthusiasm slowly morphed into hesitancy as she followed along. She plucked away at the strings with as much grace as a three-legged fox. Zenris chided himself. In the stupor of his fascination, he had nearly forgotten that she was still a novice.

"May I?" he asked, moving behind her.

Evelot nodded. His arms hovered around her, his hands ready to guide hers over the lute's neck.

"When you play, you play with the instrument," he instructed. "If you are tense, so too, will be the chord."

"Right." Evelot took a breath and loosened her limbs.

Zenris then cradled her right hand in his palm. "With this hand," he explained, "your palm is a nest, and your thumb part of the flock."

"There's not just one bird? One finger to use?" Evelot said.

"If you prefer. However, 'tis far from exciting."

With that, Zenris guided her fingers over the chords. A continuous melody sung from under their hands.

"Well, I can play it one-handed now," she chuckled.

"Oh? You have yet to take flight with the birds," said Zenris.

His hand fell to her forearm. Slowly, he led it up and down the strings, her fingers still plucking away as instructed. With his other hand on hers to hold the notes, he heard his first melody in their practice. It had been when his father stood over him and lectured him through the process. Where there was frustration, there was also love. Oh, those blissful notes of blossoming love for the craft. How shameful to have ceased recalling such splendor. Yet, to know that Evelot could experience it, there was nothing grander.

Having recited their quick tune, Evelot glanced back at him. Her smile rendered his heart useless so swiftly, its rhythm fluttered a beat too long. When those pale lips of hers moved, uttering faint words in his ear, his stomach tensed. Zenris could have drifted on the winds without a concern.

First the grass, and then her lashes that brushed her

cheeks. His jealousy knew no bounds. Zenris was certain he could caress her with better reverence than them. He could sing impassioned melodies in her ear, more lovely than the dull tune the grass rendered. If she so wished it, he could kiss her ceaselessly until that smile forever resided on her lips. All he had to do was ask.

The world tilted as he felt himself carefully leaning in. Evelot stayed rooted in his arms, her lips parted as her eyes drifted closed.

"Evelot!"

The sound of crunching grass above startled Zenris. He peered over the long grass, catching the figure of a young boy looking out from the incline. Whomever it was had yet to notice him. How strange that the boy had several features in common with—

Evelot rose, grumbling to herself. "What's going on, you eejit?" she replied.

The boy looked down at them. First, he met her gaze and then locked eyes with Zenris. Then he glanced back at Evelot. His jaw fell open.

"Tonlin!" snapped Evelot.

"D-Da!" He pointed up the path. "He needs another hand. Says it's important!"

Evelot cursed under her breath and loosed a small sigh.

"I'm sorry," she said to Zenris. "I have to go. Same time tomorrow here, aye?"

Disappointment flooded Zenris. It was too soon to end the day there. He yearned for more time, a second more if possible.

"My lady," Zenris quickly replied. "Why. . . not I go

with you?"

"What?" both siblings said in unison. Evelot frowned up at her brother, who was still present.

"I have taught you the lute. Would it not be a fair exchange by learning your ways of... however 'tis you farm?" Zenris asked.

Evelot dared not hide her astonishment. "You'd want to thresh wheat for the day? It's tasking, mind you."

Zenris grinned, displaying his sturdy arms. "I imagine it to be no different from fighting beasts in the wild."

"I thought he just played tunes for parties?" Tonlin said.

"Now he's going to help us with the wheat," Evelot snapped back at him. "Go and tell Da he'll have enough hands."

Tonlin gaped at them a moment longer before jogging up the path toward their farmstead. Evelot huffed.

"Something amiss, my lady?" Zenris teased.

"I—well, no, it's not that. Never you mind." With another sigh, she then asked, "Are you ready, then?"

"As you are, my lady."

E agerness proved to be a threat to his pride. Zenris was slow to learn the reason for Evelot's hesitancy. At first he assumed 'twas because of his status. After all, he was an idolized bard with never a speck of dirt on his pristine hands and coiffed hair. He attempted to prove himself by diving straight into his task of combing stalks of wheat for their grain. After numerous rounds of separation and grinding the seeds into flour, his hands were sore and he feared the inability to hold his lute on stage. 'Twas a relief he had until the morrow to recover from the burning ache in his muscles.

When the moment arrived for a break, Zenris collapsed against an old apple tree in their garden, his gaze turned to the dusty-rose sky.

"Tired yet?"

Evelot knelt beside him with a pitcher of water. Her smile did wonders for his exhaustion.

"I give in, my lady," he said. "In competition, your lessons were most arduous."

"And for the loser, you seem more pleased," she replied.

"My mind and body have simply been humbled, is all."

"Too humbled to replenish itsel'?"

Zenris sat up and accepted the pitcher, taking gulps until he nearly choked. He would have slept peacefully upon the ground then and there had it not been for Evelot. Instead, he grinned back at her, handing over her property.

"Thank you," he said.

Evelot furrowed a brow. "What for?"

"For allowing me to accompany you."

"You were persistent," she said before imbibing from the pitcher.

"Ah, and what a satisfactory outcome it permitted me."

"Aye, if hours lapsed toiling in wheat and sweaty

clothing were a victory," she deadpanned.

"'Tis true. Otherwise, a maiden would have suffered as such, unable to enjoy this view of the even."

There was a battle on her lips betwixt a disdainful frown and a shy grin. The latter proved victorious, all the more rewarding for Zenris. Though the day's work had worn on her, and her voice had become hoarse from shouting instructions over the millstone, he reveled at the laugh lines cupping her smile.

A squawk sounded from Jammer tucked into Evelot's hood, and he watched her flap away for food. Then Zenris leaned in and asked, "With the work now fulfilled, how will the maiden bide her time?"

"This 'hypothetical' maiden, you mean?" she said.

"Unless there is another maiden in Goldencrest with hair like new copper and a songbird's voice?"

"If that's true, you've got some explaining to do, bard," Evelot teased.

Zenris's heart raced at her wit, her proximity. He dared to nudge closer before replying, "Sing, dance, fly—if all for her answer would the bard do so."

"I recall a certain someone asking about dancing at a festival. I wonder. . ."

It appeared as though her answer were there on her tongue, but another interrupted them from the back door.

Her mother, Helga, approached and Zenris sat up straight. They may have shared only a few words prior to the work, yet she was a gentle soul who commanded etiquette. Not in the way she acted, nor spoke, but by her smile and meek demeanor that inspired humility. To Zenris, those were the same traits his mother once had before taking to her sickbed.

"Ma?" Evelot said.

"Dinner's nearly ready. Are the two of you joining us?" her mother asked.

Evelot peeked at Zenris with a nervous glance. "I-I didn't. . ."

Helga smiled at Zenris. "Of course, you're welcome to stay and eat. It's a pleasure to have another face at the table, especially one that worked the day."

"I. . ."

Zenris could not recall the last time he sat down with a large company to enjoy a meal. Not immediately, at least. His memories of such occasions were bittersweet, as he had left his party on an uncertain note. The circumstances had soured the ale, and the hearty soup had been bland. Such distasteful memories were meant to be replaced.

"If you would have me, that is, I would be delighted," he said. "'Tis not imposing on my part?"

"Not at all."

Unlike Evelot, Helga radiated with her smile, a wondrous thing that reminded him of an early morning in spring.

To her daughter, Helga said, "Go on, then. We've another plate to set."

Zenris sprung to his feet before Evelot. He offered an arm to her. Without complaint, she took it, garnering a chuckle from her mother.

"Well, it seems chivalry isn't only for knights," said Helga.

"Right you are, madam," Zenris replied. "And it does not discriminate." Zenris then offered his other arm to Helga.

She accepted with a jovial laugh that carried from the garden into the house as the three entered sideways through the back door.

Inside, the women abandoned Zenris to scour their cupboards for an extra set of utensils. Off to the side, he studied the interior of the home, finding it constricted, yet quaint. The extravagance of many inns and mansions were appealing in their own right, but Zenris had realized how isolating they were. The Wheaton home offered comforts that no amount of lacquered wood or fresh linens could parallel: the smell of a homemade meal, the tenderness of family. The thought aroused the memory of his party, causing Zenris to pause somberly.

The boards overhead creaked as Tonlin hustled down the stairs. A child-like squealing resounded from the front entrance before another three saw themselves in. More blood relatives, Zenris surmised, based on the similar point of the nose as his fair Evelot's. Yet the two other men after them appeared different. One he had only spied in passing; he was hairy and proud like an orc. That individual assuredly was Evelot's brother-in-law. The other Zenris recalled he had seen previous. His fair hair and set jaw—it was the man from the smithy.

Both men carried themselves into the room with the dignity of hardened laborers proud of their craft. As Evelot and Helga invited Zenris to a seat, the others finally laid eyes upon him. Never had Zenris come across others whose scrutiny had frightened him so.

"Good even, sirs," Zenris said, flourishing with a bow. "My lady, and little sir."

Both men glanced at one another before peering

back at him. Outwardly, Zenris maintained his composure. Inwardly, he heard the beating of war drums approaching.

"Were we expecting company, Helga?" Evelot's father asked.

"Of course, lovey. This is the kind gentleman who helped mill the flour," she chided, passing him by.

"Zenris Aspenheart. Honored to meet the head of the Wheaton household," Zenris greeted.

"Aye," Sir Wheaton grumbled.

Evelot's father regarded him curiously before taking his seat at the head of the table. The other man put a protective hand on Evelot's sister, Ulleh, and deflated in irritation. While everyone took their seats, the latter was far from discreet in his observations of Zenris. His scrutiny led Zenris to assume he was a magic wielder as well—one with the ability to make strangers squirm.

Placed beside Evelot on a creaky bench, Zenris sat with the family. Her sister's line marveled at their small feast from the table's opposite side. The smell of roast and vegetables permeated the air. Zenris saw it in the boy's salivation how hungered they were. His stomach would have been as verbal, if the smell had not dissuaded him. At the sight of the braised skin of a hearty chicken, a trickle of panic set in. He hoped the proud men in company would find it in their hearts to be understanding as he avoided the main course. To add to his troubles, he had not noticed as the family folded their hands together, and he faltered in mimicking their prayer.

Finally, bread was broken, and servings produced for each plate. To his relief, there were stewed potatoes and steaming peas to add to his meager meal.

As Zenris ate, the eyes of a curious little fellow observed him. Evelot's nephew reached for his mother's sleeve.

"Ma," he said in a stage whisper, "why don't he eat the chooks?"

Ulleh glanced at Evelot who signaled for her sister to stop him. Though the mother mouthed an apology and encouraged the boy to eat his meal, he simply ignored the gesture.

"Don't you like chooks?" he asked Zenris directly.

Zenris laughed nervously. "Of course. But I would rather they be clucking and roosting than on my plate."

The boy confusedly blinked at him before filling his cheeks with food. Compared to whispers of century-old falsities, 'twas a pleasant change of pace.

"So," Ulleh said. "Sir Aspenheart, how are you liking Goldencrest so far?"

"Very much so. It has a certain charm that many would appreciate," he answered.

"And the inn's satisfactory?"

"Absolutely. One of the better ones I have patronized thus far."

"I'd been curious mysel' what it was like, sleeping in a poster bed," Ulleh said. "I hear they're quite soft."

Zenris smiled. "A tier above a bed of leaves. Yet there is the price of a few duck feathers prodding your backside through the night."

His joke garnered a chuckle out of Ulleh. Zenris's jovial feeling returned, only to cower away at the leer on the brother-in-law's face.

"How many inns have you frequented before?" asked

the brother-in-law.

"Alas, I have not the answer. Too many to count, is the problem," Zenris laughed.

"You don't say? Suppose it was all the *merry-making* that got to you, then?" the other said distastefully.

Zenris's smile abated. "I should think not. As a public figure, and a member of an adventuring party, there are always patrons that do not take well to our presence. One would hope to be sober to either bask in the easy triumphs of our bodyguard warrior or discover their larger, stronger friend and flee to safer ground."

"And you associate with a party that antagonizes others?"

The man might as well have accused Zenris himself of being the "ill" sort of people. With an eager flutter in his heart, Zenris answered, "You know of our decorated warrior Prilthadollak, yet I am sure you have not prevailed to learn of our full ensemble. There is the quick hand of our operations, Maio, who needs not but air to unbind you from the imprisonment of the sadistic Silver Claw orc clan and pluck you from a lava pit a breath before impact. The diffident cleric, Nut, whose boundless knowledge and medicinal techniques can recover lost limbs and souls. And certainly not least, our swordsman captain, the Heiser Graymore, champion of Esmora who defended the Oglen borders from raiders at the ripe age of nine. Together, we—"

How troublesome. Zenris then realized they lacked a group name, even after all their years of traveling together.

"Well, names aside, our quest is noble, worthy of a thousand tales and accolades!"

The brother-in-law clucked his tongue, having no

response to him. Cockily, Zenris felt his chest rise. To know that the man's wife chuckled under her breath at him solidified his pride, yet 'twas Evelot's lingering smile that ruined him.

"It sounds like you have the best of adventures," Helga said.

Her husband scrutinized her with a squinting eye, and Helga added, "Don't you think so? Meeting new people, seeing what's outside?"

"Hear! Hear!" Zenris lifted his cup in a serious toast to the lady of the house.

She raised her cup as if in jest. It appeared no one else would join until Evelot elevated her cup.

"You think it, too, Evelot?" Ulleh asked.

"Don't act like you wouldn't want to adventure, Ulleh," Evelot said with a chuckle.

Ullch laughed aloud, joining them.

"He's right." Tonlin raised his own cup with a slightly trembling hand, heat aflush in his cheeks. "To an adventure, however small!" he said.

Surrounded by the family's laughter, Ulleh's son attempted the same. His cup made it to his brow before toppling onto the food. Family members scrambled to fix the table and pass around rags. On their feet, Zenris and Evelot gave aid. When their eyes met, neither withheld a shared chuckle. Anxiety had relinquished him then as suddenly as the boy had relinquished the contents of his cup.

O nce dinner had been served, and a curiously delicious "Ecclefechan tart" offered, Zenris stood on the porch. He waded in the chill night, his stomach plenty full for the small trek back to his bed. Evelot's sister and family had retired to put their son to sleep. Towering high above, the moon demanded that he rest. Zenris heeded not its demands. If he kept in Evelot's home another minute, 'twould be another minute outside of his reality.

"Aspenheart."

Zenris turned. To his shock, Evelot's father approached him from the main hall. There was a stoic air surrounding him, leaving Zenris alert on the chance he would need an escape.

"Yes, Sir Wheaton?" he said.

The farmer held his fist out, with a small pouch hanging from it. "Your wage, for an honest day's work."

"I. . . Thank you," Zenris said, accepting the pouch.

Good conscience would have him refuse it if 'twere not for Pril's previous warnings of earning his keep. When he pocketed the coin, Tarod nodded, and a beat of awkward silence passed betwixt them. The man seemed to struggle for words, judging by his frown and parted lips. Zenris decided to wait. Then, wordlessly, the head of the house walked away. Zenris remained bereft of speech.

Sparing no curiosity for her father, Evelot approached Zenris. Her budding smile coaxed a grin of his own that created an ache in his cheeks.

She stopped before him, smelling of rosemary. "How was it, the dinner?"

"Perfect," he replied, unsure of the night or her countenance he was referring to.

"As if it ever is with that shite, Yahir."

Zenris shook his head. "If I were to be offended by every impertinent inquisitor, I would have not the time to write songs."

Evelot smiled. "All right, bard."

Exhaustion wore at the corner of her lips, the same fatigue that had stolen his energy. Zenris deflated and accepted his fate.

"I fear I must bid you a good night, my lady," he said.

She nodded in dismay. "Thank you for being here. It was nice. . . having you around."

"Of course. Should you require a bard to join in another eventful supper, I am at your beck and call."

A strained silence hung over them, one that carried the weight of many unspoken thoughts. Were it possible, his words would have no leash. He would speak of the way her calloused hands felt in his palms, how her laughter held more melody than any of his compositions, how her presence alone comforted him. Alas, he was at an impasse. No word could encapsulate the feeling he held, none that he could summon to mind. For his sake, and hers, 'twas better to remain silent until the time was right.

Zenris bowed before taking his first steps into the night. A heavy sigh escaped him. That moment would have been most opportune if the fates had not captured his tongue, subjecting him to appear the oaf.

"Zenris!"

He turned around to find Evelot slipping out of the house. Over the muddy path, she hurried. Zenris's heart leapt when her boot slid out from under her. He reached out, catching her before a horrendous fall. When he pulled her to her feet, Evelot laughed, staring at him in disbelief.

"My lady, what troubles you?" he asked with a chuckle. A delightful spark of heat raced up to his shoulders as she kept hold of his arms.

"I have your answer, from earlier," she said.

"Oh?" Zenris had nearly forgotten his teasing proposition in the garden.

"I'll go with you and maybe dance, if you teach me more of the lute. Sound like a plan?" she asked.

Elation left him speechless. He kicked himself internally and said, "'Twould be my greatest pleasure, Evelot."

"Meet me tomorrow, then."

He nodded, unable to utter another word. The wind teased at her hair, and a jubilant glint in her eyes brightened her smile. Such a beguiling sight.

Zenris assumed then he could turn and leave, save whatever pride was left for him. However, she tilted toward him. His body stiffened. Then, a warmth drew across his cheek where her lips pressed a gentle kiss. The dawn could have risen and he would not have felt one ray of its comforting heat. Not to the degree those precious lips had granted him. Exhilaration pounded through him. He knew not why his body reacted in such a way, only that he did not fight back against the wordless thoughts of ecstasy racing through his mind.

His hand extended to her as she backed away, and he quickly retrieved it before she was the wiser.

"G'night, Zenris," Evelot said.

He suspected he smiled at her from the way she withheld a laugh. Evelot raised a hand and waved goodbye.

His own rose partially in the air, though moments later. Unable to turn away, Zenris stumbled backward on the chance she might bequeath him another kiss from her delicate lips. Alas, the only thing awaiting him was a discarded wagon wheel that caught his boot. Zenris toppled over backward, slamming into the ground. Yet there was no pain. No sound of little Jammer as she flapped above him, nor the sensation of her warm body flattening atop his forehead. Only the imprint of Evelot's kiss remained, and his heart was alight like a melodious choir in his chest.

Chapter Twenty

It wasn't the chill weather that made Evelot's hand quiver on Zenris's arm.

Taking to the main square on a bright day, Evelot perused through the shops with her companion. All around there were whispered conversations not of the witchling in her tattered, old cloak, but of a warmly dressed bonnie lass stealing smiles from their bard. It sounded like a compliment at first, but the longer the two went on, the more the other lasses' stares bore a hole into her head.

Regardless of the gossip surrounding her meager peasant dress and subpar braided hair, Evelot couldn't find it in herself to be bothered. Not when a half-elf bard watched her with a cockeyed grin and an attentiveness worthy of envy. It left her to wonder which made her more nervous: the lasses' ire or Zenris's devout attention.

They stopped between two corner stalls in the square, the smell of fresh baked buns and honeycombs masking the rank of the alleyway beside them. His fingers brushed across her wrist and gathered her hands in a gentle grasp. Evelot tried for a smile as her breath caught in her throat. She wanted to slap his hands away for making a thrill go up her spine, or kiss his cheek in revenge.

"Are you content, my lady?" Zenris asked.

"What do you mean?" she said.

He gestured to the town, saying, "'Tis a week that has passed us this way, strolling in town and spiriting away to the fields. Is there truly nothing else you would rather do?"

"W-well, I figure to take you round the parts that aren't rank. Unless you're up for carving into neeps and"— Evelot scrunched her nose—"pumpkins."

"My lady, not even on an excursion to the Esmoran wastes would I fret. Not when in your company," Zenris replied. "In truth, I wonder if this is becoming monotonous."

Evelot stalled with a coy look. "What? You wanting another adventure gallivanting in the Choille?"

"There is the possibility of joining me on stage tonight," he teased.

Her muscles loosened as she laughed in relief. "Ach, as if there's a chance in the hells!"

"You have proven yourself in practice, I assure you!"

Evelot fiddled with her hood, thinking about the times she'd tried and sounded more like a honking goose than a songstress. "I-I dinnae ken. . ."

"Ah, she waits for the right moment." Zenris grinned to himself before tapping her hand in acknowledgment. "Then I shall do the same."

A giggle left her. It was obviously in good fun, but her heart raced at the thought of standing on a brightly lit stage. Her comfort had increased in public, but the familiar icy chill of panic seized her when others watched her for too long. As if she could perform a song under that kind of pressure. For the time being, she would let Zenris lead the crowd with a magnificent spectacle.

Zenris's small smile stirred a nervous flutter in Evelot's chest. His hands hovered around hers, careful to close the distance. The previous times he'd done so ended with stolen moments: he would brush a lock of hair away, hold her hand for the briefest second. It was a rabbit chase to her. So thrilling, yet it always eluded her. It didn't matter if they were standing in the square. She wished for more of it, but also cowered away from acting on her feelings.

"I apologize," Zenris said, pulling her back to the present, "but I must step away a moment."

"O-of course."

Their hands fell back to their sides. The heat in her cheeks dissipated, replaced by the flutter in her chest. An urge to reach for him was almost overwhelming.

"Tarry you a while?" he asked.

Evelot nodded and gave him a small smile.

When Zenris headed toward the nearest storefront, Evelot's body went lax. She sat on a discarded crate, caressing her hands where his touch still lingered. He spoiled her that way. Whenever he looked at her—more than anyone had ever dared to—and when he smiled, it was a priceless gift. She felt more sure of herself, reaching the idea of what she wanted bit by bit. Maybe somewhere farther than Goldencrest was where her true self lied, and if it meant Zenris would be there, it wouldn't be so worrisome a thought.

But like all wax wings, they eventually melted. Their routine had become habitual, a daunder in the main square one day then picnicking in the fields the other. It was easier that way. It dissuaded Evelot from her wishes becoming too ambitious, and it kept the chaos of her feelings in check. She feared how much she was growing attached and the eventual impasse: Zenris would want for something bigger, and she didn't know if she could give it. Not when. . .

Walking through the finished festival grounds was a reminder that they'd soon wake from a melodic enchantment. Once their time was up, she didn't know what sort of reality they'd find themselves in.

It wasn't a reality she found herself willing to risk.

A scoff yanked Evelot from her thoughts. She looked to the booths that lined the main square ahead and frowned. Three men sidled closer to her, the ones she least expected to rear their ugly arses.

"Come to prey upon the innocent?" Piers said.

Evelot had promised to stay put, but she knew the alleys. It wouldn't take long to find her way back after losing the bastards. She moved toward the shadows, but Piers was quicker.

"Where do you think you're going, hag?" demanded Piers, gripping her arm. Her skin chilled under his grasp.

"Away," Evelot said. "Now get off."

"Back to your little friend, then? Don't think no one's noticed the way you ogle him."

She rolled her eyes. "You jealous?"

"What? Of some pompous lute strummer and his gaggle of stalkers? He's as much a nuisance as he is useless. But it's only a matter of time before he learns the truth."

"Get your hands off me," Evelot breathed.

Her heart raced while he kept hold. That icy panic tried to morph into mana on her fingertips, but Evelot couldn't manifest it, staring into those dark eyes of his.

"Come off it. Everyone knows why you marked him," Piers continued. As he spoke, he leaned in, his breath reeking of fish stew. "It's why you haven't fled for the woods. You want what the honest, moral people have: dignity and innocence, something that you'll never get back. Not after you sold it off for a few coins."

Evelot gritted her teeth. The other men with him chuckled at the inside joke.

With a sneer, he whispered, "Still struggling on that little dusty crop? Or do you get a thrill out of advertising the merchandise?"

The ice in her veins could've frozen over the entire duchy. She'd hated every minute of that wintery night. That was the night she'd lost her hopes of living honestly, when the seasonal cold somehow seeped into her skin and never let go.

Evelot stared down the alley, hoping, praying for an escape. Somewhere in the busy market square, Zenris was near. Either held up by fans or searching for her. Eventually he would find her. . .

No. She wouldn't ask to be saved. Zenris was clever, resourceful. So was she. Evelot tried to recount what he'd do in the moment, how he'd handle a threat that felt too large.

A gurgle of panicked laughter rose from Evelot's throat, and a wave of confusion passed over Piers and his lackeys. Taking advantage of the distraction, she grabbed her hand and tugged her arm out of Piers's grasp.

"You're pathetic," Evelot said. "As if you know who I am. After all the shite you've spewed these past few years, you haven't done as good a job to forget who you are!"

Her fear melted, and in its place a surge of energy

and the whispers of nature.

"You're worse than puke! You're a coward who sicced his dogs on me when my family was starving—all for your sick pleasures! I won't be ashamed of what I did, not anymore. So you can fuck off my arse, you manky bastard. But not before you admit that you're as guilty of fancying a witch as your ma!"

"Don't you dare mention that backstabbing who—"

With a sneer, he hurled his fist toward her. Whispers in her mind cried to a fever pitch; mana enveloped her body. With a gesture of her hands, the ground rumbled beneath their feet.

Weeds burst from between the cobblestones. Tendrils of vines stretched and grasped at the surface, latching onto anything within reach. Evelot watched as Piers and his lackeys turned pale. The other two scrambled into the safety of the square, but Piers merely stumbled back. Greenery tangled around his wrist, catching what Evelot's cheek would've. A yelp died in his throat.

Seeing him squirm, trying to cut his way out, should've given her justice. A feeling of relief that took the heavy weight from her shoulders. But it never came. Her body quaked, not from exertion of the spent mana, but for something unexplainable. While foliage wrapped tighter around Piers, prickles of doubt ensnared Evelot.

"Stop!"

A blurred figure rushed past Piers. Evelot glanced to the side. Zenris held his hand up, creeping closer to her.

"Evelot," Zenris said, the only thing he needed to say.

Her next breath was painful as she released it. One command, and the vine untangled Piers's arm. He bolted out of the alley, leaving Evelot and Zenris in the aftermath.

"Want to go," she said.

Zenris took her shaking hand. The earlier chill from Piers's hand melted away as they took off deeper into the alleyway.

Evelot didn't feel like herself until they'd trudged off the Beinn's path toward their hidden resting place. First returned was her wits and her senses, then came the realization of what she'd done. She had told Piers off for everything he'd put on her. If it weren't for an interruption, who knows what she might've done, or if she'd have the courage to do it. But that wasn't important anymore. Zenris's gentle hold anchored her in the sea of uncertainty filling her head. He didn't have to, but he held on as if it were second nature.

She hurt all the more for his kindness.

Their spot was below, a few paces away. Zenris led her closer, but her hand fell out of his. He turned back to her. Behind his braw smile sat a muddled mess of confusion and concern. There were too many things Evelot wanted to say. He'd seen a glimpse of what went on between Piers and her before his arrival. Evelot dared to wonder what he must've thought.

"Zenris," Evelot said, "I need to tell you something."

With a hesitant nod, he said, "Tell me."

She began with her magic, explaining how it had

hungrily circled around her fingers in her childhood years. How the other children laughed when she talked to the trees and plants as if they understood. A normal life wasn't in store for Evelot, but there was a yearning to be that twisted and bent like an old oak around her. It wasn't until after a handsome lad had promised acceptance in his bed, and brought her to Piers to aid her family, that her desire had withered into dust. No tears dribbled to her chin. Numbness fizzled in her chest till she finished. The past would never leave her, but she was grateful to have spoken her piece; that Zenris knew what he was involving himself with.

"Now that you know, I—erm. . . Well, I just didn't want to keep secrets from you," Evelot said.

Zenris didn't make a sound. Evelot thought she could say something else, but looking into his stupefied face only made it worse. She glanced away, but his gentle hand led her gaze back to him.

A smile sprouted on his face as he shook his head. "I am honored that you chose me as your confidant, Evelot."

The shape of him blurred; her vision clouded with tears that sprung up so quickly Evelot couldn't suppress them. Zenris laughed nervously as he brushed away the dew on her cheeks.

"My apologies. Have I misspoken somehow?" he said.

"N-no," Evelot said, and grinned with all the relief in her soul.

It was overwhelming to be comforted by him. The feel of his warm palms on her cheeks spurred her anxiety, but there was also relief. Someone had finally heard her, accepted her. That Zenris was the one who did spun her stomach into giddy knots.

Blinking away the last of her tears, Evelot gazed into his spring-green eyes. They fixed her where she stood, delight transporting her mind to a place where responsibilities and reason had no meaning. Where happiness looked exactly like him.

"Can I kiss you?" she heard herself ask.

Her whisper nearly carried off into the breeze. Zenris's lips parted in surprise. Evelot froze, horrified. If she had misinterpreted the moment—

A wee lopsided grin spread across his lips.

"To your heart's content," he said.

Her heart pounded excitedly. Before Evelot's eyes closed, she tentatively reached for his cheek. That eagerness pitter-pattered in her chest, calling for a stop. But she pushed through and closed the distance.

The warmth of his breath was a faint echo, his lips a full orchestral symphony. A sip of his lower lip turned into another, and another. She smiled against them, blissfully blind. Zenris's arms wrapped around her waist as he leaned in for more, his head tilted to capture the fullness of her kiss. The feel of his palms over her back sent pleasant shivers up to her throat, down to her curled toes.

She hadn't known it was exhilarating to hold someone until she held Zenris, and he her. All around her, she felt his embrace. It was overwhelming. Traces of mana trickled down to her calves like warm water, then to her feet. When Zenris pulled away, she heard him chuckle breathlessly.

"Evelot," he said.

She opened her eyes. His daft grin greeted her first before a gasp escaped her. Encircling them, a bed of red and gold marigolds pillowed stalks of sunflowers brushing against their knees. Evelot looked about the blossoms in Zenris's arms, flustered. But his hearty laugh brought her eyes back to his.

"Incredible," he breathed. With his eyes falling to her lips, Zenris added, "You are remarkable, Evelot."

"You wanting to make a field of flowers now, bard?" she replied.

"If you desire it so."

Evelot would've rolled her eyes, but in that moment, his eager smile coaxed a laugh from her. As whimsically as he'd given, she kissed him back and let the flowers unfurl at their feet.

Chapter Twenty-One

She could've ripped out her hair at that damned moment.

As the strands sank to her shoulders for the fifth time, Evelot huffed, scowling in the mirror. Her reflection— far from the enamored expression she'd worn the past few days—warped with frustration and worry. Time was ticking on the hour before the villager's Last Sunset, the precursor to Goldencrest's festival, and Zenris would be waiting for her.

Day after day of tender kisses in the fields had made Evelot mindlessly stumble through her chores. As she ran her fingers through her lifelessly dry hair, her countertop littered with random supplies, this time was no different.

She mentally kicked herself. She should've thought about her clothes beforehand.

"Are you done in there yet?" called Ulleh from outside. Without waiting, she turned the knob to the washroom door. "Yoo-hoo? Still alive?"

Evelot grumbled, dropping her arms. Ulleh stepped inside, locking eyes with her.

"What're you nervous about?" Ulleh asked.

"I'm fine," Evelot mumbled.

Ulleh sighed, stepping behind her. Evelot pressed against the counter of the sink, and the edge dug into her pelvis as she avoided squishing Ulleh and her swollen stomach. Her sister's chubby fingers wove through the flat strands of Evelot's hair as she twisted them into braided knots.

"I must be dreaming, seeing you dressing for a lad," Ulleh said. "Or for a cèilidh."

"What're you on about?" Evelot said, her pitch far from even.

"You don't just borrow my mirror for nothing. And how do you think there's a bairn in my womb? I had that same face in the reflection in my younger years."

Evelot sighed. There was no point in trying to fight it then. "How long have you been onto us?"

"Well, there's the town that can't shut it and all the lasses, too. And then there's womanly intuition telling me so."

Evelot hummed in thought.

"You been getting 'cozy' with him recently?" Ulleh asked.

At Ulleh's reflection, Evelot frowned in confusion.

Her sister laughed. "Must be a gentleman, then. I thought bards were notorious for sampling the village bachelors. But, you serious? No plucking at his 'lute' in the woods?"

"Ulleh!"

Her heart raced at the thought. Kisses were one thing, but imagining anything more would've created a shameful blush sure to give her away.

"Ach—fine."

Ulleh tied the main braid around the crown of

Evelot's head, then moved onto smaller braids draping down her shoulders in her curtain of hair. "I'm glad to see my sister happy."

"I've been happy before," Evelot grumbled.

"You were content, not happy. The bard came along and now you've an actual face beneath that hood."

"I. . ."

Evelot couldn't deny it. The original cloak long since burned to ash had sheltered her from countless fears. To show her face was still a challenge, but she gave herself credit for weaning herself off the hood. Hopefully, in due time she wouldn't hide from her family as a reflex.

Triumphantly, Ulleh looked around Evelot to see the reflection. Evelot stared at herself in astonishment. Where her hair had sat flat and dry like straw, Ulleh had turned her tresses into a diadem of blaze-colored braids, a recreation of their deity's style.

"It's bonnie, Ulleh," Evelot said.

"Good. Because I have something to go with it."

Ulleh waddled sideways out the door, returning a minute later with a cascade of fabric draped over her arm.

"My bastard of a husband may've gone and filled me to the brim with his seed, but you've got the figure for this, aye?"

"Wha—? But that's such a—"

"Do me a favor, Lottie, and haud your wheesht," Ulleh said. "Now, go on and put it on."

Evelot glimpsed back down at the dress. Knowing Ulleh's limits, she took the fabric and shut the door behind her in the washroom. The dress slipped on like water, unlike her many layers of thin skirts. Wool padded the insides for her to keep warm through the night; long sleeves billowed out from the elbows and her waist was accentuated by the trims of the Harvest Maiden's trinity knots. But the low neckline made her gape. No amount of shifting the dress around would change it, either.

When Evelot skeptically stepped out, Ulleh tittered with joy.

"It does fit you! Ha!" Ulleh exclaimed.

"D-do all the lasses wear something so. . . revealing?" Evelot asked, peeking down at her chest.

"Ach, don't be so modest tonight! Your bard won't be minding it. He'll prolly listen to the jewelry peddlers and buy you an Evertrue necklace. Just you wait!"

Evelot's entire face felt hot at the idea. Zenris wouldn't be that stupid to listen to the jewelers hawking their wares without a second thought. Or maybe he would.

Ulleh wagged her finger playfully before replying, "Now, stop your stalling and on you go. There're slippers by the front door for you, too."

Her sister shoved her toward the entrance of her house. Laughing, Evelot caught her in a grateful hug. Then with an anxious wave, Evelot went on her way.

The bonfire lit up for miles in the dark of night, calling forth those who wished to join the cèilidh. With each step, Evelot felt the earth thump harder to the music, her eardrums numbing to the pounding air. People cheered and hooted to the tune of drums and bagpipes in the walkway of booths and carts. She dipped through the crowds to the larger circle wrapping around the pyre. Flames licked at the sky, its heat stinging her eyes. Other festivalgoers went on without complaint, joining hand in hand for traditional dance or selling their wares over the din.

The traffic was stifling, but the smell of salted turkey legs and meat pies roused her stomach. Folks toasted tankards and Esmoran steins above her head and children zipped past her legs. Finally, the crowd thinned by the Hoarder's Tome Cache. While addressing the few curious onlookers at his wagon, Clovis waved to Evelot. She gestured back and stood off to the side, peering through the premature celebrations underway.

To think that over a month earlier, life was hardly as boisterous. Seeing the many merry faces brought relief to her racing heart. Nothing was out of sorts anymore, no fear nor death. Evelot took in a deep breath, peeking up at the sky for a sign of Jammer to comfort her. The smoke deterred the bugs, Jammer's dinner, if the smell of humanoids didn't, which meant Evelot was on her own. Any minute her bard would show. Excitement budded into anxiety. She didn't want to think of his reaction to her dress. If he did do something foolish or stared at her as if she was the sun embodied. . .

It felt like she was standing in front of the pyre. Evelot patted her cheeks and tried for a calming breath.

"Beauty becomes you tonight," said a voice behind her.

Before Evelot could turn, something gentle enveloped her head. She reached up, touching a crown of paper flowers and bowstrings. Zenris appeared around her shoulder with a loving grin.

"What's all this?" Evelot laughed.

Zenris opened his arms with a humorous air. Though his attire underneath didn't appear different from his usual garb, his feet were bare, and a long, hooded cloak sat over him like a wet rag.

"I wish not an interruption tonight," Zenris said, lifting the hood over his head. "Let us hope that our dear warrior will not notice something amiss in her room."

"What about your disguise spell?" Evelot asked.

"I dare not chance tiring early while dancing. A shame 'twould be to lose focus on such a beauteous sight." His gaze was warm as he regarded her.

Evelot rolled her eyes, her lips tilting upward in a wee grin. "Aye. Where to, then?"

Zenris only answered with a smirk as he gently pulled her into the crowd. Evelot smiled back at him. The booths blurred, and the smell of meat pasties faded to that of ash and smoke. Outside the dancing circle of the bonfire, Zenris stopped.

"After you, my lady," he said, grinning.

"No! I'm no dancer," Evelot laughed.

"Will you not keep your word?"

"I'm—"

She flushed, glancing away. It was one thing to dance for her life; it was another to risk catching the eyes of others with her bumbling about for the sake of it.

Zenris took her hands, and then replied, "Practice with me, then?"

"Practice?" Evelot echoed.

"For but one song. If then you are not persuaded, we can resume our merrymaking elsewhere."

He was too earnest, and the cèilidh stirred to life with dance partners stepping into place.

The beat itself was simple, no different from a steady horse's gallop. Evelot followed along with Zenris's sway to the drums, easing into the familiar stepping hops while he improvised. In their slow circling and mimicking of others, Evelot picked up her feet, catching the rhythm under her soles and feeling it relax her nerves.

"What grace you have!" Zenris encouraged over the drums.

Evelot grinned, doubts dissipating in a laugh.

When the song petered out, Evelot dipped away to catch her breath. People hollered excitedly at a new, rapid tune picking up on the drums. Among the cheers, Zenris cawed in jest. As if a summons, a circle formed around them, and hands shuffled them into one of the smaller circles.

The blur of the bonfire and the stomp of feet hypnotized her, and Evelot cackled aloud. Her voice blended with Zenris's and the bursts of beating drums, and her feet hummed with the vibrations in the dirt. Her cheeks ached from laughter.

By the end, Evelot's veins were thrumming with energy. Warmed up, she turned to Zenris and prepared for another round of dancing. Instead, a set of pan flutes piped in, and a woman from the band stepped up to the pyre. Her voice rose with a gentle melody. Other women Evelot's own age exited the crowd. They tugged at their partners, who separated into lines of four. It'd been a long time since she'd watched it, but Evelot recognized the Maiden's Tribute, the dance for lasses to make their affections known to their sweethearts.

As the first steps started, Evelot peeked over at Zenris. He was none the wiser, watching the display with interest. She pulled at his sleeve and asked, "One more dance?"

"Oh?" Zenris replied with an amused grin.

She yanked him into the last formation of dancers. Evelot stood with the other lasses as Zenris found his place beside the bachelors. The songstress started with a somber note, moving on with the flutes that accompanied her on a lilting journey. Evelot tried to copy the other lasses in fanning her skirts back and forth, stepping slowly toward her cloaked bard. Zenris dipped in a formal bow with the rest of his group. Then, the true dance began.

Evelot stepped back as Zenris came forth, then vice versa. The women circled their sweethearts and maneuvered with raised arms and twirling skirts. Evelot stumbled over her dress, and bashfully she righted herself each time. If she remembered correctly, they'd reached the point where the bachelor broke the chain, symbolizing their interest in either a courtship or engagement. As couples split off, the two she'd been mimicking halted. The sweetheart shook his head at his love before dipping away. Evelot panicked when the lass sprinted into the crowd, weeping. The other couples were deep into the dance, and Evelot remained stuck in one position.

A hand cupped her waist. Evelot looked back at Zenris standing in front of her. He leaned his head in and whispered directions in her ear, then they raised their arms and continued. Every word he spoke sounded heavy, leaving off on a pause that forced Evelot to nibble on her lip. She thought it was the excitement poisoning her imagination until they pulled away. His hand held her own above their heads, and the dancers stopped. That sultry glint in his gaze stifled the breath in her throat.

Only when the dancers dispersed did Evelot blink. Zenris pulled her away from the bonfire with a merry laugh. Narrowly dodging patrons and their tankards of bevvy, the two collapsed on an empty patch of grass in a heap of laughter.

"See? Nary a thing to fear," Zenris said.

"Aye, until either of us misstepped and took the entire line down!" Evelot laughed.

"Nonsense. I would have been there to catch you!"

"You and your bare feet? How's it they're not frostbit yet?" Evelot said, glancing at his toes.

"You think too little of an elf, my lady!"

"'Half-elf.'"

As if to silence her, Zenris leaned in and kissed her. Evelot squeaked; her face heated and a pout puckered her lips when he pulled away.

"Are you in need of any refreshment?" he said happily.

"What say some scran and a pint? You look famished, yersel'," Evelot answered.

With a smile, Zenris replied, "Your wish is my command."

He got to his feet and disappeared into the thickening lines of the food vendors. Evelot waited for him outside the throng, trying her best to calm the nervous jitter in her chest. When Zenris returned, he handed her a dram of whisky and a large meat pie wrapped in curiously slick parchment. She smiled as he sat beside her, his hands preoccupied by his tankard and food.

"Tatties and neeps?" Evelot asked, guessing from the smell of his pie.

"Exactly what the vendor called it." Zenris paused, and then said, "Please tell me what a 'neep' is."

"It's short for turnip," she said with a laugh and a shake of her head.

Satisfied with that answer, Zenris plunged into his food. The minced, tender mutton melted on Evelot's tongue with hints of spice and herbs, buttered crust, and gravy. She washed her bites down with sips of the sweet whisky that loitered on her tongue before its heat slithering down to her stomach. In the aftermath, her limbs tingled, and a comfortable warmth settled in her cheeks.

She'd gone on like that for a few blissful minutes before peeking over at Zenris. He watched the passing crowd in mild contentment. It was bewildering how he drank from his tankard without so much as a hoot. Evelot wasn't sure if it had to do with elven tolerance to alcohol or his own, but her concern quickly dissipated to fascination with him. The heat in her belly crackled at the thought of that fiery look he'd given her. He'd always been braw with his thick, wavy hair, firm hands, and attentiveness, but at the moment, she questioned what his lips would taste like if she laid under his exploring touch.

Evelot took the last swig of her drink. Zenris peeked over to catch her staring with what felt like a clumsy smile.

"Yes, my lady?" Zenris asked, chuckling.

Evelot desperately tried for words to say with a foggy

mind. "W-want to try the cranachan from that vendor over there?"

"A 'cranachan'?"

"Dessert. It's oats, berries, and honey with cream," Evelot said. It was sold by the local vendors, which meant the berries and oats had been swimming in as much whisky as the rest of the pished townsfolk around her.

"Mayhap another time." The peculiar tilt to his smile piqued her curiosity.

"What?" she said.

"Turn around for me?" Zenris asked.

Evelot giggled to herself as she obeyed. A moment passed, and then something shifted around her hair. It perched on her collarbone, fastening closer to her neck. When she looked down, a simple leather chain lay there with a pendant that stifled her breath. The crowned heart, spiraled prongs, and loops all formed the shape of the Harvest Maiden's symbol. It shone in the flickering light of the distant bonfire as keen as her bard.

"A token of my... affection," Zenris said, a hint of bashfulness in his tone.

Evelot spun back around, tears threatening to surface.

"You're giving this to me?" she asked. "Zenris, this is..."

This is a proposal necklace, she thought. Yet the words died in her throat. Of course he had bought her jewelry. Ulleh was right, and Zenris was probably none the wiser. Evelot didn't fault him for it. It was a bonnie gesture, no matter what it truly meant or what he meant by it.

The confidence dwindled from his face. "Is it not to

your liking?" he asked.

"No!" Evelot scrambled to catch his wrists. "No, it's not that. I'm—I'm just flattered!"

"Is that so?" he said, and kissed her hand. "Then I see no reason to stop my endeavors. Not when pleasure becomes you, my beauty."

His confident grin brought a smile to her lips. Evelot's eyes fell shut as Zenris palmed her cheek and brought her lips to his.

"It's Zenris!"

Evelot jolted. Off to the side of the crowd, several lasses gaped at them. Somehow, Zenris's hood had flipped off his head.

He smiled sheepishly with a waggle of his fingers. Any minute they'd spring at them. There was only one thing to do in that situation.

Evelot grabbed Zenris's wrists and stumbled, wrenching him onto his feet and ran.

His fans shouted as they dove into the festival crowd. Evelot's heart pounded, and with a glance back, she squealed. Several women gave chase with hollers and angered cries. The fog of the bevvy melted away to adrenaline. Evelot led her bard in dips and dodges past passersby. To her surprise, fanatics were as relentlessly terrifying as werewolves and jackal-kin.

Their call for Zenris echoed all around. Evelot scrambled to find a wedge through the footpaths that wasn't as loud. With Zenris on her tail, she led them in between the stalls where the vendors worked. Gaggles of fans fell back in dismay at the warnings of duchy security as the two shuffled sideways past the workers' protests. Evelot tried to make way for the billowing tents and their stakes stretching ropes into their path, but Zenris struggled to keep up. Between the booth gaps, his fans followed them on the opposite side of the alley.

"Over here!" Zenris called to her.

He grasped at Evelot's hand and nudged them through a slim gap. Food handlers cried out in shock as the two dodged hot plates of pies. Evelot ducked in time to avoid a tray to the face.

In the foot traffic, she let out a shocked laugh. Zenris captured her hand, and they rushed off toward the exit, fans not too far off.

Few were gathered in the main square when they arrived, leaving more room to run. Evelot heard more shouting behind them, and more fanatics that spotted Zenris out in the open.

"They'll catch us at this rate!" Evelot said breathlessly.

Zenris didn't answer as they kept running. Evelot followed his line of sight to the dark outline of the town's inn. At first she assumed he wanted to make a break for it, but half empty, the inn would provide them little stealth or privacy. Then he smirked.

"Ah-ha!" Zenris cried.

Coming out of the building was the familiar bulky figure of his warrior companion.

"Pril!" Zenris hollered.

She frowned back at him. "Heart of Aspen!"

"I require assistance, if you would be so kind!"

Whether by loyalty or fury, Prilthadollak belted out a roar. Evelot didn't dare glance back once Zenris pulled her inside. They raced past the bar counter and up the stairs.

Before she knew it, they were standing in a room, and Zenris slammed the door shut behind her.

Her lungs burned as she met his astonished gaze. Evading an entire horde of fans was no easy feat, yet they'd done it. It felt so unremarkably relieving that there rose a fit of laughter from them. Zenris's voice was hearty, melodic like a slow strum over lute strings. It was heavenly compared to her breathless cackles.

Evelot stumbled backward into something that poked the back of her knees. Zenris tried to catch her, but in vain. They collapsed onto his mattress which sighed upon impact. Then out from Evelot's mouth escaped a loud, nasally snort.

"Don't—don't mind that," Evelot said, pressing a hand to her mouth.

"How can I not?" Zenris chuckled, leaning over her. "'Tis endearing."

Evelot frowned. Zenris held her with his heavy gaze, the kind that saw into her, finding enchantment that stalled his next grin.

As his thumb traced over her lips, he said, "I may speak winsome words as a profession, but in the company of my enchantress, I speak truth."

Evelot couldn't argue when his pearly-white smile entranced her. His sigh filled her thoughts with questions of what he'd do next, and she wondered if he was feeling the same thrill she felt.

Zenris leaned in, lips above hers as if a silent request. Smiling, Evelot looped her arms around his neck and closed the distance. From little sips to skims of his tongue that tickled her, he ignited Evelot beyond comparison. The simplest massage of his palm across her waist set off a hot jitter; a small moan left Evelot.

Until he pulled away, she didn't know how breathlessly delirious she'd become. Zenris's breath, tasting of whisky, burned her cheeks. His eyes didn't flutter open for a beat, neither had his touch receded. Zenris grinned, and her heart thundered in her chest. Before his hand could slip away, Evelot pulled his wrist around to her stomach. His knuckles brushed up to her collarbone, over the trim of her neckline, and after Evelot let go, lingered between her breasts.

Zenris opened his eyes, looking into hers. She stayed silent.

His lips grazed hers softly before trailing along her jaw. Gooseflesh rioted over her skin in the wake of his kisses against her neck. A shaking sigh left Evelot. Zenris's palm cupped her breast, and a flash of heat swept down to her core.

Zenris parted only to discard his top layers. Evelot couldn't help but study him as he knelt over her. He was leaner in muscle, a noticeable chisel in his capable arms and in the valley of his chest to stomach. To her surprise, there was a slight curve to his waist. Her hand traced over Zenris's shoulder when he leaned in. Against his warm shade of brown, her skin looked ghostly.

Rising, Evelot took her skirts and lifted them over her head. Once the dress fell to the floor, and her boots beside them, she sat back. The nippy draft and anticipation made Evelot wrap her arms around her chest and glance away. It wasn't like in the dank alley where others jeered at her bare body. All the same, her heart pounded as loud as the festival drums.

"Evelot?" Zenris said.

She peeked back at him.

"You are a dream."

Her lips nervously melded into a smile. Zenris reached out and kissed her hand. Her arms fell away, but he didn't pounce. Instead, he carefully stroked the curve of her arm then gently moved to take her waist. The kisses from her cheek to her neck melted that earlier worry.

Every downward kiss coaxed her body back further until she rested against a hill of pillows. The feel of his lips caressing the slope of her breasts made her whimper and purse her lips. Zenris's straying hand left a trail of sweet heat down her waist to her thigh. Leisurely, his tongue lathered over her hardened nipple again and again. It was impossible to smother her cry. Her arms were too weak, but her toes curled at the sensation.

Still toying with her, Zenris's hand slipped over the plane of her stomach to the thatch of hair below. Evelot's grip tightened on his shoulder. She'd felt her enjoyment pooling, but it was different to have him touch her there. The voices from the past softly echoed in her mind.

Zenris's kisses slowed to wee sweet pecks over her shoulder. Evelot's hands shakily coaxed him back for a kiss. She didn't intend to entice him. A frightened, untamable shiver ran through her. She'd once feared how much she was drawn to Zenris. She'd worried she would deter him with her spiraling thoughts. But she wanted him, and she wanted their moment.

Zenris reached down, breaching her curls and skimming through her folds. Against her lips, he moaned. His knuckles brushed her burning core. Evelot sucked in a breath, making him pull away.

"Are you well?" Zenris asked.

Evelot tried for a nod.

"We can stop," he insisted.

"It's not that," said Evelot. "I. . . I liked that."

"Oh?"

She nodded. Zenris carefully leaned in and waited until she gestured once more. His fingers washing over her felt like electricity over her skin, racing with her heartbeat. Her hands balled up the bed sheets as the sound of his strokes pulsed in her ears. The rhythm married with the thunder in her chest and the heavy gasps leaving her. There was no end to Evelot's pleasure, not as he circled that entrance so coyly.

She didn't think their kisses could be more than ruptures on the border of their worlds. But on that bed, when he snagged her bottom lip, they were unspoken, fantastical promises of paradise. His tongue stroked the roof of her mouth, spearing her in tandem with his fingers. Their collective moans coaxed his pace. His strokes were growing deeper, restless. In the middle of her pleasure, she felt his thumb press her nub. There was no more withholding her responses. Every plunge, every grind against her sent a frantic pulse through her body.

Evelot crushed his lips to hers. She was at the cusp. Her body was burning, craving what he did to her.

Upon the tallest heights, a small ecstatic cry muffled against his lips. She felt his own moan before he frantically kissed his way to her ear. Hearing his breath that close, feeling him nibble on her lobe, sent shivers through her body.

He was quiet while she held him closer, and both eased back against the bed. Evelot smiled as she brushed back the locks of hair escaping his tie. It was strange to feel her frenzied heat fade, replaced by a soothing warmth from his embrace. But. . . it was comforting.

"May I join you?" he breathed.

His pinched brows and hungry eyes didn't hide how tortured he'd been. Though anxiety thrummed through her again, Evelot brought his face closer and pressed her lips to his forehead.

Zenris unbuckled his braies and tossed them to the floor. His modest length made Evelot anxiously swallow. The tip, swollen like his lips, beaded white. A shiver of odd delight passed through her.

Settling into place, Zenris kissed her back. Evelot dared to explore him, brushing her lips against his jaw, nibbling his ear the same way he did hers. Her tongue followed its shell, reaching the pointed tip. Zenris's breath hitched, but he let her continue. Having that freedom, Evelot felt that earlier sensation of ecstasy reappear with a vengeance. Her arms wrapped around his neck, and her ankles slowly crawled toward his arse.

Zenris dipped closer, his tip pressing against her core. He stopped to catch her hands, kissing them until their fingers intertwined. It quelled her fears as they fell to the bed.

With his lips to hers, he entered her. Evelot nipped at his lower lip as a subtle pain flitted down below, here and gone like a sore muscle. His first thrust had her gasp. The smell of sweet cedar cologne and sweat enveloped her like an embrace.

"You are the sunlight, Evelot," he whispered against

her brow. "Radiant, and resplendent."

"Zenris," she breathed.

Her hand trailed along his back; the feel of him grew inside.

He'd started slow until Evelot grew used to his size. Zenris dared thrust deeper, enough to make the bed posts squeak. Between stolen kisses and moans, Evelot listened to them. Zenris grunted under his breath the more he became ravished, insatiable between wet, clapping thrusts.

Evelot spared a glance up at Zenris. His brow was furrowed, his eyes lidded. He whimpered when she unconsciously squeezed him. Her knees buckled against his sides; she sank and quivered with him. She felt him dip in and clutched his hand back with a croon.

She was teetering on the edge when a warmth spread through her. Zenris choked on a cry. He shifted, bending down to kiss her once more. His lips grazed across her temple, and the weight of his breath close to her ear broke the dam. She cried out, squeezing him one last time.

Evelot thought she heard Zenris speaking, hushed and delighted. She wished she caught a few of his words, but with energy spent and the lull of alcohol in her blood, she drifted, drifted. . .

Chapter Twenty-Two

Zenris peeled his eyes open as morning light breached the curtained windows. He could not recall rolling onto his back nor pulling the sheets over the both of them. Yet there he lay beside Evelot. Her hair cascaded around her face, her braids a messy halo over the crown of her head. She murmured in her sleep as she rolled onto her front. Pressing a kiss to her temple, Zenris rose out of bed.

He stepped into the washroom, half-tempted to fill the washbasin with hot water. He decided against it as that would mean raucous plumbing stirring her from her sleep. In the counter mirror, Zenris's reflected smile was so unlike the one he'd spent years performing. 'Twas a mark of pure joy on his face, raw and ripe with emotion. No cold water could cleanse it as he scrubbed away the morning oils and brushed his teeth. The hazy memory of their night dancing and passionately embracing, the smell of her scent on his skin summoned a new sense of self. He was more than glad for it.

With the door cracked open, the faint sound of a strumming lute caught his ear. Curious, Zenris leaned partially out the doorway.

His world came to a halt. Evelot, sitting up in bed, plucked at the strings of his lute pressed to her bare chest. Her fingers gently eased into the grooves he had taught her to hold, her melody mediocre yet enchanting in his ears. His heart skipped a beat. With a perfect posture and blissfully content expression, she was a vision fully engraved into his soul.

Evelot glanced in his direction with hooded eyes, her lips curling into a small smile.

"Mornin'," she said.

He felt a lopsided grin manifest as he stepped into the room. Evelot faintly chuckled. Her eyes wandered below his hips before bashfully looking away. His other "companion", it appeared, had been basking in her glory alongside him. For 'twas as well that Zenris possessed no shame as he foolishly stood there, denuded.

He crossed the small distance to the bed. Beside her, she continued playing the lute. Zenris's body leaned in, hands hovering over hers as if to offer aid, lips dangerously close to her shoulder. Her smell of rosemary and pine beckoned him close as if a siren's call. Oh, how her body demanded to be revered. No, he could not deny her.

"Zenris?" she said.

"Yes, enchantress?" he breathed against her skin.

"I thought you told me to keep practicing the lute?"

"Did I? I cannot recall."

Evelot chuckled. "Aye."

"Oh."

His teeth softly scraped against a mole on the sea of her pale flesh before he kissed his way to the nape of her neck. Her hands slowly released the neck of the lute, and she let out a gentle sigh. He set the instrument down on the floor, crawling atop her in his reverence.

The sight of Evelot below him was greater than the stage; a treasure unlike his glimpse he once had of her in the river. She was perfect in the way her chest rose and fell, how the flush of her nipples matched her cheeks. The humble grooves of her outline were soft plush in his palms. It mattered not the smallness of her stature, nor the roughness of her calloused hands. He felt there was no end to her, both in body and in mind. Her wit and brashness, her pouts, smiles, and heady scent. They could pass days together in his bed, and still he would not know of her entirety.

He kissed his way downward, relishing in the whimpers and sighs he loosened from her lips. Under the graze of his fingertips was her skin aprickle, brazen as her nipples that begged him to tease with his tongue. The same excitement possessed him when her fingers tangled in his hair, yet it only encouraged him further down. Her smoothness gave way to the finer hairs below her knee, then to the chill of the top of her foot.

"Zenris," she sighed.

Her voice was like a command. He obediently beheld her in his embrace. The feel of her slim hands on his waist beckoned a groan from him. To be seduced by her proved too great for him. Upon his attempt to kiss her lips, she turned her head. Too self-conscious she was of her hygiene. Zenris did not fault her for it. Instead, she locked her arms around him and smiled. Her ankle slid over his rear to his thigh, causing his cheeks to clench. His eyes fluttered closed as he basked in her touch. Yet, where pleasure should have begun, Zenris struggled for purchase. They rolled over, and

Evelot landed on top of him. Victory complimented her beaming visage.

"My lady," he said, feigning surprise. To see her take charge rendered him positively giddy.

Evelot looked poised to explore him with her famished gaze. Her hands cautiously traced their way down his chest. Zenris remained still out of fear of dissuading her. He wished for her comfort after she had bravely spoken of her past. He was too proud. Proud of her, proud of their time in shared bliss, and of how breathless she had been throughout his own exploration.

His attention shifted to the necklace dangling before him. His gift around her neck. . . yes. That incorrigible pride he felt took physical form, pressing against the outline of her rear.

"Are you rushing me?" she teased.

"Beg pardon," Zenris said. "The sky looks down upon me, and she is a view most stunning."

At her satiated smile, Zenris ceased stirring. Like the sun, her extended palms warmed him, soothed him. He dared to watch as she traced the planes of his skin. Her fingers outlined the sensitive points of his ears, her long hair obscuring his view of her. By His Oaken Hand, Zenris never tired of Evelot weaponizing his weakness against him.

The more she went on, the more a sense of urgency arose from her. For 'twas as if she had to know him, memorize his features as best she could lest time slip away. Yet he knew not the reason for urgency while they lay in his bed, the day still young.

As soon as her urgent expression appeared, the image faded. Evelot bit her lips shyly, smiling to herself. She lowered onto him, her wet heat stirring his companion to attention.

"Do you desire me once more?" he asked.

Evelot took his arm and brought his hand to her cheek. She nodded.

"You need only say the word, my lady," Zenris said. His thumb stroked her cheekbone to assure her.

Evelot's shy grin pressed into his palm. "Can we?" she asked.

"Gods, yes."

She rose to her knees. That gentle brush on his shaft nearly summoned an animalistic groan from him. Her heat, her plush skin—all rendered him weak with an internal plea for more.

In unison, they stifled a moan as she bade him entrance. Her walls forcibly pressed against him. Her jaw clenched while she maneuvered herself in an explorative drag, descending and rising. Her slow pace spoke of her hesitancy. His hands went to her waist, a gesture to encourage her to do as she would.

While she tantalized him with her steady thrusts, Zenris's gaze followed the rise of her ribs. Those perky breasts above teased him. Feeling exuberant, he seized one and stroked her nipple. Evelot let out a small whimper. Zenris bit back a groan as her excitement squeezed him again.

"Zenris," she panted.

"Yes, my lady?"

"That feels good."

"Oh?" he grunted. "Does the lady wish for me to continue?"

"Please," she whimpered.

He stroked her once more while settling his feet on the mattress. Her lips pursed as he thrust with her, yet she could not withhold her pleasure. 'Twas rapturous music to him, hearing her excitement. Oh, if she thought their sounds of pleasure were obscene, they paled in comparison to her salted perfume mixed with his natural scent. All the more pleasure for him to bask in.

She leaned over him, laboring for breath. Zenris panted as he held on by her waist, propelling his hips harder when she lost momentum. He felt himself tighten inside her, his sac clenching. Her heat and hold proved too much, too mind-numbing, yet 'twas for both of them to share. He pulled her closer with his arm over her waist. His other hand squeezed her breast; she kissed his jaw before capturing the tip of his ear betwixt her lips.

He found his limit in a heartbeat.

Their cries ricocheted against the walls and into his ears. Any complaints from his neighbors were far from Zenris's concern.

Evelot fell into his arms, and with her head tucked under his, they lay in comfortable silence. Hours could have gone by, or days, but the sun was still shining when Evelot finally stirred. She curled against him, her eyes dreamily half-open to gaze upon him. His lips felt raw after indulging in her perfection for so long.

"Are you satisfied?" he asked, running his fingers through her hair.

She smiled and lazily pet his arm. "Very. Was it. . .?"

"'Heavenly' would do no justice to the woman beside me."

She pouted to herself, her cheeks aflame. "You tease."

Evelot held onto his arm as he softly stroked her hair. Her eyes peered straight through him for a breath before she brought his hand to her lips and kissed each fingertip. That moment would not fade from Zenris's memory. A sadness surrounded her that cast a shadow over the previously jubilant air. He suspected she was withholding her true feelings.

"If you are exhausted, my enchantress, what say we call on the stewardess?" Zenris said. "And break our fast here."

"No. If it weren't someone on staff, it'd be your fans that would see. You don't want to break half of Goldencrest's hearts, do you?"

"If my endeavors paint me as a villain, then I will be glad of it."

She rolled her eyes playfully. "All right, all right. I *wish* for a toothbrush and some scran. Let's go down and order before the hunger gets to us."

Zenris chuckled. "Will you go as is?"

"Sure. I figure the town won't mind a bit of tit to go with their scones," she answered sarcastically.

Zenris laughed aloud. Before she could protest, he scooped her into his arms and rose from the bed.

"If that is the case, your teats await a long, cleansing bath before their display."

Evelot giggled, and Zenris carried her into the washroom.

Breakfast was still being served by the time they appeared downstairs. Zenris assumed his cloaked identity while seated in a lowly lit corner, as Evelot was unable to mask her own. To both their surprise, the barmaid did not flinch at Evelot's previously worn attire nor cloak. 'Twas as if the devil's harlot was but a fleeting nightmare upon the town, quickly forgotten. Zenris supposed the cause lay in his lady's fair countenance. A radiant glow emanated from her, so lovely that those passing by were bold in taking no notice. Yet 'twould be a shame if so. Zenris was more comfortable being her only admirer.

As they ate and drank their fill, Zenris then said to her, "This 'haggis' that you mentioned—"

Evelot laughed over the food in her mouth. "You're a radge if you think you can try it."

"How so? Is it not edible?"

"You'd get sick if you read the list of foodstuffs!"

"I call your bluff!" he teased.

Evelot shook her head with a laugh. She swallowed her next bite, her body leaning into him in their booth. His arm went around her shoulder as he chuckled.

The flow of patrons burgeoned, and before long, the thunder of heavy footsteps parted the curious onlookers. Zenris looked up in time to see Pril take the opposite seat at their small table, her stoic expression giving nothing away.

"Ah, my fine companion!" Zenris greeted. "How kind of you to grace us with your presence."

"Heart of Aspen," she acknowledged. Her amber eyes scrutinized Evelot beside him. "The two of you look… well," she stated.

"Thank you. After a refreshing bath, we bid the day

welcome!"

Evelot stifled a gasp and blushed. She shoved at his arm, peeking out at anyone within earshot. Zenris grinned back coyly.

"You dafty eejit," she admonished under her breath.

"I had warned you, my lady, that shame would not be with us today."

"Try to contain yourself in public," Pril said, glaring at Zenris, "at least until after the festival."

Evelot sat up to finish her meal quietly. Though he missed her touch, Zenris returned his attention to Pril.

"Have heart, Pril," Zenris said. "I mean well."

"Yes, as you say. In the meantime, you have a vendor that requests you for the festival. He offers the coin necessary for our journey ahead. See that you speak with him."

"As you wish, my friend."

"Good." Pril rose out of her seat, crossing her arms. "If you need me, I will be with the hunting party."

Zenris cocked his head in confusion. "They had not disbanded?"

"They may have won the battle, but this time we search for those missing. Apparently, a handful of their strongest men have not returned since the beasts had split our ranks, nor the men sent to fetch the last of the beasts' pelts. We make for the same woods to collect their bodies, or limbs, given the time now passed."

"Ah. I see."

The hunting party and their last duties had not crossed his mind. Were it only the werewolf and his pack easily dispatched, there would be no other cause for alarm. The casualties certainly needed to be addressed.

After solemn words of parting, Pril turned and made for the exit.

When Zenris turned back to Evelot, he found her scrounging the last of her meal into her mouth. Gone was her smile, a contemplative look in its place.

"Forgive my friend," Zenris said. "She has less tact in words that matter."

"That's all right. Wasn't like death would suddenly go away," Evelot said.

Her worried glance was far from secret. It would not do to let it sour her day, nor his.

"What say we go for a stroll?" he asked.

Evelot smiled. "Let's."

Zenris paid no mind to the stirring crowds in the main square nor the odd stares that followed him. His lady's hand rested on his arm as he walked across the cobblestone; he would have glided over it if he wished. Pril may have been dour in her earlier words, yet 'twould not deter their merriment that day. Evelot and he chatted and laughed all the way to the long grass. As they basked in the last days of the autumn luminance, Zenris played away at his lute for his paramour. The tune, improvised and galloping with jubilance, paralleled his state of mind while she watched him with tired eyes.

Zenris laughed. "Am I lulling you to sleep?"

"Hmm—? No. Just lost in thought."

Evelot sat up, shivering against the wind. He opened his arms, and his cloak went around them both. His lady sat nestled betwixt his crossed legs, and her hair brushed his cheek; its woodsy scent washed away any prior thoughts.

"You seem excited," Evelot chuckled.

"Of course!" Zenris exclaimed. "I have the privilege of beholding a lady most bewitching."

"Ach, you—" With a laugh, she shifted around to where she faced him. "And how many other fanciful words have you got left to use on me?"

"Most heavenly?" Zenris offered.

"Sunlight, heavens, a bit overused, aye?"

"Picturesque?"

"I've got more life than a painting."

"Pulchritudinous?"

"Are you wanting to start a fight?"

Zenris laughed, his mirth warm on his lips. He would never tire seeing Evelot melt at his touch. Her lips that he had sipped endlessly from had not a rival in reality nor portraiture. Dare not any other bard attempt to characterize the melodious note in her laugh, nor the tapped *r*'s in her speech. Only he, if he were capable.

As he held her close, with his hands stroking her back, Zenris closed his eyes. He envisioned the neck of a phantom lute there where his fingers gently pressed. Her laughter replayed in his mind as he plucked at what he thought were the notes. Under his breath, he murmured a tune slowly connected note by note.

"Zenris?" Evelot raised a quizzical brow when he opened his eyes.

He grinned at her, and whispered, "May I kiss you?"

"You don't need to ask," she said.

At his unresponsive smirk, she rolled her eyes and tugged at his open collar. Her lips met his, and their smiles dissolved against each other. By the gods, she was a fast learner. He became victim of the little nudges of her tongue past his lips, and the fingers playing at the fine hairs of his neck. He relished in the taste of her breath, the feel of her back under his palm. If she pressed herself any closer, Evelot would hear his erratic heart. In response, he ran his tongue across her upper lip. Evelot made a noise of shock before tilting her head and chasing after it with her own.

A large bang jolted them out of their stupor. Zenris looked to the top of the hill. A simple wagon rolled past, its farmer unawares. It must have struggled over a stone.

The two looked back at one another and howled in laughter.

When the sun tired of the day and exhaustion had the better of them, Zenris walked Evelot back to her home. The trek was not far, which meant his time with her would end shortly. He savored her hand in his, stalling with as much small talk as he could conjure.

"I am honest," he said. "I wish to know the local vernacular, if but a few words."

"Are you sure? You might find it 'most difficult,'"

Evelot said, her Vestryaen accent coming along.

"Perish the thought. For example, what is 'daft'? A sort of name?"

"It means 'fool'. Which you were earlier."

"And who is to blame for that?" he said, kissing her hand.

"You numpty!" Evelot laughed in disbelief.

"What say you, my lady?"

She chuckled, stopping with him before her home. Were it possible to take back his hand, he would have relented. Yet Evelot had not withdrawn her own palm. They stood smiling at each other, the sunset's ember rays setting her red hair aglow. Her jubilance produced a sigh from his lips.

Zenris leaned in and kissed her. The gesture was quick and soft. Her lips pressed together, her eyes yet to open. He yearned to try once more.

A hush fell over the wildlife, and the wind ceased its whisper. Zenris froze; howling echoed from the wood's treeline, an ominous pitch as though in warning.

"T-the wolves must've returned?" Evelot offered.

"Yes, the native wolves," Zenris distractedly answered, pulling his gaze from the trees.

Seeing the concern on Evelot's face, he snuck another kiss upon her lips. Her shocked whimper was as harmless as her hand that batted his shoulder.

"Shall we meet tomorrow by the hill?" he asked with a laugh.

"Of course. Where else?"

"Well, if the lady asks." Zenris kissed along her cheekbone with every word he spoke. "There are my quarters."

He nibbled at her earlobe. She squeaked, breaking into laughter as her head tucked into his shoulder. Zenris apologized over his laughter and stroked her head. From the corner of his eye, the door to her sister's home yanked open. Ulleh stood there in the entrance with a grin that pierced each cheek.

"It seems we have company," he whispered to Evelot.

Ulleh waved back at him. "How's the craic?"

Evelot gaped at her sister. Zenris chuckled, pulling away from her. He kissed her hand once more and backed away.

"Tomorrow, then, Evelot?" he asked.

"T-tomorrow."

With a bow, he left her to her cackling sister.

The trek was colder in the evening, but his spirits were warm. Little Jammer trilled above his head to warn of her landing. Her claws caught the base of his tail, tugging at his hair, and she hunkered onto his shoulder. A vague citric scent blossomed from her fur as she sniffed at his skin.

Zenris concentrated on the weight of Jammer there. In his ear, mana pulled her chitters in and translated them.

Momma scent. Male scent. Male. Poppa? she said.

Zenris's eyes widened.

Male. Male. Poppa. Food?

"I fear I have not your dinner," he said.

Momma. Food.

Jammer stretched her wings and pounded against the air. He stopped to watch her travel toward Evelot's home, the sound of her titters fading.

Zenris internally replayed the sound of her clicks. He

hummed his earlier melody alongside it.

"*Your heart is an oak, whose roots stretch toward every plane.*"

His grin ached in his cheeks. Zenris took off on a run down the hills toward Goldencrest. There was much to prepare for: his performance was on the hour. But first, he hoped to steal away into his room and accomplish that which he thought he had not the inspiration to do—compose his next song.

Chapter Twenty-Three

Zenris took his bow after an hour of song requests the next morning, feeling ever the more enlivened. The crowd grew larger for breakfast, and his teeming fans called desperately as he snuck backstage.

He returned to his room, collecting a batch of parchment on the desk. Pride swelled in his chest. Too soon would he have his next composition perfected for the public. Zenris anticipated great accolades and adoration should he cast it to a larger audience, yet he wished for one sole listener to have the honor before then. A certain beauty who awaited him on the hour.

Creeping out the door and toward the main stairway, Zenris listened for any signs of fans. Only the sounds of downstairs chatter and clinking goblets met his pointed ears in the stuffy hallway. Save for a door clicking shut behind him.

"Heart of Aspen," greeted a familiar voice.

"A late rise for you, Pril? You must be quite exhausted," Zenris said.

Pril stepped up to his side. "I had risen with the dawn, unlike you who sung long into the night."

"Guilty as charged," Zenris said with a smirk.

They descended the stairs to the tavern. Though

Zenris was confident his companion would discourage lingering fans from approaching, the assembled crowd there consisted only of locals and tourists preparing for the festival. An eagerness buzzed amongst them, a new attitude most welcome after the time of innocents sheltering indoors from the werewolf's threat. It brought consolation to his heart that their efforts had played a hand in the outcome.

At the bar, Zenris and Pril took their seats. Pril dropped into hers, creating a cacophony like cannon fire that nearly sent Zenris ducking for cover.

"Do you carry the entire Esmoran army on your person?" Zenris asked, astounded.

"It is simply my weaponry," Pril said, gesturing to the arsenal strapped to her.

Zenris gawked. Three battle-axes hung from her hip belt, a claymore sword hung from her back, and what looked to be discreet explosives protruded from a pack attached to her breast pockets.

"Unless they take after the Fae Realm variety, rest assured you need only a spring trap for rabbits, Pril," he said.

"I assume that is another one of your 'sarcastic' remarks?"

"Yes, however—"

"It is of no matter. Here." Pril opened her coin purse and handed him five kingsquarters. "Your reward for hard work this week."

Zenris smiled. "Your kindness deserves generosity on my behalf!"

Before she could answer, he waved down the barkeep and ordered for the two of them. Once the barmaid scurried off with a sum of half a quarter, Pril shook her head.

"Of course you would spend it immediately," Pril grumbled.

"What can I say? 'Tis cause for celebration!"

Chuckling, he sat back in his seat. As they waited for their order, Zenris pored over his composition. His fingertips were chapped and inkstained, and an ache in his back and hands reappeared once he began reading the lyrics on the parchment. Were it not for the boisterous tavern, he would have hummed it aloud. In the back of his mind, a perfectionist's voice instructed him. Zenris preferred to hear his lady's thoughts before doing so.

"You are strangely optimistic this morning," Pril observed.

"'Tis a wonderful day ahead, is all," Zenris replied.

"The wind will freeze with cold rain soon. I assume for your feeble, papery flesh it would be most unpleasant."

"A matter of perspective, then."

Pril tilted her head in thought, then begrudgingly looked away.

There was something different about her. A guarded, secretive air that caused her to glance out the windows. Once the barmaid returned with their food, Zenris used the opportunity to observe her. Pril dug into her carnivore's delight breakfast, snapping on the chicken bones. He fought to withhold his gag. Yet her pace was too quick for the norm. She was eating hurriedly, preparing herself for something that called for a warrior's stamina.

"Is there something on your mind, Pril?" he asked.

"What?" She inclined her head. Betwixt her thin, jagged teeth was the battered flesh of a chicken breast. Zenris swallowed back bile.

"You are preoccupied with your thoughts," he tried again.

"Yes, I am."

When Pril continued chomping at her food, Zenris pushed, "Will you share them with me?"

"Very well." She swiped her hand across her face. "I will be away again for the day with the hunting party."

"The same search you joined yesterday?"

"Correct. Their bodies have yet to be found. There is concern as to if the werewolf was fully deceased, since no one can vouch for its pelt or meats from what was already gathered."

Zenris furrowed his brow. "Impossible. You had slain it yourself. Have not you scoured the woods these past several days?"

"Nearly. We assume that in the case of lost hunting party members, they searched for victims in caches the werewolf and its pack might have made."

"'Tis possible," Zenris said. "However, there are not many dens in which to keep their cache safe in the woods. The greater likelihood is that the native predators reclaimed what was theirs after having been deprived of their hunting grounds."

"That may be. The chapel will be searched once more as a possible cache, in the meantime. . ."

Her brows lowered solicitously, and she muttered, "It does not bode well to find not one bone left behind."

Pril was right. Any natural predator would surely leave behind evidence. Mayhap 'twas possible that the werewolf and jackal-kin had kept a secret room or basement below the chapel for "storage" use. Then again, having had a hand in burning the chapel to the ground, Zenris was not keen to humor the theory any further lest he admit partial blame for countless others' demise.

"Something is sure to turn up soon," Zenris insisted, a nervous sweat pooling at his collar. "'Tis nothing more to note on."

Pril guzzled her tankard of beer and throatily rumbled in satisfaction, apathetic to his response. Only when rising from her seat did she glance his way again.

"Why have you not received your meal?" she asked.

"This was my meal," Zenris said, referring to his empty salad bowl.

"Why do you only consume a rodent's calories today? Are you ill?"

"Quite the opposite," Zenris said, grinning. "I am saving my appetite for a luncheon with my enrapturing witch. There is a dessert tart awaiting me in her wicker basket."

"Ah, a 'euphemism.'"

"Wha—? No. No, I mean a literal tart."

Pril's brows pinched in frustration. Zenris only heard her grumble of "confusing humanoid words" before she turned to the exit. Customers swiftly dipped away, giving her a wide berth at the door. After waving to the barkeeper, Zenris soon followed, and swept through the alleyways to the hillside.

The chill absorbed the high sun's rays over Zenris's trek upon the dirt path. In the time he spent blowing warm air into his palms, Zenris realized how shameful he was to keep his lady waiting for him outside. Should the weather continue to act as callous, they would have to retreat indoors for the remainder of their rendezvous. 'Twas a rousing idea. Zenris could teach the lute to Evelot in the comfort of his room, while he recited the lyrics of *Our Heaven* by the distinguished Sir Adamson. All the while he would kiss the chill off Evelot's cheeks.

By the gods, he knew not the extent of his attachment. 'Twas an inebriation, and she was the sweetest wine upon his tongue. In her reserved nature lay his confidence that the affection was mutual. It had to be so.

At their hidden meeting place, Zenris found Evelot with legs curled inward for warmth while she perused her spellbook. Her hands swiveled in the air, her lips shaping inaudible words in practice of a cantation. He smiled to himself. Absorbed in her craft, energetic for the future, she was destined for greatness. Akin to the fire birds of legend, she would rise above the ashes of her former self, from that past that haunted her for too long. With his composition in hand, Zenris hoped to rise beside her.

"Zenris!"

She waved back at him, smiling and sniffling at the cold. Zenris closed the distance with a whimsical leap in his heart. In her hood there peeked the small bundle of little Jammer. She did not stir as Zenris brushed against her, placing his arm around Evelot.

"Shall we find somewhere else to sit? Mayhap some place warmer?" he asked his lady.

Evelot shook her head where it rested on his shoulder. "It'll be fine," she said. "I've got something for the cold."

Evelot reached toward the wicker basket across from her. She produced a clear bottle of bright amber liquid, gripping its neck like a hunted rabbit.

"My lady," he said, feigning shock, "'tis yet noon."

"More for me, then," Evelot chuckled.

She uncorked the bottle and offered it to Zenris. He took a swig, relishing in the spiced kick that rolled down his throat. It ignited a spark betwixt his stomach and chest, merging with the warm sensation caused when Evelot snuggled into his arms. Evelot took back the bottle and sipped. A contented sigh left her as she returned it to its place. Her hair, those soft strings of daylight, coyly batted at Zenris's face.

"How are you faring with your studies?" Zenris asked.

"Well enough," Evelot said. "It runs me down having to build resilience for spell-casting. My textbook's got stuff in there I've already learned, like keeping my herbs in a dry, cool space, and keeping soap handy for my utensils. That sort of work."

"You mean to brew more complex potions, then?"

"Suppose you could say that."

Zenris grinned teasingly. "Looking for the cure to the common cold?"

"I. . ." Her eyes cast downward, and a dejected sigh left her. Stroking her head, Zenris waited for her to continue.

"I'm worried about Ma, and Da," admitted Evelot. "He's been aching more from all the work he takes on, and Ma won't tell me what's wrong. I want them to be happy."

Though he had only seen them at the dinner table, the extent of their troubles was beyond imagination for Zenris. Mayhap he had spotted the pallor in the madam Wheaton's cheeks, or a pained grimace in the sir's.

Farmwork was taxing, certainly, yet Zenris could not say he was as concerned as Evelot.

"Suppose you find the remedy for their pains?" he asked.

"I dinnae ken. I've been working on it for years. They. . . don't seem to want the help."

"Then they settled the matter."

Evelot looked up at him, astonished. "They're family. They need me. It's just that they're being stubborn, is all."

"My lady, I mean no offense, but is it because they are your parents, or because they do not see your abilities as a boon that they refuse your help?"

She frowned at the ground, her expression falling in defeat. "I don't. . ."

Zenris wished she would become accusatory or sarcastic at that moment. The soft hum of her melancholic words struck something within him. An argument wished to rise from his subconscious against her parents. Yet it held no logic. He had no means of changing her circumstances. There was nothing he could offer her. His address changed with the tide of time, constantly on the move with adventures in store.

A feeling of gloom curled over him. Zenris had forgotten himself. He had overstepped the boundaries, forgetting their realities.

"I've got lunch, if you're up for it."

Zenris blinked back to the present, where Evelot drew cloth-wrapped food and clay utensils from within her basket. He opened his palms to what she silently handed him. With a nasally inhale, he tried for a grin.

"And what sort of local palate is in store for us today?" he said jovially.

As she rifled through the basket, she replied, "Pies and apples. With a slice of Ma's Ecclefechan tart."

Similar to the pasties the vendors sold at the earlier festivities, the triangular-shaped pies were made for convenience of travel, without the hassle of tins. A convenient method for eating while traveling the highways, Zenris noted.

"Thought you might like a wee bit of rumbledethumps," Evelot said.

"Beg pardon?"

"Rumbledethumps," she laughed. "Don't fuss yersel'. It's mostly tatties, onions, and cabbage."

He smiled in relief. Zenris waited as she said her prayers to the Harvest Maiden and then he took a generous bite. The creamy texture of mashed potatoes had absorbed the flavors of crunchy cabbage and onion, and strings of salty cheese paired with the flaky pie shell. Zenris enjoyed the mild flavor of a crisp apple afterward, then silently watched the clouds shifting on the pale blue horizon with Evelot. He was sure the earlier note of disappointment would not amount to a thing. Like their meal, this was one of many ingredients to their newfound relationship.

"Are you excited for the festival?" he asked, hoping to lighten the mood.

"Hmm?"

"The Harvest Festival. I imagine a powerful crowd will overtake the venue. However dense the audience, 'twould be an effortless task of finding you amongst them. All I must do is find the brightest, beaming smile in the evening's dark, the one that renders my heart asunder."

"Aye, and then that'll be your last performance when they rip you off stage," she teased half-heartedly.

"Ah, but I would die a happy elf."

He waited for her to correct him only to see her smile fade.

"Do not mourn me yet, my lady," he teased. "I would overcome my weak heart and play the most passionate song, sure to make any maiden weep out of jealousy."

Her lips parted for unspoken words. "Zenris, you. . ."

"Yes?"

She froze, as if those words would betray her. Zenris felt his bravado slip away as he patiently waited, yet 'twas for naught. Those evergreen eyes were haunted by thoughts that had only just struck him. Evelot had been worried about the future, one where the festival would divide their paths. Zenris was destined for the roads ahead, and 'twas plain she would stay with her family.

The enchantment dissolved around him like the shattering of glass.

Beneath her forced smile was an all too apparent melancholy.

"As you say," she said.

She finished her apple and sat beside him, facing the gray sky and dull heather. Zenris bit into the Ecclefechan tart shared betwixt them. The sweet tang of fruits and nuts did nothing to warm the chill in his chest, nor did the swigs of whisky. He was not begrudging his lady, no, not at all. She was much smarter than he to have thought of their impending departure so soon. If only fate were not as cruel to them.

With reality sealed, Zenris found it pointless that day to rehearse his composition for Evelot.

Chapter Twenty-Four

Evelot stared ahead at the Grand Granary while her thumb stroked the pendant beneath her cloak. A worried frown chiseled away at her forehead, the same as it had the past several days.

The festival was the next day. There was no time left. Zenris must've also thought of their eventual parting because he'd found ways to stay in the tavern. It was all she could do to mask her concern with a smile and excuse herself to her chores. At the moment, it wasn't false. She stood next to her ma, in line at the Granary. They had to ask for donations of chooks and feed for the coming winter, so Ma needed the extra hand. Da had been too busy with his farmhands, and Tonlin was off to meet Prilthadollak.

But she was stalling. To face Zenris before the festival would be another attempt at denying the inevitable, however badly she wanted to go. He made her forget her status as the town pariah. He made her feel like she was free of judgment, like the ground wasn't opening up underneath her.

If she attended the festival, it'd be taking a step over the chasm made by that opening. No one would be there to catch her.

"You're wearing your hood again, bairn?"

Evelot blinked. "What was that, Ma?"

Ma raised her arms. Baskets full of baked breads and produce for offering hung from her skinny, shivering limbs. The hand that patted Evelot's cheek was gentle and warm.

"Tonlin has been avoiding your da and I these past few weeks," Ma remarked.

"Oh?"

"There's a spark in his eye. I'd seen it when he took his axe a fortnight ago and snuck out the house. Been coming home later and later."

"Da going to do something about it, then?" Evelot asked.

"Him? Never." Ma chuckled. "No, your da will let him be. I ken he can sense as much as I that something changed for Tonlin. He doesn't want to get in the way of his happiness."

Evelot didn't know how to respond. Da thinking of someone's happiness before the chores? No chance. Tonlin'd been stealing away to wherever sword practice was for him and Pril. All that talk Da had did have some sway, at least for her. It'd make more sense that Tonlin got away with more because he wasn't a family oddity.

Ma smiled, looking back at her. "I thought I'd seen the same spark in you and all. But now. . . it seems a bit dull."

Evelot turned her head. Before she could argue, Ma said, "I wonder if it has something to do with a certain someone who hasn't visited the farm in a while?"

"Ma. . ." Evelot faltered in her steps.

Ma rubbed at her back, and a sympathetic smile

formed on her face. "It's all right, my wee babe," she said. "The heart yearns too much, and the mind's trying to fix it all. I don't have the answers, but the two of you will go on. There was something to cherish, aye? I'm grateful for him cause he helped you in finding yersel'. And you've got the Wheaton spirit in you. You'll weather this, darlin.'"

Evelot felt herself smiling back, if only partially. There was comfort and genuineness in Ma's words that reassured her, but in her heart an ache stirred. What truly stung, Evelot realized, wasn't a matter of ever having something, but seeing its end come on too quickly.

As she followed the line, helping Ma in offering their grains to the monk at the chook pen, Evelot took in her surroundings: the community in their temple; the main square down-hill, hoaching with people from there and afar; children that zipped around adults as they played; farmers who sold their crops and shopkeepers their wares. It was a cyclical life, but it had a purpose. Naturally, Evelot was an anomaly to their livelihood. She had a power that Goldencrest didn't. Without discarding that truth, there wasn't much of a part to play there.

Runlaris was enormous compared to Goldencrest, but Evelot only had one family. She had safety with them, in the life they'd lived thus far. On the other hand, Zenris was meant for life elsewhere, likely on the road or in sprawling cities. He had his da to search for, on top of that. He shouldn't be stopped from his goals because she was attached to him. She couldn't ask him to make a choice.

At the same time, she couldn't find one for herself.

There was no guarantee of belonging out in the world, and there was certainly no guarantee of staying with him. Either fate would smart like a knife to the gullet.

Evelot took the wire cages containing their new livestock and glanced about for Ma who had somehow slipped past her in the lower level of the Granary. Thankfully, Ma had been caught by the open entrance where a neighbor blethered on with her. At least one of them was in a better mood.

As Evelot approached, a figure closed in behind her ma. A shadowy, cloaked individual with a large build she wasn't familiar with. They leaned in, so much so it was a wonder that neither woman hadn't spotted him.

Evelot halted. A sharp grin, wicked with hunger, glinted beneath the creature's hood. A snout-like nose wiggled, sniffing at Ma's head. The figure twisted his neck and devilish red eyes leered back at Evelot.

It couldn't be.

But it was. A taloned finger rose to his thin lips. Then his hand moved closer to her ma.

"Ma!"

The cages crashed to the floor as Evelot stretched out a hand, racing toward her. Her ma froze.

Mana pinched her temples before the earth heeded her call. Evelot focused on the beast. Tendrils of vines shot in from outside the Granary, lashing at her target. Screams pierced her ears. Evelot blinked. She stood in front of her ma, prepared to unleash another attack.

Yet, the beast hadn't been struck; it'd vanished.

Evelot's eyes darted to the crowd. They all stared back at her in terror.

"Evelot?"

Ma grabbed her arm, turning Evelot to face her.

Evelot stumbled over her words. It couldn't have just vanished. She'd seen it. It was. . .

"Wheaton," called a low feminine voice.

From the upper story descended the High Priestess. Ever since childhood, she reminded Evelot of a hawk. Her flat, graying hair was pulled tight behind her head. A dark brown cloak was the only color over her pale robe-like dress that brushed the stairs beneath her. Large, dark eyes that matched autumn's rain clouds fell on Evelot.

"Is this how you repay kindness, hag-spawn?" the High Priestess said. "After years of tolerance and patience, you attack innocents in a temple of worship?"

"It was an accident, High Harvest Sister," Ma said. "Just an accident."

"Accident, my left foot," cried someone nearby.

"Get that hag-spawn out of here," shouted another, "and don't come back!"

The High Priestess watched them silently, her tanned hands clasped at her stomach. While she wore disappointment well, she let the others speak disdain for Evelot on her behalf.

Ma took hold of Evelot's shoulders, heading for the fields. When she would've felt a small wash of shame for upsetting the others, none of their jeers or insults reached Evelot's ears.

The damned beast was back.

It wasn't until they stepped inside their home that Evelot collected herself. Ma still held onto her, but Evelot sat down at the dining bench. Her steady breaths coaxed her racing heart to a slow rhythm. However it resurrected itself, that beast would not get the best of her.

"Drink up, my dear," Ma insisted, handing her a cup of water. "Try to relax."

"I-I'm sorry, Ma. I didn't mean to—"

"It'll be all right. Don't fuss. Just relax, now."

Evelot raised her shaking hand and tried for a sip. Cold water doused her throat. It was a temporary relief that almost loosened her tongue.

Of course she couldn't tell Ma the truth. Thinking about how she screamed the night it first appeared on their property, how she held Evelot's hand patiently, sent a fierce chill down her spine. Ma couldn't handle another scare.

"I-I don—"

"It's all right. I'm here, darlin'."

The front door burst open with a clash. Thundering footfalls echoed into the house. Her ma jumped, holding onto Evelot as she turned to face the newcomer.

Storming into the main room was her da. A blinding rage disfigured his tired face, twisting it up with a snarl.

"What's this I hear about the other farmer's banning us from the Granary?" he demanded. "And why're they saying you're to blame?"

Ma rose to her feet. "Tarod, it was an accid—"

"Answer me, girl!" he snapped at Evelot.

She jolted. Anything that came to mind quickly vanished. A wash of ice cold shame overcame her. Without his answer, Da only glowered. The sneer on his lip was identical to that of the townspeople. As Ma tried to call for reason, Evelot felt her da's palpable contempt.

Silently, he turned for the garden door. That sight of his back, always facing her, always creating a barrier, she couldn't bear it. Evelot leapt to her feet.

"Why can't you see I'm trying?" Evelot yelled.

Da spun on his heel.

"I've done everything I could to make you proud, to at least show everyone in this gods-damned town that I can do something right. But everywhere I go I'm reminded of what I am and what they want me to be! I am different! I can't be like you! So why can't you see that I still want to be a part of this family. Why can't you just look at me?"

She heaved for breath. Everything she'd felt, every iota of frustration and self-doubt had poured out of her. Her body wouldn't budge, and her mind fought to comprehend this sudden outburst. Silence passed over them.

"Have you really felt that way?"

She blinked back the tears that blurred her vision. Da stared at her, his expression unreadable. Too choked up to speak, she nodded and cast her eyes to the floor.

The sound of his clomping boots closed the distance. When Evelot looked up again, Da stood in front of her. She never thought she'd see him grimace against anything beyond the sweltering heat in the summer. But he did, and his remorse was too much to bear as he cupped her cheek.

"I'm sorry, bairn," he said.

Evelot grimaced, withholding a sob. But her eyes watered, and tears rolled down her cheeks before she could stop them. That dam she had built up came crashing down. She'd finally said it, and to hear him apologize. . .

Her sobs pulsed through her, racking her body so hard that Da had to still her in his embrace. She held on, and let all her emotions roll out of her, bit by bit.

Instead of joining her family at the dinner table, she opted for a daunder in the fresh air. What the others didn't know beyond her having "no appetite" was her true intentions. Evelot passed her family's crops and ran beside the edge of the woods. Moonlight shone on the horizon by the time she reached the festival grounds. The spot where she had posted one ward looked untouched. But when Evelot moved to the next, she stumbled to a stop. Where she'd buried another was a mound of dirt—the device was nowhere to be found.

"No. . ."

Evelot looked around. There was not a soul nearby, but it didn't matter. Someone did it. One marker affected meant the whole spell had collapsed. With that proof, Evelot realized her worst fear: What she'd seen was real. The werewolf was still alive, and it would take vengeance in a bloody hunt.

Evelot moved into the deserted festival grounds. Up ahead, where it connected to the main square, she spotted a crowd gathering. A makeshift stage was erected there in the center, surrounded by torches and concerned voices. Raising her hood, Evelot jogged closer to the scene.

Everyone she passed through the alleys kept their fearful eyes trained on the square where a group of people had gathered. Her heart pounded as she heard the whispers of "festival" and "trouble." Several people took to the stage, and she recognized the mayor, who turned to the crowd of locals and visitors. His son was close at hand, and a sinking feeling caused her to furrow her brow.

The mayor raised his hand, and the crowd instantly hushed.

"Good evening, townspeople and visitors of Goldencrest," he said. "Thank you for heeding my call during this late hour. I would like to address a series of problems that have recently come to my attention.

"First, as you may have heard, we locals were *visited* by a *mystery* pack of animals that took a good deal of livestock, including several of our community's finest. The loss was significant, and had it not been for the courage and strength of volunteers and our mighty duchy guard, we would have seen more terror upon our great town.

"But now, there is speculation that we haven't eradicated the threat. Some say these were savage fae creatures come to take vengeance. A 'legendary myth,' so to speak.

"I tell you that this is far from true. These rumors, based on imagination and the history of our duchies, have no ground. To make matters worse, there have been one or more persons who took it upon themselves to erect these contraptions around the limits of town."

Piers joined his father's side, his hands full with something obscure beyond the heads and shoulders of the crowd. She edged closer to the stage until she froze to a halt. Her heart dropped to her stomach.

"To whoever thought their ghoulish, artistically

designed craft would provoke hysteria, I hope you've had your laugh," the mayor said. "We will be looking for the rest of them within the hour."

Piers dropped the ward post to the stage floor. Its fragile prongs atop splintered off and clattered to the ground. To her trained eye, the mana in its cracked shell seeped out, fading into the air. Evelot gritted her teeth, her hands tightening into white-knuckled fists.

"Why not call out the perpetrator, then?" Piers announced. "Many of us locals can guess who is to blame."

The mayor motioned for his son to quiet, but Piers then turned to the crowd. "Go on, then. Show yourself. Come out, hag!"

He searched through the crowd for her. The wind picked up, blowing off her hood. When at last they locked eyes, Evelot didn't cower.

"You," he said, pointing his finger with a sneer. "You did this."

Those closest to Evelot backed away.

"I don't deny it," she said.

"Ha! So you would shamelessly admit it."

The mayor stepped between them, catching his son by the shoulder.

"Whatever the cause, it is finished," he said. "What matters is that this is settled—"

"With all due respect, Mayor Redwald, this isn't settled," Evelot said. "Because your son has damned us all out of stupid, selfish pride."

The crowd let out a hushed whisper. Their questions echoed her words. The mayor looked out at them, his anxiety evident in his parted lips.

"Pride? I have much of it in this wonderful town. I take that as a compliment," scoffed Piers.

"Good. Then you'll be to blame when the damned beast comes back!" Evelot said.

"No, I can assure you all there is no beast!" the mayor shouted.

"Those 'ghoulish contraptions' were magic wards meant to keep the werewolf outside. Now it and whatever is left of its horde will be free to hunt anyone here!" snapped Evelot.

The word 'werewolf' hung in the air.

"So says the devil's harlot that summoned the beast from the Hells!" Piers countered.

"Ach, away with you! All it had to do was sniff out your hubris and follow the trail, you fucking bastard!"

"Enough!" the mayor bellowed. When the crowd immediately silenced, he looked down at Evelot. "Girl, I've known your family and respect your father. But I won't tolerate this farce!"

"You mark my words: If you continue the festival, that werewolf will fill its gut before you've had the chance to save face with the duke!"

The mayor motioned to the side of the stage. Evelot followed his eyeline to where duchy guards waded through the crowd.

She dodged the first hand that came toward her. Two other guards maneuvered to block her exit. She tried to peer over their shoulders, but one guard sprung out and locked her in their arms.

"Get off me!" she yelled. "Get o—"

"Evelot!"

Two figures shoved through the crowd. Evelot bucked in the guard's grasp. A familiar head of dark brown hair bobbed above the sea of shoulders for a second. Zenris dove out of the throng of people in a mad dash toward her. The guard holding her stumbled back. Two more stepped in front of Zenris, blocking him.

As if to answer, a mighty roar resounded behind the bard.

Prilthadollak stomped her way through the crowd, yelling, "I've had enough of this gods-damned town! Move out of my way!"

The other guards, the one who held Evelot included, quivered in their boots. The Jinryuu warrior seethed at those surrounding her. A blaze lit within her throat, and from her unhinged jaw billowed vaporous smoke. She huffed and chuffed, the fire dying out within her.

"Evelot!"

Zenris dove around the other guards. Evelot stomped at her captor's boot. He cried out, releasing her. She bolted toward Zenris. He snatched her up in his arms and pulled her away.

"Are you injured?" he said.

"I'm fine. It's nothing—"

"For the love of the heavenly Dawn King, will everyone calm down!" the mayor shouted.

Zenris backed away with Evelot toward Prilthadollak. Their quelled companion reached for her claymore sword as if in warning to the guards.

The mayor tried for a calming breath, but it didn't do a thing to tame the red on his balding head. "There will be no beasts, no devil-worshipping or summoning, and no bludgeoning in this here square!" he snapped at the group.

"We can abide peacefully, sir," Zenris said, "but I beg of you to see reason."

"Ha! As if you can reason with someone who's been charmed by the hag!" Piers called.

The mayor raised his hand at his son, his teeth gritted in a final warning. To Zenris, he replied, "No! I will hear no more of werewolves and hunting!"

"Plug your ears and hide in your offices, but there was a werewolf in the rank of beasts your hunters encountered!" Prilthadollak exclaimed. "It has slain your people, no matter what you believe. Do the honorable thing and fight. Defend your territory!"

Many balked at her declaration, but a few in the back murmured in agreement. The mayor gaped at her before letting out an exasperated breath. He shook his head.

"Whatever sort of life or game you adventurers seek, it's not here. Please leave this square, and do not show your faces here again. Unless you wish to be escorted out."

More guards appeared around them, too many for all three to take on. They stood at the ready. Prilthadollak lowered into a warrior's crouch, waiting for the signal. But Zenris called to her, backing away with Evelot in his hold. Seeing their careful retreat, the guards let them pass. By the time they'd made it to the end of the square, the crowd's and frenzied shouts had risen to echo throughout the empty town.

Evelot numbly followed Zenris and Prilthadollak. The sky was pitch black, and the pathways were blurred. She ignored the moon as it taunted them overhead.

The mayor, and effectively the town, had dismissed

them. They were on their own to fend off the werewolf this time. Their chances were slim if the transformation had already taken place.

When Zenris stopped, Evelot finally looked at him. While a struggle for her human eyes, the tired contours on his face hung like dark shadows. His grip was firm and consoling, his sleepless smile gave her hope.

Prilthadollak groaned aloud, cursing in her native language. Evelot turned to Zenris. To her surprise, he raised her hand to his lips and kissed it.

"All will be well, Evelot," he told her. "We will defeat it this time."

"Zenris. . ."

Her hand went limp in his grasp. Whether he could see her frown or not, it didn't matter. Taking on the werewolf wasn't his problem. Zenris may have been there to perform at a festival, but they had rescinded his invitation. Cast out of town, out of work and favor like Evelot, he and Pril could leave that night if not the next day. So why fight? It was better for him to go, no matter if it hurt her to think about it.

"Cease your lovers' careless whispers," Prilthadollak hissed. "There will be a battle strategy at once!"

Releasing Evelot's hand, Zenris sighed. "What say you then, friend?"

"These werewolf creatures have an aversion to silver, no? We must collect all weaponry of such material and arm ourselves by the morrow."

"No one here has pure silver, save for the duchy guards," Evelot said. "And since they're useless, that leaves us up a shite creek."

"Then we call upon your master to aid us," Zenris

said.

"She already turned us down once before, remember?"

Prilthadollak grumbled low in her throat.

It was pointless. Without help from Beluphis, without the support of the armed guards, the werewolf had the upper hand.

"We can accomplish this," Zenris said, a hopeful smile lighting his face. "After all, we had faced it before."

"This isn't setting traps in the woods, Zenris. Killing an actual werewolf—"

"Yes, yes."

His hand went to her cheek. "But we must have hope."

"*We.*" As if it concerned him anymore. Evelot shook her head, stepping away from his warm palm.

"Neither of you have to do this," Evelot said, summoning her courage. "You can go—"

"Absolutely not. Pril and I are as much a part of this as you. Is that not right, Pril?"

"One would think to let nature take its course and let them perish, but I will defend this ludicrous town if only to sink my talons and blade in that irksome beast!" she snapped.

"See? She agrees," Zenris said.

Evelot pursed her lips. Maybe it would be better to have him on her side one last time. Whether or not for a good cause, it was still going to hurt when Zenris was too stubborn to leave. She'd have to bear it a bit longer.

Zenris then chuckled. "This. . . it reminds me of our time caught in a trap," he said.

"You're thinking of that now?" Evelot said.

Strangely, Zenris paused. His expression froze in what Evelot thought was shock.

"What's wrong?" she asked.

He grinned, wide and hopeful. "There may be a solution, after all."

"You've got a plan?"

"I cannot take the credit. For this is one of yours, only much, much grander."

Chapter Twenty-Five

The night of the festival was underway, dancing firelights and cheers of excitement filling the misty grounds. Zenris caught the melodious sounds of other bards harmonizing and strumming to passersby; if only he could do so freely in that moment.

He followed the line of festivalgoers to the entrance, an arch of white-lacquered wood decorated with bright wreaths. It stood as alertly as the guards posted there. Amongst them, Zenris spotted the mayor. A note of consternation frayed the edges of his smile directed at his guests. Exactly what Zenris had hoped for.

Nearing the entrance, Zenris stepped away from the line and approached the mayor. The guards stiffened, positioning themselves around him. Zenris held his hands up peacefully.

"I simply wish to speak with you, sir," Zenris told him. "May I approach?"

The mayor scrutinized him. Flashing his accolade-winning grin, Zenris kept still. After a beat, the mayor waved off his troops.

Zenris bowed in gratitude. "Good even. I take it the festival is going well so far?" he said.

"Yes. Now that the talk of beasts and death has subsided," the mayor deadpanned.

"Understandable. No more witches and magic to dissuade a few newcomers from making merry here, either."

The mayor tilted his head. "By that, you mean to say that you don't agree with the witchling?"

"No. Last night I was certain I was right in my cause, only to learn that I was a fool. And so, I come to beg forgiveness, sir. My companion and I will take what pride we have left and empty our rooms at the inn. Naturally, the honorable course of action would be to leave you with a humble apology."

"Yes, I see. Well, yes. All is forgiven, then."

"Thank you, sir."

Before the mayor could turn away, Zenris then asked, "If I may be so bold, may I ask for entrance into the festival?"

"You—what?"

"'Twas several nights ago that I had last spoken with one of the stage masters. We had agreed on a time for my performance, and 'twould be ever so gracious of you to allow this elf keep his word."

"I see."

The mayor glanced back at his guards and fell into a deliberate silence. His kind of authority was hardly unique. Mayor Redwald did not see his town's comfort before coin, and neither did his superiors. Zenris was worth his weight in gold, having been the first of the bards to arrive and an icon no matter the trouble he caused.

Of course, there was the possibility that Mayor Redwald had a heart. Zenris's skin anxiously prickled. He hoped there was no need for drastic measures, such as creating a distraction or taking a guard hostage. He had not the invisibility potion necessary to recreate the messy success it once brought him.

"Well, I see no harm in one or two songs played. Keep your word to the stage master, then, and enjoy what you can of the festival."

"Of course." Zenris beamed back at him. "You have my utmost gratitude, sir."

"Pleasure, it is."

The mayor's hand patted Zenris's shoulder, a signal to the guards to let him through. With that, Zenris stayed an innocent elf another day.

He made his way inside with a composed smile upon his lips. Trader's wagons and booths teemed, following the eyes of merrymaking buyers. Both local sellers and their foreign competition shouted over the boisterous noise of bagpipes and drums. His stomach roiled at the smell of roasted meat, taming into a mewl when sweet aromas arose in the former's wake. His hunger, however hidden, would have to be satiated with the nectar of victory.

Eagle to Swallow and Cardinal. Eagle heading to nest, Zenris said, sending a magicked telepathic note to his companions.

Swallow in position, answered Pril.

C-Cardinal in position. . . Do we really need to use these ridiculous monikers? We're talking in our heads for Maiden's sake!

Zenris chuckled to himself.

Oh, sweet cardinal, 'tis all a part of the fun. Fret not over it.

He imagined her sigh of frustration while weaving

through the crowd to the main stage. There, surrounded by smaller venues, it shone greater than the lighthouse of Ollthyr. Zenris's mouth dropped in awe at its size. Near the wood's edge far beyond, it stood as tall as the trees themselves, like a grand theater without seats. An accompanying band practiced before a rallying audience. The perfect display for their trap.

Behind the stage, a conclave of performers and crew members sauntered by. Zenris waded past them and their props, eyeing another half-elf leaning against the set-up. In poshly intricate vestments and sleek boots with a lit cigar in his pale hand, stood the stage master. Spotting Zenris, the willowy man coolly regarded him.

"Thought they told you to bugger off," he said with a smirk.

"But sir, what good bard would I be to stay away from the music!" Zenris teased.

In his head, he called: *Any news, Swallow and Cardinal?*

Swallow: *No sign yet.*

Cardinal: *Got nothing.*

The stage master scoffed at him. "You're lucky the other band willing to take your place got stage fright. I'll give you fifteen minutes, and nothing more."

"How generous of you, sir," Zenris said with a sharp grin, his pride stinging at the blatant disregard.

Once the stage master walked off, Zenris stood aside and waited for his call. He faced the direction of the woods, the feeling that the darkness stared back all too tangible. As the festival launched to a magnificent start, he suspected the werewolf and his pack were there, cloaked in shadow, watching for an opportune moment to strike. Zenris wondered if they would spring during the changing of the guards, or when many a festival-goer were well impaired. Only time would tell.

He hoped their plan would succeed. It had to. He wished for Evelot to remain in a home where darkness did not haunt her, not one terrorized by werewolves. Though she kept distant from him, and he was as guilty of the same beforehand, he could not bear to part from her on such a note. His heart clenched at the thought of leaving. Were their paths to split after that night, he would at least have granted her a safe home.

"You're on, Aspenlark!" the stage master called.

Zenris released a quick exhale, smiling to mask his frustration. After he sent a quick note to his companions, he recalled happy thoughts meant to bolster his performance and walked up the steps to the center stage.

Enveloped in the blaring stage lights, Zenris waved at the shushing crowd. The chipper voices of his fans drowned out the nearby street performers. Their faces were obscured, yet he was relieved to find loyal followers.

Gratefully, he dipped in a theatrical bow. The familiarity of his stage persona fell on him like a comfortable cloak around his shoulders.

"A glorious even to you all!" he said to the crowd. Many converged toward him and the stage. "Do mine ears deceive me? Methinks 'twas doves that called to me a moment ago."

Cupping his ear, he basked in the delighted cry of his fans. He grinned back at them and replied, "How I have missed you so, my lovely doves. It breaks my heart that this shall be our final night together, but I am humbled to have seen you, to have visited your beautiful home here in Goldencrest."

Clamorous sobs erupted from their corner. Zenris gathered his lute and continued, "Do not fret, for I depart with an exciting note: I present you not only with a new song, but our gracious stage master's crew to accompany it. Hear, hear for our companions!"

A quiet band of men took to the stage behind him, more attentive to setting the stage than addressing the crowd. Zenris clapped with the audience, nonetheless.

Once they were done, he jogged toward them. 'Twas a long moment to set their cues and hurriedly practice the melody. Another symptom of the stage master's indifference: not allowing time for the crew to communicate with the guests.

Finally, to the crowd, Zenris announced, "Thank you for your patience. Before we begin, I have a request: Would I stomp my foot like so"—and he did—"you clap along. A demonstration for you."

In slow motion, he coaxed the audience into participation. Zenris grinned back at them, taking up his instrument.

"Huzzah! With that, I give you: *A Thrilling Night.*"

The band started up behind him with a sextet of low, hopping notes. Zenris struck the beginning chords, signaling the audience with a timed stomp. His lurching choreography, unbeknownst to others, was as steeped in bardic magic as his voice. His lyrics of traipsing through the woods and lurking evil would have both the audience and beastie swooning.

Zenris peered out into the crowd as he carried on.

Many of them stopped, curious about the contagious melody, and some danced with him. Their hands clapped to the beat. None stirred as he hoped the villains would, and so he entered the chorus with determined fervor.

There, at the edge of the crowd he glimpsed a sturdy male figure writhing with the tune. Thick fur covered his braced arms, and his piercing yellow gaze fixed on an unassuming listener. Zenris warbled, bopping before the audience and strumming his lute. Caught in his trap, the creature mimicked his swagger. Pril was close at hand. A moment passed, and then she snuck away with her unconscious prey.

Upon the second verse, Zenris felt his mana's influence in full effect. He skipped along in a dance on stage, balancing his lute in hand. The frenzied crowd dipped with him, allowing him to see an encroaching figure as warped as the last pivot toward the stage. Zenris searched for his companions. A bystander stumbled into the beast's way. Its clawed hand curled upward, ready to strike.

A burst of mana emphasized Zenris's next lyrics. With the chorus, he stomped. His listeners did the same, and the beast froze in place. Its shoulder twitched first, and then its hips as he imitated Zenris's dance, fallen under his spell. Vines twisted around its ankles. Under her cloak, Evelot moved through the packed crowd to collect the beast in the shadows.

As he plucked at his lute, Zenris's vigor soared. He spun on the soles of his feet and belted in song. Had he not, Zenris would have missed the figure springing past the stage master and the wary band onstage.

It snarled and bucked, preparing to lunge for him.

Bardic magic pulsed through Zenris with his ecstatic heartbeat. At the last second, he leaned away from the beast, jutting and strutting with the tune. His foe's legs twisted in a similar sidestep and shuffle. Its maw hung open in shock as its body shimmied alongside Zenris.

Zenris turned back to the crowd as Pril's outline slipped behind the stage curtains and tugged the beast out of sight. His flesh prickled in excitement as he continued in song. With every stolen breath, every flick of his fingers along the lute strings, Zenris felt more than mana sweeping him into elation.

With the springing tap of his feet, magic thrust from his pelvis in time with a final, operatic cry. The audience jounced to a stop. The beasts amongst them slumped over in slumber.

Thunderous applause erupted from the crowd, his fans crying his name. He gazed upon their shadowed faces, breathless and mirthful. Yet he only searched for one.

Toward the side of the stage stood his fair Evelot. With her hood lowered, she beamed victoriously back at him. Soon, he would join her to discuss the next steps of their plans to dispose of their foes, and eventually, separate.

An echo hummed within, a yearning to sing once more. Her smile was more important than strategy with the beasts tamed.

Zenris motioned for the band behind him. He offered quick instructions before addressing the audience.

"Thank you, one and all," he said. "Before I exit the stage, I wish to leave one last parting gift. 'Tis one that I most ardently toiled at, in dedication to Goldencrest's jewel, and her radiant smile."

The crowd quieted, titillated by his mysterious reference.

Slowly, Zenris began, "*Upon yonder Choille were thistles and brush. On a bladed bed did I sleep, to discover a seedling, pouted and ablush.*"

Evelot looked marbled, frozen in shock. Their final moments were upon them. Zenris yearned to hold her, comfort her. He sang with the weight of their last night in bittersweet, whispering notes and a longing fermata. To convey the ceaseless soaring and plummeting of his heart was madness, yet he attempted to do so through his only strength. Of all the adventures to have, meeting her was the one he would carry within him to the afterlife.

Zenris opened his mouth wide for the next note—

A roar shook the night's jovial air.

Standing a foot taller than the crowd was the familiar hulking silhouette of the werewolf Alpha. His hood fell back, revealing a mane of fur for hair and a malformed snout in place of a human nose. His garnet eyes bore through Zenris with an icy glint.

Though horrified, Zenris frowned in dismay. "For shame, sir. I was singing my best before you had so rudely interrupted me."

The werewolf howled with laughter. Unable to utter a scream, the crowd slowly backed away.

"Were you now? I've only seen a feeble display of stolen work. But your song reminds me that I hunger for the little bitchling working alongside you," he replied.

The werewolf then plucked a maiden from Zenris's gaggle of fans. She shrieked for help, shaking the crowd from their horrified stupor. Audiences and passersby stampeded off amidst shouts and screams, leaving upended stalls in their wake.

Zenris caught sight of Evelot's cloak pushing through the mania. Her arm stretched outward, a peridot light sputtering on her fingertips. Pril, still somewhere behind the stage, was nowhere in sight.

"Come out, bitchling!" the werewolf shouted. "Before I use this bleating sheep as sustenance and rip out your partner's throat!"

"Careful," Zenris said. "Never underestimate a bard, sir."

The werewolf wickedly grinned back at him, sniffing at the maiden pleading for mercy in his hold.

"You've no strength in your puny limbs. And I know you've spent your mana on your songs. So, no, I think I will feast."

It opened its maw. The maiden screamed at the top of her lungs—

Thick vines cracked like a whip from the ground, piercing the werewolf's back. In his falter, he dropped the maiden from his hold. She scuttled away in a heap of sobs.

The werewolf reared back on his attacker.

"Get out of my home, you manky mutt!" Evelot exclaimed.

With a howl at the full moon, the werewolf's body twisted and writhed. Before any of them could react, what once was human ripped apart into the towering, snarling beast from the chapel.

Zenris jumped off the stage. He raced toward the werewolf while Pril charged from the side of the stage with a mighty battle cry. Beneath the shrieks of the crowd the marching of feet faintly echoed. The duchy guards had responded to the threat.

The werewolf moved to lunge at Evelot. A burst of magic coursed through Zenris. He skidded to a halt as mana settled in his throat.

"I suppose a dagger would do to smite you, lest I wield my rapier and render you jealous!" he snapped.

The werewolf growled, curling back toward Zenris. Its maw snapped open, and the flash of white teeth lunged at him—

Pril dove betwixt them. Metal clashed against teeth as her claymore caught in the beast's jaws. With a growl, it bucked and pulled until Pril swung round, sending it sprawling back.

"This ends now!" Pril roared.

Her fury created physical heat that lashed at Zenris's face. Pril raised her sword to the sky and lowered into a concentrated warrior's stance.

Cackling caught Zenris's ear. A jackal slunk toward Evelot from the sacked booths. A spark of light wrapped around her outline, and icy blue seeped into her clothes.

At the snap of the werewolf's jaws, Zenris armed himself with a hidden dagger and lunged. His foe grunted, dipping away. Zenris retreated to Pril's side before she swung down on the creature. The crunch of bone met a shrill yipe. Zenris glanced back—

Evelot ducked away from a jackal and its jaw clacked shut on her cloak. The magic surrounding her coiled about its snout. Evelot's swipe of her athame caught only air.

Zenris had to aid her.

The werewolf growled as Pril raised her claymore

sword. Its rear legs wobbled, strained by its earlier fall. Zenris snuck around as Pril's blade whistled through the air, entirely missing it. His dagger struck true into the beast's weakened side. With a resounding yipe, the werewolf glowered back at him. It thrust in a downward swipe before Zenris could retreat. He bit back a scream; hot white pain lanced through his forearm.

He grabbed at his weeping injury, stumbling back. Pril stepped in front of him and swung at the lunging beast. His foot caught on something dark. Zenris tumbled to the ground, landing on his injured arm. Grunting, he glanced down. Two jackals stirred from their enchanted sleep, their gazes latching onto him.

"Zenris!" his lady called.

Evelot disappeared behind the rising jackals. The werewolf's maw gleamed sinisterly at Zenris as it turned its back on Pril.

"Coward!"

Pril's blade sank into its hide, the tang scent of blood permeating the air. Ahead, Evelot fell back from the first jackal's jaw. The creature repeated its earlier mistake of snagging her cloak. She moved as if to join Zenris's side when the other beasts sprung at him. The first lashed its claws at him, catching his torso. Zenris gritted his teeth, yet no pain came. Only the urge to move entered his mind. His surroundings blurred as he dodged another attack and stole away a pace.

Vines sprouted from the ground akin to octopus tentacles. Evelot, in their center, pointed at one jackal. The barbed, thorny edges struck its head. The fiend roared in pain. With a leap, Zenris plunged his dagger straight into its heart. The beast helplessly whimpered and slumped to the ground.

Pril and the werewolf moved in tandem. The werewolf struck her shoulder before her blade landed. Blood coated her armor; she snarled back at the foe. Despite her pained grimaces, she raised her blade. Once, then twice she swiped. Spittle and blood flew from its sliced maw.

The beast still stood.

"Gah!"

Zenris spun to see a weakened jackal chomp at Evelot's leg before it lunged away. Red rolled down her calf as she limped backward, gasping for breath.

The other jackal spun toward Zenris. He scarcely avoided its claws, and in doing so toppled backward. A thick crack rang out behind his head, and stars burst in his vision. In his disoriented gaze, the swirling image of the jackal loomed over him.

Metal glistened at the corner of his eye. Several duchy guards enclosed their circle with their weapons trained on the beasts. Two stabbed at the weakened jackals, and the others approached Zenris's attacker. Its lips peeled back in a snarl, fixated on them.

With its attention drawn away, Zenris willed his heavy limbs to act. To rise and find Evelot. Yet 'twas in vain.

"Zenris!"

Evelot hobbled to his aid. She took his hand and pulled him up. He braced himself in her hold.

"Go," Zenris insisted. "Escape, my lady. You are injured."

"As if you're one to talk—"

Just as his hearing returned, the werewolf's howl

pierced the air. With gnashing teeth, it charged them. Zenris shoved Evelot away. Its clenched jaw hovered where they once had stood.

Pril dashed toward them and took a swing at the beast. One swipe clipped its bloodied face, and the other sent a chunk of ear soaring into the night. With the guards occupying the remaining jackal, 'twas his group left to the brute.

Evelot's athame swished in the air below the werewolf's chin. Before it could retaliate, Zenris swung with his dagger. The beast let out a pained roar, and its eyelid sealed shut from the flow of crimson rivulets.

The werewolf sneered at Zenris, who moved a few seconds too late. Its sharp claws swiped across his legs. He crumpled to the ground with an agonized cry. His body refused to move; he still breathed, if only to witness an impending, fatal blow.

"Zenris!" cried Evelot.

Pril's claymore pierced the air betwixt the beast and Zenris. With two rapid swings, she drew the beast's attention to herself.

Zenris crawled back as they battled, and Evelot nearly hopped on her wounded leg to reach him. She collapsed at his side, her shaking hands moved to her pouch while she glanced back at the beast.

"No," Zenris said. "'Tis not worth the cost. Defend yourself!"

"Just shut it and let me help you."

She uncorked a vial and put it to his lips. An acrid sludge slid past his tongue; a flutter of strength returned to Zenris.

"Better?" Evelot asked.

Her glassy eyes peered down at him, her face pale with exhaustion. Zenris wanted for her to escape; he wanted to give her the chance to do so.

The wet slap of a tongue pulsed in his ear. Zenris turned his head. Evelot shouted. Her hands flew out and shoved him to the ground.

When Zenris blinked, he stared up at Evelot. Her neck dribbled blood as the werewolf clamped down. Her shriek echoed in Zenris's ear as it lifted her up and tossed her aside.

"Evelot!"

Adrenaline surged him to his feet. The werewolf turned to him, with a snickery breath curling its lips. It dodged Pril once more and Zenris's feeble slash.

Zenris foresaw its next lunge by the crouch of its hind legs. He had no energy left to roll away. 'Twould tear him apart.

His hand loosened over his dagger. He gaped at the face of death.

Booming as loudly as lightning, a hoarse spell resounded through the festival grounds. Evelot, on her feet, fixed a pointed finger on the werewolf. Hellish fire ignited the air, dancing madly around the beast. Its wailing bellow sharpened and twisted as if a demonic opera. The werewolf shrunk to the ground, quavering and debilitated. The smell of burning flesh and fur stung Zenris's nostrils.

At last, their greatest foe met his ultimate end.

"Evelot!"

Her whimpered cries were shrieks in his ears as he sprinted toward his lady. She crumpled to her knees, her hands bearing down on her bleeding neck. Zenris fell beside her. He tried to peel away her hands to no avail.

"Stop!" he pleaded. "Let me help. Let me—"

"Get away!"

She shoved at him with quaking arms as her body writhed upon the ground. Zenris shifted and gripped at her slippery hands. Her gaping wounds puckered, darkening. From her scalp cascaded thick tufts of auburn. Sinew spasmed beneath flesh. She clutched her head as bones audibly cracked and stretched.

Zenris tentatively reached for her. "E-Evelot. . ."

"Don't. . ."

Her voice deepened as she whimpered.

"Run. Zenris—run!"

He scrambled back. Evelot screamed aloud.

On all fours, her body morphed. Fur stretched from her bare flesh and reforming limbs, her clothes tearing away under the sudden swell of her increased size. When her head tilted upward, those green eyes were there no longer. Crimson orbs bore through him, and a snarl rippled from betwixt a werewolf's jaws.

Zenris felt paralyzed in terror at its cold, empty eyes.

"E-Ev. . .?" he sputtered.

The beast reared on its haunches. Suddenly, its snarl shifted into a whimper. It shook its head. For a hopeful moment, Zenris thought there was a familiar, human-like glint in its eyes.

It looked to the moon and howled somberly. Without another thought, the werewolf, Evelot, whirled around and raced into the woods.

Chapter Twenty-Six

He shook his head, heart sinking into his stomach. "No! Come back!"

Zenris refused to believe it, for the life of him he could not. She was gone. She had disappeared into the woods. However far her feet carried her, 'twas a distance too far for him.

His body was in as much denial as his heart. He felt himself racing after Evelot, her name ripping out of his throat. Adrenaline briefly coursed through his veins before it abruptly stuttered. His feet caught a patch of grass, and Zenris tumbled to the ground. A grunted plea left him as he scrambled for purchase.

It could not be their fate. It would not be.

A hand caught his collar. Zenris yelled, kicking at whoever had hoisted him onto their shoulder.

"Do you wish to die, Heart of Aspen?" Pril snapped. "You are injured!"

"Release me! Pril!"

"It is done. She is gone!"

"No, no, no! 'Tis not—"

He squirmed against her. Evelot could not have left

him. She had not vanished. He would find her if Pril simply released him. He would get his lady back.

A growl rumbled beneath him before Pril tossed him to the ground. His back struck the earth, and the air in his lungs heaved from his chest.

Pril glowered down at him and barked, "It was a well-made sacrifice. Do not let it be in vain!"

"What do you know of sacrifice?" Zenris snapped, wheezing. "You understand nothing!"

"Enough!"

A spark of fire lit in her heavy breath. Pril chuffed, staring him down until she was at his level.

"Rage at nature," she said, "the fates or the gods. But it will do you no good."

Zenris sneered. Defiance flared through him; he rose to his feet. Pril did not understand, not that it mattered. Evelot was out there and he needed to find her. He would search all night if he had to. He could—

His body swayed. Zenris caught himself on a stage beam, and he realized they were still on the festival grounds. From the side of the main stage, the edge of the woods appeared far off, yet it could be no more than a few meters away. With all his strength, he would not survive an hour in his condition.

A noise of frustration clawed deep in his throat as he held onto the beam. He squeezed his eyes shut at the truth. She was gone.

Terror lanced through his heart.

The sound of Pril's tail swishing in the air wrenched him from his thoughts. Irritation scorched within him, the need to scream his frustration mounting.

Zenris turned to speak, only to freeze at the sight in his peripheral vision.

"Zenris?" Helga asked. "You seen Evelot anywhere?"

He felt all of his determination drain from him, replaced by guilt. His jaw clenched shut on the truth.

"As soon as we'd heard, we came. Did you see. . .?"

Helga paused. Her eyes glossed over with oncoming tears of realization.

Not only had Zenris failed his lady, he had also failed a woman who would soon mourn her lost child. He cast his gaze to the ground. Shame bore upon his chest a weight unseen and relentless in its tight hold.

Helga's drawn breath sounded akin to a sigh. A moment passed.

Her palm was warm on his cheek.

Zenris looked up to Helga's dawning smile when he should have seen misery, or grief. Anything but mercy.

Yet she took his hand, and to both of he and Pril, she said, "Come away with me, bairns."

Two days had passed since that night. Long, arduous days that solemnly meandered. Though he naturally needed little rest, Zenris's body refused him any. The stamina to help lift sacks of flour and sort the winter-stocked barns with Evelot's father unconsciously came to him. The work served as a gesture of appreciation to Evelot's family for graciously allowing him and Pril a roof over their heads, and he needed what menial tasks they offered. They aided in processing his tumultuous emotions.

When the sun was at its highest on a gray, wintry day, Zenris stopped to catch his breath. He sat beneath the garden's apple tree and enviously watched the wispy clouds.

"Heart of Aspen."

Pril stopped beside him, her arms folded.

"Greetings, Pril," he sighed.

"Your skin is ashen and your limbs are like twigs. Come inside and eat before we depart."

"Oh, my, what kind words you impart me."

"It is far from kind. It is truth."

Zenris shook his head. "I will not leave, Pril. Nor do I hunger. It has been said quite extensively."

"I know," Pril answered. "And you also know my thoughts on this."

"Yes. That I am a fool for denying food and an 'ah-ho' to stay another day.' Why is it you stay, then?"

"Because that *aho* is my ward, and my friend."

Pril sat beside him, her feet tucked beneath her in a serious martial posture.

"Of all the members in our party, you are the one that baffles me the most, Heart of Aspen," Pril said. "You make merry and laze like a feeble-minded lizard basking in the sun. But under that mask is a strong, caring soul that passionately burns like magma."

"I take it this is where you confess that you suffer the same way?" Zenris asked.

Pril frowned. "I feel nothing but the call of war to defeat injustice and my enemies."

"Pity."

"As it were," Pril continued. "You come from another culture and do as you see fit. But seeing this extremity of withdrawing yourself leads me to question why. Why do you not cut off your emotions at the source?"

"You mean my—" Zenris stopped himself. To call it 'mourning' would be an insult. Evelot could not have perished. "Why am I waiting for her?"

"Yes."

"I-I. . ." Zenris gripped at his chest where an ache slithered over his heart. "I care for her."

"Interesting."

Zenris frowned, looking up at her. "How so?"

"Because this is the first that a lover you have taken has drowned you in a stupor. All of them you had wooed and left behind the next morning, but this is the one you have stayed the longest for. The witchling brings about a difference in you."

He blinked back at her, stupefied.

"I have heard of your flesh-kin passions. Something more than leisure. Evelot is this 'true happiness,' or perhaps, 'love' of yours. Do you disagree?"

"L-love. I. . ." A shocked laugh left him. "No, I cannot disagree."

"Then that must be why she stays away, beast or human."

"What?" Zenris gasped.

"It is much like the treasure the Ancients hoarded, if you will pardon the expression. This 'happiness' of yours is something invaluable and must be protected. If it is something you equally share. And so, to protect it, there comes a time where one must forfeit their half."

Zenris sat back. Aside from the astounding observation from Pril, and a hint of her culture he rarely heard of, his attention concentrated on her point. Evelot would do something excessive. To a fault, she always put her loved ones before her own desires. Eventually, there would reach an end to the well of giving, and there would be no dreams left for her. To know that she was doing so for him brought him shame.

"I cannot abide by her wishes," Zenris said. "She cannot hide forever."

"What if she is adamant in her decision? What will you do, Zenris?"

He looked back at his companion. Instead of stoic indifference, there lay a hint of knowing patience about her; his spirits deflated. Of course he could not force Evelot to return, or to speak with him. Whether he begged and pleaded, 'twas her choice. She would choose first before hearing his plea.

Yet, he still wished to try.

"If there was a chance, I would say my piece. Though I wish it were not this way. . . I would respect her decision."

Pril nodded. "Very well."

She rose, glancing at the woods beyond. Zenris found not the strength in his heart to follow her line of sight. He feared seeing another empty path without his lady. All he yearned for in that moment was to enfold her in his arms and speak words of comfort. If but one last time.

Pril's hand struck his head. Zenris cried out.

"Look there, Heart of Aspen!" Pril said.

Zenris did so while rubbing at the spot. A speck of

ebony bolted through the air, flying as though the sunlight burned its flesh. A shrill cry came as it fell toward them.

"Jammer!"

He held out his hand for her. The little bat captured his finger and clung to him. She squirmed and wriggled in his hold, licking the salt from his palm as if it would save her from the light.

"Have you brought any news, little lady?" he asked, channeling mana to his ear.

Note. Note. Tired. Tired. Poppa, she trilled back.

On her leg was a slip of parchment, carefully tied there. Zenris unlaced it, his other hand greedily unfolding it.

If the bard is still here, send him into the woods. Your daughter needs a song of encouragement.

He was certain 'twas Beluphis's writing. Zenris stroked the little bat with his thumb, relief flooding him like cool water in the blistering heat of Aswana.

When he turned to Pril, she nodded encouragingly.

"I will stay to address our means of travel," she said. "Go."

"Thank you, friend."

Zenris pressed a kiss to little Jammer's head and tucked her into his shirt collar. He made his way into the Wheaton home to call upon them. His trek would be long despite his resolve, and supplies were necessary for the journey ahead.

Chapter Twenty-Seven

Three days it'd been since that nightmarish, foreign body ensnared her. Three days under a blur of shrieks, agony, and sleepless nights. Her memory eventually returned, but it did no good against the fits of worry and doubt that plagued her dreams. The Harvest Maiden hadn't answered her prayers at all.

She was too much of a threat to her family, awake or asleep. Her curse was like a collar around her throat. The moon's beckon was weak at the moment, but come another fortnight, it'd yank on her lead. The feelings she'd had as a beast, of a hunger so raw and vicious, were as strong as the pain of transformation had been; but these feelings were wee compared to the possibility of finding her hands soaked in her family's blood.

If anything, there was one she didn't have to worry about killing. Wherever Zenris was in Runlaris, he'd have better chances at survival. Evelot had mourned his departure before. Every time she thought of him moving on, taking another lover and forgetting about Goldencrest—about her —the pain of it tore at her insides. It was another form of torture beside her other fears. But it was the best thing for him, no matter what.

In her small sanctuary in Beluphis's home, in a cot that buried her in sheets and quilts, she shut her eyes and tried for restless sleep again.

On a day when sleep had denied her, Evelot blinked up at the ceiling. The chill from outside seeped into the room, leaving her exposed skin nubbly. Light poured in from the wee windows. She found her sheets rumpled under her chin, and a warmth against her side. What she thought was the sun held onto her hand.

She stiffened. Evelot rolled her head and found the hallucination of Zenris slumped over her bedside in a chair. His lengthy waves of hair escaped their tie and spilled over her leg. It was so lifelike, the feel of his rough palms on her hand, but warm. Like everything about him, including the breaths his illusion took, the rise and fall of its chest.

Not even cursed could she find some solace. Tears blurred her vision, threatening to spill as the image peacefully slumbered.

"Just let me go," she whispered.

It stirred at her side. She heard the loud hum of its voice, the magnified scent of its cologne in her sensitive nose, the breaths it took as—as his eyes opened. It wasn't her mind. Zenris looked back at her.

"Ev. . ."

She yelped. Zenris reached for her, but she dove out of the bed. On quivering legs, she paced back, back, until she was to the wall.

"'Tis fine," Zenris said.

"No, no, it's not."

"Please, my lady. I know you are frightened, but allow

me—"

Zenris stood there, by the bedside, blocking the way to the door. Her eyes bore into the floorboards, and she wished only to fall through them. She couldn't look him in the eye, not when she was. . .

He took a step forward. Evelot threw her arms over her head.

"Don't come any closer!" she exclaimed.

Zenris stopped, frozen with his arms splayed to show he meant no harm. As if that were possible when she was the strongest between them, when she could hear his heart racing as wildly as hers, when his natural scent made her salivate.

"I beseech you to listen, Evelot. There is no reason to hide. I wish not for you to flee any longer."

"If I can't, then you should!" she snapped. "Why haven't you left town? You were supposed to be gone by now."

"And in doing so abandon you? What kind of man would I become?" Zenris said.

"Alive. Sane. Take your pick," she retorted.

"'I would be a fool," he insisted, taking a small step forward, "and a coward. Damned I would be for taking leave when there is still hope."

"No, you can't. Undoing a damned curse? Zenris, I'm a monster—"

"Evelot, you are yourself. Right now. You will not—"

"That won't stay the same now, will it?" Evelot exclaimed. "Not when the fucking moon comes out! I can't control it. No one can!"

"'Twill be a learning curve, yes. Mayhap the use of

restraints will be a necessity in the future. But that should not stop us from working together. Do not discount the possibility, my love."

"W-why're you so. . ."

She wouldn't allow herself to cry, no matter how stubborn Zenris was in his efforts. But as she dared to peek back at him, she realized what he had called her.

"I vowed to never let you suffer alone. And now that. . ."

His whole body looked taut. His jaw tightened, and his hands froze at his side. But the moment was soon over. As he was wont to do, he plunged straight in with his next words.

"Evelot, I am besotted with you. Through tribulation and reconciliation, you have seen neither a bard nor a stranger, but this humbled soul before you. In that time, I have perceived in you more than a witch plaguing innocents. I have witnessed your wonder for the world, for things beguiling and strange and captivating. Your valor tempered with a tender heart. No curse nor beast will ever change that. So please, my love, allow me to help you."

His smile faltered at the edges, his eyes too watery to be confident. Zenris held out his hand like he had all the days before. Evelot felt the sting of tears rising to the surface. If she caved in, he would only smother her, console her. Make her feel loved. Zenris would promise to make it all better at any cost.

Her heart raced in fear. It wouldn't be right for him to treat her like that, not when things had changed. There was no hope for her, and all he was doing was putting himself in danger.

Evelot shook her head and murmured, "You shouldn't have stayed."

The anguish that fractured his sincere expression, crack by crack, made her wish for death. Zenris solemnly nodded then stepped back. Her hands fisted her skirts as the door opened and shut behind him with a soft click.

Silence engulfed the room. All of her restrained thoughts surged like a rushing stream. He'd the gumption to tell her he loved her when she was doomed to her fate. He'd loved her in all that time together.

Zenris loved her.

She looked down at the hand he'd held and brought it to her cheek. His scent still lingered in the air.

Evelot silently lowered to the floor, and let her tears flow.

When her eyes next opened, daylight had long since flown off and moonlight had taken its place, mocking her. Evelot sniffled, scrubbing at her tear-stained face. Shockingly, she felt nauseous at the thought of trying to sleep again. A growl rumbled in her stomach, and her mouth was dry. If she were lucky, Beluphis would still be in her study, and there'd be something savory or spiced to numb the dull ache in her chest.

Evelot snuck down the stairs, wrapped in her quilt of misery and listened for scuffles of life on the main floor. When nothing echoed back or struck her nose, she slunk toward the kitchen.

From the top stair of her study, her mentor harrumphed. Her scrutinizing eye pinned Evelot in the open doorway.

"So, you have decided to join the living, eh?" she asked.

Evelot looked down. "Aye, Master."

"Peh."

Her mentor entered the kitchen. Evelot peeked into the open doorway to find her scrounging through her cabinets, clanking whatever pots she'd found.

"Come in, then. Won't find food out there," her mentor called.

"No, master. I'll do without—"

"Qatiway."

With a knobbly finger, she commanded Evelot forth. The witchling entered and sat down at the kitchen island. Beluphis scrambled through a basket on the counter, one that she had enchanted to hold an infinite number of ingredients. From it, she produced several eggs, milled flour, and butter.

As she combined the ingredients in a pan hovering over a magicked flame, Beluphis said, "So, you finally saw reason."

Evelot didn't know how to respond.

"I always knew that fanciful bard would be too much for you. You made the right choice in discarding him, even if it cost your livelihood. Now you won't have to put up with his theatrics and shrieking instruments."

"Is he really gone?" Evelot asked.

Her mentor looked up from the pan with a raised

brow. "Of course. Once you rejected his pretty love confession, he left with his tail tucked between his legs. Thought I saw him shed a tear."

Evelot gritted her teeth at the shame that doused her.

"And then the bastard spun around and begged me for information about a cure. You should have seen his face when I told him. Didn't matter to him that it was somewhere beyond Aswana. He took off before I could tell him that the one able to break the curse is in hiding. Guess he'll have to lure out that sorceress with a pretty tune on his lute, if he hasn't forgotten about you first, that is? Peh, maybe not. It cost him something, mind you."

"W-what do you mean, Master?"

"You think I run a charity? I am a nature witch who bargains for information. I do not hand it out to every sob story. Ohohoho, the sort of spells I can cast with them. He needed his tongue to speak, but I will make due with the bardic magic in his hands."

Evelot paled, a gasp stuck in her throat.

Seeing her expression, Beluphis humphed. "Upa. It's a lie," she chastised. "That information isn't worth anything after a decade. That sorceress could be dead now."

After she emptied the pan onto a small plate, Beluphis handed it over to Evelot. Cloying honey and jams were set out in front of her, made with the berries from the garden. Memories flooded back; she couldn't touch the food.

After what she'd said, Zenris was rushing off to the other side of the world to look for a cure. How could she eat, knowing that?

"But what does that matter now?" Beluphis said. "He's gone, and your family is far from being eaten alive.

Maybe it would be best for you to stay in the woods. You can watch the Opening like a good little guard dog. Suppose it's fate, then. Now you can get what you want with no more interruptions."

Evelot stared at her meal. That old dream felt like a distant memory. Of course it wasn't what she wanted. But if she didn't know what she wanted now, then what was she to do?

Beluphis leaned over the counter, coming face-to-face with Evelot. "Why so glum? You are where you belong."

Evelot peeked up at her. Within her mentor's eerily calm expression morphed hardened lines, a kind of scrutiny that Evelot feared saw right through her.

"M-Master. . ."

Beluphis's fists slammed down on the countertop. Evelot jumped back with a gasp. Red mana wavered around her mentor's silhouette like a roaring flame, and her gray hair billowed in a nonexistent wind. She smelled of decay and ash. Gooseflesh raced over Evelot's arms. Beluphis's expression was worse than a glower.

"No more self-pity!" she yelled. "No more sacrifices and wishy-washy hums. For once in your life, take charge and stop being scared!"

Evelot gaped at her.

Beluphis rose to her full height, but her rage dimmed, locked behind knowing eyes. "I have watched you squander too much of your life on nothing. You wanted to be a priestess—it did not happen. You wanted to become a Guardian—it did not happen. So what? That Portal will be picky after I am long gone, as will the next. Why should it choose someone who has no desires? It already hates me, and now we are stuck together until I die!"

Beluphis shook her head, falling back into a seat magicked beneath her. The long pause between words was heavy. Evelot imagined her mentor was looking back on her life.

Finally, she said, "What do you want, Evelot? It is not this life anymore, is it?"

"I. . ."

She still had the thrum of magic in her veins, still felt the call of the wilderness beside the moon's beckon. After all that time building herself up again and again, the future she saw. . . wasn't being a Guardian. It wasn't being a dutiful daughter always there to help tend the fields. Not a life in Goldencrest, and certainly not as a damned wolf.

The outside world was wondrous, dangerous. No matter how much she wanted to have her home where she knew it best, in her family's arms and her mentor's study. A hot coal of fire burned in her chest at the realization. Her fear of a future where she couldn't anticipate all outcomes, where she might face rejection time and again, subsided. It was difficult to imagine starting a new life from practically nothing, but to stay stagnant as she had was a worse fate than what lay before her.

She wanted to study and travel. To know how different the world was.

It was time to let go.

"I thought so," Beluphis said. She leaned in to the counter and asked, "Think you can chase after the bard, then?"

"Are you sure the sorceress will help us—help *me*?" Evelot said.

"You will not know until you find her, eh?"

Evelot nodded. Warmth flooded her, and with it a sense of courage. Sitting up, she considered her mentor's hunched form. Evelot was without many things, supplies above all. She'd need to start somewhere.

"Master, may I—?"

"You do not need to ask. Everything you need is in there."

With a stomp of her foot, Beluphis summoned a large chest to the doorway. It opened with a clang, and out sprung several cloaks and bolts of fabric. Evelot's eyes widened. They'd all been from her mentor's travels decades ago. Among them, she found the familiar brown of a nature witch's cloak, and a thick, long-sleeved dress appropriate for the winter. Evelot reached out and gingerly stroked her thumb over the whorls and dark patterns. A woodsy scent wafted from the dusty old cloth.

"You better be careful with them. They were meant for war, others for spell-casting. No one left on this plane to mend them if they tear," Beluphis warned.

Evelot smiled. "Thank you, Master. Will you be all right? While I'm gone?"

"You act as if I was not alone before you came along. I know how to keep myself—eh. . . occupied."

Beluphis may have rolled her eyes, but Evelot's mentor couldn't hide it. There was sentimentality about her that softened the edges of her earlier attitude.

Evelot threw on what new garb she could and gathered her supplies. She packed her tomes, parchment, and little pouches of rare herbs into a traveling sack. As she paced about the main room, the sounds of shrill chirps and beating wings came down from the second level.

"Hello, my wee beauty," Evelot cooed, collecting Jammer from the air. "Can you do something for me?"

In response, Jammer shrieked.

Evelot went to the main door and threw it open. "Find him. Make sure he doesn't rush off too far into the woods."

With a click, the bat launched into the air. Evelot saw her off from the doorway until she was a blip in the night sky.

The woods begged her to stay in the doorway. Her heart thundered in her chest, and her palms were slick. A whole new world was awaiting her, one that didn't end at the tree lines or bounding rivers; one she had to find the cure to her curse in.

Her journey started with facing the part of her that she couldn't let go of.

Beluphis's hand clasped her shoulder. Evelot turned to her, gratitude wrinkling the corners of her watery eyes.

Trying for a smile, Beluphis said, "Though you were my only pupil, I am proud of all that you accomplished. Wherever your path leads you, know that in the chaos of the wild, there is truth."

She reached up and patted Evelot's head.

"And if anyone says otherwise, invoke my name. The world needs to be reminded that I am still alive."

Evelot nodded. "Of course. Thank you, Master. For everything."

Beluphis winked and turned back to her kitchen. Evelot faced the doorway and the frosty night. Then, she was off.

The chill air tangled in her hair, and bare branches stretched out to swipe her. Evelot raced past them and into the woods. Her legs carried her across the path of mud and leaves; she glided unlike any beast there. The sensation of her newfound strengths unnerved her, yet for the time being she was grateful. She'd catch Zenris before long.

The path became familiar in her heightened vision as she trained her sights on the blur of the woods. The shadows of their past selves stood out faintly there as if ephemeral statues. Though it felt like decades, they'd met only two months ago. Two months of trial, frustration, understanding, and encouragement. They'd been on paths that somehow intersected, creating a bond beyond what she was used to. She wouldn't cast it aside again.

Evelot called out his name. Birds took off at the sound and woodland life skittered away, but not a sight of Zenris was among them. Her throat ached with every holler, every shout. She fumbled over slick patches of grass and flew into branches that sliced her cheeks; his name didn't fade from her lips.

On a small knoll, Evelot slowed in her steps. A faint scent in the air beckoned her. Evelot ran in its direction, her heart excitedly beating the stronger the scent grew. It mingled with the smell of mud and river water, and the wee cry of Jammer.

She skidded to a stop. The burn stretched wide and low, nearly swallowing her in its open, icy maw. She studied her surroundings and sniffed at the air. He was still nearby, within earshot.

"Zenris!"

Evelot paced by the river's edge, peeking through the shadows in the trees for a sign of movement. She searched for the fallen tree that joined the two sides, finding it a meter away. A scuffle of leaves drew closer. Sprinting, she climbed onto the tree and shouted.

Ahead, the shadows stirred. On the other side of the bridge, Jammer cried and jolted into the air. Beneath her, another figure spun around.

Zenris stopped, spotting her.

"Zenris—"

Her words choked her. Only a sob escaped, racking her body. Through her teary vision, she saw Zenris race to her.

"I-I'm sorry, Zenris," she said. "I'm so sorry. I don't want you gone—"

His arms crushed her to him. Another sob left Evelot as she clung to him. His heart thundered in her acute hearing as mightily as her own pulse. Whatever she tried to say, to apologize for, Zenris hushed her with soothing strokes over her head.

"'Tis perfectly fine," he said. "I have you. I promise."

Evelot shook her head, pulling away. "My master told me what you'd planned to do. Why would you want to go halfway around the world on an assumption?"

"For a noble quest, of course."

"You—" She bit back a sob and pulled him close to her. "You're nothing but a numpty," she whispered.

"Obviously," Zenris answered, holding her back.

Though the night hardly saw activity, Evelot found her body weak and disoriented by her cursed senses. Zenris's scent burrowed an aching knife in her skull, and Jammer's wee cries pierced her ears; the sight of trees around her forced her eyes shut as she swayed on her feet.

With a helping hand, Zenris led her back to his side of the river. They sat down on frosted, patchy grass where it was less overstimulating. Evelot sucked in a breath, wrapping her cloak tight over her shoulders and head.

"Why did you leave, Evelot?" Zenris asked. "I had thought that you. . ."

"I couldn't let you go off on your own. It'll take years to find the sorceress. Decades, maybe. Just. . ."

Evelot gulped, grabbing at her cloak. "Please don't go. Not without me. I know I'd be a liability at best, or a threat at worst. But I don't want to see you go it alone on my account."

Zenris reached out to her. She stiffened as his palm cupped her cheek. His scent was still strong, and she had to clench her jaw to focus solely on the warmth of it.

"As if I could stop you." The grin on his face faded, and his hand fell away.

"What is it?" Evelot asked.

"I wish the circumstances were different," Zenris said. "It feels 'tis not of your own volition."

Evelot fervently shook her head. "No, this is my choice. I want to journey with you. Even if things were different, I'd still want this. My life—it isn't here. It's somewhere out there. Somewhere that feels as right as this."

She gently took his hand and returned it to her cheek. Zenris pulled her closer, his forehead warm against hers. As his scent clogged her volatile senses, and Jammer shuffled through their clothing for shelter, Zenris's heartbeat was like a calming tune in her ear.

His thumb stroked along her cheekbone. "Are you certain? You are free to do as you wish."

"Aye. But I won't change my mind."

"The lady is most stubborn," Zenris said with a chuckle.

"Very."

With a sigh, he kissed her forehead. "Then, let us hope Pril has made the arrangements for several days ahead."

"Thank you," Evelot whispered.

Zenris grinned at her, his tears like stars in the pale moonlight. "Always."

Epilogue

Goldencrest had woken to a dreich day, the first rearing of winter before snowfall. Those outside were bundled with thick cloaks and furs, no different from those gathering in the fisher's quarry. Yet no number of scarves and kerchiefs could dim the cacophony of sobs echoing through their alleys. With disgruntled looks, fishers loaded their docks, easing past the main dock where the noise converged.

The sight of Zenris addressing his fans was amusing, in a way. Those who weren't weeping faced the other end of the docks. The mayor—beside his arsehole son—paled as a decorated duchy guard scowled, gesticulating at the town and back to them. After their festival's uninvited guest, Evelot imagined the blame would fall on someone's shoulders. Whether that meant a change of arms was in order, or the Redwald family would be called back to Esmora, Evelot didn't know. She wouldn't miss them.

Familiar faces surfaced from the gathering fans. Evelot opened her arms to her family, who wrapped her in their embrace all at once.

"Oh, my wee bairn." Ma stroked her hair and smiled weakly, with tears staining her cheeks. "Is it really today? Of all days to leave home. . ."

"It'll be all right, Ma. I promise. I'll write as much as I can."

"You better," Ulleh said. "Otherwise, I'll breed as many bairns as it takes to send an army after you!"

"Ulleh!" their ma gasped, but quickly fell into a fit of laughter with them.

When they pulled away, Da stood in front of her with a scunnered face. He was never good at goodbyes, so Evelot hugged him before he could speak. Embracing him was still new, and she mourned the embraces she wouldn't be around to share with him. But this one wouldn't be their last.

"Will everything be all right without me, Da?" she asked, stepping back.

"Of course."

"And you have the recipes I've written for your and Ma's treatments?"

"Aye, aye. I know what to do with them."

The heat of his palm on Evelot's head made her smile. "I'll miss you, Da."

"Aye. And I, you."

It was then that Tonlin shuffled over to her side. He awkwardly looked at her, his mouth opening and closing like a surfaced fish.

"Have you gone to say goodbye to your teacher?" Evelot asked him.

"A-aye."

"You think you can manage all the regimens she set up for you?"

"Of course! I won't give up that easily!"

Evelot giggled. "Good. Maybe someday you'll be able to catch up to us. Spar with her, eh?"

"Never. She'll always be the best."

"You never know."

Tonlin blushed. She stood as tall as him, but there would come a time when he'd tower above her. He may not have his strength yet, but Tonlin knew what he wanted to do with himself. He'd make an excellent warrior in the future.

Grinning, Evelot lunged at him and snuck a kiss on his cheek.

"What in the hells, Evelot?" he snapped.

"Language, young man," their da warned.

"If you won't hug your own sister, then I'll have to get my affection out of you another way. Or are you afraid of someone seeing you with the 'devil's harlot'?"

"No! That's just gossip. Don't be so weird."

Laughing, Evelot shook her head. "All right, all right. Take care while I'm gone, Tonlin."

"L-love you, too, sis." With a bashful face, he added, "Don-don't have pups while you're gone."

Their da did a double take as Evelot burst into laughter. Tonlin smirked to himself, the gallus wee rascal.

The fans were dispersing in the background, and Zenris was on his way, so she turned back to her family. With a final wave goodbye and a few bittersweet grins, they saw her off. Evelot raised her hood and headed for the docks.

Her bard practically pranced as he joined her side. Beaming, he asked, "What, praytell, amuses my lady?"

"I'll tell you about it later."

"Oh?"

He took her hand as they approached the dock's staircase. Down below sat a small boat meant for port city traders. Somehow, Prilthadollak had convinced a commerce company from the festival to allow them a ride down the river.

It was all still new to Evelot, how connected other towns and cities were, hoaching with over thrice as many people as her hometown. Zenris had shown her a map of the landmarks closest to Goldencrest, but they were still too amazing to picture.

"So," Evelot said, thinking of their next destination, "Oglen, was it? How many times have you visited, again?"

"Several. Ah, how you could dance for days and never tire there," Zenris said dreamily. "The locals have inspired many a merry tune. When the chance arises, I will take you to one of their countless festivities."

Evelot grinned back at him, mesmerized by the joy on his face.

"There will be no making merry, Heart of Aspen!"

Prilthadollak stood before the plank leading into the boat. She watched them sternly, her arms crossed.

"Pril, 'twill not be another week before the others meet us in Oglen. Surely we can make an exception?"

"You used that excuse once, and now here we are. I will not be made a fool again."

Zenris grumbled beneath his breath, waving off his companion. As they boarded the boat, Evelot tugged at his sleeve.

"Zenris," she said quietly, "is there a Portal in Oglen?"

"Last I recall, there are at least two."

"Is it. . .?" She tried to choose her words. "Are you wanting to see if maybe he'll. . .?"

His smile was faintly melancholic, but still as bright as ever. "In days of doubt and self-discouragement, I dreamt of solace in my father's words. Yet to myself, I have not been true. 'Tis with the inspiration of your courage that I await with a peaceful heart for either reunion or parting."

Evelot nodded, amazed by his confession.

"Until such time. . ." He took her hand and planted a soft kiss there. "I am much more invested in another whom I revel in showing all that the world offers."

"You numpty," Evelot said with a small smile.

With her hand still in his, Zenris led Evelot to the stern. The ferrymen prepared their vessel and untied the boat from the dock. Evelot held onto the side, rocking with the waves as the river slowly carried them off. Goldencrest receded with the rising daylight. At the end of the docks, she spotted her family waving back at her. She grinned at them with an eager wave. She wouldn't let them see her cry. Not when she was finally setting off on her journey, the beginning of her new life.

The wind picked up and tossed at her cloak. She gasped as her hood fell back and her hair tangled with the air. Stepping back, she frantically tucked away what she could. Jammer, hibernating in her towel-wrap within Evelot's bag, didn't stir at the jostle.

Zenris wordlessly lowered her hands and fixed her hood. He was quiet, transfixed as if pondering a thought. It was true that she looked different from before. Only once had Evelot dared look at her reflection. Her red hair had turned a shade of auburn, like a lighter wolf's coat; her body had grown toned in muscle to accommodate her newfound strength, and her eyes. . . that sickly, menacing shade of red glowed there instead of green. She hated that color, hated the mutation of her body. But when Zenris was there, staring as if in awe, she could forget about that for a while.

In all their time, she hadn't realized until later how much of an impression he'd left. She wanted to have courage, to smirk back at the face of death, to be passionate and free. With time, she felt she'd be able to do so. It only required a different perspective, and a little less pride.

However, as their time together progressed, it became more than an impression. It tied her to him, a spark that ignited whenever he laughed. Whenever he looked back at her like the sun would always be alight. She couldn't leave it at happiness or passion. He was her equal, and her home.

"I love you."

His lips parted as if in shock. Those springtide eyes gave him away, though; they were full of felicity.

She grinned back at him. "You wanting to make a field of flowers, bard?"

"With pleasure."

Against his smiling lips, she let her worries all go. Her circumstances were still unsure, her future unplanned. But Zenris kissed her back, a small firm promise that no matter what, they'd weather their futures together.

When he pulled away, she felt his breath on her neck. In her ear, he began quietly singing. She recognized the lyrics, those wee tender words from the festival before it'd gone wrong. Evelot beamed, shutting her eyes as she let him take her away with his braw music.

She was positive, then and there, that it'd be all right. This was her journey and their path, side by side. No curse nor beast could take that away from them.

Acknowledgments

It's one thing to tell yourself that you will finish a writing project, but another to actually publish it. If it hadn't been for the people below to give this book a chance, the strength and confidence to have made that transition likely wouldn't have been mustered. And so, it humbles and pleases me to mention these individuals here and on the copyright notes.

To my loved ones, close friends and relatives: thank you for listening to my ramblings and speculations about the story and its lore. Without you, the notes on characters and races wouldn't have been sorted through properly or my Easter eggs been carefully tucked into the writing.

To my handful of beta readers from both online and within my writing group: thank you for your patience and care. It will always mean the world for every one of you to have taken the time out of your schedules to read my later (yet still sloppy) drafts. You have taught me much about the reader's aspect and how to move forward with my writing process, as well as more fun facts about farming and the countless drinking games from certain repetitive words.

To my sensitivity readers/authenticity consultants D.D., L.C., S.T.: thank you for your patience and time. You've all helped me build my characters and guided me toward the right steps of using inspiration of the real-world cultures and languages for this book and series sequels. I hope so much to make you proud, even if the majority of attention is directed more toward the spicy romance half of it.

To my artists, both interior designs by T.M. and front cover designs by Z.A.: thank you both for your expertise and passion. Without you, neither the main characters would have a face to put on the cover nor their emblems be proudly displayed on these pages. That your creativity and talent met this project will always be a gift to me and this series. Here's to a hopeful and fun future together in Runlaris!

To my editor, K.R.: thank you for your patience and critical eye. You've gone above and beyond to help someone with their first book and your dedication to the editorial craft is a marvel, and I'm so grateful that it's started me on this journey. Let's see in the next book if those grammar refresher courses help any!

And finally, to you, reader: thank you so much for giving this book a chance. I hope this little story was meaningful to your life, if at least to have made your day a bit brighter. There's more to come if you're in the mood for more couples, more spice, and adventure. Stay tuned for my socials on the last page if you're interested!

Glossary

Take note that for some of the Scottish/Gaelic and Quechua, pronunciations vary slightly depending on which region of Scotland or Peru (-and its neighboring countries) you visit! For context, the Scottish dialect used in this book is a mixture of the eastern coast and the Central Belt, and any Quechua is from the Ayacucho branch.

Aho ("ah-hoe"): the Japanese Romaji spelling for the word "idiot" (not as popular as "baka").

Athbreith ("affreh")- In Gaelic, it means "afterlife". But within the story's world, it refers to springtime and the month named by the elves (equivalent of April).

Bahoochie: an uncommon word for "butt" (like "fanny" in English).

Bairn: a baby/child.

Beaghan(s) ("bake-ahn". The "gh" is a faint "kuh" sound): A term derived from the Gaelic word "beag," meaning "little." One of the many races of Runlaris.

Bevvies: alcoholic beverages.

Blether: a bunch of chatter.

Bonnie: beautiful.

Braw: good-looking.

Burn: river.

Beinn ("bine"): A mountain/large hill.

Cèilidh ("kay-lee"): a Scottish dance party. For you western American readers, this'll be right up your alley.

Choille ("coi-yeh"): Scottish Gaelic for "woods/woodland".

Craic ("crack"): good chat, fun, entertainment.

Daft: foolish.

Daunder (also known as "dauner"): a stroll/walk.

Din: loud, obnoxious noise.

Don't Fuss Yersel': don't worry.

Dreich ("dree-ch." But the "ch" comes from the back of the throat like a hiss): a wet, damp, miserable day.

Duodies: The second day in the week (this system works just like ours, but counts the days in Latin instead of naming them after mythological gods. I.e., Sunday=Unidies, Wednesday=Tridies).

Eejit: idiot.

Gallus: being bold, daring (and usually borderline reckless).

The Gloaming: the time between twilight and dusk.

Haud Your Wheest: hold/shut your mouth.

Hen: another term of endearment, usually directed toward female partners.

Hoaching: really busy/overrun.

I Dinnae Ken: I don't know.

Jinryuu (jihn-ree-oo): a play on the Japanese word "jinrui" ("jihn-roo-ee," meaning "human/humanity") and "ryuu" ("ree-oo"), meaning "dragon". One of the many races of Runlaris.

Jobby: another word for "poop."

Kip: to either sleep or nap. Have a kip/take a nap.

Lovey: a term of endearment.

Manky: dirty (but when directed at someone, has a more negative connotation).

Ninanuna ("nee-nah noo-nah"): A term derived from the Quechua words for "fire" and "soul." Like the phoenix, this race named themselves after having risen from literal and proverbial ashes centuries ago.

Numpty: a word similar to "dork" or "idiot," but usually lovingly used.

Patter: chat or banter.

Pished: one of the many terms for "being drunk".

Puddocks: frogs.

Qatiway ("kah-tee-why". But the "q" is gargled): the word for "follow me."

Rank: disgusting smell.

Radge: someone acting wildly or not thinking straight.

Scallywag: someone mischievous or badly behaved (like a "rascal").

Scran: food/a bite to eat.

Scunnered: an expression for being "fed up"/frustrated/over it.

Siki ("see-kee"): another word for butt.

Skelp: To gently hit or slap, sometimes used as a parental threat (not in a serious manner. But if a stranger threatens this, it's time to exit stage left).

Tadger: in the words of Crocodile Dundee, "that's a knife" (except this one ain't made of metal).

Uchuy Achkiy (Oo-ch-wee ahh-ch-key): in Quechua, this means "little light".

Upa ("oo-pah"): Quechua word for "fool".

Upallay ("oo-pah-ll-eye." But the "ll" is like a quick "yuh" sound): the word for "you be quiet."

About the Author

L. C. Jewels hides away in their den of solitude out of the southern US heat, thinking of ways to brilliantly weave medieval romantasies while rolling polyhedral dice and researching historical and cultural fun facts.

When not thrusting their head into the wall to weave said stories, you can find them and their works at these online platforms.

www. leighcrownejewels. com
@lcjewels.bsky.social
instagram.com/leighc.jewelsauthor

www.ingramcontent.com/pod-product-compliance
Lightning Source LLC
Chambersburg PA
CBHW030100310726
48970CB00004B/1085